The
GIANT

A NOVEL OF MICHELANGELO'S DAVID

LAURA MORELLI

English translations of Michelangelo's sonnets based on
work by John Symonds and Elizabeth Jennings

Cover design by Kerry Ellis
Interior design by Shannon Bodie, Bookwise Design

ISBNs:
Paperback 978-1-942467-36-6
Hardcover 978-1-942467-37-3
Large Print 978-1-942467-38-0
Mobi / Kindle 978-1-942467-39-7
EPUB 978-1-942467-40-3
Audio 978-1-942467-41-0

www.lauramorelli.com

Davicte cholla fromba
E io choll'archo
Michelagniolo

David with his sling
And I with my bow
Michelangelo

Scrawled in the margins of a preparatory drawing for the *David*

CONTENTS

IT BEGAN ON the day our hands reached for the same silverpoint pen.

In the dust-filled light of our master's workshop, I saw his fingers first: short and slight, with knuckles too large for a ten-year-old boy. He gripped the bone stylus. I gripped it too, as hard as I could. The metal tip trembled in the air. My first thought was that my wide, thick fist would win out over his smaller hand, but when our gaze met, I saw only beady-black eyes filled with fire.

I let go of my grip.

I hardly had time to console myself with the idea that I had let him have the pen, for our master announced a competition to see who could draw the best rendition of a Moses in silverpoint. We boys wanted nothing other than to please our master. We darted to our places in the workshop, and each of us began to work as grains shifted noiselessly inside the sandglass.

I watched him, that black-eyed boy. He slunk off to a dusty corner and hunched over his parchment so that no one could see what he had drawn.

When the time was called, our master circulated quietly among his pupils. Then, he pulled the two of us by our sleeves to the front of the room, declaring a tie. That moment changed everything. We were friends. At least I thought we were then.

But in my heart, I still wanted to beat that boy.

PART I

THE COMPETITION

Florence
Summer 1501

The best artist has that thought alone
Which is contained within the marble shell
The sculptor's hand can only break the spell
To free the figures slumbering in the stone

From a sonnet composed by Michelangelo Buonarroti

FROM THE SHADE of a fruit seller's door, I watch the hanged man's body spin and dangle.

The midday bells in the tower of the Signoria have not yet begun to clang, but wavering heat emanates from the cobblestones and I feel a bead of sweat trickle from my neck to the small of my back. I press against the stone wall as a mule-drawn cart rattles by, sending up splashes of steaming mud left from the morning rain.

Do I dare to look at the condemned man's face? My calloused hand shields my eyes from the glare bearing down from behind the tiled roofs. Little more than a horrid puppet, the man's jowls are as bloated as the putrid peaches in the fruit seller's bins, his eyes bulging and crazed.

Look away, Jacopo. The voice in my head.

During the night, the Black Brothers led the condemned man to this fate. I imagine their hooded forms hoisting his wriggling body over the high window ledge and pulling the noose tight, before letting him fall against the stone wall of the Bargello prison for all to see. Now, his body unfurls from the window like a dark banner hung as a warning for the murmuring crowd of onlookers who began gathering in the square long before the first cock crowed.

For days, the condemned man's name—Antonio Rinaldeschi—has been on everyone's lips. He had forfeited not only a pile of *soldi* but most of his clothing after losing a dice game in the tavern they call The Fig (not the tavern where I deal cards; that one is in the square near where Master da Vinci's father lives.)

I was told by the old woodcarver Monciatto, though he is not always reliable, that when Rinaldeschi was laughed out of the tavern, he was filled with as much rage as shame. Passing a painted image of Our Lady at a street-side tabernacle, he cursed the Virgin's name in a loud tirade that roused the neighbors from their beds. On the cobblestones before the church of Santa Maria degli Alberighi, he picked up pieces of dried horse dung and hurled them at Our Lady.

I imagine that Rinaldeschi then wandered off in a drunken stupor, thinking that his rant was finished, if he remembered it at all. But by dawn the next day, the brown, soiled rings on the Virgin's crown drew a crowd. Someone said that one of the stains resembled a rose. People began to light candles. Hold vigils. The crowds around the dung-stained Madonna grew. By the time our archbishop arrived to inspect the defiled image, Rinaldeschi had fled the city. Great piles of melted candles littered the square, and a few opportunistic painters with meager skills were selling token pictures of the event in the alleys leading to the piazza.

When the Night Guard traced Rinaldeschi to his hiding place in a villa outside the city walls, he tried to stab a dagger into his own breast. It struck a rib instead, sparing his life. He was dragged back into Florence and sentenced to hang here from the windows of the Bargello.

If only my father could see it.

The voice in my head speaks again, but this time it sounds like my father. *Art holds the power to make us immortal,* figliolo.

Immortal.

As a boy, I believed it. As a man, I can only conclude that art leads to eternal damnation.

From the time I was old enough to hold a nub of charcoal steady in my hand, my father showed me how many of our city's makers—Perugino, Brother Angelico, even my own Master Ghirlandaio—made pictures that brought them acclaim beyond measure. It was not as in previous generations, my father told me, wagging a plump finger under my nose, when a fresco painter might be paid based on a price per square. Now, he said, patrons would be willing to pay us on merit instead.

Merit.

It was what was inside the *mind* of the artist that counted, my father said, moving his thick hand from my nose to point at his balding head. The *idea.* We could create work that inspires passion, love, tears, my father told me. It would make us live forever.

"It can inspire even the throwing of horse dung at a picture of the Madonna," I mumble, as if my father could hear me all the way from his grave outside the city walls. It is precisely the artists' ideas, I think, that have led us astray.

Our priests tell us that the turn of the half-millennium may signal the beginning of the End Times, and as I contemplate the calamities along with Rinaldeschi's head wrenched grotesquely to one shoulder on the wall above, I can only believe it to be true.

It has hardly been three years since the noble people of our city lost their heads, tossing their paintings, books, and other precious objects onto a great bonfire in the Piazza della Signoria. Even that painter Botticelli dragged his own pictures to the spectacle, and everyone watched them curl and char in the flames.

The event has left a raw, open wound in the hearts of all who craft beautiful artifice for a living.

But it seems the chaos extends far beyond our city gates. Our brutal skirmishes with Rome, Siena, and Pisa—begun long before my parents' own birth—seem to have no end. And even the unthinkable: the French have taken Milan. Our city's leaders build alliances and make enemies so quickly that it is impossible to keep score.

Who are our friends and who are our enemies? I no longer know.

Rinaldeschi's body has fallen still now. As the midday bells begin to peal, the brothers appear, their black hoods barely visible at the top rim of the wall. They reel up the body, which spins slowly one last time before it disappears over the ledge. A streak of blood, a smear from where the hanged man's hands scraped the wall as he was pulled up, is the only remaining testimony of the hanging.

I turn from the sight of streaked blood on the Bargello walls, and make my way home to the quarter of the city where my sister, Lucia, and I inhabit our parents' old house. But the farther I walk away from the executed man, the more malaise rises from the pit of my stomach.

Who, I wonder, has not left a tavern cursing his luck? Who has not felt the sting of loss at the card table, has not handed over a pile of coins to a rival, has not felt the urge to rant or throw dung when he has been dealt a bad hand? I am unable to rid my head of the image of the swinging body, for I know that it is only a curse said aloud, a roll of the dice—a hairsbreadth—that separates the hanged man from myself.

As the crowd disperses and I slip down the alley toward home, my mind is filled with only one thought. On another night, it might have been me.

❧

"L'INDACO!"

I stop walking as I hear my nickname called from the direction of the square.

I turn to see the blacksmith's son, Paolo, jogging to catch up with me. His cheeks are streaked with soot, and beads of sweat dot his forehead. His skin looks as leathery as the apron that covers the stained *camicia* he wears between daybreak and the ringing of the afternoon bell. Long ago, Paolo and I worked alongside one another in Master Ghirlandaio's workshop, both of us full of promise, only to return to work at our fathers' sides.

"Your father let you out of his sight?" I smirk, a long-running jab.

"I wasn't going to miss the spectacle," he says, gesturing behind us at the Bargello walls. "Besides, it's time my dutiful brother handles things at the foundry for once," he says, his voice tinged with sarcasm. "And you? Did you sneak away from your fresco?"

"I… I managed to," I stammer the response and hope that Paolo cannot see the look of dumb shame on my face. I cannot admit that weeks have passed since I've picked up a paintbrush.

"*Senti*," he says, grasping my forearm. He doesn't seem to register my hesitation. "You have heard the news of the competition?"

"Competition?"

"The giant," he says. "They are saying the *gonfaloniere* is calling a contest for it to be carved after all this time."

All at once, I feel the hairs on my neck stand on end. I stop walking, feeling the crowds leaving the square snake around us, merchants and artisans, shopkeepers and servants, returning to their lives after the hanging.

The giant. *Il gigante.*

We all know the block of marble that lies in the workyard of our cathedral of Santa Maria del Fiore. They say that a sculptor named Bartolommeo Baccellino first attempted to make something from the marble long before my lifetime, but nothing ever came of it. Later, another sculptor, Agostino di Duccio, took his hammer to the block, only to cast it aside in frustration. Since then, some four decades ago, it has lain discarded and abandoned.

"The giant," I say, almost a whisper. "The Signoria has seen fit to resurrect the project? Why?"

"The cathedral committee," he says, setting his wide brown eyes on me. "A large David to adorn the tribune of the cathedral. I am surprised you have not heard of it. Everyone is lining up for a chance to take on the block," he says. "Sansovino, Botticelli. Even da Vinci's name has been thrown out." The heat of the midday sun bears down on the back of my neck, as hot as a blue flame, and I wonder if my skin has already turned red.

"But L'Indaco," he continues, "there is one person missing from the list. You know it better than I. Too bad he is not here to propose his own name. He might have a fighting chance." Paolo slaps me on the shoulder. "*Buon lavoro,*" he says, veering down a narrow alley toward his father's foundry at the edge of the city wall.

"*Saluti,*" I say, watching his broad back disappear behind a gaggle of people and a large oxcart loaded with bales of raw wool.

The giant. A great David. The lowly shepherd of Israel who would become a mighty king. I feel my heart quicken in my chest, and my mind is already racing. Of course, there is no way the Signoria would give such a commission to a man like me. Not by myself. But maybe… My mind flashes with the memory of clambering over that block together with my closest friend when we were barely ten years old. If there is a giant David waiting to be freed from inside that old hunk of marble, I know the man to free it.

But when I think of his face, my gut is filled with a mixture of excitement and trepidation. Would he come home?

I feel a surge inside my chest. Yes. We need him. Florence needs him. If I am honest with myself, *I* need him. If I am to play any role in this competition—if I am to amount to anything at all—he might be the one who could help pull me out of this hole I have dug for myself.

My friend.

Michelangelo Buonarroti.

⁂

To Michelangelo Buonarroti in Rome—

IT IS ALL I have managed to scrawl on the parchment so far, for I struggle to find the words that will bring my childhood friend back home to Florence.

I ponder the blank page in the dimming light. Beyond the leaded panes of my bedchamber window, the sky has turned a distinct shade of lavender-blue that only appears on summer evenings. The aroma of my sister's pie, made with onions and the pickings of a boar carcass donated by a sympathetic, neighboring butcher, wafts into the room from the hearth downstairs. In spite of the fact that we are nearly broke, Lucia manages to feed us like nobility, night after night. We had to dismiss our last remaining servant two years ago—a shame, for the woman had served our parents for some three decades. Now my sister does everything herself.

I swallow the saliva in my mouth along with the guilt I feel for allowing my sister to live like this. It has gone unspoken, but we all know that she is past marriageable age. There is no longer enough for a dowry; no one has to tell her that. But she prefers to paint small prayer books for the nuns rather than to live cloistered behind the convent walls with them. Our father taught Lucia, our younger brother, Francesco, and myself to paint minuscule scrolls, gilded initials, leaves, and delicate figures so small that one needs an oculus to see them. With Lucia's talent at illumination, she can make a little money for us to eat. And as for our little brother Francesco... Well. He has had to work far beyond the walls of our city to keep himself warm and fed. He knew better than to rely on me.

I light the oil lamp at my worktable, and the bright chaos of color springs to life on my bedchamber walls. Around me swirl faces of serene Madonnas, martyrs in agony, hands and drapery and horses, layered one atop another, a mess of pictures attacked and abandoned over years. Ever since I was small, my bedchamber walls have been my sketchbook. My parents gave up trying to stop me years ago. Into the wooden mantel I have carved obscene figures from the time I was young. Other images awoke me in the night, flashes of brilliance that I painted in a state of supreme inspiration, but by dawn's light, they appeared dull, flat, inconsequential. Not good enough. They might send me back to my bed for days, my windows shuttered and my eyes closed so that I would not have to face my own failure.

I brush aside a stack of drawings on my desk to make room for my parchment. In recent months, the table has become cluttered with drawings of churches, and small figures of clay and gesso that I have formed with my hands. If I am to become immortal as my father wished, then the gilded pages of books to be tucked away behind convent walls seem hardly enough. Instead, the monumental forms of statues and buildings are the only path, I am convinced. Sculpture. Architecture. Fortune has not favored me in the way that it's favored men my age who have established workshops for themselves or have found important commissions in Rome—like Michelangelo himself.

I brush a layer of ash and dust from carving into hardened gesso and stone. I plunge the tip of my quill into the glass ink-well, into the abyss of the midnight blue liquid. *L'Indaco*. Indigo. The deepest blue there is. The same as the nickname that Michelangelo himself gave to me.

My *blue boy*, he said. All those years ago.

How will I find the words to lure him back home?

My friend,

I have faith my letter will reach you with some important news. Surely you recall the old block of marble in our cathedral workyard.

At last, the Signoria has decided to commission someone to sculpt it—a David for one of the cathedral tribunes.

You know the block well enough, so I need not describe it to you.

DOUBT CREEPS IN and my hand stops. It has been four long years since he left for Rome. He already has earned acclaim, won commissions from lords, cardinals, His Holiness himself. He has made a new life there. Surely he does not wish to return to his native city. Will he run his dark eyes across my letter and then stoke the fire in his hearth with it? It would be just like him to do such a thing.

But how could I live with myself if I did not make an attempt to win this commission? To not do so would mean I am meant for nothing more than painting church frescoes to pay back my failed card and dice tricks. To admit I have failed my father's dying wish.

No. I steady my hand again and begin to put ink on the page.

As you might imagine, my friend, the Signoria's plan for the block has provoked a tumult among the artists in our city. That is why time is of the essence, why I am writing to you at all. I hesitate sharing this information, but you have been away from home for so long, so I feel it is necessary to characterize the nature of the competition for you.

You should know that recently, I have turned to sculpture myself. I'm not bad, if I may say so. I am certain the two of us together could—

I scratch out that last paragraph with an angry scribble, then crumple the page. I pull out a fresh piece of parchment, carefully copying the first part of my letter onto it. Then I continue:

Da Vinci's name was on everyone's lips as soon as the competition became known, but surely I do not have to convince you he is not considered a serious candidate. I shall say no more about it.

As much as it pains me to write these words, you must know the truth. That bothersome Andrea Sansovino has nearly convinced the committee to let him take on the sculpture even though the contest is hardly underway. You know him better than I, of course, having spent so many hours alongside him in the Medici gardens.

What you may not know is that since you have been away from Florence, Andrea Sansovino has taken on many commissions that, I must say as your friend and most loyal ally, should have gone to you. I have heard from reliable sources that Sansovino is trying to convince members of the wool guild he can take the block and transform it into a David.

There are others, of course, clamoring for the commission. Your name has come up as you might imagine, but without you here in person, well, my own words and actions have found a limited audience.

Bene. I think I have painted the picture for you well enough. We both know that you and I are better suited to win this commission. The idea we discussed years ago for the block will surely convince the members of the committee.

With my strongest affection and regard for you, as your friend and closest ally in Florence, I can only urge you to come back home as swiftly as you can. I will be here waiting to work by your side. I commend myself to you. May God guard you from evil.

Your L'Indaco
In Florence

"Jacopo."

Since our parents died, my sister is the only one left who uses the name they gave me. Lucia appears in the crooked doorway of my bedchamber, wiping her hands on a rag. She approaches the table beneath the leaded windows and peers over my shoulder.

"*Cavolo,*" she says. "I cannot say that I have ever seen you write so many words."

It is true. I might sketch beautiful images of saints and women but my lettering is clumsy and inelegant. I crook my arm around the parchment to hide my crudely drawn words from her gaze. Our father taught us to draw. He never encouraged us to read or write beyond basic necessity.

"And who is the fortunate recipient of this work?" she asks.

"Buonarroti."

"He is coming back to Florence?" I see her eyebrows elevate, her brow wrinkle. I know she would be as pleased as I to see him—the old infatuation still alive—but she will never admit it out loud.

"Only if I have done my job with this letter."

"But it cannot be safe to travel," Lucia says. "The French are moving south, I have heard. And armed men of the Borgia have joined them. They mean to take Naples. You remember what it was like, having French soldiers on our streets. I would not like to be on the move right now, not without a legion of soldiers for protection."

My mind flashes with the memory of our city's eleven days of occupation under that ugly, red-bearded French king. He entered our gates weighted down under gilt armor too big for him, riding a black warhorse under the shelter of an embroidered canopy held aloft by four knights. With him, there were ranks of crossbowmen, officers with thick plumes, speaking in strange tongues. Our streets stood deserted except for young men and a few brave, old women. Everyone else, filled with terror, tucked their daughters and wives into the darkness of their houses until those smelly French soldiers left Florence with their stomachs filled with beer and their sacks filled with ransom.

"He will come. I am sure of it," I say. A lie.

But my sister is no longer listening. Instead, her eyes flicker in that way that drives me mad, just like our mother used to do. She runs her gaze across the disaster of my bedchamber. Lucia stopped complaining about it years ago, realizing the futility of cleaning or commenting on it. I see the shadow of worry cross her face as she reads new words I have written in the soffits above the window, a tirade against the noble families that make up our

Signoria. She looks as if she will say something, but then presses her lips together. She flips the rag over her shoulder and turns her back to me. "The meat pie is on the table."

My stomach growls, but I force myself to wait. First things first. I must get the letter to the courier before dusk. "Save it for me," I call to my sister, who is already halfway down the worn, creaking stairs.

I read the letter one last time. I wish I could have found better, more convincing words but I am a painter, not a poet. It will have to do. I scratch a quick, obscene picture below my name, a private joke I am sure he remembers from our childhood, just in case there is any doubt in his mind that it is I.

I fold the paper into a triangle, then bring the candle's flame to the long stick of sealing wax. Red drips splash awkwardly on the folded page. With this, too, I am unpracticed. I press my father's old bronze seal into the hot wax and watch the tiny image of John the Baptist appear as if by magic. I blow out my candle, then kiss the tiny, warm rendition of our city's patron. I descend into the shadows of the stairwell.

"But... where are you going?" Lucia says, holding out her palms in supplication. I see a healthy fire in the hearth, two neat places set at the table, a flame illuminating two matching, chipped plates, flickering on two cups of hammered copper.

"I am going to find the courier, but I will be back before the bells in the campanile ring. Promise," I say, gesturing in the direction of our parish church. I hear Lucia cluck in exasperation as I push the rough oak door open and head out into the street.

My sister takes good care of me. For that I am grateful. I do not deserve it, and if she knew the truth, I feel certain she would throw me out of the house altogether.

◈

THE GIANT IS large and ungainly, an enormous hunk of mineral heaved out of the mountains of Carrara.

I have never seen the Apuan Alps, but have heard people describe white, craggy cliffsides that loom over the Ligurian Sea. Michelangelo told me of them himself, years ago, after he returned on a barge down the Arno with several large, white blocks.

I press my face between the bars of the cathedral workyard's iron gate. The waning sunlight no longer penetrates the wooden enclosure that has been erected around the construction zone. My eyes follow a pigeon as it flutters down from the tiled dome and into the darkness of the workyard. Filtered beams emerge through the cracks between the planks, and I hear the shudder of wings as other birds explore the piles of wood, stone, and iron that litter the workyard. In the jumble of lumber and dust, the giant, that large block, lies still on the ground, its dull surface rough and dark in the shadows.

For my entire life, this marble block has lain on its side. In its discarded state, it has become as much a monument to incompletion as the cathedral itself, cast aside by two different masters over two generations. Both men, we are told, put their hammers to the giant, only to be defeated by it.

Since then, the block has lain dormant inside the precinct of the cathedral workyard where stone masons, carpenters, bricklayers, and other craftspeople spend their days, lazily working toward completion of this building that seems to be ever under construction.

Many afternoons, when Master Ghirlandaio finally let us out from under his thumb, we would burst through the doors of the studio and raced to the cathedral. Michelangelo and I spent many hours running around the block or clambering over it, stopping only to share a sweet from the bakery or a joke. Later, the city fathers had wooden barriers erected to keep out curious onlookers, thieves, and others of malintent. Now, the block and the gated workyard are part of the fabric of our city. The abandoned block, with notches nicked into the sides before their masters gave up, has become part of the landscape. Most people going about their business pay no mind to this piece of white marble reflecting the sun. But for those of us who make things with our hands, it pulls at our attention, pulls at our hearts.

Michelangelo, of course, is most aware of *il gigante*. For a while in our youth, as he worked in the Medici gardens with smaller specimens, the thought of taking his own hammer to the irascible block obsessed him. Even as we worked in Master Ghirlandaio's studio, Michelangelo once confided in me that the block tormented him. He lay awake at night, he told me, imagining himself taking his old bow-shaped drill, his beloved *trapano*, to the block.

Behind me, I hear the bookbinders battening down their wooden enclosures for the evening. Signor Battistini salutes me as he works a complicated iron mechanism that locks the wooden shutters of the shop where my sister brings her illuminated parchments to be bound. His worn-looking expression touches my heart. On a normal evening, I would stop to trade drolleries with Battistini, a bit of light consolation for a man not long ago bereft of his wife. But not tonight. I wave and keep my pace, following the winding street toward the mail agent in Santa Croce. I hope the agent has not already closed his own shutters for the night.

I am careful to avoid the area around the Mercato Vecchio, for no good can come of showing my face there.

At the fruit seller's shop on the corner, I turn onto the riverbank. The Ponte Vecchio comes into view. Even with its sagging wooden shutters and the precarious conglomeration of butcher shops perched along its edges, the bridge is always beautiful to behold. At any hour of the day or night, light shifts across its aged stucco surfaces, sometimes golden, sometimes orange. I watch a burly man pitch scraps of red flesh from a small window in the crumbling yellow stucco of the old bridge. The dregs of market day splash into the water below.

It is only then I feel the shadow.

I sense it rather than see it. I duck into a doorway, and look over my shoulder.

Nothing. I hear myself exhale.

Not again.

For days, I have had the feeling I am being followed. Am I dreaming it? I quicken my pace toward the mail agent's office.

Everyone loves old man Fabini the mail agent, with his lined cheeks and jug-like jaw. Our citizens entrust him with the most precious details of their lives: notifications of births and deaths, agreements between merchants and notaries, appeals for prayers and money, professions of devotion between lovers separated by great distances, heartfelt and urgent requests like mine.

In exchange for a small fee, it is old man Fabini's job to route each letter to the proper *corriere*. From our city, these messages disseminate far and wide. Our Florentine messengers are some of the best in the world; at least that is what I have heard. The men urge their horses across great distances on routes long established, a model of efficiency. Messengers carry letters along the dusty roads between Florence and Rome every single day.

Simple.

Still, letters do not always reach their recipients; of course I know this. Any number of things can happen. A letter can be lost in a roadside skirmish, misrouted, mislaid, or simply fall off a cart rattling along a country road. Now I worry that I should have copied my letter and had a second version sent by a separate route to Rome. Instead, I decide to place an extra *denaro* in old man Fabini's hand to ensure its arrival, even if it is the last one in my pocket. Under the best of circumstances, it should take four or five days to reach the gates of the Holy City.

I finger the sealed parchment one last time. Weightless in my hand. Heavy in my heart. I can only hope my message will reach my friend at all and that it will reach him in time.

If Michelangelo Buonarroti answers my call, then the two of us will work side by side again, just as we did long ago, he with his wild ambition—and I, with my wild ideas. Together, we can convince them to give us the commission, but only if my letter reaches him before one of our rivals clinches it.

The sun hangs low, making shifting orange and purple patterns on the surface of the Arno. Beyond, the great egg-shaped, earthen-tiled dome of our cathedral looms over the city.

In my mind's eye, I see the great misshapen block of marble lying in the workyard at the cathedral's base. Silent. Foreboding. Waiting for us, Michelangelo and me. Waiting to be transformed for the glory of God, for the glory of Florence. Is it too much to think that I will be recognized as an artist at last? For now, I will settle for a paying commission to keep the bondsmen off my back.

As soon as the thought enters my head, the shadow is back. This time, I hear the footsteps. I dare to look behind me. It is not one shadow, but two. Two large men.

My heart begins to race inside my chest.

Just ahead, I spot the familiar sight of the wooden horse pro-
jecting out over a doorway lit by a small oil lantern. I duck into
the mail agent's office.

ॐ

BRIGHTLY PAINTED BANNERS of the wool guild
flap above the heads of the crowd assembled in the Piazza della
Signoria. The midday bell sounds its familiar clang. The old
building's tall, skinny watchtower casts a foreboding shadow over
the square. I scan the crowd, seeking a friendly face among the
painters, sculptors, goldsmiths, and makers of saddles, buckles,
iron, books. Few of them will be qualified to take on the giant,
but all want to hear what will become of it.

I recognize the stooped shoulders of Master Botticelli, and
I push my way toward him. He respected my father, so I expect
that he will at least make conversation with me. He greets me
with a tight nod.

"Ciao, L'Indaco," Andrea Il Riccio, the goldsmith, squeezes
my arm and sidles in beside Botticelli and me.

"Throwing your name into the hat, Andrea?" Botticelli asks
the curly-haired goldsmith.

"Only if they want a sculpture of gold," I interrupt. "This
big." I show them my thick fingers as if to demonstrate a tiny
sculpture the size of a coin.

Their laughter buoys me.

Nearest the building, a dozen officials from the Signoria are
assembled, their dark, red-lined silk robes flapping. On the other
side, a matching dozen set of clerics and laypeople from the cathedral committee, the *operai*, cluster together. In the middle are

members of the wool guild, even more richly outfitted than they were in the days before those hypocrites threw their own fine things in the fire. I shake my head as they assemble under a tottering series of painted guild banners carried by standard-bearers, young boys in what look like stiflingly hot velvet waistcoats.

"Hypocrites."

I hear the whisper at my ear. Has Andrea read my mind? I turn to see him watching the row of the twelve good men—the Dodici Buonuomini—some of our city's wealthiest men serving a two-month term on our city's high council. Golden chains hang across their proud chests and their sober faces scan the crowd.

"Probably worried that someone will start throwing rotten fruit," I whisper back. Most of these men are known Medici sympathizers.

Suddenly, my mind is filled with a terrifying image—perhaps my first memory. I feel my father's hands lift me from the pavement and balance my small body on his shoulders in this very square. Now I can see what all the screaming and chanting is about: members of the Pazzi family and even an archbishop, hanged and dismembered before our eyes, in retribution for the fatal stabbing of Giuliano de Medici during high mass in our own cathedral.

"How fortunes turn," I say, for now the Medici family has fled to their supporters in Rome, and their partisans here in Florence are doing their best to show public support of the new republican government. "Hypocrites indeed."

But I turn to see that Andrea is no longer listening to me. "Look!" Andrea whispers, squeezing my arm again. "It's Soderini."

Shielding my eyes from the sun's blaze, I spot the shiny, bald head of Gonfaloniere Soderini, who now commands not only our city's soldiers but also our entire city, it seems. Soderini was elected *gonfaloniere* only months ago. I suppose he was as good a choice as any—he had the right experience, they said—but others disagreed. Soderini is not an old man, yet his face is lined, with deep creases alongside his nose, matched only by the ponderous folds of his long, dark robes.

"He is the one who is behind the resurrection of the giant, I heard," Botticelli mumbles.

I only scratch my head. I wonder why such a man would concern himself with a sculpture, when surely he has bigger things to worry about; after all, mercenaries from Pisa, an army from France, even Cesare Borgia's men from the Romagna, might appear at the gates of our city at any moment.

The tottering flags of the wool guild settle around a hulking bronze sculpture made three generations ago, showing the biblical Judith severing the head of Holofernes. I imagine that our people of the time saw it as a symbol of our city as a powerful foe, but as our fortunes changed and the Medici were ousted, some now see it instead as a symbol of the Medici pushing to come back and overthrow the same Signoria that had exiled them.

"Anyway, it is disgraceful as a model, for we should not show a woman killing a man," my father had said as we passed the sculpture on one of our Sunday walks. We often strolled to look at the statues around the city, especially those displayed in the covered loggia of the same square where I stand today. My father's voice rings in my head. "The lion, on the other hand," he had said, pointing to the statue on the other side of the door, "is an appropriate symbol for anyone who might try to take on the Pisans."

A man from the cathedral committee steps onto a wooden platform that has been dragged into the square. The committee stomps on the stones to make a rumble that quiets the crowd. Into the silence, the man speaks.

"For the glory of the Florentine Republic, our *gonfaloniere* and our esteemed cathedral fathers announce that they will award a commission to create a male statue from a large block of marble in the cathedral workyard. The said block of marble was badly roughed out some forty years ago. The *operai* would like to consult with the city's artists to determine if the block might be turned into a statue. If successful, it will be the first of a program of twelve prophets for the *tribuna* of the cathedral of Florence."

The man's eyes look up from the parchment to scan the ragged crowd of makers. Then he continues. "We shall open the gates of the cathedral workyard at Monday's midday bell. At that time, any qualified guildsman who might consider a proposal may examine the marble block in greater detail. After that, anyone who would like to be considered must register his name at the wool guild offices no later than the Feast of Santa Barbara."

Little more than a month. Will it be enough time for Michelangelo to return to us?

The man continues. "The *operai* will hear individual proposals up until the evening bell. The commission will be awarded to one master, who will receive a stipend for the work. He will be compensated for expenses and assistants, as well as be given the necessary scaffolding, tools, and space in which to make the sculpture. That is all."

Murmuring swells through the crowd as the people begin to disperse.

"You think they will pay?" Andrea the goldsmith asks, but Botticelli has already lurched away, with his strange gait, in the direction of his workshop.

I shrug. We artists are left unpaid all the time.

"I could eat a mule," Andrea says. "Join me?" We walk shoulder to shoulder. Before I have a chance to consider another path, we are already snaking through the alleys toward the Mercato Vecchio.

We arrive at the door of The Fig, a tavern whose name references the fruit as well as a woman's backside. The establishment, with its questionable odors and dark walls, has become an unofficial meeting place for those of us who paint, sculpt, draw, create. I hesitate for a moment, but Andrea pushes me through the door, and before I can make a better judgment, I stumble inside the tavern.

For a moment, I am blinded by the darkness, then I am hit with a cool rush of air and the smell of smoked meat. My mouth waters. Already, a dozen men are straddling the benches around a large table in the center of the room, ordering cups of watery beer. The tavern owner's wife is bringing large platters of noodles and setting them on the table along with chunks of dusted bread. Before she rests the platters on the table, the men reach their forks and fingers into the plate.

"*Buon di*," says Federico the tanner, a gray-haired moose of a man with a large backside. He drags a crooked stool over to the table, then gestures to the barman. The tavern owner nods and begins filling a ceramic tankard with our favorite brew.

"Wasting time again, L'Indaco?" Federico raises his brows and smirks behind his bushy beard. The words come out gruff and thick with Tuscan dialect, slightly slurred. Federico and the dozen or so other men seated at the long table are already into the beer.

I deliver my usual response: "Time favors the inspired." Federico taps my tankard with his. We drink.

We began meeting here back when that ugly business with Savonarola got started. The tavern seemed the only place to find levity when things got heated in the squares and on the streets. For a time, we lived in an upside-down world when ducking into a seedy tavern was the only way to avoid the debauchery outside. We folded ourselves into the familiar darkness of the card table at the same time our patrons emptied their homes of paintings, dresses, jewelry, and other riches to burn on the pyre, and chased the wealthiest families from their palaces with the clothes on their backs. Now, thankfully, that time of madness in our city's history seems closed. A new day has dawned for us in Florence, a day in which an old hunk of marble might be turned into a biblical hero.

Two goldsmiths at the other end of the table have already produced pairs of dice roughly hewn from pig bones. They shake them between their palms and rattle them onto the table. Others are already pulling coins from their pockets.

"Wait! Our dealer is here!" says a man from the other end of the table. He looks familiar, but he seems to know me. "L'Indaco, there is a seat for you!" With his scuffed boot, the man pulls out a chair for me to sit at the head of the table.

All eyes are on me now. I open my mouth to decline the invitation to deal cards, but the words will not come. How would I start to explain that I have lost one too many times, that the debt collector's henchmen are already trailing me in the streets, that they may even darken the doorway of this tavern if I am unlucky? How would I tell them that I have already gambled away everything my father left to me? That our roof is leaking and our shutters are beginning to rot? You would think I would have sworn off this tavern given everything that's happened.

Instead, I pat the front of my cloak, for there is usually a deck of cards or a pair of dice in each of my pockets. But today they are empty, my sister having confiscated the card decks from my pockets on wash day. She has not returned them.

"I am afraid I did not bring…" I start. Perhaps I am saved after all.

But before I can finish, Federico produces a deck of cards and slaps it unceremoniously on the table.

With all eyes on me, I take the deck of cards and sit. Instinctively, I begin to shift them in my hands. It's an old deck, worn by time, pliable, with old pictures of kings and queens, crudely painted. The black and red pigments are faded and cracked. Between my fingers, the cards flex, sending up a musty smell. It would be simple to palm a card from this old deck, I think. An old, easy trick. Well-practiced. At the very thought of slipping a few extra cards invisibly into my lap, my palms begin to itch.

I shuffle the deck three more times in a way that looks impressive but is all for show. Then, I bang the deck on the table and cut the cards as the matron places another copper cup of watery brew before me.

Three of the men place stacks of coins on the table. Now, all eyes are on the coins and no one is watching my hands any longer. I deal the cards for a round of *frussi*, placing five cards before each player, and the rest of the deck between us.

I can't help it; I palm two extra cards and conceal them under my own hand of cards.

"You're putting your name in, Andrea?" asks one of the men at the table. "For that sculpture, I mean. The giant."

"I might," Andrea says, wiping a layer of foam from his top lip as he spreads out the cards between his dusty palms.

"Not me," says Federico. "Those old cranks couldn't pay me enough to tell me how to make something."

"That's because you wouldn't know where to start, Fede," the barmaid says, teasing him with a slap of her rag. The men around me roar with laughter.

"If they even paid you at all," I say. A nod of agreement around the table.

"I'm not putting my name in," Federico says.

"Oh, they'll pay," the fair-haired man at the other end of the table says. "Two years' salary for one sculpture, I heard."

"I'm putting my name in," Federico deadpans. He throws an extra coin into the pile on the table.

I look at my cards now. A quick peek at the palmed cards. Not good, even with an unfair advantage.

The man across the table continues. "You are all wrong. You forget that Master da Vinci is back in town. If he wants that sculpture, all he has to do is ask. I bet three," he says. He slides three coins to the center of the table.

"Da Vinci? That old sodomite? No more than an ass-kisser dressed in purple velvet," another man teases, and everyone laughs again. The tavern owner's wife delivers a plate of fried chicken livers, and the men make quick work of them, smearing greasy fingertips on the playing cards.

I look at my hand again. Two threes and a spade. Deathly. Even with the extra palmed cards, I wouldn't bet even if I had more than two coins in my pocket.

"Why do they go to the trouble to make such an announcement?" the man across the table butts in again. "They already know who they want." I say nothing but in my mind, I agree. Most of the artists in our city have gotten ahead on lucky timing or on the merit of their family relations with those in power.

"They are giving it to Torrigiano, I heard," says a small man with a high-pitched voice seated at the other end of the table. I cringe, knowing how much Michelangelo hates Torrigiano, that it is Torrigiano himself who is responsible for Michelangelo's crooked nose, the result of a boyhood fight. My heart pounds to think what would happen if Torrigiano won the commission.

"Wrong," says Andrea. "You're all wasting your breath. It's already Sansovino's. This whole thing is a charade. There is no contest."

"It's true," Federico says, raising his eyebrows and scratching his beard as if fleas inhabit it. "I, too, have heard Sansovino may have already clinched the commission. He's been seen talking to the *operai*. He's going to see them, one by one."

My heart feels like it has leapt into my throat. It is the first name that has made me stop dealing cards. "Sansovino?" An image of the young sculptor fills my mind, his cunning eyes, his mouth drawn into a line. I cannot hold my tongue any longer. "Sansovino!" I exclaim. "How? He is not even a Florentine."

Federico continues. "I heard he has tried to get a private audience with the *gonfaloniere* Soderini. My brother saw him coming out of the Signoria this morning before the announce-ment. He was already bragging about it."

The men continue to draw, discard, and match suits of cards around me, coins stacking and sliding across the wooden tabletop as the game continues. Under the table, I feel my fists curl. The truth, which I will never admit to this group, is that I am nearly broke. You would hardly know it by looking at our fine house, which my father inherited, but we have little cash. If I am to turn things around, this commission might be my last opportunity.

I stand up at the head of the table. "Michelangelo Buonarroti and I are going to the Signoria to capture the commission." I wish I could stop myself from blurting out the words, but it is done. Everyone at the table falls silent and looks at me.

"Why would Buonarroti come back here?" Federico says. "He is working for His Holiness."

"It is *our* block," I say, gesturing in the direction of the cathe-dral as if we can all see the discarded white hunk of marble from this dark, musty tavern. This comment makes the men laugh again. "Hear me, signori," I say. "He has had plans for it for years. I know; he told me himself. We have worked on it since we were boys." The story begins to take on a life of its own. "We even have new plans for it, which we will present soon to the Signoria. You will see."

"Then where is he?" says Rinaldo the bell-maker, quiet until now.

"Still in Rome, I heard," says Andrea.

"Good riddance." I am not sure who has said it, but the others titter and grumble in commiseration.

"Michelangelo knows that block of marble better than anyone," I insist again. "He has felt it with his own hands. He is the obvious choice."

"Well, if he wants this commission, he better get here fast," says Federico.

He is right, I know, and I start to feel my palms sweat on the front of my woolen hose. It has already been weeks and there has been no answer to my letter.

"I know him," I insist. "You remember that we have been friends since we were children. He has talked to me about it for many years. He knows the block, and so do I. We can clinch this commission."

"We? We!" Andrea bellows a laugh. "L'Indaco, you have had too much beer already. And you talk too much, but I'm sure that's not the first time you've heard it."

"Forza!" Federico the burly tanner bursts from his seat. He grasps me and squeezes me with his big arm. His camicia is drenched in sweat, and his pungent scent makes me lightheaded. The gesture rouses the crowd. They cheer and laugh, raising their tankards toward us.

They are only making a fool of me.

Rinaldo comes to my aid, placing his hand on my arm. "Don't forget that L'Indaco and Michelangelo were both apprenticed to Master Ghirlandaio when they were boys," he says.

"Yes," I say, deflated. I wonder why I always manage to set myself up to be a target. A laughing stock.

Anyway, my hand of cards is bad, and even if it weren't, I have no coins to bet. I slap the cards down on the table. I swill the last mouthful of warm, foamy beer into my mouth. The man next to me studies the cards fanned out before his face, and he cannot act quickly enough to stop me from grabbing the remaining fried livers on his plate into my cheeks. Mercifully, this makes me unable to speak. The man slaps his cards face down and tries to grab my sleeve, but I weasel away. I grasp my hat and leave the men at the table, jabbing and laughing at my back. I scramble for the door and plunge into the darkness of the alley. Will they retrieve my extra palmed cards on the floor after I leave? I no longer care.

My dignity is bruised but I know I am right. I have lost faith in these fools, and I have learned that I am better off with people who are on my side. Besides, I have access to one person they do not. Surely there is one man who might take my side.

Michelangelo's own father.

If he doesn't believe his son and I can take on the block, then I don't know who will.

IT HAS BEEN several years since I last waited outside the front door of Michelangelo's boyhood home. And now, standing before the looming house made of coursed stone, I have left

behind the shame of the tavern. Instead, I am filled with anticipation. Surely Michelangelo's father will take my side. Surely he
will want his own son home once again.

I would not have called Signor Buonarroti a handsome man
even in his prime. It is more that he carries himself like a nobleman, shoulders back, befitting a man with a long lineage of wool
trading. If you saw him on the street, you might think him a
magistrate or at least a notary.

But as a house servant opens the door and Signor Buonarroti
draws me into the sitting room with a bony hand, I see that over
the course of just a few years, his hair has turned thin and dull.
The skin on his neck has begun to sag from his jowls. Still, he
carries a noble air.

"You have been painting at San Pier Martire, I have heard,"
he says, heaving himself into a chair and sighing with relief. His
statement ends in a question. I feel his dark eyes on me, beads of
black just like his son's.

The thought that Signor Buonarroti follows my work brings
a flush to my cheeks. I do not begin to tell him the only reason
I am working at San Pier Martire is to pay off gambling fines I
owe to the city. It is a little known fact that the reason Florence
boasts so many beautiful public buildings is that these spectacles
are matched equally by people's compulsion for dice, cards,
boxing, cockfights, and fisticuffs. Few of us who play such games
have the money to pay such penalties, nor do we ever see a *soldo*
in return for our work. Instead, we finance the glories of the city
with the labor of our own hands.

"Yes," I say as guilt washes over me. While my younger
brother Francesco, barely old enough to be a journeyman, has
left Florence to work with a team of fresco painters in Arezzo
and Montepulciano, I am months behind deadline and am certain the abbess of San Pier Martire is ready to strangle me with

her arthritic hands. I have only managed to avoid strangling by virtue of the fact that I have timed my work when the old lady is at the bottle or behind locked doors throwing dice herself. Still, the hired men of the *guardia* shadow me.

A striped yellow cat leaps into Michelangelo's father's lap, and the old man runs his elegant fingers over the animal. "I am glad to see you have turned into a responsible adult. We had our doubts. You were a mischievous youngster." I see the corner of his mouth turn up, and I know he is teasing me, too.

"I am the first to admit it, sir," I say. "I can hardly compare with your son."

Signor Buonarroti strokes the top of the cat's head as the beast kneads the old man's legs, then settles in his lap. "Rome suits him," he says. "He has taken on commissions for the Holy Father."

"I have heard it spoken on the streets," I say, taking a deep breath and pushing down the truth—the truth that it was nothing more than stupid luck that brought Michelangelo to the pope's door. A turn of fortune's wheel. After all, it's impossible that Michelangelo's personal charms won the pope's favor.

In my ten-year-old mind, my criterion for choosing Michelangelo as my friend was not that he was kind or even that we might be matched artistically, but rather by the fact that he was very bad. He spoke in a scathing Tuscan tongue, his vocabulary full of swear words even as a young boy. He was knotted, grubby, and walked around with a cut above his eye or a bruise on his arm. He constantly scanned the room with his shadowed eyes, seemingly waiting for anyone to cross him. All the other boys steered away from him.

He was a year older than I and had been an apprentice for nearly two years when my father ushered me into Master Ghirlandaio's studio. In those days, the workshop was filled with boys whose fathers, like mine, pushed them there. Michelangelo was the only one of us who dragged his own father there unwillingly. He was supposed to be a notary—at least a wool trader, anything but an artist—but Michelangelo prevailed over his father's will.

I see now it was volatility that drew me to him. I followed him like a hungry street dog. He was quick, deliberate in every word and deed. Everything he did, drawing a hand or throwing a punch, he did with absolute conviction. Not one of us could match that terrible, dazzling boy. He crackled with an energy like the lightning of a summer tempest.

"Surely you are proud," I say to his father.

He is more than proud, I see, for the money Michelangelo has been sending home is everywhere in evidence. Back when we were boys, Michelangelo and I stood on similar footing, inheritors of comfortable homes even if we hardly had a *denaro* in our pockets. Now, as I note Signor Buonarroti's upholstered chairs, his finely embroidered silk hose, his roaring fire, new servants in the corridors, I realize that our own home looks ramshackle in comparison, our shutters hanging off the hinges, our linens tattered and mended many times.

Signor Buonarroti had always claimed he was descended from the counts of Canossa, but Michelangelo confided in me years ago that his family had long run out of money. Twice a widower, Signor Buonarroti appears wealthy but struggles to sustain a household of five growing boys. The oldest, Lionardo, is no longer a burden to his father, cloistered behind the walls of a Dominican monastery for many years now. That makes Michelangelo the oldest, and I know from a young age, my friend has felt responsible for taking care of his father and younger three brothers still at home.

Back when both of us had our fathers, we used to compare them. Michelangelo even confided he was envious of me, having a kind father who encouraged my artistic pursuits rather than getting in the way of them. My father was large and jovial, with a broad forehead, pudgy hands, and a girth that made him look more like a butcher than a manuscript illuminator. In those days we ate meat, with garlic and figs braided and hanging in ropes from the rafters of the kitchen, and sides of beef from Chiana stored in the cold box in our kitchen. Still, my father had none of the connections or privilege of Signor Buonarroti.

Then one day I came home to find my father laid out in our house, ashen and surrounded by candles, purple drapes, neighbors, our parish priest, and my little brother trying to look brave. My sister sat hunched over with her face in her hands.

"I know your son is doing well in Rome," I say, "but, well, I was hoping he would come back to Florence, to work on the cathedral commission."

Signor Buonarroti blows air and snickers. "Come back to Florence? What kind of commission would prompt him to do that? He left just in time if you ask me. All that ugly business with Savonarola, thank God it is past. And now," he says, shaking his head, "the lords of Romagna and even those French are trying their best to rape our lands. Last year, Borgia's bands of savages burned our crops in the Val di Chiana to the ground. The entire harvest lost!"

"Bastards!" I interject.

He nods in agreement. "And they could be at our gates any day, if we're not vigilant. Return to Florence…Why would he? Anyone would be better off in Rome right now. Would *you* leave Rome if you were working for His Holiness himself?"

He has a point, but I am not ready to let go of my desperation. I scan the dark coffers of the ceiling. Painted cherubs peer down at me with their whimsical, taunting smiles. My mind searches for the words to make my case.

"But sir, the men on the cathedral committee, even the *gonfaloniere* himself, have said this sculpture is one of the most important commissions in years. It will be placed on top of one of the tribunes, high above the rooftops of Florence. It will be there for everyone to see. Surely it will be one of the most esteemed works in the whole city." I rise from my chair and gesture in front of his face. "I have written to him, begging him to come back and fight for this commission."

Signor Buonarroti pauses, frowning. "And he has responded?"

"No. Not yet. The letter has only just been sent." I lean forward and grasp Signor Buonarroti's bony arm. "Signore," I say, "I could not bear the thought of Sansovino or, heaven forbid, that da Vinci, winning this commission. Your son and I... we have talked about that block since we were boys. We made sketches, spent hours looking at it, climbing all over it."

I see his eyebrows raise at the mention of da Vinci. "It was a different time," he says.

"You could write to him, too," I insist. "You could tell him how important it is for him to be here now for this commission. You said it yourself; it is a critical time for our city. You know that better than anyone. He should be here at home, working for our new government, creating a symbol of our new state." I feel myself getting excited, talking too fast as my mother always tried to stop me from doing. "If he won't listen to me, surely he will listen to his own father!"

Signor Buonarroti looks down his nose at me, as if I am a bothersome house servant. "Jacopo," he says, pulling his arm from my grasp. "You have the power of persuasion your father lacked. Of course I am happy our republic is finally restored after that ugliness, but as I said, there are still threats on all sides. I can hardly see the rationale in tying your fortune to a statue in Florence, under the circumstances." He waves the air as if he is shooing a fly. "However significant these monkeys think their sculpture is, I can assure you that it in no way can compete with a sculpture made for His Holiness. Surely you can see the logic in that."

I feel my shoulders fall.

Signor Buonarroti wags his head. "No, Jacopo, I am sorry. As much as I would like to have my own son back under my roof, I cannot imagine why he would abandon his patrons in Rome to come back here for one meager statue."

THE WEEKS PASS. No response from Michelangelo.

In my obsession over the competition for the giant, I have neglected my own work. I have no other choice but to return to my frescoes at San Pier Martire.

I wait until the afternoon sun casts long streaks across the square and shade cools the stifling air that settles over our city in the summer months. As long as I appear in the church regularly, the hulking shadows stop following me. That's how I know the men are watching.

The Dominican convent church of San Pier Martire is filled with the aroma of plaster and dust. It has always smelled like this, I think, at least during my lifetime, when the sanctuary has been little more than a construction site. Only one magnificent altarpiece, finished two generations ago by Brother Angelico, graces the high altar. Otherwise, the convent's painting and sculptural projects have been broached and delayed, some completed, others abandoned over generations. Patrons die; families run out of interest, or money, to complete what once seemed like an inspired idea. Painters pay off their gambling debts and fines to the city, setting themselves free of the work.

Not me. Not yet.

"Where have *you* been?"

Simone, our foreman, rounds the corner of a great pillar with a new batch of plaster in a wooden bucket. He grunts, peering at me over his thick beard. He sets the bucket down in front of a skinny apprentice so the boy can mix the plaster with a broom handle. Like me, Simone is paying off fines to the city, this one for cutting down once-profitable fruit trees in his neighbor's orchard over a marriage contract turned sour.

I shrug as he passes behind me. "I have more important things to work on."

I hear him grunt again behind my back. "Like what? Eating someone else's supper? Sleeping all day? Playing a *beffa* on some poor sap with dice? I hear those are your favorite pastimes."

"I would gladly do any of the above given the opportunity."

His chuckle echoes off the walls, and I feel lighter, the way I always do when I make someone laugh. A small but satisfying victory.

I run my hand over the rough surface of the wall, examining the thin coats of plaster that have been layered in preparation for our pigments. They were laid on my last visit here. Some four weeks ago... Has it been that long?

During that time, I have heard nothing from Michelangelo Buonarroti. Instead, I have made sketches on paper, on my bedpost, on a section of wall near my bedchamber window, of a man made of marble. I have even procured some clay from a potter friend in the neighborhood, and have begun to fashion gray figures on a table in my room, the same table where I wrote a letter to Michelangelo weeks ago, imploring him to come home. Perhaps he has laughed it off with his new friends in Rome or chosen to ignore me altogether. I shouldn't be surprised.

I stand back to consider the progress other artists have made in my absence. It is a monumental project, a series of scenes depicting the life of Saint Peter Martyr. Any other painter in Florence might consider himself fortunate to take part in it. In other circumstances, it might even be a well-paying commission, but not for us. No matter how many hours we spend laying pigments on the wall, none of the compensation will go into our own pockets.

Since I was last here, part of the chapel's wall has been scored with charcoal, pubescent assistants tasked with this much like Michelangelo and I were for Master Ghirlandaio when we were boys. Today, in San Pier Martire, we work together from left to right, using the large cartoons the master has drawn on paper, then transferred to the scored squares on the wall. Later, an assistant will rough out the colors in pastel or watercolor to indicate the shades of pigment. Eventually, the fresco will begin to take shape.

My sister has completed much more work in the same amount of time, painting miniature flowers and trailing leaves in the margins of the nuns' books. My brother no doubt has made a decent living for himself, having left us four years ago for other towns in the countryside that have fewer painters than Florence, and less competition for the same paying projects. In my letter, I dared not share the fact that though I am the eldest son and my parents are dead, unlike Michelangelo, I have not been able to provide for my siblings. Instead, they have had to provide for themselves, and, if I am honest, they have provided even for me.

During my absence, one of the other painters already laid colored pigments on three of the squares originally assigned to me. I do not like the way the hand has turned out on one of the men in a scene of Saint Peter Martyr preaching, but there is no going back to fix the mistake. Once the pigments have been laid, they fuse with the wet plaster and dry into a dull but beautiful panorama of color. As much as I might like to go back and adjust the pout of a lip, the placement of an arm, the rendering of a hand, I can only shrug and move to the next square.

I pick up where the last painter left off, laying color along the hem of the robe of Our Lady. I have spent months on and off—truth be told, mostly off—laying colors based on the cartoons the master provided to us before he left for more lucrative work in Pistoia. I have grown bored with painting faces and hands, with transferring the design into the square the plaster man has scored for me on the wall. If it were not for the fact that this is the only means I have to pay my debt and fine to the city, I might have abandoned the project long ago. I have also grown bored of the other artists tasked with working alongside me.

Or I might say *had* grown bored. But today is different. There is a new painter.

A woman.

She is not just any woman. She is young and lovely, dark braids hanging down her back. A girl who paints. She has appeared with a crew tasked with another fresco in a chapel opposite our own.

I recognize only one of the men in her group, a painter I've met at the tavern, though I cannot remember his name. Even so, any excuse to earn her attention—perhaps even to make her laugh. I amble over and stand behind the woman for a bit. She does not turn around.

"You have a new master," I say to their foreman, gesturing to her.

She turns and looks at me, and I see the creases beside her eyes. She flashes her teeth but quickly raises her hand to her mouth. She doesn't want me to see her smile. I feel my chest inflate.

"What are you painting?"

The painter I recognized—Alesso is his name, I remember now—steps in. "The healing of the blind man. Master Filippo is a pain in our sides, but he does good work. Besides, Signora keeps us in line." He winks at me.

"Signora…?" I follow the man's gaze.

"My wife," he says. "Not only does she keep us honest, but she makes very good drawings," he says more loudly, but she is ignoring us now. Instead, she is concentrating intensely on the mouth of an angel in the corner of a square. If she has taken note of our commentary, she gives no indication. "It is her drawings we are using for our cartoons." I see the cartoons pinned to the wall and consider the composition. She is skilled, I think.

"We have not seen you here in weeks," Alesso says.

"That's because I have been out trying to garner support for Michelangelo Buonarroti and myself to win the *David* commission," I say loudly, gesturing in the direction of the Duomo. "Working out of the center of attention, you might say, but working nonetheless."

Now the woman turns and looks at me. I try to give her my best smile. "The rumor is Sansovino will take the commission," she says, before returning my smile with a smirk. "But now that Master da Vinci has returned to Florence from Milan, I imagine there will be a worthy competition."

"You are incorrect on that count, signora," I say. "I have written to Michelangelo, and I am certain that he will return home for it."

"Buonarroti? I thought he had left us behind long ago," says one of the young assistants.

"He has been in Rome. Working for His Holiness. Made a sculpture there of Our Lady with the Christ as a grown man on her lap. His name is on everyone's lips!" I say.

"Well, no one gives an ass's tail about him here," says Alesso. "We already have too many artists anyway. He should stay in Rome."

"I think we stand a good chance."

Simone comes out from behind the pillar, looks at me sideways, then guffaws. "We? Surely you don't think *you* will have any part in it, L'Indaco."

"Why wouldn't I?" I shrug. "I am as trained as you are."

He hesitates, as if he expects me to admit I am telling another one of my jokes. I don't, and he narrows his eyes. "Since when are you and Buonarroti friends?"

"We have collaborated ever since we were boys in Master Ghirlandaio's studio. We climbed all over that block of marble. I have already made *bozzetti* for the sculpture."

"Then you must be happy," he says.

"About what?"

"That your man is back."

"What man?"

"Buonarroti. We saw him with our own eyes last night."

I feel my heart stop. "Where?"

"We saw him coming through the Porta Romana on his mule just before the evening bell. I should have thought he would have a more fancy entourage, being the papal artist and all that." Simone laughs.

Alesso adds, "Come to think of it, he looked pretty much like the same old vagrant he always did. Just older."

"And meaner." They both laugh.

My mind races. Has he really returned? I should have re-ceived a letter. Perhaps it was lost along the road from Rome? After all these weeks... I must go to his house without delay. If we don't begin planning the sculpture immediately, our opportu-nity may be lost.

"You mean you did not know he was coming back to Florence?" the woman says.

"No, of course I did," I say, rousing the same confidence I tried to muster in the cathedral square. "Of course. After all, I was the one to write to him and tell him to come back home. He's just coming because of me. Because we planned it." I feel annoyed they are not convinced.

"I'm sure he is waiting for me now," I mumble, but I am not sure they have understood my words, or if they would believe them if they did. These ridiculous frescoes can wait, and anyway, my fellow painters here have proved little more than a thorn in my foot.

I remove my smock and scramble for the door.

❧

FROM THE STREET, I see lamplight glowing in an upper window. The rest of his father's house lies dark in the purple light of dusk. The street is silent.

Long ago, I used to lure him from his drawings by throwing pebbles at his window. Then we would run, a couple of adventur-ers under the illusion that the streets of Florence were ours to conquer.

I reach between my worn leather clogs to feel between the cracks of the cobblestones, still warm from the retreating sun.

I wedge my fingers between two cobbles and extract a pebble. Twisting my arm behind my head in an awkward, now unpracticed motion, I throw the stone at the window. It hits its target, bouncing off the leaded glass with a tinking sound like a small piece of hail. No response. I fish another pebble from the ground and try again.

I cup my hands around my mouth and yell, "*Michagniolo!*" An old woman peers down from her window and casts me a deep scowl. She reaches for her shutter and pulls it closed with a slap that echoes through the street.

"Little Michael Angel! It's me!" I try again, forcing my voice to come out as a loud whisper, tamping down my exhilaration at the thought of my old friend, returned home on my account.

After a moment, a silhouette appears in the window, then the leaded pane opens and his head emerges. His curls fall across his chin, and immediately I recognize the gnarled profile, the dark expression. I cannot help but smile and even laugh a little, seeing his familiar face emerge from the window.

"Who is there?" he calls in a gruff voice.

"It's me, friend! Welcome back to our most glorious city!" My loud voice has returned. It ends in a laugh.

"L'Indaco," he says, and I am sure I see a grin cross his face, too. "Stay there," he says, and the silhouette disappears from view.

After a few, long moments the arched doorway opens, and finally, I see the familiar form of my friend, his shoulders stooped slightly forward as if he is protecting himself from something. In one hand, he holds a lantern high enough that his familiar face glows in the candlelight. Then I feel his wiry frame in my arms. I squeeze him with all my might, and I feel I might burst from happiness.

He presses his palms to my chest. "*Piano!*" he says. "You will crush me, you pack ox. *Sant'Angela*, what have they been feeding you?"

I pat my paunch with my hand. "Tripe, liver, beef steak... Only the best Florentine specialties. But then, you would not know. You have not graced us with your presence here in such a long time."

"You have been eating for me, too, then," he says.

I follow my old friend into the darkness of his house, and once again I lower my voice to a whisper. "They are sleeping already?" I imagine Signor Buonarroti and Michelangelo's young brothers sprawled across their poster beds upstairs, perhaps moved to the lower floors to escape the heat.

"No. Out at our country house. It is too hot for them in the city, they say. Ha! They should come to Rome."

I follow him across the patterned tile floor, but instead of taking the broad staircase, he leads me into the shadows of the kitchen at the back of the house.

"You want something to eat?"

I shake my head but pick up an apple from the bowl, then follow him to the back stairwell. The heat hits us like a wall as we climb the stairs, and I understand why the family has moved out of the city as a respite.

We step into Michelangelo's bedchamber. It is neat and orderly as it is only when he is away. His canvas mulepack and a few papers and books are strewn across the worktable.

"You received my letter," I say finally, breaking the silence.

He nods but says nothing. He places his lantern on the large wooden desk, and I study him in the lamplight. He looks the same as always, but his face has taken on a harder appearance, with dark lines reaching from his crooked nose to either side of his mouth. His hair falls greasy and tousled over his cheeks.

In the flickering light, I cannot see if he still bears the cuts and scuffs on his knees and elbows as he did when he was younger, but his doublet is dirty and smudged, no doubt the same one he was wearing when he entered Florence on muleback the night before.

"And somehow you knew I was here already. No doubt you heard it in the tavern." He grins now, and I see the edges of his eyes crinkle. For a moment, an image of the boy I always knew returns to his face. "Am I right? Il Porco is the font of all information, after all."

"All critical information, yes."

He smirks.

"But no, I heard it at San Pier. I... I don't go to the taverns much anymore." A lie. "Haven't played dice in months."

He nods. "I'm glad to hear it." Then his face turns serious and he studies me with his black eyes. "You are well," he says.

"Yes," I say, shrugging and taking a bite of the apple. "I am busy with my frescoes at San Pier and other nonsense..." I rush forward and grasp his forearm. "But *grazie a Dio*! Finally, you are here! I was beginning to worry you hadn't received my letter. The commission! It's all anyone in town can speak of. I fear the city fathers are close to making a decision. We do not have much time."

"The block," he says, scratching his brow with dirty fingernails. "Yes. Well. It has taken them years, hasn't it, to decide what to do with that old thing. Why now? I suppose it is a sign of the new Florence."

"Yes! The new Florence. The time is now." I begin to pace. "They say our enemies could appear at the gates at any moment, but I swear you would never know it! The rich are indulging themselves as never before. It's as if none of that crazy business with the bonfires ever happened. They are commissioning new paintings, new sculptures. There are new frescoes in every church. New spectacles, each one more debauched than the next. Medici or no Medici, the pigs are feasting to the point of excess in our city once again."

"Hmm," Michelangelo narrows his eyes. "Pigs get fat. Hogs get slaughtered. At least they do in Rome."

But I don't let his jaded assessment stop me. "Little Michael Angel, think of it!" I wave my arms as if our names are written in the stars. "You and I! We have been waiting for this our whole lives. They are throwing out names. Da Vinci, Sansovino. Sansovino! Can you imagine? They say that he has already been to see the *gonfaloniere* in person! And talking to each of the *operai*, going to their houses, breaking bread with those old mossbacks, trying to convince them he can take the block…"

I am pacing the room excitedly—I can't help myself—but at a certain point, I realize Michelangelo has stopped listening to me. I turn to find that he has flopped on his back on his large mattress, all but his legs hidden behind the heavy drapes that obscure the bed.

I stop talking and push aside the netting meant to keep the mosquitoes from the Arno from turning us into bare bones overnight. Inside the enclosure of the curtains, the heat is stifling. I can smell the filth of his body and his stained doublet after days on the road.

"L'Indaco," Michelangelo whispers, and I see his face soften. For a moment, we consider each other in the silence. He grasps my hand and laces his fingers through it. I feel his gnarly, bony fingers, as rough as sandpaper, in my pudgy ones, our palms sealed together in a firm grip.

"I have missed your ranting. It has been a long time." The left corner of his mouth turns up, a crooked line.

"But you... you are the same as always," I say, though that is not entirely the truth. He looks the same, same gnarled frame, same crooked face. He is still young, but Rome, I see, has turned him from an intense youth into a man. His face has become more angular, as if his features have finally come into focus, including the flattened bridge of his nose. In the lamplight, I can see the whiskers across his chin, the veins knotted and protruding from his forearm, once prematurely muscular from his nonstop hammering.

It was he who gave me the nickname L'Indaco, for my black-blue eyes the color of the indigo we used in our pigment dyes. The name went to my brother, too, which made no sense for his eyes are green, but I guess people want to ascribe the same traits to the younger brother as the older.

We worked alongside one another on Master Ghirlandaio's projects for several years, whispering to one another while we set the plaster in wet squares. Michelangelo wanted me next to him because I made him laugh, he told me. At night, I would lie awake and think of things I could say to him the next day that would bring a smile to his face, or even better, make him throw back his head and squint his eyes in laughter.

At the end of my first year in Ghirlandaio's studio, my father praised me for winning many competitions for my talent, for drawing came easy and early. I easily passed over the other boys by drawing figures and drapery with the pen and the charcoal. Michelangelo praised me, too.

We lost our mothers around the same time. His succumbed to that moment in the childbed when birth and death are so closely intertwined. I lost my own to the rushing waters of the Arno, shortly after my little brother was born. My brother Francesco never had an image of our mother to hold in his head.

But then one day, Lorenzo, our Magnifico, asked Master Ghirlandaio to send his two best pupils to the palace. There, he said, he would see to their tutelage, would provide them with down-filled beds, fattened goose at the table, and the best teachers. To my utter dismay, I watched Michelangelo and Francesco Granacci pack their pens and charcoal and walk across the Ponte Vecchio, never to return to Ghirlandaio's workshop.

It was the last time Michelangelo and I worked side by side, not because he lived happily inside the Medici gardens, but rather that fate swept us into a whirlwind. It wasn't long before his illustrious patron died, the Medici family nearly went bankrupt, and the angry crowds chased Il Magnifico's heirs from our city. Michelangelo set off to seek new patrons in Venice, then in Bologna. The pestilence took our Master Ghirlandaio to the Hereafter, and I returned home to my father. Then, our city lost its mind for a span of time that now seems a strange nightmare. Michelangelo followed fortune to Rome, and others here in Florence got ahead by sheer luck or connections to patrons with deep pockets. Then my father died, I started playing games in the taverns, and my own fortunes turned.

From then, we did not see each other any longer. We went long years without writing or hearing from one another. Our paths diverged. He flourished; I floundered. And I never ceased to rid my mind of the image of him walking away from me over that bridge, all those years ago.

"Angelino," I whisper into the darkness of the draped bed. "Think about it. The time is now for us to make a symbol of our city. We can do it, after all these years. You and me. Just like the old days."

He continues to lock my fingers with his own, but he looks up at the drapery above his head as if seeing something far beyond the confines of the bedchamber. I am left to wonder what has happened in Rome that has hardened him, brought deep creases to his forehead and cheeks.

Finally, he squeezes my hand and lets it fall. "It is just a silly sculpture," he says, swatting the air with his gnarled fingers as a fly swoops drunkenly into the shadows of the bed.

But I look into his dark eyes and I know better.

I watch his jaw set. To me, to someone who knows him so well, I can see he is hungry for it.

But behind the hunger there is something darker, something that has me worried. As certain as I am that we will clinch the commission, *he* is not sure we will win.

"HE'S IN THE latrines."

My sister appears from her bedchamber, where she has been dressing for dinner. I lift my chin toward the back door, the one that leads to the narrow row of stinking pits behind our garden.

Finally, we may start. It didn't take much to lure Michelangelo to our table, but all the same, I feel restless, fidgety. I want to get the design settled so that we may put our names on the list as contenders to take on that accursed marble block, at last.

Lucia picks up a wooden spoon to stir the pot of stew over the fire. She has let her hair down in the style of a maiden set to lure an engagement. She has traded her worn linen shift for the only dress she has for more serious occasions, not worn since our father's burial. My sister's stew, started before the hens began their morning cacophony, fills the house with the aroma of thyme and the meat brought from the Val di Pesa. A fire crackles in our hearth, and steam from the copper pot rises into the air, bringing color to her cheeks.

I can resist no longer. Michelangelo's leather-bound sketch-book calls to me from where it lies on the worn planks of the tabletop.

Is Lucia watching me? No. She keeps her back to me while she stirs the pot.

I tip open the cover of the sketchbook with one finger, hoping to catch a glimpse of the David in progress. Instead of sketches, the initial pages are full of script, neat, angular cursive drawn in iron gall ink. Many of the passages are crossed out, the pages stabbed with the point of an ink pen as if in haste or anger. Notes and half-formed thoughts are neatly captured in the margins. I open the book flat and continue to shuffle the pages.

From the corner of my eye, I keep watch on the back door. Michelangelo has always been notoriously vigilant, ever nervous that someone might steal his ideas before he had a chance to bring them to fruition.

Finally, behind some two dozen pages filled with script front and back, the sketches begin alongside the words. Rendered in smudged charcoal and ruddy pencil, I see a jumbled series of men's hulking backs, of legs, arms, faces, hands, men carrying blocks, twisting, turning, throwing rocks, carrying swords. Men of action. Powerful, writhing bodies.

Lucia comes to my side and closes the leather cover, pressing the binding straps over my hand so I am forced to remove it or be crushed.

"Stop it," she whispers, setting her large, brown eyes on me. "He trusts you."

I relent, pulling my hand out of the pages. I step away from the sketchbook just as Michelangelo opens the garden latrine door. As his stooped form appears under the low beam, I see my sister straighten her back and smooth her skirt with her palms.

"Signorina," he says as he steps into the kitchen.

She smiles brightly, then looks down as if she doesn't want him to see her eagerness. "Signor Buonarroti. It has been a long time. Please. *Tutti a tavola*," my sister says, gesturing for us to sit. "Before the stew gets cold." Behind us, she ladles steaming stew into chipped, ceramic bowls.

We all cross ourselves and mumble a perfunctory thanks to God. Then Michelangelo curls his arm around the bowl as if he fears we will steal it from him and lowers his face into the steam. He grunts below his breath as he slurps loudly from the spoon.

A few seconds of awkward silence. My sister shoots me a cautionary glance from across the table.

"You have brought your sketchbook," I say, holding Lucia's gaze.

"Mmm," he says, his mouth full. Long moments of silence follow, the only sound the three of us scraping our bowls with our spoons. The familiar flavors of my sister's handiwork warm my cheeks.

Michelangelo's bowl is quickly emptied, and Lucia rises to refill it. "I already knew your sister was gifted with the brush and the pen," he says, watching her cross the room. "But I see she is talented in more ways than one."

"*Grazie*," she says. Her straight, white teeth flash again before she brings her hand to her mouth in a self-conscious gesture. Her cheeks are pink and flushed. She looks beautiful. I watch Michelangelo's face, which has already turned back to the bowl. He lets the steam rise to his cheeks again.

"I have missed this," he says. "Florentine home cooking."

"You don't eat well in Rome?" she asks.

"Well enough. But it's not Florence."

He does not look up again, but I see she is elated with his attention, that she craves the affirmations of this gnarled, little man. For some reason, I think, it has always been impossible to resist his strange power, which pushes and pulls you at the same time. She is no more immune to it than I. I see my sister watching him, hanging on his every word. I know the feeling, for I have felt it myself, and immediately I am filled with compassion for her. I wish I could tell her to let go of the idea that she will ever turn his head. His love is the stone, his art. Unless he has more to tell me from his stay in Rome, he has never given himself to a woman. Before he walks out our door, he might have left Lucia's heart behind in pieces, and he will never know it.

"Little Michael Angel," I say, eager to turn the conversation to matters of business, "we must go to the Signoria first thing tomorrow and put our names on the list."

"Already done," Michelangelo says, breaking a hunk of bread from the loaf in the middle of the table, and dunking it sloppily into what is left in the bottom of his bowl.

"You have already recorded our names? Thanks be to God," I say, exhaling audibly. "Well then, it's settled."

I feel relief wash over me, knowing we are officially in the running for the commission. In recent days, crowds have formed around the gates of the cathedral workyard. The city fathers have even installed armed guards to dissuade maldoers. If the public were not aware of the block before, they are now. The Signoria's announcement has attracted a host of annoying windbags who suddenly want to be experts on art—those who want to comment, give their opinions, suggest, be involved, say what they would do if they were the ones to win the commission. Nobility appear in scores, if only to show off their latest belted tunics, circle-brimmed velvet hats, silk brocades, and gems around their necks. They collect around the workyard, sharing opinions, competing for ideas, wanting to be seen.

"You must tell us about Rome," my sister says, before I can say anything else about the commission or try again to get him to show us his drawings.

Michelangelo says nothing, but wipes his wispy beard on his sleeve and reaches for his sketchbook. He opens the worn leather cover and turns over the first few pages of script. Lucia casts me another searing glance, then stands and begins to clear our plates from the table.

"That is a lot of words," I say, as he shuffles through pages of elegant script.

"I have been writing sonnets," he says. I marvel at the elegant, practiced handwriting and immediately feel ashamed of the chicken scratch I sent him in my own letter. I remember when I visited him at his father's house, after he had been in the Medici gardens for some time, learning with Lorenzo the Magnificent's own son. I watched him dip his pen into the inkwell, then carefully draw the nib across the parchment, showing me the deftness in his hand that had turned from drawing figures to making beautiful letters. He fancied himself a writer and worked hard on his sonnets and quatrains, even long ago.

But I feel I may burst. "Angelino… The sculpture. The *operai* are saying it is to be a David, high up on the tribune of the cathedral. A boy king, perhaps like the one of Donatello."

One of the drawings catches my eye, a finely drawn sketch in red ink, showing the head of a man with a square jaw and large, staring eyes. Alongside it is a hand facing up. I pick up the paper carefully from the table and bring it closer to the oil lamp so I can see the lines. "What is this?"

"A colossus," he says, fingering through the other pages of his sketchbook. "I sketched it in the ancient forum. The head alone stands four times the height of a man."

"A giant?" my sister says.

"Si," he nods. "There are many in Rome, marble sculptures from the antique age, some painted, some white. Some life-sized. Many larger."

I fail to imagine this sight as much as I fail to imagine the great cliffs of Carrara marble that lie to our southwest, those that Michelangelo tried to describe to me for years. He shipped a block of marble to make a great Hercules years ago, bringing it back to Florence on a barge on the Arno. Nothing ever became of the project, but I will never forget the pages and pages of sketches my friend made of the marble masons in the quarries, no less than the sight of the shining block strapped across the deck of a river barge.

In the sketchbook, I run my finger across the arm of a man. The drawing is filled with pulsating life, through the veins of the forearms and hands, through the bulging tendons of the neck. Next, there is a beautiful young man, neither fully god nor fully human, but somehow, both at the same time.

"That one is my favorite," he says. "Apollo Belvedere. I have gone to observe and sketch it many times. The guards in the papal palace know me by name now. They open the gate when they see me coming." I see his chest fill with air.

"They are all naked," Lucia says, and her face flushes again. "Why is that?"

Michelangelo presses his back against the chair. "They were heathens in those days, of course. But better to show the divine beauty of the human form, not to mention the human body as nothing more than a beautiful and mortal veil of divine spirit."

"You are revealing your Medici training again," I say.

"Apollo," he says, ignoring my comment and pointing with one finger. "It is in the collection of His Holiness. The ancients saw it as a human manifestation of a heathen god, but I say rather that the perfect human body draws us into contemplation upon the perfection of our Creator."

"And we are to make something like this for the block here," I venture.

Michelangelo waves his hand. "Impossible. The problem is the block here in Florence, our *gigante*, is no longer freshly quarried. It's been sitting in that workyard for more than a generation. It's been exposed to the rain, the wind, the sun, left to dry out. It is bound to be brittle, difficult to work."

"Not to mention the fact that it has already been butchered by Agostino di Duccio," I say.

"Exactly!" he says, slapping his palm on the table. "One is limited by the constraints of a narrow block that has already been partially worked."

He quickly shuffles through to the last pages of his sketchbook. Toward the back, there are countless images of a youth, a slighter figure. Some of them resemble the *David* of one of our city's most celebrated sculptors, Donatello. Other sketches reveal an older, more developed man with slings and rocks in various positions. Some from the front, some from the back, some with arms out, some with supports, some details of feet. Pages and pages of drawings. There are also sketches of the block, unmistakable. I feel my heart surge as doubt retreats from my mind. Michelangelo has been thinking about that marble block for a long time.

He spreads out several parchment pages across the wooden planks of our dining table. "Yes, the block was badly cut, but there is no need to add anything else. I am sure of it." He has drawn several versions of a tall, narrow sculpture without any protruding appendages.

"The trick must be to convince the committee," my sister says. "It is no longer as in the days of your Medici, when they gave you commissions for specific things to create. Here, in the hands of our new leaders, it seems that you must prove yourself instead."

I watch a shadow fall over his face. So much has happened, I think, since Michelangelo has been in Rome, that I hardly know where to begin, nor do I know what his own associates have told him about affairs in Florence. Michelangelo does not respond, but he taps his finger on his pursed lips.

"But I think Soderini would have more important things to do than think about a sculpture. Doesn't he have a new army to command?" My sister has a point, I think. Instead of engaging bands of freelance mercenaries, our governor general is now training a standing force to protect our city. We have seen their bright, new uniforms in the guard stations of each of our gates, and lines of men patrolling the squares.

"True enough, *cara*," Michelangelo says. "But you forget that one way to corral people's resolve is to inspire them through ancient heroes."

"Do we really need another hero in this city?" Lucia sighs. She collects cutlery to take to the wash basin. "*Per l'amor di Dio*, let us get on with our lives. We have had enough of heroes."

"Especially false ones," Michelangelo says. We all know he is talking of Savonarola though none of us dares utter his name. None of us wants to relive the time when that crooked priest roused the masses against one another in a brutal public renunciation of the excesses of Medici rule. He fanned out his roving bands of followers, little more than boys, across the city, knocking on every door. They demanded vanities of every kind—paintings, dresses, cosmetics, books, fans, playing cards, wigs, even spirits—and threw them into a great bonfire. But it wasn't long before the priest's rants fell on deaf ears, nooses were tied around the necks of Savonarola and his followers, and another bonfire turned their bodies into clumped ashes in the Piazza della Signoria. Chaos followed. Someone let goats and horses run through Santa Maria Novella. For weeks, acrid smoke hung heavy in the air as opportunistic kids set fires in squares across the city.

"The symbolism of a biblical David is not lost on Soderini, I assure you of that," Michelangelo says finally. My sister and I sit in the silence for a few moments, contemplating the idea. "There is a reason they call Soderini the Lion of Judah," he continues. "He is meant to defend Florence and govern her justly. It's obvious." Neither my sister nor I might have seen this, but it is clear as day when it comes from Michelangelo's lips. "It doesn't have to be a living man. The new hero might be... symbolic," he says.

"A new hero for Florence," my sister says, drying the last bowl with a dishrag.

He nods and sets his black eyes on her. "Yes, my lady." He bows toward Lucia as if he might have once addressed a woman of the Medici household. "A new hero. A beacon for the people. Larger than a man. A colossus. A giant."

<hr />

HE HAS STARTED without me.

I turn from the closed door of Michelangelo's house and try to comprehend his younger brother's words.

"He left at first light," Giovan Simone said, looking at me with wide, brown eyes, a face so similar but so much more innocent than his older brother's. "You might find him at Santo Spirito," he said before he pressed the striped yellow cat back into the shadows of the house to prevent him from darting into the alley, then closed the heavy door.

I feel the sting as if Michelangelo has pushed me away with his own dirty, scarred hands. I thought we had agreed to begin together?

But… the old haunt. Of course. He was lured by it, wanting to visit as soon as he returned home.

I never understood the appeal of spending days in a monastery crypt, but Michelangelo loved nothing more than drawing there among the corpses being prepared for burial. Victims of old age, disease, strange accidents. His old friend, the Augustinian prior of Santo Spirito, had long ago allowed Michelangelo in to sketch cadavers. How like him to go directly there on his return to Florence. Years ago, Michelangelo had even carved a wooden crucifix for the prior in exchange for the privilege of spending untold hours among the dead.

Somehow, Michelangelo was able to detach himself from the idea of the bodies in the crypt as real people. There with his sketchbook, he entered another world. The results are undeniable: he has drawn great men of myth and biblical history who breathe, men whose veins pulse with blood. From the dead, he has imagined men larger than life.

I turn and make my way from the Buonarroti home in Santa Croce toward the Oltrarno section of town, south of the bridge. The vendors along the narrow streets leading to the Ponte Vecchio have opened the hatches of their shops and begun to put out their wares for the day. Bread. Metal pots and pans. Linens. Oil lamps. Vinegar.

Self-consciously, I look behind to see if I am being followed. I do not see the men anywhere in sight.

Michelangelo must be expecting me to come find him at Santo Spirito. He knows I will find him there. Then, at last, we can begin.

Along the Ponte Vecchio, I pass the line of stinking butcher shops perched precariously along the edge of the bridge. I stop at the apex of the bridge, the only place not crowded with shops. I stop for a moment and swing my legs over the railing.

Our old meeting place.

After he had left Master Ghirlandaio's studio for the Medici gardens, Michelangelo and I used to meet most middays on the Ponte Vecchio. Together we would sit side by side on the railing and watch the river waters rushing far below our feet. We would banter back and forth about painting, sculpture, our friends, our enemies. Around us, the bustle of shopkeepers, carts stacked high with animal carcasses to be cut up and sold, the banter of daily negotiations did little to dissuade us. We would watch the bird seller with her wicker cages, and men carrying water in buckets with wooden beams propped across their brawny shoulders.

Sometimes we sat on the north side, where we watched the egg-shaped dome of the cathedral hulking over the tile rooftops, an uplifting sight that drew our vision away from the dismal slaughterhouses along the riverside. Other times we sat on the south bank, where we watched the *tiratori* dyeing the fabrics that bring our city riches to this very day.

Michelangelo would walk up from the fold of the Medici family's Pitti Palace and I from my crumbling house. He always brought something to share, some delicious morsel he had pinched from the palace kitchen on his way to meet me on the bridge, hidden deep within his pockets or his knapsack. Sometimes we would share a ripe pear, a piece of bread still warm from the oven, pecans coated with sugar and roasted in a pan; sometimes a less choice piece of beef or pork the cook had set aside for the hounds but that Michelangelo had managed to nick before coming to meet me.

Sitting on the railing of the bridge, he would recount the wonders of the palace in such detail that I might imagine I had seen them myself: the many sculptures of metal and marble, his joy in learning new things about poetry and dance, his privileged access to hundreds of ancient texts in the library, how he worked with a tutor alongside the duke's own children to learn to compose music and letters, his conversations with the learned ladies who sought his company. Some days I imagined that I, too, might be plucked from Master Ghirlandaio's studio, as he was, and invited by the duke, but day after day, I only worked alongside my father. I only created small things, swirling letters, decorative leaves with a flourish of gold, marginalia hardly worthy of note.

Sometimes, I waited a long time on the bridge for Michelangelo to arrive. While I waited, I would swing my feet back and forth, then look between them and wonder what it would be like if I leaned forward and let the heft of my body fall into the rushing waters below. I imagined how it would feel, the world receding as the water closed over my head, what it would feel like to watch speckles suspended in the green, to hear the muffled water sounds as I let the cold Arno fill my nostrils and then my lungs, letting the darkness embrace me like an old friend.

Is that what my mother experienced in her last moments?

To be fair, she didn't jump. One day, not long after my brother was born, she simply stepped into the cold, rushing waters by the riverbank of the dyers, and let the Arno close above her head. Sometimes, I think she was brave to do such a thing.

But just as I might begin to feel sad—and maybe a little angry—at my own mother, inevitably he would appear. Then we would talk, laugh, and share a treat from the palace kitchen. Soon enough, my imaginings of jumping into the river would dissipate like morning fog on the surface of water, rendered powerless under the splendor of the sun's rays.

The memory makes me smile. I continue my walk across the bridge, and after a short walk, I cross the threshold into the church of Santo Spirito.

Even in the blackness of the crypt, I would recognize him anywhere. He stands before the bloated body of an old man, leather sketchbook propped against his hip, working with a fine silverpoint pen. I recognize the silhouette of his stooped shoulders, the unruly hair that looks as if he has just risen from his bed, the worn smock smudged with charcoal and marble dust. The air hangs ripe with the tang of death, like a withered arrangement of flowers whose rotting stems coat the vase with slime. For a moment, my stomach churns. I feel as though I might flee from the crypt, gasping for fresh air, but Michelangelo seems not to notice the stench.

"Ahem." I steel myself against the malodor, bracing myself against a door frame and clearing my throat. "It seems I have caught you with another naked dead man. You didn't get enough of them in Rome?"

He turns, and the left side of his mouth turns up in a crooked smile. "It turns out that there aren't any mortuaries there that will let me in."

"I see. So this place of darkness and death is a pleasure savored only in Florence."

His short laugh echoes through the vaulted crypt, and the flame of a lone candle shudders. "Yes, my blue boy, you could say that."

"I should have thought you would be in the cathedral workyard instead. After all, we have a sculpture to make."

"Already been there."

I feel my jaw drop. "You have already been to see the block? How did you get in? They keep the gate locked now."

Michelangelo says nothing, but fishes into the pocket of his canvas shift and produces a large iron key.

"You have a key... to the cathedral workyard?"

He nods, but already he has returned his eyes to the bloated forearm of the dead man on the table.

"How did you manage that?"

"Salviati," he says.

Giuliano di Francesco Salviati was elected to the cathedral operai earlier in the year. Who had not heard of it, considering the public celebration that went along with his investiture? Paired with the election of members of the Mancini and Giugni, the cathedral's governing board now includes some of the most powerful families of our city's wool trade and its guild, the Arte della Lana.

"Salviati." I can only guffaw. "How?"

Michelangelo suspends the pen in midair and stares into the darkness. "Simple. He brought me the key himself. Do not forget, L'Indaco, that my family still has connections in the wool trade, even if most of the profits now go to others."

It is true, I realize. The Salviati and Buonarroti are neighbors in Santa Croce, the beating heart of our city's wool industry. Both claim to be related to the Medici by marriage. The truth is that Signor Buonarroti is only a small-time city functionary who clings to this pedigree, but I see it still counts for something, if only a key.

"You have already drawn the giant?" I gesture to his sketchbook.

He nods. "Mostly measuring." Over the greenish, bulging abdomen of the cadaver, Michelangelo thumbs through the parchment leaves. Reluctantly, I leave the security of the doorway, which might hold me up in case I faint of the stench. I cross the room, inching my way closer to Michelangelo and his sketchbook. In the flickering candlelight, I begin to see sketches of hands, shoulders, veins, but mostly words, again that looping, elegant script, and numbers, too, perhaps measurements made by his metal square.

"I suppose we should calculate for the weight of the sculpture on the buttress of the cathedral." I think about its dome, that red-tiled, egg-shaped form that defines the form of our whole city. I try to imagine the twelve figures the cathedral committee has planned, mounted high on the tribunes, figures of ancient prophets looking down to the hot streets below.

He does not respond. His eyes focus only on the bluish, swollen fingers of the dead man's right hand. I feel suddenly than I am an annoyance, an interruption, but I try again.

"That will be a lot of weight high up above the city."

Michelangelo stops sketching now. "No," he says, shaking his head.

"No?"

"No, L'Indaco," he says again, an exasperated tone in his voice that only confirms my suspicion that I am annoying him. "If this bid is successful, I will make sure the sculpture does not end up positioned so high that no one will see it." He gestures as if we could see the cathedral dome from the dankness of the crypt. In the candlelight, I see his eyes flash. "It is as I have told you, my blue boy. This David is to be a symbol of Florence, a symbol of the new republic."

I shrug. "If not up there," I gesture, as if I, too, have the power to see the cathedral dome from the depths of this dark place, "then where?"

He takes his eyes off the body and his sketchbook for the first time since I entered the mortuary, and sets them on me.

"In the square. Before the Signoria."

IF WE ARE to make a sculpture that will last forever, a giant that might stand before the town hall of Florence itself, then we had better get to work. The date for the contest quickly approaches. I have seen the many sketches in Michelangelo's folios. If he can design something, then so can I. Surely.

The empty page looms before me. I tap the nub of chalk on my knee.

Behind me, in the large, empty chapel off the nave of San Pier Martire, I hear my fellow debtor guildsmen scraping mud from metal knives, mixing pigments into wooden pails. The church is filled with the echoes of the work of their hands, their petty arguments and observations, their laughter. Normally, I would relish the thrill of engaging them in conversation, in funny stories, contributing nonsense of my own, but not today.

Instead, I have taken myself to a quiet chapel closer to the high altar, a chapel built by a family many years ago, its paintings now darkened by the smoke of a thousand candles lit over the generations, its air still and stifling. It is here that I have taken out my paper and a stick of red chalk, far from the prying eyes of my fellow guildsmen, where they are laying pigments in the wet plaster of the bright, new chapel, where light streams through the windows and conversation fills the air.

A simple shepherd brave enough to stand before a giant. A boy brave enough to stand before the Signoria. One to stand before all of us Florentines. How to bring such a boy to life?

I stare into the blank page again as if it is a mirror, as if the paper might reflect back to me what direction I should take. This design, this giant, is my chance to regain the artistic footing

Michelangelo and I shared as boys. We can be equals again. We can work together. I know it. It will be just like old times.

Then, I think about the small crowds who have begun to form around the cathedral workyard, and my hand halts. Florentines once passed this discarded hunk of marble every day without it drawing notice, but news of the competition has sparked renewed interest.

If I am honest with myself, I do not think much of impressing the crowds around the cathedral gates. Instead, I want to make a drawing that will make my friend proud. And so I begin as he does, sketching many different possibilities for a David. I've sketched just as I've seen him do it in his own book, individual studies of arms, torsos, faces. My chalk stands poised over the paper for long minutes before I finally place the tip on the page and begin to draw a head with curling locks of hair.

"L'Indaco." Simone pokes his head around the corner. "We could use a little help. That is, unless you were planning to spend your day in here instead?"

"Nicer ambiance, if you ask me," I say, sweeping my arm toward the shadowed, smoke-stained niches of the chapel.

He shakes his head, then comes to look over my shoulder at the drawing emerging on my page. The curled hair of the boy king unfurls from a lined brow. Not bad, I think. At the least, it's a start. "You going to the workyard on Thursday?"

"Why?"

"The block," Simone says. "They're raising it upright so all the contenders can draw it in preparation for the competition. Thursday at the noon bell. You coming?"

"Yes, I have heard." A lie. "Of course I'll be there. Thursday. The noon bell."

❧

"YOU LOOK TERRIBLE."

So does the state of his bedchamber, I note. Drawings and dust scatter around the room, so that in a few short days it has become nearly as unkempt as my own.

"Kind of you to say." Michelangelo runs his hands through his greasy curls but doesn't take his eyes off his worktable.

With one hand, I push open the shutter of one of his windows. The wood resists for a moment, and then the iron hinge creaks under the pressure of my hand. Daylight streaks through the window. Sounds of merchants and wool workers starting their workday waft up into the house. I push open the shutters on the other window, and Michelangelo stretches out his palm against the rays of light streaking into the room. The light illuminates the worktable, littered with a dozen gesso and wax models, sheaves of parchment with hands, arms, heads, faces drawn upon each folio. As the light fills the room, I see a long table against the wall, a dozen candles burned down to nubs, the wax having dripped over the stained wood.

I set my own leather-bound portfolio on the table. "You have not slept?"

Michelangelo's bed remains made up, as if the maid did her duty days ago and has not returned. His dark eyes have sunken into his head, ringed with circles. His skin looks sallow and gray. He is wearing the same stained shift I have seen him in since he came through the city gates weeks ago.

"I don't remember," he says. For a few days, Michelangelo has disappeared. I see now that he has not left his bedchamber, has only been working on the models. On the table before him lie scraps of vellum, scraped to erase the images beneath. Hollowed-out rabbit bones refashioned into quills. Small glass pots of ox-gall ink that have dried black at the edges. I peer over his shoulder to a sheet of paper with nothing but different variations of a hand holding a stone.

I press my palms onto his shoulders and begin to press my thumbs into the tight knots that have formed there. I can smell the sour, dank smell of the base of his neck. Under my hands, I feel his shoulders loosen and drop.

"You have worked out a composition for the block?" I ask, rubbing his shoulders vigorously.

From behind, I see his head shake. He runs his fingers through his hair. Then he gestures with his hand, the kind of gesture that would normally accompany a heartfelt statement, but the words don't come. Instead he approaches one of his wax models and runs his hand over it, turning it toward the light streaming through the window. A man, a boy? A youth, standing with his head turned to his left shoulder.

Michelangelo has always chosen to work like this. In his younger days, he worked for days, weeks at a time, without sleeping, producing copious amounts of work, while I, for all my equally sleepless nights, have rarely produced more than a series of ridiculous, meaningless images on my bedchamber walls. He used to come to my house exhausted, falling into a heap on my bed or in a kitchen chair. Later, we might share a meal and tell tales of art and our colleagues. There was no one else who made him laugh like I did, he told me.

But today, he is not laughing.

On the table he has formed a half dozen *bozzetti*, the wax and clay models used to form a preparatory study for a sculpture, a kind of sketch made of earth. I see that, in each of Michelangelo's models, the arms have been posed differently. In one version, the youth stands with arms outstretched. In another, David holds his sling back, ready to fire a shot. In this way, Michelangelo has brought the drawings on his pages into three dimensions.

But as soon as I see his models, I realize my own drawings pale in comparison. I press my sketchbook under a stack of papers. I will not show it to him after all.

"I don't have it yet, L'Indaco," he says.

"Don't be ridiculous! We have made a successful sculpture together before, have we not?" I turn to face him. "Whatever happened to that cupid we made? Did you ever get it back?"

He waves his hand in dismissal. "Our so-called patron, Milanese, told me he would sooner smash it to pieces than return it to me." He gives a disgusted growl.

"No matter," I say. "It opened your passage to Rome. And it led to His Holiness himself."

"I suppose you are right," he says.

"Of course I am right. We can do this. Besides," I say, running my hand along the *bozzetto* he has made of wax, "this is genius! We will clinch the commission with no problem." I tap the back of my hand against his shoulder as if to wake him up to the realization.

He smiles at me briefly, a tight grin, then he turns the *bozzetto* around to look at the back. "Let us not kid ourselves, L'Indaco. I am young, unproven. Sansovino? If you ask me, he is just blowing perfume up their asses, and I think the *operai* know it. But Leonardo... let's face it. Da Vinci has spent a lifetime proving himself, here and elsewhere. You have not lived outside Florence, but I have heard his name spoken in Bologna, in Venice. If he wants the commission, they will give it to him. That much is as certain as the Arno flowing to the sea."

"But he is not a sculptor," I say. "He has made it clear that he considers sculpture beneath him."

"None of it matters," he says. "All he has to do is say he wants the commission. They love him already."

"Bah! Underneath that lavender silk cape and *acqua vita* he is just a smelly old man."

Michelangelo barks a loud laugh, then walks to the window and looks out into the clear sky. "You speak the truth," he says.

For a moment, I feel the old satisfaction of having made him laugh, but when he turns back to me I see the shadow has returned to his face.

"I, on the other hand, L'Indaco..." He shakes his head. "The *operai*... They are wool traders, not artists. They must see exactly what the composition will be. They will not take an unproven sculptor at his word. They are men of commerce who need to be sure of success before they will hand over a giant marble block the height of four men. No. If I am to win it, I must *show* them."

I consider his words. It is true that our patrons, for all their learning, sometimes have trouble visualizing a final work of art. A *bozzetto* helps them understand how the final work will appear.

"But this is the part I don't have yet. Sculpture. It must not be just an object of beauty. It must be that, of course. But it must also serve a moral purpose, as much as the Judith in the square, or as much as any of the Davids before this one. Do you see, L'Indaco? It is to be a symbol. Whether they know it or not, it's why the committee has seen fit to resurrect that damnable block in the first place."

I consider his words in silence for a moment. "Sansovino is planning to show the David at the instant when he pulls the sling back, ready to cast it at the giant," I say.

Michelangelo's brow furrows, and he sets his eyes on me. "How do you know this?"

I hesitate to tell him that this particular bit of gossip was procured over a hand of dice, but he knows me.

"Il Fico." I shrug.

Michelangelo puffs in exasperation and shakes his head. "The tavern. Of course."

"They said he was bragging about it!" I continue. "Sansovino said he was planning to add other pieces of marble from the workyard in order make the arm." I reach my hand behind my back as if I, too, were about to hurl a stone.

"Sansovino is an idiot."

I see the tendons in the sides of his jaws, as if he is chewing something. Finally, he says again, "*Imbecille*. If Sansovino has any skill as a sculptor—and that, my friend, is to be doubted—then he must know you cannot put the arm like that." Michelangelo crosses his arms, then raises his index finger to bat it briefly against his lips. "The question *is* in fact what to do with the arms. The way the block was worked out before, they removed too much from what must be the rear view. The key is to decide how to make the arms look right. There must be a solution other than making the arm out of a separate piece of marble and attaching it."

I pick up a piece of parchment where he has drawn a hand holding a sling. "Or, I say you could have the David holding the sling over his shoulder. That way, you convey movement within a closed form."

He pauses for a moment, deep in thought. Then he grasps my face with his grubby hands and kisses my forehead. "I love you, my blue boy."

"Don't foul my hair," I say, and he laughs.

With the recognition of my idea, and the laugh, he has admitted that I am valuable to him. It is all that matters.

"I have heard something else," I say, eager for more praise. "They are opening the workyard on Thursday morning. They are going to raise the giant."

"I have heard," he says. "But I already know the block. I don't need to go. You have already seen I have my own key." He pats his pocket with a chalk-stained hand.

"But if we are to be considered serious contenders, I think we should be there, to make a showing. If not for ourselves, then for the *operai*, for our future patrons. Surely Salviati or some of the others will be there."

Michelangelo hesitates, then he nods in agreement before turning back to his *bozzetto*. "Yes," he says, "I suppose you have a point."

"*Bene*. Then I will be back before the noon bell. We will walk there together." I push him on the shoulder, and he stumbles sideways under my heft. "Get some sleep."

OUTSIDE THE GATES of the workyard, the artists of our city have assembled. I feel my shoulders slump as I realize that anyone we might have expected is already there. I recognize several faces from a distance: the soft-cheeked painter, Sandro Botticelli; young Ridolfo, the son of my boyhood teacher, Domenico Ghirlandaio; and yes, Andrea Sansovino, the sculptor who has risen to fame in a city that is not his own and who, I must admit—if to no one other than myself—has talent in his hands. They are laughing, slapping one another on the shoulders in forced camaraderie, but I can already see they are posturing even before the gates have opened.

Michelangelo and I walk shoulder to shoulder toward the group. The day is young, but the sun has already cast black, raking shadows across the alleys and stones. I imagine that few of these men have laid eyes on Michelangelo Buonarroti in four years, even if they have heard of his return, for he has remained holed up inside his bedchamber or in that dank crypt the entire time, working on drawings and on our *bozzetti*.

Sansovino spies us before any of the other men. From the corner of my eye, I see Michelangelo's hand make a fist, but he does not change his gait. He continues forward. If Sansovino feels surprised or threatened by his presence, the only evidence is a flash of recognition in his eye and a twitch of his mouth.

But before the two men are forced to exchange pleasantries, a cloaked prior arrives with a large, iron key. The chattering men fall silent, the gate opens with a groan, and we file into the shade of the workyard. In the shadows, the giant lies prone on the ground, surrounded by dust and clutter, just where it has lain for two generations.

To my surprise, there is already one contender inside the workyard. He is dressed in an elegant fashion, indistinguishable from the finely dressed members of the cathedral committee who crowd around him. If anyone did not know Master da Vinci already, they might take him for another one of the *operai* tasked with deciding who will take on this discarded marble. The committee members exchange words with da Vinci, facile and confident, as if he himself is the proprietor of this dusty workyard. His hands are elegant and manicured, with no sign of paint. His long beard has turned gray, spilling out over his silk gown the color of pale roses. He is telling a story, and one of the men laughs. In the shadows, a dozen brawny stonemasons' assistants have gathered, hanging on like servants, eager for Master da Vinci to say the word so they might spring to action.

Michelangelo moves into a patch of sunlight and crosses his arms across his dirty shift, his jaw set. He says nothing, but I watch his eyes follow one of the apprentices, a youth barely old enough to be called a man, whose broad upper back and shoulders evince his years of labor among the stones.

Soon enough, it becomes clear why Master da Vinci seems already to have taken control of this operation. One of his own contraptions, some sort of hoist, will be used to lift the impossibly heavy block to an upright position. Da Vinci gives a simple gesture of his hand, and the stonemasons' apprentices move into place, turning a large, horizontal wheel as if they were beasts of burden. The wheel operates a large screw, which creaks inside its wooden casing. A series of ropes and pulleys brings the contraption to life. Soon enough, the block of marble shifts across the sand and sawdust strewn across the ground. Da Vinci has positioned his contraption so that the widest end of the marble will remain on the ground, while the narrowest end tilts upward toward the sky. The motion seems effortless. Within a matter of moments, the block stands upright, the height of four men, and gleams and sparkles in the sun.

I cannot stop myself. I burst into applause. It is only the realization that I am alone in my glee—and a glance at Michelangelo's dire expression—that stills my hands.

All the same, there is a collective gasp of awe. Only Michelangelo stands with his arms crossed, regarding da Vinci suspiciously. The artists circle the block. While the stonemasons' boys unlash the thick ropes from the marble, we pace around it, sketchbooks in hand. A mantle of profound silence falls over the workyard.

It is clear why there was a question as to whether the marble could be salvaged at all. The block bears the scars of two masters, over two generations, who attempted to tame this great hunk of white and failed. A large nodule protrudes from one side. The beginnings of an arm? A knee? It is hard to say. Was it the knot of a cloak for the original David? Or just a quick mark that would help guide the rest of the work? We will never know. Other sections of hatch marks have marred the surface, evidence of a battle between this chunk of marble and a claw chisel, the marble block abandoned to its victory.

"Are we certain that this beast can be turned into a sculpture?" says one of the members of the cathedral committee, his brow furrowed. He has voiced aloud what all of us must be thinking.

"Of course," says Ridolfo Ghirlandaio. "It is only a matter of the right tools."

"Ha!" says Sansovino. "So says the painter."

I cannot hold my tongue. I lean in and whisper to Michelangelo. "And so is Da Vinci—a painter and maker of crazy contraptions, to be sure—but a sculptor? Surely he is not a serious candidate."

"But this project will be easy," says Master da Vinci. Has he heard me? He gestures broadly and smiles at the *operai* to ensure that he has continued to capture their attention. "Sculpture is only a matter of labor, gentlemen; there is no creativity behind it. In the end, it is a purely mechanical operation, generally accomplished with great sweat, which mingles with dust and becomes converted to mud. A sculptor's face quickly becomes plastered and powdered all over with marble dust." He pauses and looks directly at Michelangelo. "That is why, when sculptors go around town, people mistake them for bakers."

The workyard is filled with a burst of laughter. I see Michelangelo's jaw set even tighter.

"*Bene*, signori," one of the robed men says, quieting the crowd. "We shall expect you to announce your intentions to the committee, including Gonfaloniere Soderini, on the feast of Saint James. We will hold audiences inside a hall of the Palazzo della Signoria. You have ample time to prepare your proposals.

For now, this is the time to evaluate the block. You have until the afternoon bell."

The men swirl around the towering block of marble with their sketchbooks. All but one.

Michelangelo's eyes have turned black. It's an expression I have known for years; I stop in my tracks. In the face of each person in the workyard, he sees an enemy. I remain frozen, hoping I won't be included on his list.

Throughout the proceedings, though there has been a lot of conversation, he has said nothing. Everyone has come prepared with paper, pen, and chalk. During the entire event, he has not opened his own leather-bound book, but rather has gripped it to his chest. Of course he has not needed to sketch. His notebook is already full of sketches of the block. Some of those sketches were made over a decade ago. He has no need to draw it now. He leans against a pile of lumber, his arms crossed, the toe of his scuffed mules wedging a rock from the dust.

"There is no contest," I hear the man next to him whisper. "It is rigged. I swear. They have already decided to give it to da Vinci. Did you not see him? He holds them in his hand. They are enchanted."

Another nods his head. "If Master da Vinci wants it, all he has to do is ask."

Suddenly, Michelangelo springs to life. I hear a puff of air escape his lips. He begins to march toward the iron gate, toward the beating sun of the street.

"What about you, L'Indaco?" Michelangelo growls under his breath, but his eyes face forward. "Are you with me or against me?" He doesn't wait for my answer.

For a moment, I turn back to look at the white block towering above our heads. My feet feel buried in the dirt. He is already far ahead of me, no more than a silhouette against the streaking, beating heat of the sun. All of the other artists watch his back, his heavy footsteps kicking up dust in their wake.

I tip my cap briefly toward the men, then I skitter after him like a stray dog.

❧

IT TAKES BOTH of us to carry the box.

Michelangelo has adapted one of the wooden crates the wool traders use to carry bales of raw and spun cloth from the countryside into the markets. On either side of the box, he has nailed short pieces of rope to serve as handles. Inside, he has carefully placed his stucco *bozzetto*, a miniature model of the design. We've filled in the empty spaces with hay procured from the horse stables at one of the city gates in order to prevent the model from shifting inside of it. I watch him secure the lid, then I pick up one side while he holds the other. The box is not heavy. Michelangelo's servant woman holds the door open as we pass through it and into the streets of Santa Croce on our way to the Piazza della Signoria.

Already, my heart is racing. Hope rises through my veins.

The goldsmith at the corner is opening the shutters of his window as we pass with our box. The wool dyers in Santa Croce have begun their work for the day. Women move their mending contraptions to their windows, seeking fresh air before the heat of the day presses down on us. Sounds of the shopkeepers fill the streets, echoing off the stone walls of the quarter. Someone is heating oil in a large copper basin on the corner.

"Shall we stop for a bite?" I ask, as the smell of fried dough fills the air.

"Is that all you think about? Food?" Michelangelo growls, but he doesn't look at me. Instead, his eyes flicker back and forth, scanning the street as if he is waiting for someone to spring out and steal our box.

I know his heart is racing, too. I am sure of it. The anticipation crackles the air like summer lightning. I do what I always do in circumstances like these. I attempt a joke.

"*Angelino*, you know what a virtuous Sienese woman and *bistecca alla fiorentina* have in common?"

No reaction.

"They're both very rare."

But he does not laugh. His face seems to have turned to stone, as hard and impenetrable as the great block of marble itself. As the tall, skinny tower of the Signoria looms in front of us, I feel my gut clench. Michelangelo looks straight ahead, not speaking.

When we turn into the piazza, the statue of Judith slaying Holofernes catches our attention, its bronze surfaces glistening in the sun. We pause before her, the gilded woman wielding a sword over her head, victorious over the evil tyrant at her feet. Like the David in our box, she is an underdog, an unlikely hero. In a flash of divine power, she has wielded her weapon and brought down a powerful enemy. A formidable defeat.

Michelangelo exchanges words with the palace guards. For a few moments, we wait, balancing the box between us. I try to imagine the *bozzetto* inside turned into a giant version of itself, standing here alongside the Judith at the doorway to Florence's town hall, but my mind fails to envision the sight.

They open the gate for us, and we sidle in with our box. I feel my chest swell with excitement, thinking how impressed the cathedral committee will be with our design. Michelangelo has fashioned David as a strong youth, one hand holding a sling at his shoulder—my own suggestion. The other holds a stone at his side, the rock that will slay the enemy.

In the courtyard, another sculpture of David fills the space.

"Donatello," I whisper. It is the sculpture Michelangelo has drawn and described to me so many times, a bronze rendition of the boy hero that once stood in the Medici gardens. Finally, I have the chance to see it with my own eyes. This rendition of the David is not what I expected. Although his foot presses down on Goliath's head, the boy has long, slender legs, a pubescent torso, and a large, floppy hat festooned with flowers. He seems silly, flippant, compared to the intense, brave figure we have designed.

"He looks like a girl," I whisper, but again, Michelangelo ignores me.

The long stairway to the audience hall was paved with marble centuries ago; its treads are now worn across the middle. Palace guards observe us from the upper galleries as we make our way up the stairs with our box in hand. In an upper corridor, muffled voices echo from behind closed doors. We wait. It is difficult to say whether time is passing quickly or slowly. I expect to see other artists here to present their ideas to the committee, but I do not see anyone.

Finally, a set of hulking doorways down the hall open and we see Sansovino exit the chamber. I feel the box quiver; Michelangelo has flinched. Sansovino clutches a leather-bound sketchbook under his elbow, and his mouth has pulled into a wide line that I cannot interpret. A smile or a smirk? Either way, he looks smug. His eyes flash toward us, and he finds it within himself to acknowledge us with a nod. Michelangelo and I nod back, but we do not exchange words.

A man in a long, black robe gestures for us to come forward. We stand and walk to the door.

"Buonarroti?"

"The same," says Michelangelo.

Through the narrow, open slit of the doorway, I see a row of a half dozen *operai* in their silk-lined robes seated at a long, wooden table. One man taps the table idly with the tips of his fingers. Another shuffles through paper. I recognize the face of Salviati, the old man on the cathedral committee who gave Michelangelo his clandestine workyard key.

Michelangelo walks through the doorway, and I follow, helping to carry the box into the room. For a moment, I am disoriented, overcome by the audience hall. Far above our heads, the ceiling is designed as gilded, octagonal coffers. The walls are covered in paint and gilding from floor to ceiling. It is the most luxurious, extravagant room I have ever seen. For a moment, I stand and marvel that I have had the privilege of stepping into such a place. It is quiet, the only sound the clearing of a throat. Behind his fist, Salviati smiles and nods at Michelangelo. Another man gestures to the guard at the door. We set the box on the floor.

The guard at the door hesitates, then holds up his palm. "Only Master Buonarroti, please. His is the only name on the list." Michelangelo's gaze softens toward me for a fleeting second, then he turns to the men in the room.

My feet feel stuck to the floor. Words will not come. Only one name on the list? How can that be?

Finally, the guard presses me back through the door, into the hallway. I see Michelangelo's face turn toward the men at the long table. At last, he turns to lift the lid from the box.

The corridor is cast into shadows as the heavy, walnut door closes in front of my nose.

⁓

THREE DAYS GONE.

It is only the arrival of a letter from the *guardia* that rouses me from my bed.

"Get up, Jacopo," my sister says, her brown eyes wide with fear of the messenger who darkened our doorway. She presses the folded parchment onto the bed next to me. I glance down at the red wax seal with the lily, the official mark of the Signoria. My sister has already broken the seal, has already read the words inside.

"He said that if you don't return to San Pier Martire and finish that fresco, you will owe twice what you lost in the taverns," she says. "Why didn't you tell me about this before? Jacopo! *Per l'amor di Dio*, get up!"

I manage to rouse myself to a sitting position at the edge of the bed as my sister loudly claps open the shutters.

"Failing that, they say you will be sentenced to the Stinche Prison. The *Stinche*, Jacopo! What will become of us then? Our family's good name!" An image of the looming debtors' prison in Santa Croce appears in my head. "Our father would die of shame." But I try not to think of our parents. Lucia snatches the linens off my bed and shakes the dust from them out the window and into the alley.

I rub my palms across my face, scrubbing the skin in an effort to move blood through my body. Behind me, I hear Lucia's frantic fluttering around the room, dusting surfaces and tidying objects on my worktable, as if putting things away or delousing my sheets might rid us of the Signoria's debt collectors once and for all.

After a few moments, I feel her hands come to rest on my shoulders, pressing her palms down. "Jacopo, you cannot stay in bed forever. Please. You must tell me everything now. And for God's sake, what happened with that sculpture—the giant?"

How do I begin to describe what happened? How the hours passed, but there was no sign? No sign of his *bozzetto*. No sign of his box. No sign of him. How do I explain how I passed the hours sprawled on a stone bench in the square, drawing patterns in the dirt with the end of a stick and watching pigeons peck small crumbs from the ground? That as the evening bell sounded in the tower of the Signoria, I threw my hat in the dirt in frustration, then let my rumbling stomach lure me home so my sister might feed me? That those silly frescoes are the least of my worries? That I have never felt more worthless in my entire life?

I shrug Lucia's hands from my shoulders, but I do not respond. There is a period of thick silence, then I hear her sigh. She may guess well enough.

I DON'T GET out of bed.

In spite of Lucia's sighing, fussing interruptions, I wallow in my own self-pity for a few more days.

With my eyes squeezed shut, my mind winds through tortuous images of the past. Did I only imagine that we were friends? My mind searches for evidence, reaches for memories that might lift me from the darkness.

The one that rises to the surface is the memory of a *beffa* I once played on Michelangelo when he least suspected it. My younger brother, along with two other boys from Master Ghirlandaio's workshop, were there with us that day. As we sat on the ledge of the Ponte Vecchio, all in a line, I suddenly wrapped my arms around Michelangelo and pretended I was stopping him from falling into the water, when in fact he was destabilized and felt like he would tumble. He fought back, and we wrestled like that for a few moments, me squeezing his wiry, strong frame against my larger one. I felt his lungs fill with air, then he pressed against me with all his might.

By chance, at that moment two visitors from England were passing on the bridge. Thinking we were engaged in a real fight, the men jumped to try to separate us. It occurred to me to yell, "Sirs! Please help me! This poor young man loses reason at changes of the moon. You see yourselves that he is trying to throw himself from the bridge!"

The men seized Michelangelo with all their power. The more he yelled that I was the one who was mad, the tighter the men held him. Soon a large crowd gathered. The Englishmen bustled Michelangelo into a nearby inn, all the while lamenting the poor boy's madness. The other boys and I laughed all the way back to Master Ghirlandaio's studio, knowing well enough that one of us would be the victim of the next prank.

And now? Is this all an elaborate prank? Is he paying me back for all the times I made him the butt of my own absurd follies? But just about the time I have convinced myself that it is nothing more than a bad joke, my mind reaches for the dark memories instead.

We were about fourteen years old, I think, the first time I saw Michelangelo get beat up. He had thrown his fists before, of course, but never had I seen him bloodied. Most of the apprentices were too afraid to get close to him. He was not a big boy, but he was intimidating, formidable in a way that most boys in that in-between stage of life could never be. As much as his arrogant temperament might have raised others' ire, there was something about him that stopped them from pushing him to throw a fist.

Torrigiano was different.

Pietro Torrigiano was one of those boys our parents warned us against playing *palla* with in the square. I knew little of him, but could never understand how he was chosen, alongside Michelangelo, to create sculpture in the Medici palace gardens. Torrigiano was proud and swaggering, his brow permanently knit as if he were born angry. Come to think of it, Torrigiano and Michelangelo were equal in arrogance, so it should have been easy to see the conflict. They were bound to come to blows. It could only end badly.

One afternoon, I was waiting for Michelangelo in the alley outside his house. I was bouncing a leather ball against the wall behind the houses, bantering with the bird seller's son while the birds squawked and fluttered their feathers at us, then peered at us with strange, beadlike eyes from inside their wicker cages. When he finally came around the corner flanked on either side by his new friends from the Medici gardens, I saw that he held a bloody rag to his face.

"What happened to you?" I scrambled behind the boys into the cool darkness of his kitchen. Michelangelo's family maid gasped and let go of her broom. She moved as quickly as her plump form would allow, fussing in dialect for the boys to move out of the way so she could take a closer look. She sat him down and removed the rag. His eyes were swollen and dark, his nose pushed in, the bridge of it already sunken and flat.

"It was Torrigiano!" said the boy next to him, his eyes wide. "We were in the Carmine church. That's where Master sent us to draw the paintings of Masaccio," he told me.

Pietro Torrigiano. Of course.

"He is a mule's ass," the other boy said. The maid clucked loudly.

"How did it happen?" I pressed.

Michelangelo waved his hand in dismissal while the maid pressed a clean rag to his nose. The blood was turning dark and crusting. "He is too easy riled. I made a comment about his sculpture and he punched me," he shrugged. "That's all."

I was enraptured and honestly, a bit in awe that a sculpture could make someone come to blows.

"To be fair, Michelangelo made a valid criticism," one of the boys said.

After that day, the bridge of Michelangelo's nose was permanently flattened. It accounted for a strange, crooked profile that I would come to recognize from afar. I heard later that Lorenzo de Medici was so angry with Torrigiano that he sent his men in search of him to punish him. I also heard that Torrigiano never showed his face in the palace gardens again. Michelangelo, meanwhile, received a respectable daily wage. A pile of freshly culled partridges and sweet cakes delivered to his father's door. A cloak of violet silk. The distance between us grew.

At last, I rise from my bed.

As I press the cool water over my face in my dark bedchamber, for the first time I understand what Torrigiano must have felt. I now understand the impulse he had to hit Michelangelo, that flippant, gifted man who made you love him one minute and want to strangle him in the next. How difficult to untangle awe, jealousy, love, hate.

How did I misunderstand?

Why did he allow the door to close in my face, to shut me out of the presentation of the *bozzetto*? I am as qualified as he is; surely he knows it. I was the one who called him here from the start, the one who told him of the commission. Without me, he never would have won it, would never even have known of it until it was too late. I did all the groundwork to ensure success. And what gratitude did I get?

But after my initial burst of indignation, I feel despair rise up from a deep pit inside my soul, that familiar, dark blanket of oblivion. In the end, I know he was not trying to deceive me. It's simply that he never intended for me to be part of it. If I felt entitled to work on the giant, then it was my own doing, not his. I feel the sting of how things used to be when we were boys, he already far ahead of me, and me struggling along behind, barely understanding my own place. There is the old familiar feeling, that experience of working alongside him, only to see him pull ahead of me, to see others bestow accolades that I never got, would never get.

And although he has said he loves me, I feel hate well up in my breast against my better judgment. I think about his black eyes now, so like those strange birds, and where once I saw friendship and potential, I now only see the gnarled face and arms, only the snubbing. I feel nothing but hatred, perhaps more for myself even than for him.

His words repeat inside my head.

I love you, my blue boy.

I heard the words, and I thought I loved him, too.

And now, I feel something I have never felt before, something that goes beyond envy, perhaps even beyond hate. Talent and magnetism can make you love someone, but it can also make you come to blows. Between my desire to embrace Michelangelo and knock him unconscious, there lies only a hairsbreadth.

LONG BEFORE I turn the corner into a small piazza bordering the Mercato Vecchio, I know there is blood. The sound is singular, a communal roar that verges on madness. By now, red rivulets will be running into the cracks between the cobblestones.

The fisticuff matches in the Mercato are a dirtier, bloodier version of the *calcio* that draws crowds to Santa Croce each autumn, when the flags and loud chants of each quarter fill the streets. Those games, however brutal, are supported by the Signoria itself. They may draw smaller crowds, but the fights around the taverns, I think, have their own appeal. They are more immediate, more exciting, more violent.

Another communal cry, a frenzied whooping. The skin on the back of my neck tightens, and I taste metal in the back of my throat as if I am the one who has been punched.

Since the competition for the giant was first announced, I have succeeded in avoiding this narrow warren of streets leading off the Mercato Vecchio, an area teeming with taverns, baths, and inns, thinly veiled hotbeds of debauchery. But it is the only place I can think might soothe me, where yes, I might lose my soul, but where I might also drown the sting of rejection. At least for a while.

Chiassolino. Panico. Porco. Malvagia. The taverns in this part of town have names that fill your mind with hidden body parts and depraved ideas. Il Fico, a dirty hovel on the corner, is the one whose name connotes both a fig and a lady's most intimate treasure. It's the place where I lost my last *denaro*, the place where the *guardia* did a sweep and I, caught in their net, was handed a fine and a sentence to do service as a fresco painter at San Pier Martire. That sentence has haunted me for many months now. I avoid turning down the street, for I intend never to cross the threshold of that particular tavern again. And perhaps I am no longer welcome.

I pass a small, unassuming door, the nearly hidden entrance to our city's one public brothel. I hesitate, but move quickly down the street. Once, when I had just about given up hope that I might be able to attract a woman on my own merit, I considered it briefly. But then, a painter friend showed me his oozing sores, the result of a visit there. It swore me off any temptation I might have had to patronize the ladies of the night, even those at the official whorehouse sanctioned by the republic.

As I move into the narrow alleys feeding the *piazzetta*, the crowd swells and the chanting rises in the air. I press my way forward until I can glimpse the two fighters at the center of the circle. I recognize the bigger one, a bear of a man called Buffo, who is a regular competitor and frequenter of Il Fico. He is broad-chested and mean, with close-set, dark eyes and a single, thick eyebrow across his wide forehead. He sidesteps, his fists balled near his chin. Across from him, a much smaller, wiry man I have never seen, skips back and forth like a cricket on hot coals. I am not sure if the twisted expression on the little man's face is one of pain or determination. I push my way forward into the mass of bodies, and press the back of my hand to the shoulder of a man next to me. "Who is that?"

The man shrugs and keeps his eyes on the fighters. "I do not know his name, but they say he is from the Val di Chiana and has flattened the biggest fighter in Pisa. We're about to see if he has earned his reputation." He must be a worthy contender, I see, for the front of Buffo's crumpled linen shift is already coated in blood and his woolen hose are ripped. An ugly gash has bloomed across his left cheekbone.

Two shabby men sitting on wooden boxes pushed up against a stone wall—judges of this crude spectacle—lean forward with their elbows on their knees. Those who handle the purse have dragged a rickety table through the door of the Porco tavern. They have collected coins in woven sacks, guarded by several other large men I recognize as regular fisticuff contenders. They have a stake in the fight and will get a cut of the pot if they have predicted the victor correctly. On a piece of parchment they have scratched how much each bettor has waged.

It is all illegal, of course, but today, like most days, the *guardia* has better things to do. Besides, they could never suppress all of the gambling schemes that unfold in Florence on a typical day. There are too many bettors and not enough men on the Signoria's payroll to track them all.

I feel the familiar urge to place my wager. I press my hands deep down into the pockets of my paint-stained shift. I feel a single coin lost in the scratchy linen pouch.

"Name?" asks the man at the table.

"Torni." I press my coin down, and the man scratches my name on his page. "I place my venture on the new man."

No sooner have I laid down my coin than I hear the roar of the crowd behind me. The wiry man has knocked Buffo to the ground in a single punch. The big man's face hits the cobble-stones. His black, swollen eyes close, and his bloodied mouth huffs in defeat. There is a communal bellow of glee.

Winners push past me to be the first at the money table to claim their winnings. The big men guarding the loot push the crowd back, their shouted commands lost in the uproar. The losers skulk back down the alleys out of the piazza, some still with smirks on their faces, even if they lost a few coins in ex-change for the thrill of the fight.

At the table, the men press two coins into my palm. In less than a minute, I have doubled my money. That old feeling—a rush of joy—washes over me. If I can turn one coin into two, just think what I might do with a full purse. Next time. With a pleasant jangle of metal in my pocket, I smile and press my way out of the crowd.

⁓

INSIDE THE CHURCH of San Pier Martire, there is only talk of Michelangelo and his giant.

"I heard the Signoria is paying him six broad florins of gold for the sculpture," a young assistant says.

A fortune.

"And giving him an allowance. A place to live," another adds. "And as many assistants as he wants."

From the door of the church, I have an unobstructed view of my chapel, the one where I am supposed to have finished painting some forty squares of fresco by now. They have braced a large, wooden scaffolding between the soffits of the arches. One of the journeymen is standing atop it, filling in patches of sky with light blue and green pigments where the wall meets the arch. Below it, two assistants are mixing pigments in ceramic pots.

On one wall of the chapel, my fellow guildsmen have nearly finished the scenes from the life of Saint Peter Martyr. I look at the serene face of Saint Anne with a gilded halo. Dust-flecked sunbeams illuminate the dull, white-washed surface that has been scored into lines, waiting for our pigments. Waiting for me. My part of the job—an entire wall that must be painted—stands out, vast and empty.

My heart sinks.

As my eyes adjust to the cool dimness of the chapel, I see the woman painter. Alesso's wife. She sits quietly on one of the benches against the wall. The men swirl around her in a mess of buckets, scaffolding, whistling, talking, humming. On her lap is a leather-bound sketchbook open across the cool, linen work shift and scuffed leather apron of the type the men wear. She has tied her hair in a loose knot at the nape of her neck, and is bent over her paper in concentration, running a piece of red chalk across the surface.

"L'Indaco! We have not seen you." Simone is stirring rabbit glue in a bucket.

"*Bof.*" I shrug my shoulders. "I have been occupied."

How could I begin to explain that I have been in bed for days, though I have not truly slept? I feel sluggish, as though I am walking in mud. I don't tell them that I am wearing the same wrinkled gown I have been wearing for days while lying on my back, staring at the ceiling, trying to push the images of Michelangelo and his *bozzetto* from my head.

Before I can formulate a response, our journeyman peers down at us from high atop the scaffold. "The reason you have not seen him is because he has been working on the new David," he says. "The *operai* have made their choice."

"And they chose *you?*" Simone says. He stops stirring his glue and looks up wide-eyed, then looks around to the others to see if he has been caught in one of my tricks. "Is that true?"

"Him and Buonarroti," Alesso says. "I heard it at Master Botticelli's studio. Sansovino is madder than a mule with a mouthful of hornets. He stomped out, and no one has seen him in days." He chuckles under his breath.

"*Da vero?* You are taking on that block of marble?" asks one of the apprentices.

Silence. Everyone stops what they are doing, and I feel their many eyes on me.

How could I begin to tell them the truth? That I have not slept for days? Every time that sleep overtakes me, I wake in a cold sweat. Then, in the quiet darkness, the truth washes over me like a wave on a wintry beach. The truth that there is no "us."

There never was. There was only "he." He and his *David*. His giant. I am not part of the story at all. I never was.

"You are taking on the giant?"

I turn to see the signora leaning against the pillar, her sketchbook clutched against her chest. Her full attention is on me.

"*Bene.*" I step into a pool of sunlight on the patterned marble floor. "You know, we—he and I—have been preparing drawings. Models." I sniff loudly, and it echoes through the church. "The planning has kept us busy and so that is why I have not been here." But I don't look them in the eye. Instead, I begin busying myself with refolding some tarps I have brought from the shed my sister and I use to store painting supplies at the back of our withered garden. "It went well." I turn my eyes back to the floor. "Very well."

News of the giant seems to have spread across town already, but Michelangelo has not come to see me. I do not even know what I would say if he did. The disappointment and disillusionment have sunk to the pit of my stomach.

"Well then, we will not be seeing you around here anymore," she says. I feel the looming white space of the partially frescoed wall behind me.

"Yes," I say, realizing that I am right back to where I was before I wrote the letter that called Michelangelo home. Without a patron, without a commission, as broke as ever before and indebted to this community of nuns who are still waiting for me to finish my fresco.

"Why is everyone talking about that Buonarroti?" Her words echo in the vast space. "What makes him so…?" Everyone turns to her. "I mean, I never heard of him before he left for Rome."

"We have been friends for many, *many* years," I say, my chest inflating. "I am his oldest friend. He is," I make a hand gesture as

I search for the right word, "talented," I say finally. "And some-times a giant mule's ass."

She smiles, bringing her hand to her mouth in a coy gesture. For a fleeting moment I feel a weight lift from my shoulders.

"He is beautiful to look at?" she asks.

I stop folding. "If you like a hunched, little man with a flat face, I suppose."

I see the corners of her eyes wrinkle, and she laughs out loud this time.

"Do you think you could introduce me to him?" I see her big green eyes shine in the filtered light. "I mean, if he is so wonderful to win such a commission—in spite of being flat-faced and small—then I would like to meet such a man."

"I… Well, yes. I mean, I can introduce you to him at any time," I say. "We are very… close."

⁓

ANOTHER DAY.

Another fight.

Another few coins in my pocket.

My success at predicting the victors of street fights has con-vinced me that my luck may extend to the card table. Inside Il Fico, I quickly splay four kings and a queen on the table, scraping a pile of coins away from Il Riccio, who only scowls at me. At the Malaviga, I am down to two coins before I draw three of a kind.

I admit it. Here and there, I have helped myself with a trick. A lightning-fast bottom-dealing of cards in which I retain the kings for myself at the top of the deck. It happens so quickly that no one sees. Two cards stuck together with a dot of soft wax. A special card palmed into my cloak and saved for the right moment. The occasional trick, along with my continued streak of luck, keeps me afloat.

Fortune doesn't favor me every night, of course. Many times, I forfeit whatever I've gained at the card table, even when I employ a sleight of hand to my own advantage. On those nights, I walk home with the consolation that at least someone has called my name, has invited me to the table, has laughed with me, has kissed my cheeks or grasped my shoulders. That someone has seen me for who I am, not for who I am supposed to be.

On those nights, I slip silently into the house after Lucia is asleep.

❧

IN A SMALL square on the edge of the Mercato Vecchio, I watch a group of boys pull a fighter, unconscious and bloodied, from the pavement. As the crowd disbands and disperses down the alleys, I find myself drawn to the street-corner shrine where a man named Rinaldeschi once threw dung at an image of the Madonna, a man I saw hang on the walls of the Bargello with my own eyes. For a moment, I rest my eyes on the faded paint, the dried wax, the wilted stems in the cracks of the stones.

But then, I recognize a familiar face. Filippo Dolciati. It has been years.

The painter I knew as a boy, one of those weeded early from Domenico Ghirlandaio's studio, ambles around the edges of the square. He is rummaging through the detritus of market day, a pile of rotting tomatoes and scraps of cabbage left behind by an untidy market vendor. He has spread out a paint-stained piece of linen on the dirt and has propped several panels up against the wall of a fruit seller's shop. They are small, crudely drawn pictures, and quickly turned out, I imagine, but full of bright color, with an appeal that is hard to define but undeniable at once.

"Putting together a feast?" I ask.

It takes him a moment, then his eyes light up in recognition. "Jacopo Torni! It has been a long time." He smiles, then lifts up a husk of bread he has rescued from a rubbish pile behind the tavern. "The only critics are those who have not sampled it," he says. "Signora Lucci makes salted black bread and an *erbolata* that would make a nun cry, even if it is two days old. They throw out more food than they put on the table. I never understood that. Want a bite?"

I grasp the heel of dark bread from his hand and bite off a stale piece. I seat myself cross-legged on the linen cloth beside him. "Not bad," I say with a muffled voice. Then I pick up one of the small paintings from the ground. "How is the trade?" I ask, tapping the crudely painted image.

He shrugs. His stringy hair hangs ragged below the rim of his worn cap. He is skinny, his gown rumpled. He looks and smells as though he has been sleeping on the street. It must be at least five years since I last saw him. Two of his teeth in the front have turned black with rot, and one is missing.

"The usual," he says, counting on his fingers. "I've sold twelve pictures so far today."

I pause. "Twelve pictures? Before the midday bell?"

"*Affermativo*," he nods. "Not bad for a Tuesday. The fight has brought out a few customers." He gestures to the crowd of people retreating from the square.

I look at the pictures more closely, and try to see something different this time to account for their appeal. There are several Madonnas, straightforward as might be expected, and a few saints, especially those who are patrons of the churches near the market. I pick up a larger square panel that shows nine scenes, constructed as a story read left to right, top to bottom. There is a scene of the hanging of Savonarola, the priest who nearly brought our city to its knees just a few short years ago.

I squint at Filippo through the sun that has risen high in the sky. "And you get how much per picture?"

Filippo stands now to survey his collection of small panels propped on the ground. "For smaller pictures like the ones of the Madonna, I collect a *soldo*. For the larger ones, three. Let's see, twelve pictures, of which two were larger…" He hesitates. Bread in one hand, he waves the air with the other. I was never good at calculating figures in my head, but I can see he has made more money than I would have ever made on the street.

"You mean you will go home today with ten coins in your pocket?" I say.

Filippo shrugs again. "More if there is a funeral mass or a marriage in one of the churches." He slaps my shoulder with the back of his hand. "They are dupes for pictures after they come out of listening to Father in the *confessionale*."

"But the guild…" I do not know what else to say. The guild strictly forbids painters from working outside its statutes, and for selling pictures on the street. Filippo is breaking the rules on both counts.

I do not need to complete my thought for him to understand. "Sì," he says. "I've been caught. More than once. I even spent three months in the Stinche," he says, gesturing with his thumb toward the great, walled prison in Santa Croce. "But the day they let me out, I set up my shop here again. What am I to do? I must feed myself. I am not like you, out there working on high-paying guild commissions of your own." His eyes dazzle in the sunlight. "Tell me of your work."

I hardly know where to begin. "I have been occupied. I have been preparing for the commission for the giant." Immediately I regret it. The wound is raw. I feel a pang in my gut to even utter the words.

He looks at me with a blank stare. "What's that?"

"You don't know about the competition for the statue? The block in the cathedral workyard?"

Filippo continues to look at me blankly. I sigh. It is a relief to find one painter in Florence who does not know, does not even care about Michelangelo and his giant. I press my back against the stone wall of a building and feel my shoulders relax. I take another bite of the black bread, and we sit together in silence for a few moments, watching a cluster of noble ladies around a display of ham hocks hanging in one of the market stalls.

"So. What do you do to avoid the *guardia?*"

"I've become good at it," Filippo says, taking another bite of his pear. "They know me around here, so sometimes someone will tip me off that the roosters are on their way. And if I see them, I quickly grab the corners of my blanket, throw it over my shoulder, and run. And I know all of the good places to eat." He gestures to the alley behind the tavern. "Pipo in the Malviga tavern will let me run through the inn and out the back door into the other alley."

"Do you think I could try?" I grab one of the panels from the stack of blanks holding down the corner of the linen blanket. I grasp his palette and brush, and then start to sketch a picture of a bearlike man with close-set eyes and a single, bushy eyebrow. With a few strokes of the brush, Filippo recognizes that I have created a likeness of Buffo the fighter.

Filippo's cracking laughter draws the attention of two men who are leaving the betting table. They come to see what I am painting. Pretty soon they are laughing, too, and a small crowd gathers. It's just a few strokes, only a few roughly hatched lines, but I must admit I have caught Buffo's essence.

"*Cavolo*, you are pretty good!" Filippo says, punching my arm with the back of his hand.

"What did you expect?" I say. "I am trained."

"*Dio*. You could make a good living here."

⁓

"HE WAS HERE."

My sister sits under the window, catching the last bit of day-light as her fine brush makes a gilded leaf appear, as if by magic, on the frontispiece of a small religious book. I recognize her fas-tidious rows of leaves and trailing vines, her neatly organized pigments on a small palette beside her, just as our father taught his oldest child, his dutiful daughter.

"Michelangelo Buonarroti," she says, when I look at her blankly. Her jaw is set tight, and she studies my face for a few long moments before returning to painting. "He came to see you. He waited for a bit, but then he left. Why aren't you talking to him anymore?"

I busy myself with straightening pots on the shelf.

I hear her sigh. "You missed dinner. I saved it for you." She lays down her tools, then searches my face. "Where have you been, Jacopo?"

"I… I have been working. I went back to San Pier Martire. Are you happy?" I shrug. I hope she does not see the color rise to my cheeks, as much for my half-truth as for my reaction to the news that Michelangelo has come to seek me. The truth is that I cannot face my frescoes—or my colleagues—at San Pier Martire right now. Anyway, if my lucky streak continues, I won't have to worry about my debts anymore. I just need to stay in the game long enough. She doesn't need to know.

"Where... what did he want?" I stammer.

Lucia wipes her brush on a rag. "He said you should meet him at dawn tomorrow. In the cathedral workyard."

* * *

"L'INDACO! I NEED you."

He walks toward me in the golden light, a crooked man in a soiled, white canvas shift amidst a pile of marble, stone, wood, and dust, which rise behind his silhouette like a heavenly cloud.

I have been awake all night trying to find the right words to say to him. That I am angry. No, beyond angry. Aggrieved. That he had no right to treat me that way. That he owes me an apology. That all I wanted was a piece of the work, a role in the commission. That he has taken advantage of me, of our friendship. That I am done with him once and for all. That he is a giant pig's ass.

But as he comes toward me with shining eyes and a wide, tight grin, I am silenced. He needs me; nothing else matters. I have waited weeks to hear these words.

When he comes within reach, I open my arms. Soon, I am slapping his back with my palms. He squeezes me back, grunting under my heft. All that comes out of my mouth is a sigh of relief.

"Come." He pulls me by the sleeve.

What else can I do? I follow.

⁓

IN SPITE OF the early hour, there is a swirl of activity around me in the workyard. Several large mule carts have been wedged before the iron gate, bearing stacks of freshly cut timber from the hills beyond our city. Stonemasons and carpenters move back and forth across the dirt, heaving flatbed wagons stacked with sawn boards.

In the bright morning light, Michelangelo examines the tools laid out on worktables that have been arranged along one wall. Point, claw, and tooth chisels. Rasps and mallets of various sizes, free of marble dust, freshly turned out of the blacksmith's forge. Sticks of charcoal, newly cut. The *operai* have provided everything he will need to begin.

If I have arrived expecting an apology, I soon accept that it will not come, at least not now. It's not the sort of thing that would come easily for Michelangelo anyway, especially not in front of an audience. I am not the only other artist here. To be sure, any project like this demands many hands. Nothing in Florence is made without a team.

Michelangelo has chosen well, I judge. There is young Ridolfo Ghirlandaio; his uncle is training him to take over the studio of the father he lost when he was just a boy. My old friend Paolo the blacksmith. Francesco Monciatto, a woodworker who has fashioned many of our panels for portraits. Andrea Il Riccio, smelling of the taverns.

We collect around the worktable, each man in good humor. There is an atmosphere of levity, of the promise of an important work of sculpture. Each of us is filled with anticipation for what Michelangelo—the winner, the one chosen by our city's most powerful men—will direct us to do. I pull myself up beside him, more ready than ever to begin this work, at last.

The first task, Michelangelo tells us, is to construct a wooden enclosure around the marble block, with some extra space to work. This, he says, will ward off curious onlookers, and allow him to focus on the task at hand.

While Michelangelo begins to describe in detail the design of the wooden structure he has envisioned, I grasp the handle of a small claw chisel on the table. Then, I pull my sleeve down over it, so that only the claw is visible at the end of my sleeve, a crooked and horrible-looking skeletal hand. Already, I see that Andrea is smirking.

For a few moments, I raise my claw-hand above Michelangelo's head as if preparing to grasp him from behind. A looming, frightening ghoul. Then, I act as if, instead, I will coif his hair with the claw. Soon enough, all the men are laughing.

Michelangelo hesitates, seeming to wonder what he has said that the men find so humorous. Then, I gently lower my claw-hand to Michelangelo's scalp and begin to massage his messy curls. Only then does he turn and swat my arm.

"You're a *buffone*," he says, but I see only half of his mouth turn up. More of a wince than a smile.

I shrug. "What? You should thank me for the improved hairstyle." But Michelangelo ducks away from my claw-hand and walks toward the block, shaking his head. We follow.

At the center of the workyard, the giant stands like a beacon, sparkling with light on its eastern side. Since the day the cathedral fathers and Master da Vinci made a show of turning the block upright on end, it has been braced by several iron rods lashed together with linen straps. I see that Michelangelo has also directed an effort to clear the space around the base of the block. Where there was clutter, there is now only dirt. A mason's apprentice is sweeping the area around the base with a large broom made of rush.

"Where is your brother?" Ridolfo asks Paolo.

"He wasn't invited," Paolo responds, flicking his eyes briefly toward Michelangelo.

I respond quickly. "Believe me, you don't want Paolo's brother here. He's so contrary that if he drowned in the Arno, you'd have to go upstream to find him." I've already started them laughing and it's just the kind of joke Michelangelo might appreciate, I think. I turn to judge his reaction—a laugh, a smirk, even a tight grin.

But as I turn to judge if I have gained his approval, I see that he has selected a large mallet and a sharp-ended chisel from the tools on the table. I watch him drag a wooden ladder across the dirt and prop it against the block. He climbs halfway up the block, mallet and chisel squeezed under his arm. He stops at the place where a large nodule—the beginning of an idea—was carved by Agostino a generation ago.

Michelangelo says nothing, only runs his hand over the knot. He carefully places the chisel. We fall silent. Even the other laborers in the workyard stop and watch. Michelangelo raises his right arm and strikes the nodule with three loud blows. Ring. Ring. Ring. The metal reverberates on the marble. The swiftness and sureness of it takes my breath away. Four more strikes, then the knot flies off, thudding into the dirt in a small cloud of reddish dust. For a few long moments, there is nothing but stillness and filtered powder in the workyard.

"Ha!" I hear Michelangelo exclaim from the top of the ladder, his gruff voice echoing in the space. He has claimed the block for his own. He climbs down the ladder and lays the mallet and chisel on the table. He claps his hands together, sending up a puff of white. He looks at me. Finally, a smile.

"Now we may begin."

Everyone cheers.

Dragging a stick across the dirt, Michelangelo roughs out a rectangular area around the base of the block. The carpenters begin removing planks from the carts and laying them out so they can be cut into regular lengths.

After a few hours, a wooden frame is laid around the base of the block, and we begin to raise the side planks and nail boards across them. The work moves swiftly.

While we work, I do my best to keep the men entertained. I pretend to stab one of the stonemasons' assistants in the back with a saw, until he chases me across the workyard and I am forced to scale a ladder to feign escape over the wall. I steal a drink from another stonemason's canteen. I lead the men in a round of a popular tavern song about a bishop who looks like a woman. Even the head carpenter's father, an ancient-looking old crow, joins in singing.

All the time, I watch Michelangelo's face. Over the course of the day, his expression softens. That old familiar tight-lipped grin, which I have not seen since his return to Florence, wipes away some of the hardness that his time in Rome has etched onto his face.

Not everything is forgiven. Not yet. But here in this dusty place, our giant will take shape. We will work together again, just like in the old days. And maybe in time, I'll get my apology. Everything will be as it should be. I can hope.

AS THE SUN makes its slow progress across the sky and then sinks behind the wall of the workyard, my hands turn more raw, more sore. The men slow their pace. One by one, they sit on a stone or a pile of wood, the familiar rumble of the stomach luring them to stop. Michelangelo shows no sign of stopping to eat, of even slowing. He has not strayed from the block, his eyes only set on the work before him. He runs his hands over the surface of the white marble, feeling its crevices and contours as if he were assessing the health of a horse or a prized hunting dog. He climbs the ladder and descends. He tinks lightly on one section of the block with the tip of a chisel. Then another.

With the help of a half dozen men, a bucket of iron nails, three cartloads of lumber, and a lot of singing, a large, wooden enclosure has been erected around the giant. A narrow door has been fashioned and hinged with iron locks and a rope to keep it closed. The carpenters have even fashioned a trap door in the ceiling of the box that can be opened to the sky or closed to the elements. A great box has taken shape around the marble hunk.

Andrea Il Riccio heaves himself onto an old wooden beam beside me and wipes his brow with a dirty rag. "Your sister," he says.

"Lucia? What about her?"

"I have seen her at Battistini the bookbinder's shop when I go to buy my paper."

I shrug. Lucia brings her newly painted folios to Battistini to bind in leather casings on behalf of the nuns.

"I have seen her there more than once," he continues, setting his eyes on me as if to judge my reaction. "Lingering. That old bookbinder seems happy to have her in his shop. He should be lucky to find any lady to darken his doorstep, I suppose, with his wife gone to God and all…"

Old man Battistini? And Lucia? No one could deny her the right to look for a man, but still, the idea makes my head swim, and I can only huff in response. Right now she is probably examining the beans and tomatoes in our sparse courtyard garden in preparation for dinner. I imagine her gently twisting their stems to judge their ripeness, careful not to pluck one too soon or too late. She is a good woman, I think. Frugal. Sensible. That much should be obvious to any man looking for a wife or a mother for his children.

If I could feel a spark of excitement for her, it might help ease my conscience. Instead, the only empathy I can muster is for myself. What might become of me if Lucia were to leave our father's house for that of another man? I think of the pitcher of watery beer on my nightstand. My chamber pot, ever emptied. Each day's hot meal. My mended hose, hung on the line.

I stare out at the men lounging across the workyard and feel as I always have: surrounded by earnest souls who are always working, always employed with their hands. Somehow, I stand in the middle of this relentless industry, but at the same time, strangely apart. What, really, do I have to show for myself?

"Huh." I don't know what else to say about Andrea's suggestion that something might be brewing between my sister and the widower bookbinder. Andrea stands and brushes the dust from his shift.

"See you tomorrow?" I say.

He shakes his head. "No. We are done here."

"Done? What do you mean?"

"My father told me he was sending me here just for today," he says. "Michelangelo's only paying a day's wage for our work.

There arc to be no assistants. The Signoria said they will pay, but he will not accept."

I stand back and look at our handiwork. A large marble block inside a wooden box. When Michelangelo closes the door to the wooden box, no one will know he is working on a sculpture. He will disappear from view. No one will see him—not the passerby on the street, not curious onlookers pressing their faces through the iron gate. Not even the laborers toiling in this very workyard. He will be invisible to all.

And then, the truth hits me like a kick to the gut. Inside the new wooden box, there is only room for one man.

I WILL NOT be a sculptor. Not even a sculptor's assistant. Not much more, perhaps, than a builder of a wooden box.

But how could I possibly accuse Michelangelo this time for making me believe I was worthy to take on a giant marble block? I have only myself to blame.

So, maybe I have spent a few weeks at the dice table to soothe my soul. Maybe I have stuffed my pockets full of plums looted from a neighbor's tree, one whose branches have overgrown the wall of the garden where it was planted. More than once, I have staggered home down the urine-drenched alleyway behind the Porco tavern as dawn breaks. Lucia is none the wiser.

But after just a few weeks of leaving Michelangelo behind, at least I am a successful street painter. It is a good arrangement as long as I don't get caught.

Filippo Dolciati and I take turns painting, peddling our wares, and keeping watch for the *guardia*, who make a sweep of the tavern area at least once a day, or perhaps worse yet, an official from the painters' guild who might ruin our prospects for another commission.

Filippo has made a series of small pictures narrating the story of Rinaldeschi, the hanged man accused of throwing dung at the Madonna. They are selling briskly. He has standardized the story in a series of squares, beginning with the man throwing the *caca* at the painting, followed by his arrest, and ending with his body swinging from the walls of the Bargello. The pictures of Savonarola on the gallows, Filippo tells me, once sold all day long, but they have become less popular. People are not interested in that story anymore. Who wants to go back over that ugly chapter in our city's history? He has abandoned the subject.

Filippo and I are not simply *madonnieri*, for only a few of our pictures are devotional in nature. In fact, people seem to like our irreverent, ridiculous mockeries more than the Madonnas. I paint prostitutes with melons for breasts, asses dressed as monks and priests, bearded men in the guise of noble ladies, other distortions and travesties inspired by miniatures in the margins of my father's illuminated books. One of my most popular pictures shows Buffo the fighter with oversized muscles and a tiny *pissolino*. I relish the moment of recognition when fight spectators pass our blanket. Inevitably, they leave with a picture, or at least bent over with laughter.

Not only does their approval and appreciation bring me joy, but I have also made a little money. I begin to collect a few coins in my pocket. I am giving a cut of my earnings to Filippo, and both of us are giving a cut to the tavern owner who has allowed us to set up shop in front of the Porco. Most days, my intention is to buy ingredients for my sister's stew on the way home, but as soon as the coins rub together in my pocket, I cannot stop myself from trying to amplify my earnings at the betting table.

What is the harm in wagering a coin on a cockfight or a bare-knuckle brawl? What is the problem with predicting the outcome of an innocent game of *calcio*, of joining a hand of *primera* or *frussi*, or rolling the dice with the regulars at the Porco as they cheer my name from the counter? What harm is there in dealing a card from the bottom rather than the top of the deck? It is all in fun.

Most of the time, I go home empty-handed. The tavern owner has started a tab.

Other times, though, I win. A small sum, usually, but a win all the same. The barkeeper puts my coins in the leather belt at his waist and scratches my name off his list. At those times, the old feeling returns, and my cares disappear. I spread the cards in my hand or spill the pig-bone dice on the table, and I feel full of anticipation, the same as if I were going to meet a lover. Everything is full of possibility.

I do not tell my sister where I've been. As she works diligently, perhaps she imagines me lying on my back on the top of a scaffold, laying blue pigments on the ceiling of a chapel. Gambling is evil, she might say. At least they say so from the pulpit of our parish church.

But I ask, really, what harm can it do? It is merely a game.

BUFFO IS BACK in the fighting ring of the piazza, and once again, I wager that he will lose.

The match is one we've seen before, his opponent a thickly muscled tanner's son from the hovels along the Arno, a mean-looking boy with long, red scars down his back, probably the result of his father's lashing. Buffo's wounds, sustained in his last knockout with the young fighter from Chiana, seem to have healed; they are now blended with the deep marks permanently etched into his broad forehead and lined cheeks.

I empty my bag of coins on the betting table, watching them spill out like a pile of rocks. The money man's eyebrows fly up.

"You sure about this, L'Indaco?"

"As sure as I am that the barman's wife is 'visiting' the priest right now."

The man smirks and makes a mark on his page. "All right then, into the wolf's mouth!"

"May the wolf die." I press my way to the front of the crowd for a good view.

The fighters circle and swing, their huffs and grunts audible above the jeers of the crowd. It only takes a few minutes. Soon enough, the tanner's son is flat on his back on the cobbles, his face and his hands bloodied. Buffo raises his own bloody hands skyward as the crowd roars with delight.

For a moment, I feel I'm the one who has been punched in the gut. Time seems suspended, and the world goes quiet. My pile of money, weeks' worth of coins exchanged for my street-side paintings, brushed into the communal pot with the sweep of an arm. Nothing left in my own pockets.

The crowd pushes past me, beginning to disperse from the square. In a few moments, the square will stand empty once again.

I snap back to life. I jog to my makeshift painting workshop, little more than a swath of linen spread on the ground, with a small display of pictures. Buffo reigns victorious, at least for today. I expect I will sell a few pictures to the crowd. Afterward, surely I'll reclaim reward at the card table. I must. A dry swallow. I can't go home empty-handed tonight.

"Ciao, Jacopo."

Andrea Il Riccio, the curly-haired goldsmith and sometime-bronze-sculptor who frequents the same card tables as I, squats down and picks up one of my pictures, one of a woman's face made entirely of fruit.

"You're pretty good at painting figures. You looking for work?"

"Aren't we all?"

He laughs. "I suppose. Just make sure the guild doesn't catch you, that's all. Say, some of us have begun to meet with Master da Vinci on Thursday mornings. Now that he is back in Florence, he is taking on assistants here and there."

Leonardo da Vinci is taking on assistants. Would he take on a street painter? A failed sculptor's assistant? A failed... A failure?

"Even if we don't get hired," he continues, "it only seems like a good idea to take advantage of any time he is willing to give to us younger artists. Have you been to any of the meetings?"

I shake my head.

"He likes to talk. We simply stand around and listen. The Servite brothers have provided him a studio and other rooms in their monastery at Santissima Annunziata; he is painting a large altarpiece for them. If it's cold or rainy, we meet in his rooms at the monastery. If the weather is fair we meet at the Loggia of the Signoria. You should come."

"I will consider it." I clasp his hand as he offers it, then press my hands deep down into my empty pockets. "I'm feeling lucky."

❧

LEONARDO DA VINCI left Florence years ago in shame. He was put on trial for sodomy and chastised for an abandoned commission. I don't blame him for escaping to Milan. In my father's time, we heard the story on the streets everywhere, but now, it seems that no one in the city remembers any such transgressions over the years he has spent up north. No one has anything bad to say about Master da Vinci anymore. I have heard some call him our city's greatest painter. Until today, I have only observed him from a distance.

Through a maze of dark corridors, I follow the squat form of a monk into the silence of Santissima Annunziata. The monk's wooden block sandals clop on the stones, the only sound. At a small door, he gestures for me to enter. Another dark hallway; at the end, another doorway. This time, I hear the din of voices.

I take a deep breath and raise my fist to knock, but the door budges under my hand. Inside, I recognize not only my fellow card player, Andrea Il Riccio, but the familiar faces of several other members of the guild of Saint Luke, milling around a large table in the center of the room.

Ridolfo Ghirlandaio spies me when I close the door. "L'Indaco! Come. Join us."

I make my way across the large vaulted hall, perhaps an old monk's dormitory or dining room that has been turned into a makeshift studio. There are several tables covered with drawings, wooden contraptions, pots of pigment, and gesso-covered panels. The other painters have made a circle around one of the tables, and I press myself into a small space between two men. They pay me no mind. I look around, registering the familiar faces. All of the men around the table are guildsmen, artists with commissions, with workshops, and assistants of their own. I imagine that many may not recognize me at all.

At the head of the table stands Master da Vinci. He is an old man now, I see, past the time when many grown men have passed from this life to the World to Come. His hair has turned to gray frizz, his face lined like a thin veil of crepe. Yet there is an understated elegance about him, as if he were in the full bloom of youth. He is the very opposite of the Servite brothers, with their tattered robes belted with rope. As Master da Vinci raises his arm to speak, his rose-colored velvet cape falls open with a line of embroidered tassels and gilded threads of the kind that fine ladies weave into their hair and the bodices of their dresses. His dark purple hose match the velvet cape.

I look down at my own linen gown, nearly threadbare now, in spite of my sister's careful diligence in stitching the moth holes and the small rips where the threads have worn thin. I wonder how I have been invited here, among these successful men, these learned makers, clustered around this artist who appears as a kind of biblical orator, a prophet in a hooded cloak, hanging upon his every word.

"Painting involves greater mental deliberation than sculpture," the master is saying. "Painting is also of greater artifice and wonder than sculpture. It is therefore more esteemed and more valued. Painting is the most noble art. I'm sure you will agree, signori."

Is Master da Vinci trying to justify why he did not win the commission for the giant? Or perhaps he never put his name on the list for consideration by the *operai* at all? I keep my questions to myself for now.

"But Master," one of the younger men says, "is there not a role for sculpture at all? Does sculpture in a public place not help teach biblical stories to ignorant people, especially those who do not read?"

"You have just described most of the citizens of Florence," says Andrea, and several of the men around the table nod in agreement.

Master da Vinci raises a slim hand, and everyone falls silent. "Yes, you are correct that public sculpture serves to teach and inspire the uneducated. But my friends, consider! Sculpture is made by the most mechanical exercise, often accompanied by great sweat and marble dust, which forms a kind of mud daubed all over the sculptor's face. His back is covered with a snowstorm of chips." A bark of laughter.

Encouraged by the response, Master da Vinci continues. "The exact reverse is true of the painter. The painter stands before his work, perfectly at ease and well dressed," he says, rubbing his palms across his silk gown as if he is the perfect exemplar. "He adorns himself with whatever he pleases."

"But the role of public sculpture is that it must be symbolic, do you not agree, Master?" one of the men asks. "Think of the Judith and the lion before the Signoria."

"The Judith is a symbol of the Medici partisans," an older man snaps, his eyes bulging and flashing in the evening light.

"You would do well not to let anyone hear you say it," another voice at the table adds.

I feel as if I may burst. What of the new sculpture Michelangelo is creating inside that accursed wooden box?

Again, Master da Vinci calms the crowd with a mere gesture of his hand. "And you all would do well to pursue painting, gentleman, mark my word." He gestures around the cluttered studio, and, as if he hardly sees the cobwebs or dust-covered tables, he says, "A painter's house is always clean and filled with charming pictures, and often he is accompanied by music or by the reading of various and beautiful works, which, since they are not mixed with the sound of the hammer or other noises, are heard with greater pleasure. The painter moves a very light brush dipped in a delicate color, the nobler of the two pursuits without a measure of a doubt."

"You did not want the commission for the giant yourself, then, Master?" I blurt. For a moment, the only sound is a kind of rushing in my ears. Every pair of eyes in the room is on me. I watch a shadow cross over the master's face.

"We have enough marble sculptures in this city," he says. "You have only to look in any of our squares. At the Loggia of the Signoria. At the Orsanmichele. I have more important ways to spend my time." He gestures to a table filled with stacks of drawings and small wooden and metal models of various contraptions I cannot begin to fathom.

"With all due respect, Master, that's not what the *operai* think," an older man presses. "The Signoria has already paid him to hire assistants, though he refused," says Ridolfo. "He is alone inside that box in the workyard. You have witnessed it yourself, have you not, L'Indaco?"

Suddenly, all the eyes in the room are on me again.

"You are a sculptor, son?" Master da Vinci sets his focus on me.

"Well," I hesitate. "I am the son of the illuminator Torni. Mostly I paint, sir. Frescoes."

"Very good!" Master da Vinci raises his eyebrows. "Stick with painting, young man. As I have said, it is a nobler art. When you are an old man like I am, you will be glad you followed this advice."

FILIPPO DOLCIATI IS nowhere to be seen. I sit cross-legged on our cloth outside the Porco tavern, running my brush across the small panel. Today it's a scene of a woman with melons for breasts, which I have calculated sells better than any of my other works. There are no crowds, the market having moved to another part of the city until Saturday. The air weighs heavy and damp under my collar, and a wet mist coats the air in a white haze.

Eventually, the mist turns to heavy raindrops, pelting the tile rooftops like small pebbles. I am forced to stack my small, painted panels, gather the corners of my canvas tarp, and tie it in a knot. I slip into the crooked door of the Porco tavern.

For a few moments, I stand with my back to the wall and let my eyes adjust to the dim light. I hesitate. Tied around my waist is a sack full of coins, worth two days of work on the street corner. Maybe I should just take it home and add it to our coffers? It took me weeks to recover what I lost in the last fight, after all.

"Jacopo!" I see a familiar face at one of the card tables.

What would it take, I wonder, to bring home enough to pay off all our debts? Could I double my purse? Triple it?

Again, the call of my name. Now there is whistling, the waving of a hat, the raising of a glass. The spark of recognition. Acceptance. The men at the card table. They have spied me and now, there is no turning back.

I slide into a narrow bench along the card table, where a group of men have laid out a deck of *frussi*. Pen, ink, glazes, gilding. Knights. Knaves. Hunting horns. Hound tethers. Game nooses. The cards are exceptionally beautiful, a fine deck likely once made for a more wealthy man. I wonder how this deck ended up in a dirty tavern, and I think my sister and I could easily create a deck like this. How much would a rich man pay?

Stick with painting, young man. Master da Vinci's voice echoes in my head.

At the table are several artists whose faces I recognize. A young man who used to work for Piero della Francesca raises his hand when I remove my hat. Filippino Lippi, an older painter who has remained a loyal assistant to Master Botticelli for years, squeezes my shoulders.

"Eh, Jacopo!" he says in my ear. A hiss. "Come. Care to wager?"

⁂

HE IS BACK again.

Though I cannot make out the words, I hear his gravelly voice rise up the stairs from the lower level. My sister's whispered response is barely audible over the din of neighborhood children playing in the alley behind the house.

Through the orange light I perceive a crack in the battened shutter of my bedchamber. My stomach growls, and I surmise that it is evening. No wonder he has chosen this hour to appear. The smell of Lucia's cooking wafts up the stairs.

I don't remember how many days I have lain sweating in my bed, the shutters closed to the outside world. Lucia has tiptoed around me, leaving trays of fruit and bread on my desk, refilling the ceramic pitcher on the table, removing my chamber pot, and making fitful attempts to tidy the supplies littered around my bedchamber before making an exasperated sigh and surrendering me again to the darkness.

A few times Lucia has tried to lure me out of my bedchamber with the promise of food. "A meat pie," she says, or, "Signora Gramchi has brought over a bounty of persimmons from her garden outside the walls."

I growl a response, and she shuts the door.

How could I begin to tell her that instead of working on a grand fresco scene, instead of collaborating on the *David*, I have spent weeks sitting on a street corner drawing prostitutes, then gambling away what few coins I earn at the card table at Il Porco, a place in which I have promised her I would never set foot again? That after weeks—no, months—I have nothing to show for myself at all?

I must appear as a snarling hermit to her. I wish Lucia could see instead that I want nothing more than to lift this shadow of overwhelming shame, that she deserves to care for a husband instead of her undeserving brother. It is years past time, and perhaps she is well past the age of marriage anyway. Somehow her own fate became lost in the chaos of our parents' death, our brother's itinerant work, my own failure to live up to what I was tasked to do as the eldest son. It should have been my job to marry her off before it was too late, before she became too old. Instead, she has contented herself to take care of me rather than *me* caring for *her*, as our parents would have expected me to do. She quickly took the place of our mother, doling out words of advice for me, cooking and cleaning after me, admonishing me. I realize now that she has shielded me over the years, has tried to save me from myself. She is the only one who has stayed by my side when things go dark.

It is this realization, more than Michelangelo's gruff voice, that prompts me to sit up in bed, then to get up and splash water on my face.

When I reach the bottom of the stairs, I see the two of them, their backs to me, hunched over my sister's worktable under the window where a small book lies open. With his grubby hand he turns the pages, examining my sister's minuscule illuminations.

"This one is not for the convent?" he asks.

"No, it's for a young lady near Santa Maria Novella," she says. "Her father has commissioned me to decorate it. I am taking it to Battistini the bookbinder as soon as it's finished."

That bookbinder again. I'm not sure if it's the talk of Battistini or the presence of Michelangelo that has brought color to her cheeks, light to her eyes.

I lean against the doorjamb, running my fingers through the greasy strands of my hair. They haven't seen me yet.

Michelangelo has always had a strange allure with the ladies, I think. He's always known what to say in any situation, when women crowd around him to watch him sketch, to listen to his words. As he grew from a boy into a man—dirtier, darker, ever more stooped—he had women, even beautiful noblewomen, always in his company. Even one of the most esteemed ladies of our city tried to catch him before her father betrothed her to another family in Siena. I, friendly and gregarious to all women, even those not so beautiful, could not manage to attract or keep any one of them. I never understood it.

Michelangelo picks up the small page on Lucia's worktable and runs a crooked finger across her fine wisps of leaves and decorated initials. "Petrarca," he says.

"Yes," she says, satisfied with his recognition. "The lady reads it in addition to her prayer books. Her father allowed her to have these decorated as well. I am copying an ancient text from the library at the monastery at San Marco, but this is a welcome change from the same decoration I do. For this one, I can put my father's pattern books away."

"You have learned your father's lessons well, but do not underestimate your own way with the brush. You are gifted in your own right."

"It is kind of you to say," Lucia says. From the light of the hearth I see her face glow again. I want to call out to her, to tell her to stop engaging with this deceiving man, that he will only lead her down a path with no end, that he will only break her heart. But then she turns and sees me standing in the doorway.

"Jacopo," she says. "You are up."

"L'Indaco," Michelangelo says. The old, familiar, crooked smile crosses his face.

"Please," she says to Michelangelo, "join us for dinner." My sister stands and begins to busy herself in the kitchen. She fills our copper cups with a dusty bottle of wine. Our neighbor has shared with us from his vines in the countryside, near the place where Michelangelo's father owns land. Michelangelo sips the wine and remains silent. My sister goes to the hearth, ladling large spoonsful of stew into bowls. She places a loaf of bread on the table. Michelangelo tears off a piece and begins to chew. He remains silent; so do I. I drain my cup in one gulp and refill it. The wine fills my cheeks with grapey flavor. I refill it again.

"I see that you eat well, L'Indaco. I thought I might take advantage myself." Another awkward silence follows.

Into the silence, Lucia says tentatively, "We don't have much food, but you would never know that by looking at him." She pats my stomach before she steps out of the room.

My cup is quickly drained, and I refill it again. Michelangelo and I eat in silence for a few moments. When Lucia comes back, she has tidied her hair, exchanged her soiled apron for a new one, and tied it carefully at her waist. She grasps the spoon above the pot on the hearth, then refills our bowls. I watch him closely, feeling the malaise well up into my chest.

"I should think you would have enough to eat at your own house," I manage to say finally.

"Jacopo!" my sister chides me. "Don't be rude! We are always happy to share what we have."

I stand and pull another bottle of wine from the cabinet, open it, and refill our glasses. I drain mine in a single gulp. Lucia glares at me. Then she turns to Michelangelo.

"You are making progress on the giant?"

I cringe. Do I really want to know what is happening in the walls of that box? After he has shut everyone out?

He regards me with his black eyes for a few moments before answering. He chews the piece of bread in his mouth slowly, then says, "The carpenters have helped create a lever and a series of straps to help secure the block. It allows me better access as I sculpt."

"That sounds ingenious," she says. "Doesn't it, Jacopo?"

Michelangelo nods. "It's managed to tilt the block back so the marble dust will fall away onto the floor as I carve."

"Is that so you won't look like a baker?" I cannot help myself.

A sarcastic scoff from Michelangelo.

I continue to pour the wine. My sister widens her eyes at me again, but I do it anyway. She is not my mother, after all. My questions grow bolder.

"Is that not true? That you just pound away at the marble all day, covering yourself with white grit, so that you look as if you've been slaving at the ovens?"

He scoffs again, but he doesn't laugh this time.

"That's what Master da Vinci said," I say.

"Is that so?" He is looking into my eyes now. "And now you're spending your days with that perfumed daisy?"

"Maybe. It's better than working on some stupid sculpture where I am not welcome." I feel my heart begin to pound in my chest. "Besides, painting is the nobler art."

What I want to say is that I am angry with myself for not understanding that he never intended for me to be part of the commission. It was all about him. I feel mad that I duped myself into thinking that I was part of it, when I was only considered good enough to be a hired hand to build the enclosure around the giant block.

I want to yell that *I* was the one who wrote him a letter calling him home, that I pled with his father, that *we* were the ones to take the block. Not only am I not welcome inside that filthy, little box I helped build with my own hands, but I am not even allowed to see the sculpture inside. How did I not see this coming? How was I so stupid, so naive as to be blindsided? It was my letter, my doing, that brought him back home, my own efforts that brought him to Florence. It was my sweat and hard work that built the box around the marble block. And then, just about the time I have finally begun to wipe my hands of Michelangelo Buonarroti, he shows up at our door to give my sister some kind of false hope and to pilfer our meager stores of food.

But somehow I do not know where to begin with my words. Instead, I push my chair back, and it clatters to the floor. I roughly grasp the front of his collar in my fist. With one arm I lift him by his shirt into a standing position.

My sister jumps to standing. "Jacopo!"

I pull his face close to mine. I can see the whites of his dark eyes, can smell the wine and onions on his breath. For a few long moments, we stand like that, me holding him up by the front of his shirt, the only sound the heaving of our breath at one another's necks.

Michelangelo grasps my forearm. Though he is smaller than I, his grip is bruising.

"Jacopo, stop it immediately!" my sister yells in vain.

Finally, I find it within me to say something. "You were going to work on this damned sculpture by yourself all along, weren't you?" We continue to grip one another by the forearms, standing face to face. "When were you going to tell me? When? You never intended for me to be a part of it! You only wanted to use me as a cheap labor when it suited your own timeline."

"L'Indaco, you know I work alone," he says, quietly at first.

"That's ridiculous! Name one artistic endeavor in this city that was completed by someone working alone!" I throw his arm to the side. "If it weren't for me you would have never had the opportunity to take on that block! You would never have even known about the stupid competition!"

"And if it weren't for me, you would still be lying in your bed or even worse, drunk in the gutter next to Il Porco!" His eyes flash, and we stare one another down for a few long seconds.

"*Testa di...*" I begin to spit the words out between clenched teeth and rush at him again.

Lucia gasps. I doubt she has ever heard me use such language.

Michelangelo grasps my fist now, throwing it to the side. I feel the callouses on his palm. We stand chest to chest now, circling each other like I have seen Buffo and the other bare-knuckle fighters in the Mercato Vecchio.

Lucia tries to wrench her body between us. "Stop it! Both of you!" She puts a hand on each of our shoulders and attempts to pry us apart. I see the veins roil across the surface of Michelangelo's forearms, the result of years hammering blocks of marble.

"You think you're so important?" I say, but in truth I know he could probably knock me on the ground with one punch if he set his mind to it. I push my sister behind my back.

"Both of you have had too much to drink!" she yells, but she gives up trying to stand between us. We stand in the grip of one another's hands. Our eyes are locked. For a few long moments, I stare into black pools of his irises.

Then, I feel his grip on my arm loosen. His hands move to my shoulders, and he pulls me to his chest, whether an embrace or an attempt to squeeze the life from my body, I do not know. I feel him exhale. Then he places both hands on my face and pats my cheek, almost a slap. Affectionate. Painful.

"My blue boy," he growls, then lets out a low chuckle.

I am defeated.

With the nickname, he has defused a fistfight. With derision in his voice, he has stung me harder than if he threw the punch. I wish he had thrown his punch instead. He considers me neither a threat nor a rival. I am not a worthy contender. I never was.

"Thank you for the stew," he says to Lucia, but her eyes are only on me, wide and on fire. Listening to my own breath huff, I stand at the door with my sister. Michelangelo ducks under the door jamb and stumbles out. Together, we watch his silhouette stagger into the darkness of the street.

PART II

THE WAGER

Florence
1501-1503

The marble not yet carved can hold the form
Of every thought the greatest artist has,
And no conception ever comes to pass
Unless the hand obeys the intellect.

From a sonnet by Michelangelo Buonarroti

FROST STRETCHES ACROSS the Arno like a great
sheet of glass covered with a patina of potash and lime. Under
the wooden eaves of the Ponte Vecchio, doves fluff their feathers
against the cold. The dyers have closed up some of their warehouses and vats of boiling concoctions along the river until the
water is warm enough for the workers to wade in again with their
bales of wool. Two of the fruit sellers have battened their doors
until spring. Winter has laid its quiet mantle over the city; the
heated passions of the summer and early autumn seem long past.

I have not laid eyes on Michelangelo for more than two
months, not since the scuffle that separated us at the same
time that it served to launch me out of my melancholy. I have
avoided the streets around the cathedral workyard. I am certain he is there, invisible to the world inside his wooden box,
mallet and chisel in hand, breathing vapors into the cold air.
Frozen metal in his hand. A woolen shawl wrapped around his
head and neck. Silent except for the soft ping of the chisel or
the scrape of the claw. No doubt, by now he has begun to free
the figure from its marble prison, frozen inside as if encased
inside a block of ice.

No matter. I keep myself occupied. Now and then, I dabble at my frescoes at San Pier Martire, at least long enough to keep the henchmen off my trail. But mostly, I sit on the cold cobblestones or hop up and down on my blanket, rubbing my hands together and puffing warm breath into my fists while waiting for that small burst of joy when a customer picks up one of my small pictures and laughs. Filippo has been free from the debtor's prison for weeks, and together, we make a small living. The *guardia* has increased its surveillance of the Mercato Vecchio, so our movements have become more furtive. The crowds that congregated for the summer fistfights have dried up, as people want to stay inside for one of the coldest winters our elders can recall.

Eventually, though, Filippo moves away from me. "You can have this corner, L'Indaco," he tells me, though he does not meet my eyes. "I'm going to try my luck near the Porta di San Frediano."

"I'm sure I'll find you swimming upstream in the Arno, instead!" I holler, but he doesn't laugh. Doesn't even turn around.

"He'll never sell a picture sitting next to an old city gate." I address my mumbled comment to Our Lady in the street corner shrine, her once vibrant paint now faded. We have dubbed her the "Dung Madonna," for it is here that Rinaldeschi paid the price of his own life.

I chuckle to myself, but in my heart, I know it's not for sales prospects that Filippo has moved away from our makeshift shop at the corner shrine. Filippo simply no longer wants to hear me ask to borrow money. He sees through my stories about sick friends, my broke uncle, the poor orphans who need coins in their box, the thugs who jumped out at me in the alley and emptied my pockets. "You won't believe what happened!" I say, and I see that he doesn't. Not anymore. I have not repaid him; I admit it. As the days pass, he has appeared at our old corner shrine less often, and now I am alone.

On my way home in the evenings, sometimes I feel an urge to stop at Michelangelo's house, to poke fun at our almost-fist-fight, to tell him how many *soldi* I've made selling pictures on the street, to hear news of his family, to commiserate about my nearly abandoned commission at San Pier Martire. But he would say something mean or mocking. He would interrupt me for loftier talk of his David, about chiseling the face of a giant from marble, of his invitations to the homes of the cathedral committee. For all I know, if I knocked on his door, his servant woman would tell me he is dining with Soderini himself tonight.

And if I did stop by the street where Michelangelo's house lies, and he answered my knock, if he invited me in, what then? My deepest fears might be confirmed: that I am nothing more than a fat, lazy excuse for a guildsman, toiling away at a faded street corner shrine, with no wife, no children to pass my art on to, never able to rise beyond an apprentice to a great painter, sooner or later dead from exhaustion or excess, while the rest of the world crowds around Michelangelo and calls him a genius. I might conclude that my own work, my very life, was pointless.

So I stay away.

What I cannot seem to turn my back on is the card table. Whatever coins find their way into my pocket seem to vanish. I cannot turn away from the compulsion to wager my bet at the table.

Most nights, I walk out of the tavern, sick to the pit of my stomach, contemplating all sorts of things to make me feel better. I sit at the gambling table, only focused on the next hour, the next two, how good the thrill of chance will make me feel. But I leave with empty pockets and the stark realization of what I could have done with the money instead. Then the guilt sets in.

I promise myself that tomorrow will be a new day, that I will have a fresh start.

But the next night, I find myself drawn to the Mercato Vecchio as if under an enchantment, and without knowing how I got there, I find myself seated in Il Porco or Il Fico, at one of the card tables—playing with either the house decks or ones fashioned with my own hands. I crave the feeling, that rush of bliss that trumps even the happy effects of mild inebriation. But instead of bringing home a nice piece of meat for Lucia to prepare, I cannot stop myself from slapping the extra coins down on the table.

Next time. On one of these turns, I will beat them. I am sure of it. One day, I will win their stacks of coins, and who will be laughing then? My sister and I, we will be living as we should. I can call my brother home from the country, and we can live out our days without having to lift a finger. In the long run, it is more than luck. Those who don't lay enough on the line do not understand that it requires skill and dedication, a willingness to invest. If I keep going, my experience and skill will eventually pay off. I am bound to win, and win big.

A BLAST OF fire lights up the night sky in white, a moment of daytime in the midst of darkness. In that flash of brilliance, I see his face. I stop in my tracks.

Michelangelo Buonarroti.

He stands at the edge of Piazza Santa Croce. Like everyone else who has come out to see the fireworks and festivities of San Giovanni, he turns his face to the sky. In the blinding light, I see that his expression is full of wonder at the spectacle of the *fuochi* in the sky. The pops and blasts are just one part of the celebrations of our city's patron. Along the river's edge and in the squares, men launch projectiles and burn powdered metals and charcoal in open tubes. They pack gunpowder into metal contraptions to create rockets small and large. *Girandole. Scoppi. Razzi.*

In every church of our city, the guilds and nobles have donated thousands of candles, some small and simple, others elaborately crafted and towering over our heads. Over the course of a single night, these *ceri* are lit simultaneously across the city. Every year, I look forward to the energy of this celebration, when the lights create a magical atmosphere unlike any other night of the year. Sumptuously decorated and gilded wax creations are displayed inside and around the Baptistery, where crowds dressed in their own quarters' bright colors press forward, chanting and singing the songs of their ancestors.

I push my way into the crowds that assembled hours ago, progressing as a pushing, excited mass from the Palazzo Vecchio to the Baptistery. They are already stirred into a frenzy thanks to the annual game of *calcio* in the Piazza Santa Croce, where men dressed in the blues of Santa Croce, the whites of Santo Spirito, the reds of Santa Maria Novella, and the greens of San Giovanni, leave every year with dirt-stained breeches and bloodied, bare chests. And now, as the sun sets, the city is filled with blasts of light and color, filled with song and revelry.

In the next white flash of light, I see the marble dust coating Michelangelo's greasy hair and caked into the creases of his cheeks. He is not alone; in fact, he has attracted a small entourage. In the intermittent flashing of the fireworks, I recognize the faces of some of my fellow guildsmen: Master Botticelli and Filippino Lippi. Francesco Monciatto, a woodcarver who's prepared panels for many of my fellow painters. Ridolfo Ghirlandaio, our master's son. In the center, Michelangelo stands, arms crossed, the inkling of a smile on his lips.

I approach the small knot of men, moving slowly alongside them but not engaging. I hesitate. Do I go up and talk to him? Do I make a joke? If I did, I would have to get through these opportunists who are only trying to win the favor of the one man chosen by the Signoria to craft a sculpture larger than a man. Surely it's the only reason they have to show loyalty to a person who has never known how to earn a friend.

But before I can resolve to turn and walk away, he sees me. He pushes aside one of the artists hanging alongside him. It is too late for me to duck into the anonymity of the mob.

"L'Indaco!" he yells over the noise of the crowd. A blast of white in the sky, and then darkness. His face is shrouded in shadows now, and I only hear his voice. "I haven't seen you in a while."

I shrug. "Maybe you weren't looking in the right places."

"What? Where is that?"

"Only the most reputable institutions of the city."

"Ha!" A loud scoff. The entourage circles around him again, enveloping me. The men hang onto another, grasping handfuls of a shirt or pressing a shoulder so they stay together as we are carried into the mass of people swelling into the piazza. I am swept up into their nest of sweating, pressing flesh. I feel Michelangelo's grasp on my sleeve. Another flash of light. I see his teeth now. He is smiling. He pulls me alongside him, and as a group, we are funneled out of the square.

Near the Piazza della Signoria, we catch up to the parade procession. Along the street, there is a wooden barrier and torches overhead. Over the heads of throngs of onlookers, I catch sight of a man outfitted with a shining halberd and emblems of the wool guild, astride a muscular, beautiful horse. Behind him, men on horseback as far as the eye can see: dyers, bankers, silk workers, physicians and furriers—members of guilds large and small. The lifeblood of our city.

Behind this long procession, there is a line of mules and water buffalo, each beast snorting and heaving to pull the weight of a large float. The float bears a wooden contraption meant to resemble a small building painted and gilded with angels. Our tight knot of men presses forward into the throngs lining the street to watch the procession.

"Di Cosimo…" Ridolfo says. "He usually creates something surprising every year."

As the procession passes, I see that the buffalo have been draped with white and gilded fabrics to make them appear as angelic beings themselves. The writhing crowd presses me forward, against Michelangelo's back, so close that I inhale the metallic tang of the sweat on the back of his neck. Then one of the men tugs my sleeve, and as a mass of bees on a honeycomb, we move together down the street.

BY MIDNIGHT, WE are all singing loudly through the streets like a bunch of drunks. All around our little knot of men, the flames of thousands of candles come into brilliant, sharp detail. As we walk through the streets, it's as if I can see the whole city from the perspective of a bird flying high across it, thousands of individual flames flickering in the night. On the Arno, skiffs drift along the water, appearing like fireflies on a summer night.

Somehow, in the altered light, I see my city with a clarity I have never experienced. Beautiful. Enchanting. Magical. Larger than me, but I am one with it. I close my eyes and let the sounds of the frenzied crowd carry me. I let the bodies press me forward. At the center of the circle, Michelangelo is our beating heart. My hand reaches for his sleeve.

Ours is an unprecedented generation. It's as if God has pre-destined those of us staggering through the streets like fools to make a mark on history. It is preordained. Together, we have the power to make something miraculous, something never before seen. Our art might endure forever. We might be immortal. Can I imagine myself part of it? Maybe I just need to hang on.

Before dawn, I finally make my way home. Market vendors are still hawking their wares to crowds of revelers in the squares. Rounding the corner into the Mercato Nuovo, I see several long tables set out in rows. Vendors of fruit, fish, and poultry have set up their baskets and makeshift tables, taking advantage of the foot traffic funneling out of the squares. The aroma of food fills the air, and I feel a rush of saliva fill my cheeks.

The poultry vendor, a ponderous, sweating woman with a crown of braids and flushed cheeks, has arranged a display of large hens, their necks wrung, on a table. She has fallen asleep on a stool. Her head lolls to her shoulder, much as the hens on her table. Her son, only slightly bigger than the chickens himself, runs his small, grubby hand over the feathers of one.

"Pssst," I whisper to the boy, one eye on the sleeping woman. "You ever seen a dragon breathe fire?" His eyes are wide and shining. He shakes his head slowly. "There's one just around that corner." I gesture. He turns his head but hesitates. "Really," I say. "Don't you hear it?" Behind us, there is the hiss of fire and the cheer of a crowd. His wide eyes glow in the candlelight. "Go have a look before it's gone."

The temptation is impossible to resist. The boy steps away from the chicken table and scampers around the corner. His mother sleeps.

As a blast of fireworks cracks overhead, I grasp the supple neck of one of the chickens and stuff the bird into the pouch at the front of my apron. It just fits, a few of its burgundy feathers sticking out. Quickly, I funnel my way into the rear of the crowd, leaving the poultry seller—and Michelangelo and his friends—behind me. In the chaos of the *fuochi*, I do not believe anyone has witnessed my trick.

I have never stolen anything before, nothing of importance. I feel my heart race at the same time that my mouth waters to think what Lucia will be able to make with the chicken.

"Collecting chickens, L'Indaco?" My heart runs cold. I turn to see Francesco Monciatto the woodcarver, who has detached himself from our group of men. Has he witnessed my prank?

"Bringing it home to my sister for the pot." I press the feathers into my pouch. "You are working with Michelangelo now, are you?" Immediately I regret asking the question in case the answer is yes.

"Me? No. He works alone; you should know that. Ha! Actually, I've been working with di Cosimo." Monciatto gestures to the fireworks. "I made some of the banners and floats for this parade, in fact."

"Di Cosimo," I say. "Isn't he…" I bring my hand to my head in a gesture of questionable sanity. Di Cosimo is one of our city's most important painters, not to mention a designer of unforgettable public pageants.

"Di Cosimo has been commissioned to orchestrate a pageant for the feast of Saint Agata. He is creating banners, floats, flags, garlands, you know, everything that is needed." He stops and presses my arm. "He is looking for some assistants and good painters to help. You would be great. Are you interested?"

"Well, I have a few obligations," I say, scratching my head. "But I might be able to fit something in."

"*Benissimo.* Give us a few days to clear up this mess," he nods at the back of the float ahead of us, "then come to di Cosimo's studio. I'll make the introduction."

∾

ALL THE WAY home, I pray that I will slip into the house unnoticed, but when I press the door with quiet hands, I see my sister's silhouette in the glow of a neglected fire, her arms crossed.

I pause in the doorway and study her face, the deep lines creased alongside her mouth. We look at each other in silence for a few long moments. I inhale the familiar scent of smoke and onions. The last embers crackle in the hearth. Near the back door, I spy a small puddle of water where the rain has beat a steady drip through a leak in the roof.

"Did someone die?" I say finally, trying to cut through the thick atmosphere that has descended on the kitchen. I place the wine-colored hen on the table. An offering.

Lucia narrows her eyes at me. "Where have you been?"

I gesture at the chicken. "At the *fuochi*. And the poultry seller."

"And then..."

I shrug. "And then what?"

"And then where else?" She crosses her arms across her chest, her eyes no more than slits.

"That's it," I say, fidgeting with the ties of my shift.

"The debt collector has sent you another notice," she says, then sighs, as if it is a relief to reveal the information. From under her crossed arms, she produces a folded piece of parchment, sealed with the red wax of the Signoria. She stands and slaps it on the table. The fear is gone from her face this time; all I see now is suspicion.

Without breaking the seal, I pick up the parchment and throw it into the fire.

Lucia opens her mouth into a perfect circle. "Jacopo! In the name of God! You cannot just ignore those men. They know where we live!"

"Don't worry about them." I shoo her with my hand. "I am working on it."

I move to go up to my bedchamber, but she plants her body in front of me, her hands on her hips. After a few moments of silence, she looks me in the eye. "Are you gambling again, Jacopo?"

I laugh, a brief, high-pitched hack. "Me? Why do you ask?"

"What are those cards?" She points toward the staircase. "The ones in your bedchamber?"

I raise my eyebrows. "You have been sneaking around in there?"

"No one else is going to clean that mule stable. I found them when I was tidying your worktable."

"It's a commission," I say.

"A commission." She does not budge, only crosses her arms. "For playing cards."

"Yes! *Per l'amor di Dio!*" I meet her gaze. "Everything is under control. I promise."

"I want to believe you," she says, "but it seems I am the only one putting food on our table these days."

I gesture frantically to the bird on the table, as if a single stolen chicken could make up for all the times she has gone to the market and paid for food from her own pocket.

In return, I get a searing gaze. "The roof is leaking. Where is the money for that?" she says. "You said you were saving up for that in the back of the ledger book. But when I went into the drawer, I found the book but the back pages were empty. What happened to it?"

When I do not respond, her eyes go big and brown. "Jacopo. Many times I have not said anything when you came home with spirits on your breath. It's because I do not want to hear you lie to me. I do not want to hear the words I know are not true. And so I have forced myself to remain silent. More than once. Because I knew you would tell me you weren't betting money on cards or dice. I wanted to wait for the right time to carry on a calm dialogue about all of this, but I can no longer hold my tongue."

"You know me. When have I ever given you anything to worry about?" I say again, but I can see that the debt collector's letter has rattled her.

"Jacopo," she says, "you have let me down so many times. You are intelligent, you are gifted with your creations. I do not want to see you throw away everything as you sink down into this... melancholy of yours." She sighs and begins to pace the room. "Enough times I have accepted your lies, told myself that it is only temporary, that it is not so bad, that we can bear it, that you will eventually stop and find gainful employment instead."

"You're the one who's lying here!" Deep inside, I know I am only lying to myself. "You... exaggerate."

She doesn't waver. "Only you can decide how to squander your own time and money. I cannot stop you from throwing away every florin you make; that much is clear. But you must understand," she says, lowering her arms and setting her brown eyes on me with a steely gaze, "that your choices do not only affect you. Our fortunes are tied together. They always have been, whether or not you want to admit it."

I turn away from her, busying myself with tidying our felted capes hanging on an iron hook by the door. "I swear to you that things are not as bad as you think. You can trust me."

She looks at me sideways. "Trust is earned through action, not through words, Jacopo."

And trust is fragile. I know that now. What could I do or say to earn it back?

She continues. "Have you never considered that while you and our brother might choose to work, I have to rely on you? The three of us. We must rely on each other." From the corner of my eye, I see her press her face into her hands. "And now… I cannot even get married," she says.

For a moment I am struck mute, hating myself for ignoring this obvious consequence of my own actions. I have gambled away Lucia's dowry. She has no hope of marrying now. In a dark corner of my mind, I feel only relief that she is stuck here caring for me, until we are both bone dust, for who else will do it? I will never admit it aloud. And I have nothing to give her in return for her labors.

The hen on the table draws flies. I think about all the money I have gambled away over the years; it is more than I could ever calculate. It would have amounted to a very handsome dowry for her; even fifty broad florins might have been enough to start. It would have given her the life that my parents might have wished or even expected. But I have already frivoled away the bride price our father set aside for her. I have made it several times but given it all away at the card table.

I sit at the table and put my forehead in my palms. Lucia has become my keeper. She could have asked me to leave long ago. She would have had our parents' house. She would have been fine with the pittance she earns illuminating books. My choices have sent us down this path. For the first time, she has unburdened herself, has told me exactly how I have hurt her.

"You want to get married," I say quietly. It is all I can muster.

She scoffs and her face turns pink. "What did you think, brother? If I had wanted to live a contemplative life, I could have taken my vows long ago. You know that. Why do you think I have not joined the sisters?"

I press my face into my hands. I want to shut my ears, but she continues.

"When you say that you are done gambling, I want to believe you. *I do.* But I cannot walk away now. You have made it our problem. My problem." She stands and slams her palms on the table in frustration. "If you want to go spend the rest of your days in the gutter, that is your choice, but I cannot afford to be out on the street with nowhere to live."

For a long moment, there is only the sound of a slow drip through the hole in our roof.

"I've written to our brother," she says softly.

"What for?!" I yell, more from shame than from anything else, for it falls to the older brother to care for the younger ones. Just look how Michelangelo has cared for his own. Just look at how I fail.

"We don't need Francesco to come home! Everything is fine."

Her expression is pained. I know she has lied for me—to friends, family, neighbors. She has said that I was working and earning money when she was the one who kept us afloat. She has looked the other way when the evidence and the consequences of my debt have mounted all around us. And if Francesco bails me out, what would stop me from bleeding our little family dry once again?

"Look," I say finally. "The debt… Yes, it was assigned to me to pay back a fine. Yes, it was for gambling. I admit it. But the fresco project at San Pier Martire. I'm paying it back through my labor there. *Capito?*"

"I know." Her words come out little more than a whisper.

"How?"

She shrugs. "I deduced as much. No one had to tell me. Jacopo, you must find paying work now. If you are only working to dig yourself out of a hole, then how are we to go forward?"

A deep, heaving sigh. "The giant…" I stare at the ceiling as if God could hand down a reason why things worked out the way they had with Michelangelo. "I was deluding myself that I could work on it."

She begins to say something about the giant, then stops herself. "You have gone to Master da Vinci. Did he give you work?"

I wave my hand and shake my head vigorously. "Those are not my people. They are all fakers who think they are better than everyone else."

She slaps her rag on the table in exasperation. "You cannot afford to be choosy! We are talking about paying work!"

"I have sold a few little pictures," I say, gesturing as if to make the size of my little boards.

"On the street corner?" She crosses her arms again.

"I have been looking for better work." I shrug. "I promise."

She sears me again with her large, brown eyes. In that moment, I hate her.

"Like what, Jacopo?"

I hook my thumb in the direction of the waning festivities in the streets. "Monciatto the woodcarver says there is work in di Cosimo's studio. Just now he told me. Di Cosimo? That crazy man who organizes all those pageants."

Lucia grasps my forearms with her hands and squeezes them tight. "Then for God's sake, you must go, Jacopo. First thing to-morrow morning. No more excuses. I am coming with you."

&

IN SPITE OF the fact that he is one of our guild's busiest paint-ers and a genius at staging public spectacles, Piero di Cosimo lives more as a beast than a man. His house and workshop occupy an entire city block. Vines have overtaken the walls and doorways so that I hardly know where to enter.

When I finally find the unassuming entryway to di Cosimo's studio, I stop for a moment and ready myself. The only thing that matters now is making a good impression. A lot is riding on my employment here, not only for myself but also for Lucia. What a relief that I was able to convince her to stay behind at home. I push my shoulders back and brush my stained shift as if it might improve my appearance. And what an ass of myself I would have made if I had brought my sister along with me to vouch for my skill. The men would surely have laughed me all the way back out into the street.

I step inside di Cosimo's walled orchard, then hesitate. The fruit trees look as though they have never been trimmed. Steam rises into the branches from great copper vats, and the smell of animal glue and boiling eggs hangs in the air like a smothering cloud. I make my way through the tangled branches, an improb-able forest in the city, to an open door where there are voices. Men working. The acrid smell of vinegar and pigments.

"Monciatto the woodcarver sent me," I say to a boy whose apron falls to the top of his soiled clogs. The boy disappears into the clutter and I wait, trying again to appear relaxed and confident. I feel the grin on my face quiver.

Inside di Cosimo's studio, I see that things are not much improved from the outside. The floors look as if they have never been swept. Every tabletop is cluttered with paper, models, brushes, and banners. The carcasses of great parade decorations lie dormant, burdened under the weight of teetering contraptions long abandoned. There are hollow wooden angels. Papier-mâché figures as tall as a man. The head of a fearsome dragon with wild eyes and a lolling tongue.

While I wait, I stare into the face of the dragon, widening my eyes to match. What do I have to be afraid of? I stick out my tongue and try to twist it sideways, matching the expression of the unlikely beast.

"Jacopo!" Monciatto says. I quickly collect myself and reassume my swaggering, confident posture. "You've decided to join us. Come!" When Monciatto turns away, I make one last wide-eyed face at the dragon before following Monciatto's back into the depths of the studio.

The space is cavernous and filled with warm light from leaded windows high up on the south side. For each of the dozen or so assistants, there are at least two cats. I make my way through the clutter, feeling the warm swirl of feline forms around my ankles. Other cats lounge on the tabletops, on fragments and pieces of disused carnival floats, on the cool dirt floor, or high in the dark reaches of paraphernalia discarded from years of pageants and spectacles.

"We are getting ready for the next parade already," Monciatto tells me. "Master di Cosimo has asked all of us to recommend our friends. There should be work here for a while. Master!" he calls to a sagging wooden screen in the corner of the studio. I stand behind Monciatto and peer inside.

Seated on a low, wooden stool, Master di Cosimo is little more than a potato of a man who looks as though he has never washed. He regards us with round, bulging eyes like those of a toad.

"Master, this is Jacopo Torni... L'Indaco, they call him. He is a guildsman skilled with fresco and illumination."

Master di Cosimo stands, teeters. He waddles over to us, then looks me up and down with a skeptical, twitching eye.

"Who is your father?"

"Master Torni. The illuminator. May God protect his soul." I cross myself and hope that Master di Cosimo can't see my hand tremble.

Di Cosimo's toad eyes go wide, then he nods. He lays a meaty hand on my shoulder and his mouth turns into a wide grin. He grasps my hand.

It only takes an instant. I am hired, if only thanks to the credibility of my dead father.

⁓

I AM SURPRISED at how quickly I fall into a comfortable rhythm of work. Somehow, amid the squalor and chaos, di Cosimo's workshop is productive. I find myself among a happy cadre of apprentices, painting the colorful arms of our city's major and minor guilds on long fabric banners. I recognize the golden eagle of the merchants, the lamb of the wool guild, the gray stripes of the shoemakers, the iron calipers of the blacksmiths. In other corners, assistants are grinding pigments, cutting fabric, painting trees in the backgrounds of small panels, stirring glue in pots for papier-mâché.

Banner painting. It's not what I thought I would be doing with my time, and I'm not sure I will even admit it to Lucia when I go home. Making ephemera is hardly the path to immortality our father described, even if it was his own reputation that sealed my employment in this very studio. But it is paying work and my sister would remind me that I am in no position to turn it down.

Master di Cosimo emerges from behind his wooden screen every so often to survey the work of his assistants, then waddles away again. There, he cuts himself off from the rest of the studio while he mutters to himself and captures words and pictures in a great bound book on a wobbly wooden stand. The workshop is run by his assistant Giusto, who is already a master and foreman. I quickly assess that Giusto is the true overseer of the workshop, circulating and commenting, directing and correcting.

I spend the day painting the same leaping ram, the symbol of the butchers' guild, against a series of yellow fabric banners. By midday, I have gotten pretty good at rendering the strange, twisted horns of the animal from nothing more than two pots of pigments and a handful of paint-stained brushes. With friendly banter with the other painters at the table, the hours pass quickly. Toward dusk, we are directed to a back room of the workshop, where several women sit, sewing. On long tables, they have stretched out rolls and layers of painted fabric. Their chattering stops when the other banner painters and I step into the room.

Suddenly, I am pushed sideways and I stumble.

"Oh! Forgive me." A young woman has bumped into me as she is unfurling a roll of painted fabric. There before me, more beautiful than any of the angels painted on panels in di Cosimo's workshop, is a girl, fine and delicate. Around her head is a halo of hair the color of carrots. Her face is full of freckles and her eyes a beautiful shade of chestnut. "Are you hurt?'

I smile. "Never been better."

She nods and moves to the table.

Monciatto presses his elbow into my side as if to warn me from being distracted. "Di Cosimo churns these out so quickly that he has brought a few women into the studio to sew them." I watch the girl as she settles at the worktable to sew. Her hands make tiny, careful stitches, fixing each banner to a golden cord. She measures with a long stick before adding the next one.

I pull up a chair and lean in conspiratorially. "Signorina, you and I share something in common."

"Is that so?" She flashes her large brown eyes at me, but her hands stay busy with her stitches.

"Yes. I too have been brought in here for my special skills. From my... large... productive... workshop." I lower my voice so that Monciatto won't hear my fib.

"Oh?" she looks at me skeptically. "And what workshop is that?"

I hesitate. "Perhaps you will not have heard of it, signorina, as we only take on special commissions."

"Like what?"

I grasp a piece of paper from the table and make a quick sketch, one of my most popular female figures composed with melons for breasts, and grapes for hair. With a few practiced strokes of the pen, I finish the drawing and push it across the table to her. "As I said... special."

For a moment, she only stares at the drawing, then at me. Then, I see her face transform. I see the white, straight teeth, and then she throws her head back and laughs so hard that I see her red tongue, the small nodes at the back of her throat. Then she buries her face in her hands. When she moves her hands away, she is wiping away tears of laughter with them.

Making her laugh gives me a jolt of energy, a high like I have not felt since that night of the candles and fireworks. I feel my heart swell with joy. It is just like when I was a boy, when I used to make my mother laugh, only two hundred times better.

❧

ELATION PROPELS ME across town, as far as the cathedral workyard. The whole way, I review my exchange with the red-haired girl. I think of what I will say tomorrow to make her laugh, even to bring a smile to her face or make her eyes dance. My feet feel as if they are floating above the cobblestones.

In the dimming light of early evening, I stop at the gate of the cathedral. The workyard is desolate, all the laborers having gone home for the evening.

All but one.

Before me stands that wooden enclosure I helped to make with my own hands. I hear the muffled ringing of the chisel on the marble, the scuffling of his clogs on the rungs of the ladder. Michelangelo has disappeared into his box again.

I pause for a long second. Surely whatever incited us to come to blows has now passed, after the night of fireworks and the strange, magical energy that swept us up as one with our city. The fight was stupid after all, on both of our parts. Surely I might sit with him and share a swill of watery beer? Surely we can both laugh about it now? Why do I let him get under my skin? We are friends after all. Aren't we?

I press my hands deep into the pockets of my shift, jingling to-gether the coins that Master di Cosimo has pressed into my hand after a day of painting banners for the butchers' guild. An honest day's work. And yet so little. So much less than the fortune that Michelangelo is being paid for his sculpture, it is laughable.

What would it take, I wonder, to match Michelangelo's payment? Much more than a handful of coins. But on a good night—a great night at the card table? How much would it take to pay off all our debts? For a moment, I allow myself to imagine what would bring a smile to Lucia's face. To erase the creases in her brow. To fix our leaky roof. To show her, once and for all, that she was wrong about me. To put all our troubles behind us for good. To redeem myself.

I press my hand on the wrought iron gate, and it unlatches, then opens a crack. Nothing is stopping me from walking inside. And yet, I cannot bring myself to cross the threshold.

I press my hands into my pockets again to make sure the coins are still there. Not much, but enough to wager. Enough to stay in the game. Maybe even enough to win big.

I move down an alley headed toward the taverns. This time fortune is on my side. Just maybe.

⁓

THE FAMILIAR CRACK and shuffle of the cards com-pels me to the table. I slide onto a worn bench and hunch my shoulders alongside a man dealing from an old, ragged deck. He stacks and restacks the cards, then lays them out in a fan shape. I reach into the leather purse attached to my belt and pull out a few of the coins I have earned in di Cosimo's studio. I run my fingers across their hard, dulled surfaces before tossing them on the table. The dealer stacks them before him, making a mark on his paper to track my wager.

"Wait. Jacopo is a superior dealer." My curly-haired friend Andrea the goldsmith is back at the table, along with three men I do not recognize. "Give him the deck." Without protest, the man hands me an old, cracked stack of crudely painted cards. Each of the other four men produces his wager, a jangle of roughly engraved silver *denari*.

I shuffle the cards, beating the bottom of the stack on the table. I deal two cards to each man. I watch Andrea's chin shift left and right. His dirty fingernails arrange the cards in his hand. The second man huffs out a breath of air. The third places his cards face down on the table and keeps his hands in his lap.

I palm a second card underneath my draw, knowing the men are occupied with studying their own hands and will never see my well-practiced trick. "No one's bidding?" I say. The men shake their heads. I pass out two more cards to each man and wait until each considers their hand. I arrange the cards in my hand so that cards of each suit stand together.

"Curly, you start," I begin.

But Andrea only shakes his head. "Pass." He discards two cards and draws two more from the deck.

"Me too," says the second man. He discards two more cards and draws two more. Then he slaps down his four cards on the table and crosses his arms over his chest.

A good start.

Suddenly, the tavern door flies open. Buffo's commanding presence fills the doorway. His appearance in the tavern sends up a communal shout, and the great bear of a man salutes as he swaggers his heft into a table. Instinctively I duck, thinking about the crass pictures I have made of his genitalia over the last weeks, but he does not take note of me. Instead, he is surrounded by a group of scraggly, dark men. He looks better since the last time I saw him. His lip has a long wound and his eye has turned shades of purple and green, but it is no longer swollen.

"Come, signori," the third man says. I feel his leg bouncing under the table. "Numerous thirty," he says. He stacks five more coins on the table and keeps his cards. He must have a primero already. Blast! His eyes dart over to me, a nervous glance.

My turn. If I am lucky—and if my palmed card helps as I think it might—I may double my bet. Hoping for a maximus, I discard two of my cards, and draw two more. I try to keep my facial expression in check so no one will suspect my hand.

The fourth man. "I bid Numerous 32 and 10 coins." He lets the coins fall into a stack from his cupped palm. Their familiar ring sends me back to study my own hand.

"Pass," the third man says.

The fourth quickly discards two cards and draws two more. I feel his leg bouncing frantically under the table.

I consider my hand. Although I already have more than 60 points, I feel certain that Andrea has a better hand than he is letting on. I discard two of my cards, hoping for a maximus that might win the game, but my cards disappoint. No one else has covered the third man's wager. Reluctantly, I reach into my purse, pull out another coin, and clink it on the table. "Where is Filippo Dolciati?" I ask. A distraction. I palm another card.

"You have not heard?" says the third man, sitting across from me. "Yesterday the *guardia* picked him up at the corner by Il Fico."

"Sì," Andrea chimes in. "I heard this morning that he was fined and thrown into the Stinche. He must be waiting for his brothers to bail him out."

Before I can respond to this news, I see that the second man has slapped down a strong hand of cards.

"Primero 61." He displays a row of rotting teeth.

I say nothing. My heart has begun to pound. Reluctantly, I add another coin to the pile on the table as I watch the corner of the second man's mouth turn up. He can either keep his hand, pass, or match my wager. His mouth twitches back and forth. After a moment's hesitation, he puts in another pile of coins.

The third man discards two cards and picks up two more.

"Pass," says the fourth.

We count.

The second man and I both have primero, so we count our point totals. He has 61; I press my cards down. I have 58.

"Ha!" The man stacks my coins on top of several others and scrapes them into a small bag, which he quickly places into the folds of his gown.

"Care to make another bet, Jacopo?" Andrea asks me.

I reach into my pocket and feel the last coin left, a deeply tarnished *soldo* a fine-looking lady paid me for a miniature Madonna and Child. Reluctantly, I pull it out of my purse and slide it across the table. It looks small and insignificant compared to the others.

"I'm out," says Andrea, slapping his hand of cards on the table. He slides his rickety chair back from the table and runs his palms along his thighs.

As he speaks the word I see the second man, who has been silent up until now, put down the winning hand. Another stack of coins goes to him. In the middle of the stack is the last coin I earned on the street. The last coin to my name.

❧

HIS VOICE.

It is distinctive, and even from the top of the stairs I recognize the deep sound, the Tuscan dialect spoken with a sharp clip, that I have come to know as his alone.

Lucia has complained that I have been in bed for four days, but I no longer know if it is day or night. I hear the familiar din of the church bells, the feet of passersby, shop doors opening, neighbors' voices, kids throwing a leather ball in the street. Inside, it is all the same: the darkness, the rank odor of my room, the sour smell of my own skin, the dirty woolen blanket over my head. I sleep when I can, sleeping to forget. I go to bed and I pray that I will not wake up, that I will not have to admit to Lucia after all that I have nothing left, that I have lost what little I have earned.

I must get up and return to Master di Cosimo, she pleads with me. Yes, it is a paying job. I know. But more than that. It is a job in which I am tasked with making things that will last only weeks, maybe months. I will turn out beautifully painted objects that will end up in the garbage heap of Master di Cosimo's studio, soon forgotten, ultimately discarded.

To think that I am the source of Lucia's pain is almost more than I can bear. She would be better off without me, I think. I should have sat on the edge of the bridge and let my weight pull me down into the icy river. I was stupid not to take advantage of it when the idea struck. She might be better off with a bereavement stipend from the painter's guild than with a brother who cannot provide, who has squandered her dowry, the one thing that stands between her and a union with an honest man.

I should have unburdened her then, but I was too much of a coward to do it.

I hear their voices downstairs, his and my sister's. They are whispering loudly, talking under their breath so that I cannot make out their words. I am not strong enough to face Michelangelo Buonarroti. Not now. How could I pretend that I am good enough to consider us friends, equals, after everything that has happened? Did she fetch him in a desperate attempt to lure me from my bed? Did he come of his own accord?

Soon enough, I realize that his appearance at our house is not about friendship at all. No. He is hungry.

My heart goes out to Lucia, whom I hear scraping together a few pieces of cured speck from the ice block, the last bits left over from better times. After a few moments the aroma of the boiling pot wafts up the stairs, beans and asparagus she put away last spring in glass jars, and that we have rationed out day by day so I can hardly stand the smell anymore.

She is feeding him. I know she wants to. She would not accept anything less.

At least there is wine. Our father put away enough for a lifetime before we had to sell our shares in the winery outside of Florence. But as for food... We have already gone through most of our stores for the winter. I know that Michelangelo's own house is full of men and his maid is a poor cook, but he at least has the money to eat well enough that he doesn't need to rely on my sister to cook for him. Why is he preying on us, pretending to be helpful when he's only serving as a greedy mouth to feed for a family that can hardly feed itself?

I do not want to see him.

No.

The truth is that I do not want him to see me. Not in this state.

Still, I do not feel it within my power to get out of bed. I run my palms over my greasy hair and gather my wrinkled bedding up under my chin. Surely I could knot the sheets and tie them to make a cord long enough to hang onto, while I slide out the window, down the stone façade of my house and onto the street. Or hang myself on the way down.

But before I can think of an excuse or tie my sheets in knots, the door creaks open and his shadow darkens the crack.

"L'Indaco," he says, his voice as deep and gravelly as if he has a mouth full of stones. He knocks gently on the door with the back of his knuckles. I pull the woolen blanket off my face and watch him in the flickering shadows.

He says nothing, but opens the door the whole way. He takes a sideways glance at me curled up in bed. He walks to the hearth and stokes the fire with a long, iron poker. Then, he heaves his weight onto the edge of my bed and puts his dark eyes on me. I glimpse the hard edges of his face in the shadows. He looks horrible, as if he has barely survived some tragedy. His head, his face, his entire body is covered in fine, white dust and grime, and I imagine that no amount of boiled water, lavender, or lime soap will remove the layers. Powdery, white dust fills the fine lines that have developed across his cheeks and the deeper ones on either side of his mouth.

"You don't look well," he says finally.

"And neither are you queen of the Carnival," I say. I see the corner of his mouth turn up. He runs his hands across his greasy hair.

"Your sister has prepared a meal for us."

"I cannot face those beans another day," I say. "And I don't recommend them unless you want to spend the next week farting inside that box of yours. Mi raccommando."

He snorts out a laugh and pushes the woolen blanket off my body. "Forewarned. Well, at least we can enjoy a glass of wine together. Surely I could tempt you?" I feel his coarse palms on my thighs, and he jiggles me in an attempt to get me up.

I sit up, but the effort makes me dizzy and I flop back on the bed. "My sister has sent you, I suspect?"

He hesitates. "Friends help one another, no?"

I shrug. Our alliance has hardly been equal. But there it is. The truth. Is it some form of apology? I do not dare to ask.

The silence stretches out between us. "You have been occupied," I manage to say.

"Yes, about that…" he starts, staring at the fire in the hearth. "I… You know I work alone, L'Indaco. Always have."

"I know," I say. "But that's not how it looks to me. Seems you have a team of admirers everywhere you go."

"*Bof!*" He swats his hand. "They are just opportunists. Anyway, I am not very good at working with others." He makes an attempt to meet my eyes, but I see the words do not come easily for him.

"No," I say, "but you have in the past. Do you remember that time when we pretended we were throwing you off the bridge?"

He laughs. "Ah yes. That *beffa*. You and your little brother. Clever. Took me a few years before I forgave you for that one."

My head starts to clear and I sit up, finally. "Ha! Those English people were convinced that you were mad. Do you remember that one man, what he said about…"

"L'Indaco," he interrupts, his face suddenly dark and serious, "I understand that you might need a loan."

I search his eyes to see if he is bluffing, but they are nearly invisible in the shadows. "I don't want your money—or your charity."

"But I am now in the thankful position of being able to help you if you need it," he says. "It is the least I can do as I have not always treated you as a friend." He squirms.

I feel this is the closest thing I might get to an apology, and I nod my head and close my eyes in acknowledgement.

"It's all right," I say. "I am working now. Nothing like what you are doing, of course. Little more than ephemera for di Cosimo's pageants. But working all the same."

"Good," he says and jiggles my leg again with his dust-covered hand. "Di Cosimo. He is *pazzo*, but occasionally there is a flicker of pure genius. And what you are doing is a worthy task. And, I think it is all right to," he waves his hand as if searching for the right words, "lower your standards of perfection sometimes." He sees something in my face and hastens to correct himself. "What I mean is that you do not have to attain perfection to feel worthy. If you continually reach beyond your capacity, you will always feel disappointed. Set your expectations at a realistic level and you will never fall short."

Once again he has managed to insult me without meaning to. I feel a burning sensation rise into my throat; it is enough to finally push me out of bed. I stand up at once and begin pacing the room.

"That is easy for you to say!" I cannot meet his eyes, so I look at the window as if it were open and I could see the view to the river, all the way to the cathedral workyard. "You and your commission, your raise, your admirers, your... your giant." I feel a scoff roll off my lips.

I hear him sigh behind me. "L'Indaco, it was not meant as an insult. Please." I feel him come to stand behind me; he places his hands on my shoulders. I feel a tingle ripple down to the small of my back as his thumbs press into my shoulder blades. A startling jolt. He leans into me, and I feel the swing of his hair against my cheek. "What I mean to say is… Everything is a work in progress. You can only go up from here."

"What makes you so sure?" I close my eyes and feel his hot breath at the back of my neck.

"Because you are a creator in your heart. Besides that, you are well trained—by your father. By Master Ghirlandaio. You only lack the power of your own conviction. If you believe it, then others will, too." I feel his hands tighten on me. My shoulders fall under his grip.

"I am nothing. I am not like you." It comes out as a whisper, but I feel my heart pounding so hard inside my chest that he must hear it.

"On that count you are incorrect," he says, almost a whisper.

I whip around to face him, pressing my hands on his shoulders. For a few long moments we stand like that, our hands on one another's shoulders, like goats locking horns or wrestlers about to push each other to the floor, hanging in that suspended moment before one yields to the force of the other. For a moment, I wonder if we will once again start a fight that will end with him slapping my cheek, chuckling, and walking away. Or if he will pull me into a tight embrace instead.

"Prove me wrong," I say in a loud whisper. I grasp his shoulders as tightly as I can, feeling that if I let go I will crumble to the floor, and then the tears will begin to fall. That is the last thing I want him to see. I feel the heat rise to my cheeks and his muscles push against my broad palms as he meets me with renewed force.

"Prove me wrong!" I spit out the words again.

I watch his dark, beady eyes flicker in the fire. "*Bene*. Come to the cathedral workyard when the sun rises tomorrow, *amico*. I will show you."

❧

AS SOON AS I enter the gate, I hear scraping inside the wooden enclosure. The workyard is deserted, the guildsmen prohibited from working on the Sabbath. Michelangelo never believed that rules applied to him.

Dust hangs in the air, and I make my way through piles of lumber, stacks of limestone blocks, sawhorses, and hand tools. I knock softly at the door to Michelangelo's wooden enclosure, and from the other side, I hear him fumble with the latch.

Inside the wooden box the air is warm and still. Although closed on all four sides, the top of the wooden enclosure is propped open to the sky. Morning sun filters into the space around the hut, dust motes and marble powder suspended in the gilded pools of light. The smell of damp stone hangs in the air, coating my throat and nostrils with fine powder.

He reaches out a hand coated in white, and gives me a short squeeze of the shoulder. Then he heads off to a large, makeshift worktable wedged into the corner.

Before my face, a foot the size of my torso. I gasp at the scale of it. "The *operai* must be very happy with you," I say.

He shakes his head. "They have not laid eyes on it yet. No one has seen it. Only you."

"Working on the Sabbath, I mean."

"Hmm," he says, scratching his head. I realize then that he has no idea what day it is.

For a moment I stand and soak in the light and the silence of the workyard. The great hunk of marble fills the space, as tall as three men. Much of the body has been roughed out but not yet smoothed. Still, from the awkward block, slowly, a colossus is taking shape.

I walk around the base of the sculpture. On one side, the block is still in its rough-hewn state. At first I perceive that he has done nothing with it, that it remains little more than a long hunk of marble turned upright.

On the other side, though, he has drawn a silhouette in charcoal on the face of the block. Then he has worked inward from the face, always working from that side, drawing the figure from the stone as if it were to be a relief instead of a sculpture in the round. The gesso model that we had carried in the box those months ago stands in the corner.

He picks up a *gradina*, a short, metal claw with a toothed cutting edge at one end. He climbs a few rungs up the ladder, and wordlessly, begins to remove marble. It is as if he is drawing with pen and paper, revealing muscles, skin, sinews in the same way he has brought vitality and life to the male form even with a pen and paper, as if the figure can breathe and move.

"You do not worry that your patrons have not seen your work yet?" I lean against the worktable and direct my question to his back, high up on the ladder now.

He shrugs. "Nothing is certain," he says. "It could go away at any moment. Borgia could change his mind about our ransom and come through our gates right now. Or the French. They've already gathered at the gates of Rome. Who knows? The Medici partisans of our own city might have already plotted to slit Soderini's throat in the middle of the night, for all I know." I stop to consider that his knowledge of these larger forces far outstrips my narrow view of events in our city.

"So I don't know if this project will see the light of day, if they will change their minds," he says, gesturing with his chisel. "All I can do is my best work. Move forward. To use my skill to make something as beautiful as I am able. Plus, they are paying me to do a job. Just as you," he says, locking eyes with me and reminding me of the scuffle that got me out of bed once again.

He makes a few crosshatches with his claw chisel, as if he were making a tentative sketch with his ink pen. They have the same effect: rounding and bringing out the depth of the figure.

I begin to walk around the block; I see the large foot, toes, a knee begin to emerge, rising up from the marble as if the body were a sunken ship rising up from the ocean, one side fully formed, the other lost somewhere below the surface, waiting to appear.

"The boy king is trapped inside the block," I say.

"Precisely." He cannot help but smile that I have understood him. "It is my job to release him. To release the colossus inside."

Above my head, he has already completed the right hand, the one that holds the stone. Michelangelo has carefully chiseled the veins on the back side of the hand, and for a moment I believe that blood must be flowing through the marble itself. I feel all the latent tension of a young man preparing to hurl the stone at a giant, a beast of a man that no one had dared to challenge before.

Near the worktable, another wooden ladder stands propped against the wall, so tall that it reaches to the opening at the top of the box.

"Take a closer look," he says, gesturing to the ladder.

The wooden steps lashed to the two vertical poles creak under my heft. I have never felt at ease in high places. I do not dare to look down at the earthen floor of the box. Instead, I look up. From the top of the ladder I turn my face to the spring sky. The sun breaks the edge of the box, and a bird flies over my head, peering down at me with a black eye, questioning what I am doing there at the top of the ladder, what I am doing there at all.

I dare to turn my body. At the top rung, I find myself face to face with the boy king, the David. About three-quarters of the face has been roughed out. Michelangelo has used a small drill to form the pupil of the right eye, as well as some of the neat curls of the hair; part of the hair disintegrates into the mass of the marble. One eye has been carved out, and a knitted brow; the lips curl in intense concentration.

I peer into the eye, into the soul of this boy hero, the one who is about to sling a rock that will knock out a giant, an impossible foe who no one would have believed possible to defeat. The face of this man-child is fierce, defiant. His brow is knotted above his nose, and he gazes out into the distance, toward the enemy that he is not sure if he can overcome. At the same time he is tense, coiled, and wound tight like a spring. He is brave but not quite confident. Now, standing face to face with this boy hero I see the uncertainty, the moment of getting ready, of facing a great enemy. He is not sure if he will win.

At the same time that I look into the face of a boy, I feel I am looking into the face of a god made flesh. But my friend has not slavishly copied a pagan statue he has seen in the ancient squares of Rome. No. I am looking into the face of God made into divine man. I am in touch with the divine. The divine of creation of man.

For a fleeting moment, I have glimpsed immortality, the immortality that my father always said was the highest aspiration of those of us who make things for a living.

More than that. I have glimpsed immortality, yes, but now, looking into the face of this new *David*, I know that immortality is not achieved by some stroke of magic, by some sudden windfall as in a game of cards or a roll of the dice. The glory has to go with hard work, with security in your own conviction. The way to immortality is paved with showing up inside a little box every morning to claw at a discarded block of marble. It's losing hours of sleep sketching a hand holding a stone four hundred times. It's a lot of marble dust.

There is no magic, no glory. It is only a small man attempting to do something big.

And I see now that this sculpture, this giant, is the result of nothing more than days, weeks, months of hard work; the talent in the hands and the dedication to see something through to completion. It is nothing more than the result of having the courage to pick up a sling, throw a rock, and see if its hits its target. I have never understood it until now.

"Ha!" I exclaim from the top of the ladder. Beyond that, I am rendered speechless.

Below me, at the base of the ladder, Michelangelo sharpens the flat end of a chisel, scraping the blade against a sharpening stone. Then he meets my gaze, and we stay like that for a long time, watching one another, immersed in the filtered light.

ॐ

I RETURN HOME to find Battistini the bookbinder lingering at our doorway. I stop in my tracks. Before he spots me, I duck under the awning of the cobbler's shop at the corner.

My sister is there, too. Lucia talks softly to the bookbinder, standing at the threshold in plain daylight, as if she has no cares in the world for the old women across the street who are undoubtedly peeking through the cracks of their shutters.

Neither of them has spotted me. For a few minutes, I watch them talk together and share a quiet smile. Then the bookbinder brings her hand to his cheek, holding it there for a moment before he says goodbye, turns, and walks toward the river.

Later, I enter the house to find my sister fidgeting with the brushes on her worktable, her cheeks flushed, unable to look me in the eye.

❧

I RUN UP the stairs to my bedchamber and flip my wooden chair over onto the floor with a loud clatter. With one sweep of my arm, I send all the drawings stacked on my worktable fluttering to the floor.

My hands shaking, I crumple several half-finished sketches and feed them into the hearth. New flames leap to life. I ball more drawings into my fists, years of inadequate attempts to represent hands, feet, faces, trees, architecture. One by one, I toss each ball of parchment into the fire, watching them char and dissipate, tiny, black flecks in the gray draught. One by one, I burn them all. Everything. All the sketches of all the subjects I have done over the past years. Every sketch of that accursed giant.

Now, the playing cards. All the cards.

In a frenzy, I rummage through all the places around my bedchamber to see what's left. There are stashes of painted playing cards in the drawers, stacked under pots of pigments, stuffed into and under the straw of my mattress.

Frussi. Naibi. Bassetta. Cursed games.

How many hours have I spent painting card decks with brushes loaded with vermilion, charcoal black? How many hours have I spent flicking my wrists furiously, sending the cards scattering across the table? Some old and worn, some with edges frayed and rubbed smooth from years of shuffling. Others newly printed in black on large sheets, then hand-painted by myself or another poor, unknown guildsman.

Batons, swords, cups, coins. Kings, queens, knights, knaves. How quickly I could palm one into my pocket and replace it with another. How well I could read the hands of my opponents. How easily I could produce a card from a narrow, nearly invisible drawer in the edge of a table. What did it amount to?

Nothing.

If I ever believed that winning a card game requires skill, then I have utterly deceived myself. I have nothing to show for all my so-called skill at the betting table.

Because of this compulsion, I cannot raise a dowry large enough to send my sister off with the man she loves. I can't even put food on our table. And my little brother has had to seek his fortune far away.

I light a long match. One by one, I light each card.

When the flames lick the tips of my fingers, I toss the cards into the hearth. I watch them snap and burn in the flames, the bright colors disintegrating in the fire before my eyes, vibrant images of red and black.

None of it matters. Not my cards, not any of my pictures.

If I am to amount to anything at all, I must start again.

IN THE NAME of getting out of the money hole I have dug for myself, I resolve to get Master di Cosimo's help. I follow the waddling artist through the alleys of San Lorenzo, looking for a chance to talk with him, to ask for his favor upon me, and for an advance against my day wages so I may begin to save a dowry for Lucia.

But I find myself vying for di Cosimo's time and attention among many others who seek it, now that the normally reclusive artist has left the hovel of his studio and walks the streets of Florence. I file in behind nearly two dozen others who are paid from di Cosimo's purse.

There is something about Master di Cosimo, I think, that is intimidating. This authoritative air seems at odds with his rotted teeth, wispy hair, and high-pitched voice. Assembling around him, we make a striking collection of artists and makers. Embroiderers. Goldsmiths. Makers of bronze and silver. A handful of painters. We have all come together to make di Cosimo's latest pageant more fantastic, more spectacular than the last one. We follow him from the shade of an alley into the blazing square before the church of San Lorenzo, listening to him describe in great detail the procession he has planned for his latest public spectacle.

"*Attenzione!* There is a lot to cover, gentlemen." Our master has wrapped his potato body in swaths of linen that hang down in dirty pieces, making him look like an ancient glutton who has taken to drink and spent weeks living on the streets.

"And ladies," says the red-haired seamstress—Maria—whom I have come to learn is the daughter of Andrea del Sarto, one of di Cosimo's most successful pupils. The other assistants laugh.

"Then I must make a correction," says di Cosimo, bowing to her. "*Signore e signori*, there is much to discuss."

Over a stretch of spring days, an unprecedented heat wave turns Florence into an inferno. Along the Arno, water birds collect under the shade of the bridge. People swim in the rushing river. Food spoils in the markets before our very eyes. A man hangs from the gallows by one foot just outside the city walls, his body black and rotting in the sun. Flies swarm.

Master di Cosimo does not appear to notice the heat. He seems to occupy another world than the rest of us anyway; he takes note of the things no one else sees. In addition to those of us who toil in di Cosimo's wrecked workshop, a handful of finely dressed noblewomen, wives and daughters of the wool and silk guildsmen, who will sponsor this year's festivities, follow behind in an entourage. In exchange for their largesse, the ladies get a preview of the event from di Cosimo himself. The ladies collect around him, sweating in their brocades, layers of silk and linen, red woolen caps and sheer headdresses.

The studio master, Giusto, follows close behind with a small book and a piece of black chalk, taking notes and sketching quick, labeled diagrams while Master di Cosimo talks. I look for an opportunity to wedge myself alongside Giusto so I have a chance to talk with Master di Cosimo, to ask him to pay my wages directly to an account for Lucia's dowry.

"Master, we admired the red flower garlands you prepared last year for Santa Maria Novella's floats. Will you be doing those again?" A lady with a broad bosom steps in front of me and gestures across the square with a sweep of her lace-trimmed hand.

"No, signora, we have something else special planned for you." Behind her, three other well-attired women cool themselves with delicately painted paper fans, pressing forward to hear di Cosimo's description of the new pageant. There are gems on each finger and layers of brightly colored silks. They have broken at least some sumptuary laws, I think. Perhaps many.

They are smart and sophisticated in their tastes, the wealthy of our city. One might even say insatiable. They understand the symbolism of Heracles and Diana. Of the Trojan War. Of the founding of Rome. Of many other mythological scenes for which Master di Cosimo's floats are famous. These elaborate things will be spoken about for months afterward. No doubt the feast of San Giovanni has already been the topic in these ladies' fine salons for nearly a year. They will be the envy of their friends when they announce that they have been privy to di Cosimo's plans for the next pageant before it has even been unveiled.

"When the Heracles float arrives in this square," di Cosimo is telling the group, "that's when those of you dressed as heralds will hop down from the edge and continue to the ox float behind. You will know when you hear the flautists begin to play their parts." I have seen the floats beginning to come together in the great cloister of Santa Maria Novella, where the Dominicans allow Master di Cosimo to rehearse his parades so the floats will remain out of public view until they are ready for the procession.

Mercifully, we move to the shaded side of the church. "And this year," di Cosimo continues, "we shall do something that has never been seen in our city; you are the first to hear of it, and I trust you will keep it a secret." They won't, and I'm sure di Cosimo is expecting them to spread the secret like wildfire through the city. He continues. "We shall gild a living child!" There is a collective gasp, not only from the ladies but from some in our clutch of artisans as well.

"A golden child," di Cosimo says again, and I see the expression of smug satisfaction at the reaction he has incited. "The dawn of a new day in our glorious city, personified in the form of a gilded youth."

"A gilded boy!" one of the ladies exclaims, and a new murmur rises among the crowd. Several of the noblewomen clap their hands in admiration. They chatter among themselves, whispering their excitement into one another's ears.

"Who shall it be, Master di Cosimo?" I ask.

"Young Nello," he says. My eyes search the crowd for Nello, a boy no more than ten years old, who washes paintbrushes and mixes pigments in the workshop. He is nowhere to be seen.

Di Cosimo walks off in the direction of the markets, his entourage following like a pack of dogs. The red-haired seamstress, Maria, trails along from the back. I slow my pace and pull in beside her. "A golden boy," I say. "A symbol of the new Florence. Do you find young Nello worthy of such a designation?"

"He probably has no idea, poor boy." She smiles. "But Master di Cosimo is in charge. Nello hardly has a choice." Then she gestures at Master di Cosimo walking ahead of us and lowers her voice to a whisper. "Sometimes I think he looks like a toad."

I strike a pose to mimic the funny, staggering gait of di Cosimo. I begin walking behind the artist, imitating his bow-legged progress, which is indeed like a giant frog walking on its back legs. Maria puts her hand over her mouth to extinguish her laugh. Everyone else is paying close attention to Master di Cosimo, so she and I share our private joke without either of us having said a word. My favorite kind of *beffa*. Just as di Cosimo turns around, I turn my back so that he does not see what I'm doing. He does not break his speech. He is so wrapped up in his explanation of the upcoming pageantry that he does not notice us at all.

"And then," he says, "just before we reach the Piazza della Signoria, our buglers will spring ahead on horseback, galloping into the square at great speed."

I mimic what di Cosimo is describing, pretending to be riding a horse and playing a bugle. The girl has detached herself from the gaggle of ladies, hanging behind so she can get a better view of my antics. Her eyes sparkle, and she makes no attempt to cover her laugh.

Before us, two of di Cosimo's sons and a daughter are following their father, bored expressions on their faces.

"And his children look like little frogs, too," Maria whispers, her hand cupped in my direction. "It is a lie that di Cosimo only makes beautiful things."

"It is true," I say, cupping my own mouth to whisper in response. "That is because Master di Cosimo makes his art during the daylight, but he makes his children in the dark."

She sniggers again, pulling a lock of red hair into her mouth.

One of the noble ladies' daughters has caught sight of us, has seen us laughing. As we turn into the Piazza della Signoria and the imposing town hall comes into view, the ponderously dressed girl slows her pace to join us, to see what we find so humorous. No doubt, she must find what we are discussing more interesting than the meaningless blather of her mother and her friends. The girl's mother has taken di Cosimo's arm, a colorful butterfly on the wing of a gray moth. She hangs on his every word as the artist leads her on a personal tour of the city's visual delights. She does not realize that her daughter has broken off from the group of noblewomen, slipping away to join the ranks of us lowly craftspeople.

Master di Cosimo stops before the main entrance to the town hall. "It is an unfortunate circumstance that the sculpture of the biblical *David* by our Master Donatello is not able to be seen behind these stone walls," he says. "It is truly one of the masterpieces of our city."

"Surely the one being made by that Michelangelo cannot compare," one of the noble ladies offers.

"Master," another asks, "are you of the opinion that Signor Buonarroti's sculpture will be more beautiful than Donatello's?"

Di Cosimo shrugs, but I see his eyes sparkle. "Why not, signora? He may not be as well known here in his native city, but few people realize that he has made beautiful sculpture of Our Lady and Our Crucified Lord in the Holy City. Word of it has spread even as far as Venice."

I raise my finger toward the two women whose attention, by some stroke of fortune, I now hold. "Mark my word, ladies," I say as if the noble daughter and the seamstress might occupy the same world, "the giant will supersede any of the sculptures ever made before. Even the sculptures you see here in the loggia of the Signoria. Even the *David* of Donatello. In fact, any sculpture in this city."

"How do you know this?" the noble daughter says, scowling in my direction, an expression no doubt copied from the adults in her household.

"Because I have seen it with my own eyes."

The red-haired girl's eyes widen. Several other artists have heard my comment and have stopped in their tracks. "You have seen the giant?" she says. "The new *David*?"

❧

HE'S GETTING A RAISE. Twelve broad florins. Is the giant really worth that fortune? If I am honest with myself, yes. Perhaps more.

I contemplate the sum while brushing a layer of white varnish on the cornices of a makeshift building that has been hastily constructed atop one of di Cosimo's wooden parade floats. Above my head, a pair of swallows reels swiftly in the blue expanse of the sky, then disappear from view. It's a shade of blue so perfect that only God could have conjured it, and all I want to do is to capture it, to pull down just a little of that heavenly beauty, to preserve a bit of its divine Creator.

From my spot high on a ladder, I survey the large cloister. Around us, the parade floats are beginning to take shape. The cloister has become a staging area for the floats. For this spectacle, di Cosimo has envisioned a heavenly city, a series of makeshift temples contrived of wood and paint that resemble the buildings of antiquity. Around us, white columns. A vision of a heavenly city. One of the older Dominicans, Brother Maffeo, circulates excitedly among the floats, sanguine in his brown robe, hood pulled back to reveal his bald pate and ring of short, graying black hair.

For any other artist, this divine sky and these fantastic, imaginary scenes might inspire a work of art for all ages. But in my case, surely it is only a burnt offering. As I watch my fellow guildsmen swept into greatness, my own works remain in the shadows. And while Michelangelo Buonarroti stands inside his stinking box, earning a salary that will keep his father and brothers rich in wine and pork fat for the winter, I stand slathering a layer of varnish on a sad-looking, papier-mâché replica of St. Peter that may be burned in di Cosimo's fire pit by Christmas.

"You almost finished, L'Indaco?" I turn to see di Cosimo's foreman, Giusto, approaching from across the monastery square where the floats are lined up in a circle, workers on each side to finish the floats before the parade. Giusto is a serious man; I like that about him. I respect his dedication to protocol and decorum, just as he seems to enjoy my irreverence for such things.

"*Pazienza!* Inspired genius cannot be rushed," I say. I look the statue over, one of two dozen floats that will be part of that procession alone, one of dozens throughout the city. "Anyway, I hope old man Peter will be happy with it. I don't want to get to the hereafter and have him tell me the likeness wasn't flattering."

The men working around the base of the float chuckle, but I am left staring dolefully into the crudely painted face of Saint Peter, and out into the future. As this fake city of God, this brilliant ephemera, takes shape around me, I feel the darkness licking the edges of my mind. The familiar abyss. For this moment, I'm hanging on to the splendor of white and gold taking shape around me. If I let go, I might fall into the black—quiet and comforting at the same time that it consumes me.

Perhaps I should simply put down my tools and go to the Mercato Vecchio. Find Filippo working on his small pictures. Try my luck again at the cards. A wager. Perhaps my only chance at a fortune.

"I'm sure Saint Peter will be satisfied with you, L'Indaco," Giusto says. "You going back to those frescoes at San Pier Martire after this job is done?"

I shrug. It's not that I don't intend to finish those frescoes. I know it's my obligation. It will hardly help me make enough money to dower my sister. I have every intention of getting back to it. I do.

"Sure. Unless someone from the Signoria sees my work here and decides to hire me to paint Soderini's bathroom."

"Let's hope he hires both of us!" he laughs. "Or perhaps Michelangelo will still need your help with that *gigante*."

I feel the hairs on the back of my neck bristle. "I wouldn't count on it. No one's paying attention to what we're doing here, anyway. Especially *him*. Surely you know that, Giusto."

Giusto looks around, hands out and shoulders shrugging. "What do you mean? You're here with us, aren't you? You're painting, making your way as an artist and being paid well enough in the bargain. You could be out fighting the infidel, or... or serving on a galley! You could be stomping through horseshit in the plow fields."

"You make it all seem so glamorous," I say.

"Listen," he says, putting an arm around my shoulder. "Here's the truth. What you need is a wife, my friend."

"A wife? Yes, Giusto, yes, that will solve *all* my problems! A hen to peck or a shrew to shrill, another set of skeleton fingers pulling on my ears."

Giusto shakes his head. "Not all women are like your sister."

"Don't even say the word, Giusto, you may conjure her like a demon!" We share another chuckle. "Anyway, an artist must be married to his art. That's the advice I've heard—even from Michelangelo Buonarroti."

"Thank goodness I didn't listen to that!" After a moment of consideration, a gentle breeze drifting through the courtyard, Giusto looks at me over the bridge of his nose. "Many of us married men are successful."

"I know, I know," I say, taking a step back to get a better look at the massive waste of time I've been working on. "What do you say to me, Giusto? Love is... love is a bird that lands on your shoulder, it's a... a sunbeam that finds you?"

"No, my friend, surely not. But you can always go hunting for the bird. Am I right, Brother Maffeo?"

I shake my head and glance around, the monastery around us seeming like the perfect place not to have such a conversation. But Brother Maffeo only dismisses Giusto's irreverence with a wave. The old monk must be used to the artists' banter, I think, perhaps even enjoys it.

"That's time I could spend painting, Giusto, perfecting my craft! Does Michelangelo Buonarroti go chasing scullery maids? Does Master da Vinci?"

"They don't have to," Giusto says. "The maidens come to them… in droves."

Brother Maffeo peers up at me at the top of the float. "Giusto speaks the truth, however crude, my friend. If these men succeed in glorifying the Lord with their talents, then the rewards come. That's the way it is in our world, you see? Achievements attract other achievements."

After a sad moment to reflect, I must admit, then, that failure attracts failure.

We look up at the statue of St. Peter, destined to be seen only once before being destroyed. Hours of work doomed to be fleeting, with no trace of it only days after a brief celebration. I glance over at Giusto's own statue, of St. Luke. The soft face seems so human, I can hardly keep from being moved. I step closer so I can admire it in greater detail, the sadness of the expression touching me deep in my heart.

"Well," Giusto says. "You are friends with Buonarroti. Why don't you ask him about it?"

FOR ONCE, HE is not inside his box. I find Michelangelo sitting in the shade of a willow tree on the bank of the Arno, one of our old spots. He has brought a small bound book of pages, and I see his hand move quickly with a nub of gray charcoal. I see men whose bodies writhe across the page. Horses so vivid that I can almost smell the earth as their hooves tear into the wet ground.

Before us, a group of men bathe themselves in the Arno. Most of them are tanners or tanners' assistants, young men who do the backbreaking work of preparing hides for the leather trade. It is a horrible way to live. They are crooked, their skin leathery with cuts, muscular to an almost unnatural degree because the intense physical labor of the job. This spot has always been one of Michelangelo's favorites, second only to the crypt of Santo Spirito.

We both started out like this, making drawings around the city, imagining what could be, turning the face of a beautiful young girl in the market into the Virgin Mary. Turning our balding guild treasurer into Saint Peter. We spent hours in front of Donatello's statue of *David*, back when it was accessible for everyone to see and Donatello was long dead but far from forgotten. In order to teach us, Master Ghirlandaio had us set up in the shade of the loggia of the Signoria for hours, drawing the Medici lions and statues of antiquity. Here I am again, back to what our teacher taught us, back to the powerful bodies of superhuman men.

But those drawings once got us in trouble. The Cupid. A prank that quickly got out of hand. Years before he left for Rome, Michelangelo was given a key to the monastery garden at San

Marco so that he could come and go as he pleased. He used to sculpt there, and was working on a Saint John for Lorenzo di Pierfrancesco de Medici, a banker and much younger cousin of our duke. I used to seek him out in the verdant peace of the monastery garden. I brought him food and told him stories while he carved a beautiful, small Saint John of marble. I kept him company, he said.

There Michelangelo had also started working on a small, sleeping cupid, which he told me was based on some ancient sculptures he had seen of the same subject. The sculpted boy was no more than a toddler, his pudgy body resting on a stone. When Lorenzo the banker came for his Saint John, he was struck by the cupid instead. He told us that the cupid would fetch a much higher price in Rome than it would in Florence. I suggested that Michelangelo age the stone so that it might look like the ancient sculptures he was trying to imitate.

I meant it as one of our many practical jokes, but Michelangelo and the banker Lorenzo clearly saw it as a way to fetch a higher price. We consulted our goldsmith friends, who helped us etch it with some of their malodorous chemical concoctions. Their treatment nearly gave our cupid the ancient patina. Then we took the little cupid to the Arno and rubbed it in the grey dirt, the same place where the potters pull the clay to make their pots.

We showed it to Lorenzo, proud of our trick, and he quickly sold it to a banker named Baldassare del Milanese, a rich man with a palace near the Medici. It was only later that we learned Milanese did business in Rome and took the sculpture there. Then we heard he sold it to Cardinal Riario, the nephew of Pope Sixtus, for two hundred ducats! When Michelangelo heard about this turn of events, he launched into a rage, for he himself had earned only thirty crowns for the piece. What we didn't learn until later was that Milanese was the biggest trickster of all, for he had not sold it as a sculpture by a Florentine artist, but rather had passed off the cupid to Cardinal Riario as an ancient Roman statue.

I watch the back of Michelangelo's curly head as he sits on the riverbank. He is completely engrossed in his work. How far we have diverged since those days, I think.

Eventually, Cardinal Riario heard the rumor that he had paid a fortune for a fake, crafted by a young Florentine sculptor named Michelangelo Buonarroti. He returned the cupid to Milanese and demanded his money back. At the same time, he dispatched a trusted friend, another banker named Galli, to Florence to find the man who could make such a sculpture as to dupe even one of the most sophisticated collectors of ancient art.

When Signor Galli visited his home, I watched Michelangelo make a perfect drawing of a hand, a test that was enough to convince Galli that he was indeed the master who had made—and faked—the Cupid. Michelangelo also confessed to it. After that, Galli sent Michelangelo to Rome with a handful of letters of recommendation. I should have seen back then that I was likely to be left behind.

And that is how Michelangelo ended up in Rome in the first place. It was our doing, our artistic trick, that sent him there. Michelangelo left right away, in June of that year. Among the many letters of recommendation was also a letter of warning addressed to Baldassarre del Milanese, but the man refused to return the sculpture to us.

By that time, I had already started playing dice and card games in the taverns for money. After all, if I could trick people instead of making art I didn't feel worthy of, then it seemed a reasonable way to earn a few coins.

Now, all these years later, I heave myself into the long weeds beside Michelangelo and hand him one of two pears I have pilfered from the trees behind di Cosimo's studio. "I should have thought I would find you here."

"L'Indaco." He gives me a fierce grip of his hand in greeting, and I see beads of sweat across his forehead. His shirt sticks to his back. "The heat inside that box is infernal. I had to leave it for a bit."

We sit together and eat our pears, watching the men sink their hulking bodies under the surface of the water. Michelangelo tosses the finished core of the pear, and it splashes into the brown water.

"I should have thought you might be able to afford your own food, given that raise you got." I slap his arm with the back of my hand, feeling its hard angles under the linen.

"Hmm." He stops chewing and shakes his head. "The word is out, I see. I might have guessed."

"Kind of hard to keep a secret in Master di Cosimo's workshop."

"I suppose they have not put me in a favorable light," he says, perhaps fishing for a compliment. I don't want to tell him no one has spoken of it since; it is only my own pride that is bruised. "You are settled there, then, with di Cosimo?"

"I suppose. I am trying to raise money for Lucia's dowry. I thought she was beyond marriageable age, but it seems she has a suitor."

"Battistini the bookbinder," he says, keeping his eyes on his page.

"How did you know?" I exclaim.

He turns to me. "How did you *not* know, L'Indaco? It seems that you are not very discerning when it comes to affairs of the heart."

I snigger. "And you are, signore?" I say, though I must admit that he attracts ladies all day long. He could have any one of them, even one of those rich ladies who constantly seek his company.

"Whatever the case, you should help her get what she wants. She is deserving."

I feel the weight of his judgment sink under my skin. "What are you working on?" I say, eager to change the subject. I slap the page he is sketching.

He lets out an exasperated sigh and closes his sketchbook. "The Signoria... They have given me a new *David*."

"Another one? Another giant?!" I cannot help but guffaw.

"No, no, not a colossus. A smaller one. Bronze," he says. I see the tendons of his jaw tighten. "It is to be a gift for some French nobleman."

"Well, then, surely that is a good thing?"

He scratches the scruffy crop of whiskers that has sprouted across his jaw. "Working for politicians, popes... It is never straightforward, L'Indaco. It never comes without the expectation that I will dance on the end of their strings like a damned puppet. You cannot control their timing. Not to mention that things with the French could turn sour at any moment. Much better to work for a wealthy trader, in my view. And it's just that... between the giant and my other commissions... I find myself overloaded."

"You should count yourself fortunate," I say.

"I suppose. But it is more complicated than that." He sighs. "Just before I received your letter—back when I was still in Rome—I signed a contract with a cardinal in Siena for twelve large sculptures for an altar inside their cathedral."

"A large commission! That can only be a good thing. Wherein lies the problem?"

"How am I to get those done? Also, there's the little problem that, in the contract I signed, it says I agreed not to accept another commission for three years." He pauses, looking to see if I understand the conflict. "They have already arranged for my *conduttore* in Carrara to send three hundred *migliaia* of marble to Siena for it. Now they are writing me letters, telling me that they have heard about my commission here for the giant, threatening me and telling me that the works are due. Meanwhile, the Signoria has only given me six months to complete the bronze *David*, and the colossus is not finished."

"So, tell those Sienese idiots you got a better offer. Walk away."

He shakes his head and pulls idly at the long grass between his knees. I watch his eyes follow one of the tanners into the water, where the young man ties a small skiff to its anchor. "It doesn't work like that, L'Indaco. Besides the fact that the Piccolomini own nearly everything in Siena—and would block my prospects there forever more—when you sign for a commission, you should never abandon it. It causes nothing but heartache. Believe me." He huffs, almost a laugh, and I see that he speaks from experience.

"Then you need help," I say tentatively.

He waves his hand dismissively.

"I know, I know. You work alone. So you have reminded me," I say, scratching my head. "So, just send the cardinal some of these drawings." I tap the page where Michelangelo has sketched the muscled buttocks of one of the tanners on the riverside, exaggerating the sinews in his thighs and lower back. "Give him the idea that you are working on it here in Florence. Tell him you are making progress. Send him one of those *bozzetti* of yours. Send him the one of the giant. They will never know the difference."

Michelangelo tears several pages from his bound book and presses them into my hands. "Here are my preliminaries. You want to fool the Sienese? Then you do the drawings."

"Me?"

"Why not?" He shrugs. "You are trained. I'll pay you if it means getting those hounds off my back."

❦

AT SUNRISE, I place a few worn-down sticks of red and black chalk into a burlap sack. A nub of charcoal. My father's silverpoint pen. If I am to convince the Sienese patrons, then my drawings must look like Michelangelo's. They must pulse with life—with the muscles, sinews, and hulking shoulders of the tanners along the Arno.

"You're up early. Where are you going?" My sister stops chopping bitter greens.

"To the river," I say. "I need to start working on the drawings Michelangelo has assigned me. Those works in Siena…"

"And what time will you be home?" A note of suspicion in her voice.

"Around dinner?"

She narrows her eyes. "You don't have it in mind to go to the taverns?"

"I already told you. I am finished, I swear it!" I huff, but Lucia only turns back to chopping loudly with a sharp blade. "I have burned every last one of those cursed cards. Go check my bedchamber! You will not find any." I wait a long time for her response, but she does not meet my gaze. She only continues pressing the blade down so hard that it mars the wood. I see I won't convince her with words, only with actions. I grasp my sheaf of parchment and my bag of sketching tools. "Good day!" I slam the door and head out into the fog.

Why can't she see I am only trying to do something for *her?* Only trying to make something that turns into money? Only trying to make something that lasts.

At the riverbank, the sun streaks over the rooftops, burning away the thin layer of fog as if by magic. The lazily flowing water reflects the ochre-colored façades of the wool warehouses. Ducks bob on the surface, watching for minnows. A starling calls out as it flies overhead. My attention turns to a cluster of youths huddled around a nearby tree trunk. They're throwing dice, I'm certain of it. My fingers drum nervously on my stack of paper. I resist the pull to set down my things and go see what luck the fellows have found. Instead, I scrub my cheeks with my palms and pull a fine sheet of flat parchment onto my drawing board, a smooth and level piece of solid pine.

With the ringing of the morning bell, the wool warehouse shutters clap open. A teenaged boy bears a creaking cart of raw wool to the riverbank. A skiff loaded with cabbages glides by.

On my page, I sketch a few lateral lines that might converge at some mythic point over the horizon. A warehouse door with its worn shutters. A quick caricature of the boy and his creaking cart. I pause to consider Michelangelo's own drawings: passionate, rebellious, spirited. Writhing men who appear not as they are, but as they might be if they were divinely inspired. As they should be. Gods made into men. Men made in the image of gods.

I pull out a new blank page. This time, I draw the boy with the cart in a different way. I focus on the face, the hands. I try to turn him into something different. Something more. Can I transform this youth—the son of a dyer just doing his job—into a sculpture worthy of a cardinal's tomb?

"Your shading is clumsy." The voice in my head again. But somehow, it's his voice. *"The hands! The soul of your subject is in the hands. Yours are… they're lifeless."*

"How do I do it then? Show me!" I crumple the page. One of the boys at the dice game turns at the sound of my outburst. A lone, crazy man crumpling paper and talking to himself on the riverbank.

The truth is Michelangelo *has* shown me. Over and over again.

"The power comes from showing the tender hands of a small child, cradled in the bony claws of an elder," he had told me. "It is in the soul of the viewer and it must be in the soul of the artist. That is something our Master Ghirlandaio failed to show us. If you have loved, if you have suffered, then you will know what to do. Do you see, L'Indaco?"

But surely I've suffered as much as anybody, and not by my own choosing.

"You won't find inspiration at Il Fico, my friend," Michelangelo had said. "No artist could ever function under such debilitation."

"I don't go there anymore," I'd insisted, but I wasn't sure at the time that he believed me. I'm not sure he'd believe me now. I press my charcoal to the page.

The boatmen and dyers make unwitting subjects, transporting their fish, their foodstuffs, their wares, while my charcoal stick scratches out the lines and shades. There is beauty, yes. But for the artist, the process is not merely to show life's beauty; it is life itself. Just as the pencil and paper play their part, so too do the hand and the eye. Instinct and training guide the coal to the paper. Every stroke wears down the stick a little further. It's like the life of an artist; the daily sacrifice that only reduces. No day can be restored just as no line can be returned to the coal. Commitment, daily dedication in its purest form. Perhaps that is what Michelangelo and his giant have shown me above all.

The moments turn into hours as I feel myself, at last, pulled into that swirl of energy, not a creator but a participant, almost as much a spectator as anyone who might view my drawings later. This is where I've been deficient. It's more than just skill, it's about purpose. And I lack that in my life; I cannot deny it. Listening to Giusto, I would think love would give me that purpose, that focus, but I feel in my heart that there is a masterpiece lurking somewhere inside me that will bring my success; it will bring my acceptance and acclaim to me. Perhaps even love—one day. *After all*, I have to ask myself, *who would praise a man of such minute accomplishment? No. A worthy woman will expect a man of accomplishment, a man of reputation. And I am not those things yet. Not only am I not those things. I struggle even to put food on my sister's table.*

The noon bell. I watch the clutch of youths gather dice and coins into their pockets, then disperse. The dyers lay down their work and trudge home for the mid-day meal. I look out over the river, wondering if I will ever find inspiration for that masterpiece, the creation that will make the rest of my dreams come true.

For now, perhaps it is enough to have earned a few coins in an honest manner.

I slip my drawings into my bag. At Master di Cosimo's studio, there is more paying work waiting for me. For that, I am grateful. I tuck my drawing board under my arm, and head toward di Cosimo's workshop near Santissima Annunziata.

One day, perhaps I will make something great. For now, I just need to make a living.

THE ORCHARD BEHIND Piero di Cosimo's studio amounts to little more than a wild, primeval forest. Abundant. Untended.

Under a citrus tree, a collection of great copper vats stands ready to boil the glue we make from animal fat brought in on carts from the countryside. Against the main building where we assistants work, a variety of makeshift, lean-to sheds have been assembled to protect more fragile items from the rain and sun. Inside are stacks of wood, leftover metal poles rusty with age, elaborate harnesses for horses and mules, hundreds of other bits and pieces of parade accoutrements: discarded, repurposed, neglected, reinvented. Each piece stands ready to be transformed, remade into new never-before-imagined visions for the delight of di Cosimo's public.

Master di Cosimo himself is invisible to us, only because he has holed himself up again behind a makeshift screen, designing fantasies on parchment. We know he is inside because of the gaggle of cats that has collected around the entrance to his hovel. Outside, steam rises from a small pot where he boils the eggs that make up most of his daily diet. The man rarely stops for a meal. He thinks little of such matters other than his flights of imagination.

In the dirt path that runs through the middle of the orchard, we have ordered the *carretti* into a line, dodging chickens who peck the dust at our feet. From here, we will roll them through the streets under cover of darkness and canvas tarps, all the way to the cloister of Santa Maria Novella. There, we will set up a temporary workshop to assemble everything for the final days before the latest pageant begins. Now, on the inside of the workshop, I have understood how Master di Cosimo's magic amounts to little more than a few ingenious tricks, many hands, and untold hours of labor.

"L'Indaco." Giusto pulls at my sleeve. "Master di Cosimo wants you to be in charge of operating the mechanical doves during the procession."

"Of course," I say. "I am at the master's command." I have also been tasked with overseeing the assembly of the banners that will hang from a false façade of an ancient temple.

"Good." Giusto slaps me on the shoulder and then goes off to oversee a small knot of assistants who are rehearsing the scene where the gilded boy will be revealed. They have asked little Nello to remove his clothes. Bewildered, the skinny boy fingers the long, frayed ties of his undergarments. He holds his arms out while a group of men argue about how the boy should be pos-tured when he appears—to the great surprise and delight of the audience—from the door of a white temple mounted atop one of Master di Cosimo's most elaborate floats.

In the courtyard, the youngest apprentices are stacking wood for a giant bonfire. An older journeyman has instructed another group of assistants to throw the painted banners we made for the feast of San Giovanni onto the fire. I watch the triangles, my own handiwork of horned beasts against a yellow background, char and curl. Another set of my work, up in flames. So much for immortality. I think of Michelangelo, making great works of art that will last for eternity, raking in money from the pope, from the Signoria, while I toll away on fabric banners that will soon enough be burned on the pyre. I only hope that my drawings for the Sienese might lead to something that lasts.

I find Master di Cosimo at his worktable, rifling through a pile of dusty costumes. He wipes his hands on his dirt-stained smock and mutters to himself. He is like an ancient troll living in the squalor of a forest hovel. A pile of hard-boiled eggs are stacked in a bowl, and two of the cats sit on the table next to it. A black cat paws an egg toward the edge of the table. As I approach the table she widens her yellow eyes, the slit in the middle goes narrow, and she leaps to the floor.

"Master," I say. I knock on the side of the screen, which looks like a piece of country fence repurposed as a wall.

"My boy," he says, and I wonder if he calls me this familiar name because he cannot remember my actual one. There are so many of us in and out of his workshop. How could he possibly keep track of us all? We are all just his people. Day laborers. Skilled painters, carpenters, seamstresses, sculptors. His mouth spreads to a wide grin. "Nice work on the banners," he says, gesturing to the bonfire with a gnarled hand. Then, he reaches into a narrow drawer of his table, and counts my day rate in coins in his palm. He hands the money over to me.

"Thank you," I say, feeling the comforting heft of coins in the pocket of my leather apron. "I am glad you are happy with my work, sir." I hesitate. "Master di Cosimo, I have been working on banners and other ephemera for a time, but you might know that my primary medium is fresco, learned from my father and Master Ghirlandaio. If you have any work in that area, sir, I should be honored to help you."

"Noted," he says, raising a finger in the air like some ancient orator. "Now, let's get started bringing the scaffolds out to the carts."

"If I might, Master di Cosimo, I had one other thing I wished to discuss with you," I say. "About my payment." How do I begin to explain? Many of the wealthier families of our city have dowry accounts at the Monte dei Doti or with prestigious banks. I can only think of one solution. "I wonder if you might be willing to pay my day labor rate to another person. To a notary. In Santa Croce."

He pauses, lowering his theatrical finger. "You are in some kind of trouble?"

"No, it's not that," I say. "I just… I just would prefer that the money be placed with the notary so I can save for… an obligation. My sister's dowry."

Mercifully, di Cosimo dismisses me with the wave of a hand. "Yes, *senza dubbio*. People have many reasons why they might not want to be paid directly. Some men—and women—do not even tell their spouses about the work they do here. Others are in debt," he says. I try to find words to explain, but he continues. "It is none of my business. You send your notary here and give me your authorization. I can entrust the day rate to him."

Di Cosimo steps out into the sunlight without a further word, and I am left standing in the shed. For a moment, I bask in the simple joy of an honest day's work and an honest day's pay that won't be squandered in the taverns.

❧

BY THE END of the day, after loading the carts in the heat, I am exhausted. My body feels as though it weighs double, but still, I walk home feeling happy. I have work. Paying work. A few coins jangle together in my pocket, the last remaining cash payment made by Master di Cosimo. And Michelangelo has promised me paying work in passing on his drawings for the cardinal in Siena. I walk home humming a cheerful tune to myself. I try to decide whether I should share the news with my sister that I have begun in earnest to save for her dowry, no matter how modest.

But when I arrive, my positive mood evaporates. Lucia is pacing the kitchen nervously, her paintbrushes and her miniatures abandoned on the worktable.

"Jacopo!" she grasps my forearms as I duck into the house. "They have come."

"Who?"

"Those henchmen."

My mind races with the image of the shadows who once trailed me for months around Florence. I have been free of them for some time. "Roosters… here?"

"Yes," she says, her eyes wide and desperate. "Two large men. They didn't send a letter this time. They came in person for you. They said that the frescoes at San Pier Martire are nearly done, but that you have not been seen there in months. That you owe the city a large sum."

I take her hands in mine. "Everything is fine. I have already told you. I have paying work with Master di Cosimo. Even Michelangelo has given me work for the Piccolomini family in Siena. They own everything there."

She is rattled. "But Jacopo," she continues, "these men don't care about any of that. You either pay them what you owe or you must go there and finish those frescoes. I don't want to see those men at our door again, do you hear me? The fact remains that you owe the city of Florence a large fresco to pay off your debt. For the love of God, please stop whatever else you are doing and go there! Jacopo. I don't want to think what they might do to you if you don't comply."

꩜

INSIDE THE CHURCH of San Pier Martire, the air smells of fresh pigments and glue. It is disturbingly silent. Only my shuffling footsteps sound on the dusty tiles, and my sniffle echoes across the vast, empty space.

I step tentatively into the chapel, the place where I have come often, but not often enough. Everyone else is finished. Simone, our assistants, that lady painter. The makeshift scaffolds have long been dismantled, save one. The cloths, buckets of plaster, sizing, pigments have all been loaded into mule carts and dragged away. Now, the space feels strangely void, filled only with dust-flecked sunbeams and a riot of color. The church is empty. All of the guildsmen have moved onto other projects. There is no one left. Only me.

I step closer to examine the work of my colleagues. On the walls of the chapel, regular citizens of Florence have been stirred to life with pigment, as if by some magic. In the hands of my fellow guildsmen, I recognize a baker turned into Saint Dominic, a street whore in the guise of an angel. Above my head, a bright, ultramarine sky sparkles with gilded stars.

Already, the image of Saint Peter Martyr with a sword lodged in his balding head is beginning to turn green and shiny with mildew. This is a problem for frescoes in the churches that lie closest to the Arno. Every few years, the river swells, spilling over the banks and ruining the work of many dyers along the riverside. Sometimes, it takes weeks, even months, for those enterprises to clean up the mess. And occasionally, the dampness takes hold, working its way even underneath our newly laid pigments, so that the bright colors are marred by a green patina or black spots that spread like a plague.

My eyes scan the fully completed images of Saint Peter preaching, of the saint healing a boy's leg. Then, there are more usual scenes: the wedding where Jesus turned water into wine, and another depicting the feeding of multitudes with only five loaves and two fishes. Finally, I move across the chapel to the section assigned to me. There, it is only white. Only the white of the plaster and a few roughly scored lines in charcoal, each one a *giornata*, a day's work. Apart from that, it is a rainbow of color punctuated by blank.

In the white squares, one of my guildsmen has left me a parting message. He has scrawled my name hastily in charcoal. L'INDACO. Beside it is a silly face. I can almost hear their voices, their taunts, their laughs, echoing inside the church. *Where did he go, that blue boy?*

Shame fills every part of me, welling up from the soles of my feet and making my chest shudder. Shame. Crushing shame. Nothing more. How will I ever find it inside of myself to finish this work?

A sudden draft swirls around my ankles, as if the church itself has drawn a gasp.

I sink to my knees on the stone tiles.

IN THE END, the work for Master di Cosimo must continue and my job is simple: to operate a series of mechanical doves that appear to descend over a parade float bearing the Virgin Mary. Giusto tells me that my part comes just after a choir of boys dressed as white birds, and just before the float with the trumpeters and great vases spouting fire.

It promises to be one of di Cosimo's most stupendous displays, one that the noble ladies have spread throughout the city thanks to di Cosimo's private preview with his closest circle of patrons. Already, throngs of young and old are pressing into the

streets, precariously close to the slowly moving wooden wheels
of the parade floats.

But the celebration goes well beyond the procession of elaborately staged floats. In the Piazza dei Giudici, there is a fountain
spouting rose water, piped from the Arno and mixed with flower
petals collected by di Cosimo's own children. There is a play with
the miracles and life of John the Baptist, with our own Ridolfo
Ghirlandaio, chosen because he is such a delicate young man,
dressed in the guise of the saint. There are floats pulled by people
dressed as giant birds with real feathers. Mules carted in from
farms in the countryside, decorated with pelts painted like lions.
Other of di Cosimo's assistants are clothed as personifications of
Love, Jealousy, and Chastity. They step out from the doorways of
makeshift temples to recite verse or sing a song.

Another float is pulled by giant oxen, their horns gilded, their
bodies covered in flowers, wreaths around their necks. Shepherds
follow, bedecked in leaves and garlands. Water buffalo dressed in
the guise of elephants pull a float with a man dressed as Julius
Caesar as Triumph and Victory. He is accompanied by six men
at arms with gold armor and torches. Other grooms carry tro-
phies. Behind them, men blast long horns, while riding wild-eyed
horses draped with tiger-striped pelts.

From my vantage point atop the temporary triumphal arch—
made of little more than a makeshift wooden frame skim-coated
with plaster—I watch the drama of the story unfold. The animals,
the costumes, the realistic-looking architecture made in just a
few days' time; it is all incredible to take in from my bird's-eye
view over the city. I marvel that Master di Cosimo could dream
the entire program into existence only from his own mind.

At the designated time, I steady my hands to fly the mechanical doves di Cosimo has designed high above the heads
of the crowd. Another two assistants move clouds, little more

than wooden frames covered in cotton wool, to simulate clouds suspended with windlasses and on ropes. A little girl is lifted down like an angel. As shrill, singing voices ring out through the air, men dressed as the four cardinal virtues personified appear alongside a small golden temple. It's from this temple that Nello, our gilded boy—the very image of the birth of a new age—is to appear.

We wait.

But Nello, our gilded child, does not burst forth from the temple. Instead, he falters. His slim form wavers in the doorway of the little temple, swaying with the motion of the float. The crowd explodes in cheers at the sight of a gilded boy, but already, I can see that things are not proceeding according to plan. He stumbles again, then falls to his knees. I drop my stick holding the strings to the mechanical doves and wave my hands frantically above my head to alert the mule drivers below me. They have not yet seen the boy fall to his knees and then roll into a ball in the middle of the float.

The crowd reacts first. Suddenly, there are shrieks from a few close onlookers. From my high vantage point above the parade, I watch the crowd rush toward the curled-up golden boy like a great swarm of insects. The streets, once lined with rows of spectators, disintegrate into a chaotic tangle of sweaty, yelling human bodies, swelling and pushing toward the parade floats, which have come to a halt. The mass of people surges forward, parting only to let a wailing woman—the boy's mother?—snake her way through the crowd.

I stay high inside the makeshift arch for some time, waiting to see if the parade will start up again, but instead, several men drag poor little gilded Nello from the edge of the float. I watch the sea of sweating bodies part to let the men, the golden boy, and the wailing woman through the crowd.

The gilded boy is dead. Dead beyond any doubt. His skin sparkles in the sun, but the life has left his body. Now, he resembles little more than a bronze statue carried away by an adoring crowd. A beautiful, tragic image of fleeting beauty.

After a while, the crowd loses interest, and instead of staying to see the rest of the parade, they disperse down the narrow alleys like grains of sand in a hundred sieves. The floats, so wonderous only moments ago, stand still and abandoned, leaving only the tiger-horses dipping their heads up and down and side-stepping nervously against their reins.

☙

IT HAD SEEMED like the idea of a lifetime, but now, with poor Nello's gilded body pulled away from the edge of the float, di Cosimo's parade has been declared a disaster.

Well after dark, I work alongside di Cosimo's other assistants and a team of day laborers to dismantle the floats and move everything back inside the great cloister at Santa Maria Novella. The atmosphere is a mixture of shock, frenzied labor, and hushed voices. No one knows what has caused the boy to die, but surely, they say, it must be the effects of the gilding. Master di Cosimo is nowhere to be seen. Giusto is agitated, sweating, tying up ropes on the floats, his face ashen. Well into the darkness, we disperse.

The moon rises high in the night sky. I make my way out of the cloister and into the street, a feeling of disquiet over me. Along the river, a bank of heavy clouds leaves only a single bright sliver of moonlight along the edge of a black ball. Before me, the familiar outline of the Ponte Vecchio stands as a hulking shadow over the wavering surface of the Arno. Just as I arrive at the entrance to the bridge, I catch sight of a familiar scene.

It has been months, but I recognize him immediately. Filippo Dolciati. He is little more than a slim silhouette leaning against a stone wall, his blanket spread out before him, his small painted pictures leaning against the doors of the closed shops on the bridge.

"L'Indaco! My friend." he calls. "I wondered whatever became of you. Where have you been?"

"Working," I say. "I've been doing pageants with Master di Cosimo," I say, gesturing in the direction of the piazza where, just hours before, chaos had ensued. "And I might ask the same of you."

Dolciati shrugs. "Me? Back in the *prigione* again," he says, gesturing in the direction of the Stinche jail. "Didn't correct me, I guess." He smiles. "The roosters caught up with me one more time; it happens. But listen! There is a big fight planned for to-night, and the winning pot is supposed to be large. You should come."

A strange mixture of excitement and apprehension rises within me, like a tingle along the back of my neck. I do not want to tell him all that has pushed me away from the Mercato Vecchio.

"I might as well finish up here for the night," he says, gesturing to the pictures left on his blanket. "Not much traffic any-more. A group of us are getting together at Il Fico tonight. That fight… If you have not heard of it, then surely you have been away for a while." He punches my shoulder. "Come. Let's have a drink and some dinner. I had a good day today," he says, gesturing to the pictures on the blanket.

"Me too," I say, chuckling nervously.

"Then let's go," he says. "Maybe we'll even try our luck at the *frussi* table. Or with the ladies. What do you say?"

I hesitate. Can it hurt? Surely my sister won't know if we go to the Mercato Vecchio. She expects for me to be working the parade until the wee hours of the morning. But as I watch Filippo begin to pack up his meager pictures and his groundcloth, the more malaise rises into my gut. We begin to walk in the direction of the taverns, and all the while, I grasp blindly for an excuse to turn away.

"Jacopo!" Again, my name, but this time, it's coming from the other end of the bridge.

The voice is familiar, but all I perceive is the dark silhouette heading toward the old market. My heart begins to pound, and I face the man walking across the bridge, not knowing what lies ahead. Is it one of those henchmen who has paid a visit to our house? Filippo stands and sets down his sack, then wipes his hands alongside his legs as if he is preparing for a fistfight.

"Jacopo!"

A familiar voice. My mind struggles to place it. And then finally, a familiar outline of a face. His face, when it finally appears in the pale light, confirms what suddenly leaps in my heart. A tremendous smile.

Francesco. My little brother. He has come home.

PART III

THE SLING AND THE BOW

Florence
1503

*Be quiet and don't make friends of the associates of anyone,
except for those of God; and don't speak of anyone, neither
for good nor for ill, because one never knows how
things will turn out; attend only to your own affairs.*

Michelangelo Buonarroti, in a letter to his brother Buonarroto

MICHELANGELO'S HOUSE IS filled with the aroma of freshly baked, sweet Easter bread, of flowers and spices. Around us, our fellow guildsmen and their families make a festive cacophony. A belly laugh fills the air. There is the sound of clinking silver and glasses in the courtyard of the house. A curly-haired toddler screeches as she chases Michelangelo's orange cat around the spindly olive trees in their large, terracotta pots.

A party. It's just what we needed, I think, so when an invitation from Michelangelo's father arrived, the three of us—my brother, sister, and I—walked shoulder to shoulder to my friend's large house near Santa Croce. And now, at a table laden with grapes, cheese, and bread, I tear off a piece of husky crust, soft and warm from the oven, and share a piece with my brother.

"Is he a kind man?" Francesco asks me.

My brother's green eyes are, as ever, speckled with gold. I still see him, the essence of him, behind the changes—a sharper jaw, longer hair that brushes his shoulders, a few lines across his brow. Faces change over the decades with the expense of living, but the eyes remain the same, I think. He searches my face, too, perhaps thinking the same thing, but his expression is concerned.

"Battistini the bookbinder?" I say. "Yes, from what little I know of him. He has a reputation for being honest. At least, he doesn't swindle his customers the way the others on the bridge do."

"I'm not talking about how he treats his customers, brother. I'm talking about how he treats Lucia," Francesco says, his eyes bright and sincere.

For a long, silent moment, we watch Lucia from across the room. She has seated herself on a bench in Michelangelo's courtyard, within a cluster of women, the wives of gilders, embroiderers, saddle makers. My sister has done her best with the few gowns she has. She has washed her hair and pinned the curls in a way that has become fashionable among the Florentine ladies. She has pulled the pearl earrings that once belonged to our mother out from the drawer.

Battistini the bookbinder must be here, too, I think, milling around somewhere within the grand rooms of Michelangelo's house, where we have been invited by his father to celebrate the end of Lent and the Easter festivities. In addition to our fellow tradespeople, there are finely dressed wool merchants and other collectors eager to be seen by their peers. Like moths to a flame, they have been drawn to the house of the master now famous for his marble sculpture in progress, the giant that everyone is waiting to see appear from behind the box.

If I were smart, I might be circulating among these potential patrons in search of work, I think. Instead, I stand at the food table and ponder my brother's question. I press my hip against the table laden with Easter delicacies—quails' eggs, Easter bread, narrow spears of asparagus pulled from the garden that morning. Two servant women refill the plates with tender leaves of purple radicchio brought down from the Veneto. I have not stopped filling my cheeks.

I swallow a bite and shrug. "Yes. I think the bookbinder holds her in esteem, but if I were in his shoes, the truth is I would just be looking for someone to help take care of all those children." The bookbinder's wife, claimed by pestilence, left behind her husband and four growing boys.

My brother chuckles, but then he pushes me gently. "Lucia deserves someone who will respect her." I know he is right.

Since my brother has returned home, it's felt as if we are children again—Lucia, Francesco, and me—ambling down the street toward Michelangelo's house in Santa Croce. Toward a party. Toward fun.

Our brother has told us that he finished his work in Arezzo, the group of painters having completed their contract there. Anyway, he told us, his master had decided to take on a project with another patron in Montepulciano, and the group of painters from Arezzo disbanded. It seemed a good time to come home, he said, to answer Lucia's letter. He gives me a sympathetic smile, but mercifully, does not mention anything about our sister's plea to help the wayward brother, the one who cannot seem to stay away from the card table.

As much as I resented my sister's letter to him, I am still happy to have Francesco back home. I squeeze his shoulders. My brother, in the flesh. My heart feels lighter than it's felt in a long time, having him back. I thought that I didn't want Lucia to call him home, didn't want him to return. I didn't want his sympathy, didn't want him to rescue me from myself, but I was wrong to want him to stay away from Florence. My heart feels whole. I must make sure it stays way, I think. The important thing is to make sure Francesco doesn't come to resent me as much as Lucia does. I must make my best effort to keep everything in order, everything as it should be.

"*Signore e signori!*" The commanding voice of Michelangelo's father fills the courtyard. Signor Buonarroti is not a large man; he is wiry like his sons, but his presence fills the space, and a hush replaces the din of the party.

"First, I would like to welcome you and wish you all well on the feast of Our Risen Lord. As you are in our home, you are family. Please partake of our bounty, which we readily share with you. We have had a good harvest of grapes this year thanks to the new investment that has been put into the vineyard in Chianti," he says.

I stuff a shard of salty pecorino cheese in my mouth. The abundance, I see, goes well past cheese, eggs, meat, bread, almonds, and wine. The guests stand in awe of the newfound wealth everywhere in evidence in Michelangelo's house. His boyhood home looks better than ever. The corners are swept, and the dining table is laid with a bounty like I have not seen in many months. The servants busy themselves, cutting pieces of a roasted lamb with sharp knives. Michelangelo's father has stepped into his role as patriarch, swirling *vinsanto* in his glass. According to the whispers throughout the house, Michelangelo has bought a large country home with vineyards in the hills outside of Florence.

I try to imagine what our own home might look like if I had saved everything I earned instead of gambling it away. At least, I think, our roof might no longer leak.

"Second," Michelangelo's father continues, "I am proud to announce some wonderful news, news of my son." The man's eyes search the courtyard for Michelangelo, and it is only then that I see him, for the first time this night. He has been skulking in the shadows at the edge of the crowd, wearing the same soiled shift as ever, his hair greasy, the shadows of his face dark. He paces in the courtyard walkway, hands laced behind his back.

My brother and I follow his stooped form with our eyes. With his father's prompting, he finally steps to the edge of an arch, where there is a pool of light. Only then does he give an awkward grin and a reluctant wave to greet the crowd.

"Our Signoria, in its wisdom," Signor Buonarroti says, "has recognized the achievement of my son's *David*, which, as you know, is in progress in the cathedral workyard. And now, they have decided to award him a new commission!"

The crowd falls silent.

"A commission for not one, not two, but *twelve* additional sculptures of marble to adorn the tribune of our cathedral of Santa Maria del Fiore!" he exclaims. I hear nothing but gasps and whispers around us. One of the guests squeezes Michelangelo's arms, and another slaps his shoulder, but Michelangelo's face remains frozen, a thin-lipped smile. "Twelve sculptures of the Apostles, each to be four *braccia* and a quarter in height, in honor of God, for the fame of our whole city."

Twelve marble sculptures. I let the information sink in. All this time I have been either avoiding my obligation at San Pier Martire, or making ephemera for a disastrous pageant that has lasted only a few hours. Meanwhile, my old friend hides inside his box, working quietly to make sculptures for our cathedral tribunes that will last for eternity.

"The best part, from my view at least," says Signor Buonarroti, "is that each of the sculptures will be delivered year after year, which means that my son will be staying at home in Florence for a long time to come. At least twelve years."

Applause and cheers break out across the house. My brother claps his hands together. More people crowd around Michelangelo, pumping his hands and slapping his back.

For days, I think, all of Florence has talked of nothing but the death of di Cosimo's gilded boy, of Michelangelo's giant inside the wooden box, of the rumors that Piero de Medici's supporters are plotting to bring the family back to power. And now, we will have something new, fresh, to speculate about. Michelangelo and a new commission. A newly constructed workshop on the via da Pinti. A salary of two gold florins each month, plus expenses, not to mention payments for his other works.

"Things certainly seem to have changed around here," Francesco whispers, nodding to Signor Buonarroti's layers of velvet, to the new women doing chores in the house.

Now, Battistini the bookbinder appears in the courtyard. He greets the ladies sitting on the stone benches, and I see Lucia's face light up in a bright smile.

For a few moments, my brother and I watch the interaction wordlessly. Finally, Francesco says, "You're wrong, brother."

"What do you mean, wrong?"

"I mean I don't think she's concerned about taking care of the bookbinder and all those boys. That's not what's stopping this union."

I huff. "Yes, I know. What's stopping it is that there is no dowry. Let us not delude ourselves. I'm sure Lucia has shared with you all the details of our... situation." I cannot meet my brother's eyes. Instead, I watch Lucia say something to the bookbinder that makes him throw back his head and laugh.

"No," Francesco says, shaking his head. "That's not it, either, Jacopo. My brother." He hesitates, seeming to search for the right words. "It's not the lack of a dowry or concern over taking care of so many children."

"What then?"

He looks at the floor. "I rather think what's stopping our sister from getting married is that she feels that her primary duty is taking care of *you*."

❦

"IT'S ABOUT TIME I see this giant."

I can hardly blame my brother's curiosity, as much as I dread setting foot back inside that wooden box in the workyard, with its stifling heat and its undeniable confirmation of my own inadequacy.

But Francesco, with his gentle insistence, leads me through the tangle of street traffic until the hulking brick dome of Santa Maria del Fiore appears over the rooftops. He has turned into a competent, responsible man, I think. He carries the best of our family's traits: our mother's olive complexion, her even features, her patience. He is enthusiastic, interested in everything, filled with energy and hope. Time and rejection have not yet taken their toll. I can only hope he fares better than I.

Even more than that, Francesco has convinced me to bring along the drawings I have made for the Sienese project. They are good, I think, a productive use of my time along the Arno. I am not sure they are ready to share with Michelangelo, but my brother has convinced me to carry my leather sketchbook under my arm all the way to the Duomo.

We find the cathedral workyard quieter than usual. Only a handful of stonemasons mill around the cluttered enclosure, working halfheartedly. A black cat perched on the arm of a winch watches us suspiciously as I knock two times on the half-opened door to Michelangelo's box.

"Who's there?" His gruff, familiar voice.

Through the crack in the door, I can see that the air inside the box-turned-workshop is a swirl of marble dust and pungent solvents. Makeshift worktables are now arrayed with dusty tools, plaster *bozzetti*, stacks of pages, a few smaller marble blocks, half-worked, marred with the familiar scrapes of the claw chisel.

"Your favorite fresco painter!" I call.

Michelangelo, caked in marble dust, approaches the door and greets us with a crooked smile. "*Piccolo* Francesco!" He rustles my brother's unruly curls. "How did you know he was my favorite?"

Francesco's face flushes pink. "I am not worthy of such praise, master." We laugh and step into the box.

"Your little favorite painter insisted on seeing the *gigante*," I say. "I tried to persuade him it wasn't worth seeing, but…"

Already, Francesco is frozen as if suspended in time. He stands before us, looking up at the colossus as the world falls away from his view. The wooden door in the roof of the box has been propped open to the sky. A fine coating of white dust hangs in the filtered light, and the nearly finished sculpture appears as if it has been carried here by angels, carefully set down in a great vortex of heavenly powder. Moments of heavy silence pass between us.

Finally, I break the silence with a whisper. "You have finished it."

Michelangelo only shrugs. "Hardly," he says, climbing a stepladder with his claw-shaped *gradina* in his hand. Francesco and I watch as he quickly, confidently refines the details of a tree stump that serves to stabilize the colossus as well as give the idea of the field where the boy-king raised his sling all those centuries ago.

"What do you mean?" Francesco asks. "What more could you possibly do to it? It's already perfect."

Michelangelo doesn't respond right away. Instead, along the right calf of the *David*, he carefully drags the chisel as most painters might handle a brush or a pen. He has cross-hatched the surface of the marble just as he might cross-hatch on a piece of paper, carving out small indentations which might draw shadows when the light passes in a certain way. With these crude tools, used for many generations, he has portrayed the vitality of the muscles and the veins, drawing life from the mineral. Just as David confronted the giant Goliath with his sling, so has Michelangelo confronted the giant block of marble with his weapons—the sculptor's tools.

"Well." He turns to us now from the top of the ladder. "They may be ready for it, but I am not." He hesitates. "But I know I have to finish. I cannot afford to wait, after all. Our fates may change at any moment."

"You think they would change their mind about the commission at this point?" Francesco asks.

"Ah, but my favorite little fresco painter," Michelangelo says, seating himself on the top of the ladder, "you have been away from your native city for too long. They are telling me that this colossus is to be a symbol of our new republic. All fine. But just how long will Soderini be in power? That is the question."

"Surely there is not enough support for the Medici to return!" says Francesco.

Michelangelo shakes his head. "I believe you are wrong. And even if the Medici don't return, those French idiots could be back inside our gates at any moment."

"I wouldn't bet even one of their gilded chamber pots," I add.

He shrugs. "It is better not to get involved in politics, my friend. Anyway, what can we do? We cannot afford to express our allegiances. All I can do is finish my work as quickly as possible and collect my salary," he says, gesturing to the near-finished *David*. "After that, it is out of my hands."

But he is not ready for the world to see the sculpture. That much is clear.

It's only then that I see it: another sculpture. In the shadows of the box, I see a lady's hand in marble. A heap of drapery. A foot. The sculpture is hidden by tarps and stark shadows.

He sees me looking at the sculpture. "That one really *is* finished." Michelangelo descends the ladder and removes the tarp, revealing an exquisitely beautiful seated Madonna.

Francesco's jaw drops. "You've completed this one at the same time?"

He nods. "Plus two *tondi*—one sculpted and one painted."

"You're… you're *painting* now?!" I cannot stop my voice from squeaking.

He nods again. "Agnolo Doni the wool trader. He's paid me for a painted Madonna." When he sees my eyes search the shadows of the box, he laughs. "It's not here, L'Indaco. If it were, it would be ruined by all this dust. I've been working on it in my bedchamber."

Francesco is now circling the completed sculpture of the Madonna. "The Signoria has commissioned another work from you already?"

"No," he says. "That one is for a cloth merchant in Bruges. It's being shipped there on one of the river barges in a few days' time. That was an easy commission. Didn't take me long and they've already paid me for it. Four thousand florins."

Four thousand florins. I feel my blood run cold in my veins.

I am so floored by the thought of a patron paying Michelangelo four thousand florins for a sculpture of Our Lady that I hardly notice he has stepped over to the table where I've left my sketchbook. When I see him open the leather cover and begin to leaf through the pages I sketched while sitting on the banks of the Arno, I scramble over and do my best to stop him. But he only raises his hand to block me. I see him pick up the page with my sketches of the dyer's son and his wheeled cart. He examines it for a long time without saying anything.

Then, he raises his eyebrows and raps the page with the back of his knuckles. He looks at me and smiles. "Not bad."

ON ANY NORMAL day, the thought of Michelangelo—with his new contract for twelve marble sculptures for the cathedral tribune, his additional private commissions, his fortunes, not to mention his ability to provide for his entire family in grand style—might have been enough to lure me back to my bed. There, I might languish for days, enveloped in dark oblivion, my shutters battened to the insults of the outside world.

But my brother is stalwart in his support of me, and it is he who launches me out of the house, hands on my shoulders, steering me toward Master di Cosimo's workshop. Master di Cosimo pulls Francesco—a painter who has worked for leading patrons in Arezzo in spite of his youth—into the chaotic fold of his workshop. Just like that, he welcomes Francesco as seamlessly and quickly as he has welcomed me, a fool who has nothing to show for himself, a fool whose only protection against his compulsion to the table has been to burn his last playing card.

Avoiding the *mercato*, with its fights, its dice and card games, is only possible thanks to the fact that Francesco walks home with me from Master di Cosimo's workshop each evening. As long as I stay away from the taverns, I can't give Francesco the same reasons I've given Lucia to resent me. Beyond that, I look for his approval as much as he might have once looked for mine.

ᘒ

ALONG THE HIGH wall of a neighborhood convent, a slit
of an opening catches my eye. I look both ways, then I run my
fingers inside the lip of the donation box. It's become my habit,
this checking of the charity box on a narrow street leading to
Master di Cosimo's studio. One day, I pocketed two *soldi*, either
placed there moments earlier by a well-meaning donor, or left
behind in the box by an inattentive novice whose job it is to
check the box and bring its contents to her Reverend Mother.
Either way, finding those coins gave me as much of a thrill as if
I had won them at the card table. And, yes, it has prompted my
return day after day.

"*Buongiorno*, Signor L'Indaco."

A familiar voice. I turn to see Maria, del Sarto's red-haired
daughter, making her way down the street toward di Cosimo's
studio. She narrows her eyes when she sees my hand inside the
convent charity box.

"Signorina! And a good day it is! As a matter of fact, it's such
a good day that I've decided to share some of my bounty with the
sisters." I flash my most valiant smile, and hope she has believed
I've been putting coins into the box rather than taking them out.
I remove my hand from the slit and dust my palms together. The
two of us walk in step toward Master di Cosimo's house.

Over weeks, the shock and shame of the dead gilded boy
has lingered in Master di Cosimo's studio. The assistants whisper
that not only has di Cosimo made payment to the boy's family,
but he has even sent a cured ham hock from Valdichiana and an
entire wheel of pecorino. It's no wonder, I think, that our master

sccms filled with eagerness to put the parade behind him and plan for his newest project.

As we assistants gather around his table, di Cosimo unfurls a large parchment sheet. A dozen of us crowd around, watching him make small, sure crosshatches along the underarm of a mythological creature, some unknown species of dragon.

"We have a new patron!" he exclaims, then mumbles to himself unintelligibly as if we are not there, as if his hasty drawings might communicate much more than words spoken aloud. And they do. With only a rough sketch, I recognize a Madonna and Child enthroned, surrounded by saints: Dominic, John the Baptist, and a few others whose identities elude me. The scene unfurls with a rolling landscape filled with verdant hillsides, spindly trees, and a variety of fantastic, snarling beasts with menacing claws.

With a straight edge and several dramatic strokes of his pencil, di Cosimo draws a grid over his sketch. A fresco. That much, I can deduce. I exhale. At last, we will have a project that is not ephemeral. It is not a design for a fake church façade or a flimsy triumphal arch only meant to last for a few hours or days. It is not a design for a banner or flag that will only burn, nor a flower-covered mule, nor a vessel or creature made of papier-mâché. From this cartoon, di Cosimo's assistants will lay out the grid work for the design that will then be transferred to a fresco wall.

Light filters into the studio; dust flecks hang heavy in the air and great motes of debris brush along the stone floor under the wooden table. "Our patron is a leading member of the wool guild," di Cosimo tells us. "A wealthy man. I have already made portraits of his wife and daughters. His country house lies just beyond the walls to the west. The family would like to paint over the walls of the old church there, as the ancient pictures have faded and no longer look fashionable." On a piece of scrap wood lying on the table, I watch di Cosimo sketch a schematic, which I perceive to be a design that will cover the spandrels of the arches. *A ceiling.*

"How will this work, master?" Andrea Il Riccio asks.

Di Cosimo looks up from his drawing, his hair standing straight up on top of his head, as if he's pulled a woolen blanket over his head in the wintertime. He grins at the young man with yellowed, crooked teeth. "How will it work? We do our paintings, and then we are paid. That is how it will work."

Il Riccio pushes back. "But I mean, we have not done a fresco, at least as long as I have been here."

Di Cosimo raises a finger. "No, you are correct. Fresco is not my favorite. And besides, few patrons want fresco anymore. They want the latest—oil on panel or canvas—things they can hang in their houses and show to their friends. And portraits! Portraits are the most lucrative of all. Across our city, the wealthiest men are having portraits of their wives painted right now, I assure you! But we will not turn down major projects such as this, and that is why I am assigning a team who has experience with the fresco medium."

Di Cosimo makes a few more hatch marks on the underside of the dragon. "Painters on the project will be Stefano, Gianluca. The two boys from the orchard warehouse will serve as apprentices," he gestures. "Finally, Jacopo Torni and his little brother." He points to us with his chalk.

I nod. A paying job. Lucia will be thrilled. "I am grateful for the work, Master di Cosimo. From whom should I take direction for this project? Will you be overseeing it?"

Master di Cosimo looks at me for a moment with wild eyes, misunderstanding. He scoffs a bit under his breath and mumbles something again unintelligible. "I shall stay here in Florence. I have my workshop to oversee, plus I have commissions for Signor Rosso, for the Pugliese, for the brothers of the Annunziata." He waves his hands as if sorting his commitments into invisible buckets. He scratches his head and mumbles again. Finally, he looks at me with his clear eyes and his words come back into focus. "I will come to see the job, of course, but my team will complete the work. And so as I was saying, my dear Jacopo, it is *you* who shall be in charge."

BEYOND THE WALLS of our city, a bee sinks over a bank of abelia that has overgrown the ruins of an ancient farm. It joins others, all buzzing contentedly as they gorge themselves on golden-white flowers. Green terraces wind around the periphery of a hillside, covered with a bounty of olive trees and vines heavy with pale, green grapes. Here, the hills unfurl as if someone has spread a green blanket over a field of melons. The country homes of our prosperous merchants are enclosed behind high walls, where you can see the tops of trees—pears, peaches, plums. Beyond, there are fields of sunflowers turning their black faces to the light. Out here, beyond the walls of Florence, far from my friends and my demons, I feel I can finally breathe.

The church where our new frescoes will stand lies just beyond the view of our city walls and of the great tiled dome of Florence cathedral, yet it's close enough that my brother and I can return home on muleback at the end of each day. Most nights, though, we sleep on wooden cots set up in a side chapel of the church, as we work until it is too dark to return home.

In total, there are six of us. I am the foreman. My brother, having worked on fresco projects in cities near and far, oversees the two primary painters. Di Cosimo has sent two younger apprentices to score the lines and boxes for our pigments, to mix plaster and paint, to clean brushes and tools, and to clean up after us.

Over several days, we have erected wooden scaffolding across the interior of the chapel, bracing long poles into holes carved into the walls. When we are done, our assistants will fill the holes with plaster so that no one will ever know they have been there. Our youngest boys rough the surfaces of the walls with small axes, making it ready for our pigments to stick. For days, their scraping fills the air with sound and dust. Behind them, our painters smear a layer of rough *arriccio*, a mixture of lime paste and sand.

As we begin our work, I think about the frescoes I worked on at San Pier Martire, a project again abandoned, and how the dampness from the Arno crept in and threatened to grow mold on the walls. I decide to try mixing different materials with our plaster—a bit of vinegar, a splash of white wine. Most days, it amounts to little more than a mess. But I keep experimenting.

Father Ormanno, the old priest who presides over the church, visits us each day. He seems eager to share a joke or a story, and to watch us work. He asks what I have tried mixing in the plaster today to prevent the green mold. His bulging midsection belies gluttonous habits; his bald head is speckled with sunspots the same color as his tattered robes. He must be lonely out here all by himself, I think.

Occasionally, our patron appears in the church with his wife and children, staying for a while to watch us work. I can't help but stand in awe of his noble demeanor, his kindness toward us as he stands sweating inside an ever-changing rainbow of woolen caps, belted and pleated doublets, colorful hose. He shakes our hands, asks us questions, gives each of us an encouraging word. Signora moves along the chapel aisles as if floating, her layers of silk petticoats sliding noiselessly over the patterned marble. Her brocaded dress swells out like a giant tent, her breasts bound tightly with ribbon, pearls at her ears and entwined in her graying hair.

Finally, the day comes when the surfaces are prepared and we are ready to map out Master di Cosimo's design on the walls. Di Cosimo himself appears for this part, dismounting from his mule with some difficulty, and waddling into the church bent over from the travails of the journey. Our men hold the cartoon square to the wall, pricking the design with a needle, then pouncing it with a sack of black carbon dust until an outline is made. Master di Cosimo carefully oversees this process, for it's in the transfer of his Madonna surrounded by strange dragons and beasts that our images will spring to life. Squinting, he watches us transfer his preparatory cartoon from the paper to the wall, making small adjustments and mumbled comments as he goes. After two full days of work, he finally nods his approval and returns to the city.

In the evenings, our little team of painters rests along an ancient stone wall. We bask in the glow of the longer summer days, peacefully regarding the rolling red earth, skinny cypress trees, gnarled oaks, and sapphire skies. I watch the wispy clouds roll by as I peel off small bits of ham I have picked up at the market or sweets made especially for the celebration of a local patron saint. As the sun sets and the air cools, I feel my body let go of the knots around my neck and shoulders.

By candlelight, I open my sketchbook and work on the drawings Michelangelo has assigned to me, those that might fool a cardinal in Siena. I do my best to mimic my friend's style—large, ponderous thighs, backs, and shoulders. Writhing men in the image of our divine maker. Men in the guise of God.

But as I flop on my cot at night and close my eyes to the colors barely visible in the flickering candlelight, doubt creeps in. What right do I have to be in charge of this project? Why did Master di Cosimo put me here? I do not have my own workshop. Even after the years of tutelage under Master Ghirlandaio, my profession has amounted to little more than a bedchamber littered with crude wall paintings, abandoned projects, a stifling, impotent loneliness. What right do I have to be here among these painters?

I awake in the morning thinking that I must be intelligent, that I must have something to contribute as I watch the squares fill with color, day by day, but by noon, I think that I must be the stupidest one of di Cosimo's assistants. Surely it won't be long before they discover I am only here because of my father's reputation and di Cosimo's mindless assignment of me as their leader. That I myself am not a real artist. By nightfall, I live in terror that one of the other assistants will look over my shoulder and say, "What are you doing there? Have you ever painted a fresco before?" Worse yet, someone might laugh not at something I have said, but at *me*.

As I lie on my back on the scaffold, paint and dust falling on my face, in my hair, on my clothes, I think that one day, Master di Cosimo will realize his mistake in putting the likes of me in charge of a whole church fresco. Surely it was an error on his part. I am terrified that someone will call me out, tell me that I am not really qualified to do this job, to be in charge of this project. Someone is going to find something wrong with my work. For who am I to be in charge of anything?

ON THE FEAST of John the Baptist, my brother and I
return to the city, and to news of Michelangelo and his sculpture. Considering the peace of the countryside, I am reviled by
the smell of rotting food, the press of sweating bodies, the filth
of the simmering street. In the alleys, the markets, the windows,
and doorways, the news is upon everyone's lips: the city fathers
have ordered one of the wooden walls of the box surrounding
the *David* to be removed. Soon, everyone in this moldering city
will—at last—be able to view the giant in progress.

Master di Cosimo has called us to prepare the new decorations he has designed for the feast day of our city's patron, a
three-day extravaganza that will extoll the power, the grandeur,
the invincibility of Florence. But after the disaster of the gilded
boy, the very symbol of our city, I wonder if anyone in this city
still believes in it.

In addition to overseeing the fireworks, di Cosimo has prepared themed *carretti* for each neighborhood, covered in garlands of papier-mâché flowers, each in the color of each neighborhood—green for San Giovanni, blue for Santa Croce, white
for Santo Spirito, and red for Santa Maria Novella. The city has
commissioned his workshop to create elaborate staging for the
candles that each man fifteen years of age and older is obliged
to offer at the altar of the Baptistery for the feast. Di Cosimo
has designed a fabric ceiling for the streets surrounding the cathedral and Baptistery. It is little more than an oversized awning
hung on cords, but it has magically transformed the area into a
stage for our procession. We are covered by a vast, ornamented
firmament of gilded stars that sparkle in the light of thousands

of candles. In addition to di Cosimo's commissions for public spectacles and decoration, private houses, palaces, and work-shops across the city are adorned with flags, banners, flowers, and colored awnings.

It must be one of Master di Cosimo's most ambitious pro-grams for the Feast of San Giovanni but none of his assistants is paying attention. They can only speak of the *gigante*, can only speculate what will appear when one side of the old box I helped create with my own hands finally falls to the dust of the cathe-dral workyard. In their minds, they already foresee a spectacle more impressive than the one taking shape in our workshop and on the streets outside.

The clamor around the new *David* is enough to bring me to Michelangelo's door. To my great surprise, his brother tells me my friend has holed himself up in his room and will not come out. And now, it is my turn to lure him from his bedchamber again, rather than the other way around.

He must have known I hesitated outside the door of his bed-chamber, for I only rap my knuckles against the wood one time before he opens the door.

"It has been a long spell since I have seen you, my friend," I say, entering his bedchamber with a tentative step.

He grunts but otherwise says nothing, only heaves himself to the floor at the end of his bed. He grasps the hairs on the top of his head as if he might pull them out from their roots. Around him, myriad drawings and pages of looping script lie scattered.

"What's that?" I take a deep inhale. "Smells like sour grapes in here."

He doesn't laugh. Doesn't even offer one of his crooked grins.

I finger an array of brown ink drawings on the table, quick but expert sketches of legs, feet, hands. Muscular. Powerful. The hooded face of a woman, turning her head as if she has just been startled by a visitor at her door. I run my finger down the edge of the table to another stack of folios, these completely covered in his looping script. Words and lines are scratched out, rewritten. On another table, a slab of clay has been half-molded into the head of a man.

I don't look at him directly, but I am watching from the corner of my eye. "Your name is being spoken across the city."

"I don't want to know," he says, raising his hand as if deflecting his face from a blow. "The sculpture is not finished."

"Did they ask you if they could show it?"

He nods.

"And you agreed."

He stands, pressing the front of his shift with his palms as if the gesture might improve his haggard appearance. "It was not my wish, but my protestations were ignored. After all, they paid for it. What can I do?"

I am certain he is unhappy about having his work shown before it is finished; I know he has been working hard to push it as far as possible. I imagine he has been working for weeks in order to do as much as one man could do before today.

"But these public exhibitions," I say, "people want them. Not long before you came back to Florence, there was a public showing of Master da Vinci's cartoon of the Holy Family and Saint Anne at Santissima Annunziata... Even now, I hear that Master da Vinci will show a portrait of Francesco del Giocondo's wife, Lisa, even though it is not yet finished." But I stop myself; it is clear that mentioning da Vinci's name is the wrong choice of subjects. He is pulling at his curls again. I try something different. "I am going to see your David when they unveil it tomorrow morning. Will you be there?"

Silence.

I should have known better than to ask. He begins pacing around the room, idly arranging papers and testing the squeak of a shutter.

"You and the rest of the idiots in town. Little more than sheep following the latest fashion."

But I don't let his comments define me anymore.

"What, are you afraid they will only speak of the small *pisello?*"

"Ha!" A small, sarcastic huff. He shakes his head. "Not that. Soderini has said that the nose is too big."

"What? Too big?" I approach him, wagging my hands. "What does Soderini know about sculpture? About noses? He is a politician," I insist.

"One with a big nose himself," he offers, and now it is my turn to laugh.

"So fix it," I say, shrugging.

His eyes widen. "Fix it? Fix it! What is there to fix? The nose is fine just as it is. I would like to see Soderini do better himself."

"Of course you are right. So, you don't want to go to the unveiling." I shrug. "Your choice. But, Little Angel," I grasp his forearms, "listen. Gonfaloniere Soderini is your patron, no?"

"No. The cathedral committee is."

"And who is their superior?"

He nods in recognition.

"Well then, what do we do with our patrons? We please them."

He scoffs. "I'm not going. And, L'Indaco, there is nothing wrong with the nose!"

"That may be true, but…"

"Of course it's true!" his voice booms through the chamber.

"Our patrons," I repeat myself quietly. "We give them what they want. You said so yourself." I watch his face, slowly considering my words. "Just be grateful that Soderini didn't say anything about the *pisello*." His expression softens. "Hey," I say, giving his cheek a soft slap, "if we can make a cardinal in Rome believe a brand new sculpture is centuries old, then surely you can figure out a way to 'fix' a nose on a face that's way up there above our heads."

"What do you mean?"

"An idea!" I say, and it's my turn to pace the room. "You keep a fistful of marble dust in your pocket." I walk back and forth quickly, filled with a vision. "While Soderini is watching, you pretend to chisel a little away from the nose, then let the marble dust fall from your hand, grain by grain. He will never know the difference."

"L'Indaco," he says, "I am never sure if you are an idiot or a genius."

But I can see that he will be considering my idea long after the great orange ball of sunlight sets over the Arno.

THE NEXT MORNING, Michelangelo stays home. Undeterred, Francesco, Lucia, and I walk together to see the unveiling of the giant. I love nothing more than to walk shoulder to shoulder with my brother and sister through the streets of our city. Despite the gaps in our age, the gaps in our understanding of one another, since Francesco's return, we have become a team.

As we approach the area surrounding the cathedral, the crowd thickens and boisterous chanting fills the air, echoing under di Cosimo's painted tarps that shelter the streets. I watch di Cosimo's gilded stars shimmer in the morning light as we work our way to the gates surrounding the cathedral workyard. We press through clusters of bakers, housewives, nobles. Along the raised sidewalks, opportunists hawk everything from apple cakes to small wooden slings—children's toys in the guise of the sling David used to slay his giant.

There is already a great swell of people pressing up against the wrought-iron gates. I cannot see over their heads, but from my vantage point, I perceive that one of the four sides of the wooden enclosure has been removed. I can see the great, marble boy-king from the waist up, still protected by three sides of the box, still kept from hungry onlookers rattling the locked iron gates.

Even still half-hidden, the sculpture takes my breath away. Everyone presses forward to catch a glimpse of a young man larger than life, with no armor, taking on a goliath that no adult man was brave enough to face. My friend has captured the moment just as the youth has caught sight of his enemy. His body has just begun to tense. His right hand is beginning to curl, fingering the stone that will be loaded into the sling. He stares into the distance with an intense expression, as if he is contemplating taking the sling from his shoulder and loading it with the stone just a moment from now. It's a sculpture about potential, about being brave. It is unspeakably beautiful.

"A marvel," someone nearby says, their loud whisper traveling through the air to the ears of the crowd.

"They will be lucky if that sculpture goes anywhere before it's destroyed," I hear a man grumble. "Those Medici agitators have already designed a plan to demolish it, at least that's what I heard." My heart stops. Is that true?

Two women toward the front of the crowd giggle, whispering to one another. They press their way out of the crowd, and my brother, sister, and I push our way into their space. Now, we have an unobstructed view of the sculpture. From this distance,

I can appreciate that Michelangelo has created a colossus in the spirit of those works of antiquity he studied in Rome, a perfect man-god in the body of a beautiful youth. But this David is no Hercules, no Apollo. He is not a god but rather a man who dares to be god-like. A man who reflects the divine nature of God as his own image. Surely this colossus surpasses anything that might have been made by the ancients. Blood runs through the boy's veins. A fierce, human spirit seems to pulse through his muscles. He is a man, yes, but more than that, he is a symbol. He is Florence. He is us.

Then, to my great surprise, Michelangelo emerges from behind the wooden enclosure. My heart skips a beat. Somehow, he managed to pull himself out of his bedchamber to face the harsh light of public scrutiny anyway. It is more than I have ever been able to do. I am stunned.

But he is not alone. A small entourage of men from the wool guild and cathedral committee walk behind him, the hems of their robes collecting layers of dust as they follow Michelangelo around to face the sculpture. They must have entered the work-yard from a locked, private entrance inside the cathedral. Now I feel silly for asking if he wanted to walk to the unveiling with me. Of course, it makes more sense for him to have these important men by his side instead.

When the crowd catches sight of Michelangelo, a few people begin to clap, and soon, a communal roar of applause and whistling rises into the air. Michelangelo only acknowledges their approval with a tight-lipped smile and a dismissive wave. Then he turns back to the small knot of officials standing around him. The men gaze up at the *David*, awe and excitement etched on each of their faces.

Then, another surprise. Soderini himself.

The *gonfaloniere* appears from behind the wooden enclosure. I recognize the tall, lean man by his stooped shoulders, the deep lines alongside his mouth, his layered black robes, his stiff leather cap. His stern expression breaks only for a moment as he acknowledges the crowd with a nod and a smile. Another round of obligatory cheering and a small burst of uninspired applause erupts, but it pales in comparison with the admiration heaped on Michelangelo.

For a few moments, I watch Soderini and Michelangelo confer, speaking to one another out of earshot. Soderini stands with his hands clasped behind his back, staring up at the face of the David and nodding his head as Michelangelo gestures some sort of explanation. I strain to hear, but I cannot make out any words.

Then, Michelangelo breaks from the crowd of officials and grabs a wooden ladder from the shadows of the workyard. It's the same rickety ladder I used weeks ago to climb up the sculpture-in-progress and stand face to face with the biblical hero. Michelangelo braces it against David's abdomen, then climbs to the top. From the ground, the cluster of officials and the spectators grasping the iron gate watch in silence. From one pocket of his worn leather apron, Michelangelo produces a small chisel and mallet. Then he places his hand in another pocket, fishing inside. My heart begins to pound. Has anyone guessed? How could they? His back is turned to us.

The crowd falls silent as we listen to the gentle tap and ping of metal on the marble. The nose. Michelangelo's face draws so close to that of the David as if to kiss him. One face white, godlike. The other dark, crooked. Both intense. Both intent on the mission before them.

But then, we see small grains of marble dust begin to fall from the face of the giant. Everyone watches as small shreds of white glisten in the sunlight as they fall from high above. The officials watch the marble dust collect at their feet.

"What is he doing?!" Lucia whispers to me.

I shrug. "Improving it?" I can't help but smile.

It only takes a few minutes. Michelangelo descends the ladder, replaces his tools in his pocket, and claps his hands together to remove the dust.

Gonfaloniere Soderini looks up at the sculpture again, then claps Michelangelo on the shoulder with a nod of approval. Then, our general turns to the crowd and raises his hands as the people at the gates roar in unison again.

I throw my head back and laugh.

"What's so funny?" Francesco looks at me with a puzzled expression.

How can I tell them that Michelangelo has just accomplished one of the greatest public pranks in our city's history? I am elated with the feeling that I might have played a small role.

❧

"YOU WOULD BE proud of our brother." Francesco smiles at Lucia from across the table.

The smell of Lucia's *pici* with a sauce of tomatoes and milk fills our small house. I feel content and comfortable in the bosom of our modest home—my siblings and myself huddled around the table together, just like old times.

"On what account?" She looks at me with an expression of exaggerated, mock skepticism. She grabs a hunk of stale bread from the middle of the table and rips it into pieces.

"He may have solved the problem of mold ruining our frescoes."

"Is that true?" Now Lucia looks genuinely surprised.

"Please don't say it," I wave my hands in protest. "You'll tempt the fates."

"No reason to be humble, brother!" Francesco insists. "He has been mixing crushed marble and lime to our plaster mixture. We think it might help inhibit the ravages of moisture, especially out in the low-lying areas in the countryside."

"Stop," I say. "It won't even work... probably."

"I think you may be on to something, brother," Francesco says, turning to Lucia. "It's a brilliant innovation, really. It may bring up costs—or at least allow us to charge higher wages."

"Until an eager apprentice steals the idea from us."

Lucia clucks and swats at me. "Why do you always think of the worst? Perhaps instead, your name will be spoken far and wide."

I try to explain. "Every artist dreams of that one major work, a piece so magnificent that it propels and consecrates his name through eternity."

"Easy for you to imagine for yourself," she says. "But a woman like myself can hardly set her mind on such a dream."

"And what do you dream, sister?" Francesco asks, shooting me a cautionary glance.

"Well..." she begins. Then she shakes her head and shoos us as if we are pests in her garden.

"What is it?" Francesco prods. "You should not keep secrets from us, of all men."

We eat in silence for a while, but something seems to be hovering over our sister which neither of her brothers fails to recognize. Francesco keeps sending me little glances over our meal, wordlessly telling me that I need to pry.

Finally, I clear my throat and say to Lucia, "If you're worried about my work, I can reassure you that Francesco and I are
in good hands. We will be employed with Master di Cosimo for
some time." I offer my brother a little nod and a wink and we
both turn our attention to Lucia, a nervous smile on her face.

"No, it's… it's not that." The tone becomes more somber
and she clearly knows our curiosity has been piqued.

I say, "So, what troubles you?"

"What doesn't?" But her answer comes too quickly, followed
by an echoing silence. Then she stands and clears her plate from
the table.

ROCKING DOWNHILL ON muleback through the city
gates, I already feel the clutter in my mind begin to dissipate. Our
small team of fresco painters follows; my brother's pack mule is
loaded with leather satchels full of fresh pigment blocks, brushes,
and oils procured from the vendors in our city. We wind down a
dirt path into a dusty olive orchard, the sound of cicadas nearly
deafening in the hot air. Behind us, we leave the steam, the
filth, the spectacle, the madness of the city. We leave behind the
frenzy of the feast day pageants. We leave behind Michelangelo
and his giant.

We arrive at our job site to find a small group of visiting
Spanish merchants. They are lodged nearby, Father Ormanno
tells us, in the great country house that sits on a hilltop surrounded by olive trees and vines heavy with fruit. Our patron,
the wool merchant, wants to show his foreign visitors the artistic

wonders of Florence. I am only left to wonder why they might consider our little country church one of them.

Our patron, his family, and the Spanish merchants follow us into the chapel. The merchants have brought their wives, sons, and a few servants along on the journey, and I marvel that they have traveled such a distance in silks and brocades so fine and elaborate that they would easily break every sumptuary law in Florence. The women are draped in pearls and gold, enormous earrings hanging to their shoulders. Braids loop around their heads, studded with sparkling gems. They carry black lace fans the size of meat platters and wear ponderous skirts that scratch across the straw strewn around the stone floors of the chapel.

"I do not mean to impede your progress, gentlemen," our patron says, "but Master di Cosimo said we could come and view your work. My colleagues have traveled from Murcia to see the work of our renowned Florentine painters and sculptors. I thought they would like to see your frescoes."

I lead the group over to the wall where we have been working for the past months. The place is a mess. There are pieces of di Cosimo's cartoon, scattered pots of drying pigments, fragments of papier-mâché confections and wooden scaffolding scattered around the room. I step over the broken husk of a papier-mâché monstrosity I created by gluing together the parts of several discarded parade creatures from di Cosimo's studio, then stringing them from the scaffolding to frighten the life out of our assistants when they least expected the horrible creature to fly down from the ceiling. My brother reads the embarrassed expression on my face, and he whispers to one of our young assistants to tidy up.

All of us stand before the white walls newly scored with the charcoal outlines of Master di Cosimo's design. Through a translator—a tiny, older woman dressed in widow-black—our patron describes what he has commissioned Master di Cosimo and his assistants to paint for his family chapel. The translator gestures animatedly to the walls as she conveys the information to the Spanish contingent. They nod their heads in understanding.

"Jacopo," our patron says, "you might explain better than I how you will go about putting color on the walls."

"Of course," I say, but I look at the job before us and inhale deeply. The truth is that it is only through the grace of God—and my brother's steadfast support—that I will have the courage and wherewithal to complete such a great task.

"We work square by square, a *giornata*, as much as we can do in a day." I wait for the small woman to translate into Spanish, a language that sounds, to my ear, at the same time foreign and familiar. "As we go, the *intonaco* plaster will cover up the lines. My brother and I will be responsible for most of the painting, especially the figures." Francesco waves his hand and smiles at the group as they listen to the little woman's explanation. "Our boys mix finer sand with more lime, then spread it piece by small piece. We try our best to hide the lines between the squares; my brother is good at that."

I watch the group run their eyes over the freshly drawn Madonna, saints, platters of loaves and fishes taking shape on the walls. One of the men, a stocky gentleman with a large, floppy hat and sharp eyes, asks more questions about our techniques and the subject matter. Through the translator, they are all listening to me. Suddenly, it dawns on me that they recognize me as the master. Me. The head of this project. All of the other workers have fallen away, and they are all watching me, listening to me. I am the master of the work. I can hardly believe it myself.

As the group moves on to view the rest of the chapel, one of the Spanish ladies lingers, her face bright and intelligent. "Thank you for your explanation," she says to me in perfect Tuscan.

I gasp. "You didn't need that translator after all!"

She laughs, her crinkled eyes just visible behind a fan ornamented with carved bone and ivory. "No. My father did so much
trade with the Florentines that he made sure we had a tutor in
the house to teach my brothers. They continue his work, after
all. I made sure I learned some Tuscan, too. So, I know some of
the language, but I have never traveled here before. I pestered
my husband until he finally allowed it. We brought our sons so
they might understand their family's business better."

"And you have come all this way to see us…"

The lady, who tells me her Christian name—Isabel—bows
slightly. "We are here for our trade, true. But it is more than that.
We have heard that Tuscany is a place of incredible achievements. That there are wonders seemingly ordained by God to
occur just now; not as in hundreds of years ago, when the sky was
said to be dark and the towns rife with disease and corruption.
The talents of a man like yourself might have been wasted in
that callous time, no? My husband thinks only of our purse, but
I believe our travels here are no celestial mistake, no happen-
stance. Destiny seems to have placed us in just the right place
and at just the right time."

"But I'm afraid you may have been deceived, signora," I say,
bewildered at the lady Isabel's assessment. "We are only humble
guildsmen working in a simple country church. Some of us
are working only to pay off debts…" The lady looks confused.
"Anyway, our work here does not convey what we Florentines
can do. You will find many more things of artistic interest within
the city walls, if I am honest."

"Tomorrow," she tells me, "we will go into the city. Then we
will see as many artistic glories as we can. We have heard that
there is a marble sculpture unlike anything else in the whole
world," she tells me, her dark eyes wide and filled with wonder.
"A giant."

I imagine that the Spaniards will be so taken with Michelangelo's *gigante* that we will not see them again. However, over the course of the following weeks, while the men do business in the city, the Tuscan-speaking Spanish lady brings the wives of her husband's associates to watch us work. I welcome their visits, lifted by their interest and enthusiasm for the color taking shape on the walls.

ISABEL THE TUSCAN-SPEAKING Spanish lady is back again in our humble country church. She seems to like watching us paint. She picks up my leather folio filled with the sketches of the sculptures for the Piccolomini altarpiece, as well as several designs for small churches. I try to stop her, but it's too late. She is already thumbing through it.

"You have a talent for drawing architecture," she tells me. "Have you designed a church we could see, Master Torni?"

Master. I blush. "I dream of making a church someday, signora, but I do not imagine I will ever have such an opportunity."

One of the other ladies asks her something in Spanish. She turns back to me. "May we see some of the other work you have done in the city?"

I hesitate. What more can I show? The truth is that I have nothing to show for myself, and I would hardly invite a lady to view the crude pictures on my bedchamber walls.

One of our young assistants stops grinding pigment and says, "Jacopo, haven't you painted frescoes at San Pier Martire?"

I freeze. I try my best to ignore him, for the question of the old frescoes in the other church loom over my head. It has been months since I have been there to paint. I still owe the city a certain number of florins in fines. More than I care to realize. I have every intention of going to fulfill my debt and finish the painting. But the more time that passes, the bigger the problem looms over me. I do not begin to describe this to the Spanish ladies.

"It is better to see my work here, signora," I shrug.

"You have your own workshop in the city?" she asks.

"No. I am only the foreman on this commission. I work under Master Piero di Cosimo. Besides, there are other artists in the city who are better than I."

"I believe you have underestimated yourself, *señor*," she says, thumbing through my sketchbook again. "You have immense talent in your hands. I see no reason why you should not be the head of your own workshop. In Spain, you would be considered a great master."

◌

I'M PUTTING THE finishing touches on a saint's face when I see Father Ormanno waddle through the dim church, replenishing melted candles on their wrought-iron stakes with new ones.

"*Padre!*" I call to him.

The old Father Ormanno and I are the only two people left inside the church. My brother and our assistants have already finished for the day. They are sitting outside on the stone wall enclosure of the church, wiping their paint-stained brows and watching the dusk fall beyond the hills.

I gesture to Father Ormanno as I walk toward the ancient confessional propped in the aisle of the church. I press myself into the cramped space and sit on the worn seat. For a few moments, I breathe in the stifling, stale air while I wait for the old priest to join me on the other side of the confessional's metal grate. Father Ormanno hesitates, then I see his ample form move toward me. He leans into the tight space, where I sit waiting. Sweating.

"What can I do for you, Jacopo?"

I take a deep breath, cross myself, then bow my head in his direction. "Forgive me, Father. I have truly sinned. You see, I... Well, where shall I begin? I..."

But the priest's pudgy hand reaches into the narrow box. "Come out of there, my friend," he says.

"But *padre*... I only wanted to give you my confession."

He pulls me by the front of my smock, and leads me to a church pew. From our seats, we have an unobstructed view of our frescoes in progress. My newly finished squares are still drying. I heave a deep sigh.

"Now, tell me..." Father Ormanno says. "What troubles you?"

"You see, *padre*," I glance around nervously—at first back at the confessional, then around the vast, empty space of the church. None of the other men are to be seen. "I've been working things out, asking myself the difficult and necessary questions of life, and... Well. I don't like the answers I've come up with. I think certainly a wise and holy man like yourself will have insight."

"How long since your last confession, Jacopo?"

I scratch my head. "Well, it's not for having missed services, I... I've been busy getting ready for Holy Week, you see."

"We should never allow secular commitments to lead us astray, even from regular confession."

"I... I agree," I say. "Completely."

"What do you have to confess, my friend?"

"Well, *padre*. I... I don't even know where to begin, really. I... I feel like I'm a good Christian, and my sins, are..." A long stretch of silence.

Father Ormanno gestures. "It's all right. The Lord knows the secrets of your heart."

"Right, yes, of course, but... but you don't." I chuckle out of nervousness. I clear my throat and go on, "Well, on the one hand, *padre*, I've had a bit of a bad time with cards and dice, see..."

"You've been in the taverns?" His bushy eyebrows raise.

"Me? No! No, not now. I've been staying away from them, mind you, busying myself with my work, but... I know it's a failing. It has been. In the past."

After a brief moment to consider, Father Ormanno answers, "To know the weakness is the first step toward turning it into a strength. We are all of us tempted by Satan. If you resist the temptation, this is a virtue, not a sin."

"Yes, I... I have been staying away from the dice and the cards of late, *padre*. But I do have debts, which I've hid from my sister for years. If she discovers them, she'll be terribly disappointed in me, my brother as well. But my pay for these frescoes will go a long way to settling those debts."

"Only right."

I nod, knowing I haven't gotten to the worst of it. "And the taverns too, I'm not nearly the patron I used to be. But... abstinence is a little more difficult than I thought it would be. Not that I paint with a tainted mind; I don't. I love my work, and I don't want it tainted in that way."

"I know this of you. And your resolve is admirable. As I said, to resist these temptations is a virtue, not a sin."

"And I'm grateful for your merciful assessment, *padre*. And it's not merely the games, but the company, the sense of comradery. I… I do enjoy a bit of libation. I can't lie to a priest in a church, confessional or no."

"You can always be forthright with me, son." Father Ormanno says. "But there are other ways to clear your mind. Like a walk along the Arno."

"Truly said, Father. I tried walking along the river, a mile a day for two weeks."

"And what, if anything, did it bring you?"

"It brought me miles from my home!" I laugh, but he doesn't seem amused by my little joke. "Really though, there's something else, I… it's my work, *padre*."

Father Ormanno looks up at the frescoes my brother and I created, renderings of the wedding feast and the feeding of the five thousand. He smiles. "It seems you and your brother have made yourselves worthy servants of the Lord."

"I… I'd like to, Father, I really would, but it seems I've been… ignored. Maybe overlooked. That is, my gifts go unrewarded, unrecognized."

The father seems to give this further thought. "Is fame so important as the blessings of God?"

"Not fame necessarily, just… well, all of us who toil, at whatever labors, crave some reasonable reward. With the Lord, after all, it's not about the greatness of my accomplishments, but by His grace that I'm redeemed." Father Ormanno nods, but I have to add, "Down here, accomplishments go a long way."

"And?"

I hate to have to say it, but I know it has to be said. "I… I look at my fellow guildsmen, their workshops filled with assistants. So many different projects and all of them finished. But me? I… I'm… I'm lost, to be frank. I'm searching for my masterpiece, the work that will win me the patronage I need, that any artist needs. And in the meantime, all I've left behind is a… a series of experiments; unfinished, unrealized…"

"But you've learned from those experiments, have you not?"

"Of course. But there is one thing that plagues me more than all else, *padre*. It's my sister. She is a woman of God. She wants to marry. But I am ashamed to say she has spent up her beauty, her youth, her years of starting a family… All taking care of me. I have been a burden to my family. And there has never been enough to dower her properly."

"A good woman deserves our respect. Our protection. And then? You must be patient, be as kind to yourself as you are to others." He looks back up at the frescoes. "Look at these two works of art here, my son. Think of the joy and wonder they will bring, not just to the congregation here now, but for years to come, for generations, for as long as this church stands on this ground and the spirit of the Lord lives in the hearts of those who come here. It's a great thing you've done, divine in its way. Be of good faith, Jacopo, and know the Lord will answer all your questions in good time."

"Good time," I repeat. "Time is… it's a thief, a villain, a liar! It makes promises it can't keep, it tricks you and turns you from a young, eager spirit like my brother into a… into a frustrated failure like me."

"Failure? My son, you're a survivor. And no man who survives can be called a failure."

This sounds like a riddle to me, one I can't instantly understand. "But… how can that be, *padre*?"

He reaches out and touches my chest. "Let hope renew your heart." He rises from the pew.

"What is my punishment, then, *padre*?"

"Punishment?" He shakes his head. "Seems to me that you have punished yourself enough." The old priest puts his pudgy hand on my shoulder. "There are times when a soul needs confession, Jacopo, and other times, just a friendly ear."

FROM THE SCAFFOLDING high above the chapel, I watch one of di Cosimo's boys lick his thumb and attempt to smear a drip of paint into the cloak of Saint Peter. He smooths the brownish-red pigment, trying to hide his mistake in one of the folds of the saint's cloak. He thinks no one is watching. Silly boy. He has much to learn about painting drapery. Someone needs to stop him before he makes another miscalculation. In the crook of another scaffold, my brother crouches in intense concentration, his face nearly up against the wall. He has not seen the boy's mistake.

I set down my brush where I have been working on the ponderous thigh of a cherub, lying on my back while dust and paint fall on my hair and face. I swing my legs over the edge of the wooden platform, my stomach reeling at the vertiginous sight below. Then, my feet search for the wooden rungs.

As I make my way slowly down the ladder, I survey the colors that have already long dried, already fused with the wet plaster. Vast landscapes of green and brown, with fantastic trees, craggy rocks that do not exist in the real world, and di Cosimo's strange beasts grazing in the fields. The main figures—saints, the figures of Our Lord and the Madonna—are mostly done, their drapery turned out by those working their way up the ranks in di Cosimo's workshop. I stop to examine the left hand of Saint

Paul. The fingers could have been better placed, but it may be too late to make a change. I continue down to the next rung.

In this section of the wall, the assistants have left blank ovals for the faces. After my brother and I have finished painting the fleshy *putti* in the spandrels, we will work our way down the wall to fill in the blank spaces with faces of the main characters. During this dry work, *a secco*, we will add the fine details. Expressive eyes, mouths. Details of hair, drapery, hands. The gilding of haloes, hems of robes, applied with an odorous pot of fish glue. We take our time.

Farther down the wall, Francesco and the other boys are working on new squares. We paint in two- to three-hour windows, for the paint dries quickly and there is no going back to fix anything. My brother and our assistants stab and move their brushes across the wall. In the silence, I hear only breathing, the clatter of brush handles against buckets, the creak of a scaffold, the occasional hum or a line of a tune echoing in the silence. Minute by minute, we apply the paint in thin layers. Day by day, the squares of the fresco cartoon fill in with terra verde, ultramarine, yellow ochre, azurite, gold. The assistants come to me, ask me for help, ask for my advice, ask me to check their work.

Now and then, someone yells a joke, and the sounds of laughter or mild annoyance echo through the church. They have picked up my habit.

The Spanish lady's compliments have given me the courage to continue, the audacity to keep painting even when I might otherwise have questioned my ability or stopped. Besides, my brother, our other painters, and assistants are counting on me.

When I reach the bottom of the ladder, I stop and look up at the expanse of the wall. From here, I no longer see the minutiae, the blank ovals left to be filled in, the apprentices' small mistakes, the hands that could have been better formed. Instead,

I see a comprehensive cycle—an epic drama of saints, humans, dragons, and other creatures—unfold along the walls. It is a riot of color, and it takes my breath away.

⁂

THE NEXT TIME I swing my legs over the side of the scaffold, I look down between my feet to see Michelangelo staring up at me.

"Little Michael Angel! What brings you to the far reaches of our territories?"

His dust-covered face tilts upward. "Your sister said it might be worth my time to come have a look at your frescoes."

"Lucia." A momentary panic. "She is all right?"

"Fine as always. I saw her in the market." Now, I see his eyes scanning the squares Francesco, our assistants, and I have spent weeks bringing to life. I make my way down the heaving wooden rungs of the ladder, hastily lashed together by one of our youngest apprentices. Michelangelo stands close to one of our squares, hands on his hips. He runs his fingers lightly over the folds of a garment painted in green.

My eyes scan the colors, too. In recent days, it's been hard to pull myself away. There's always another detail which could enrich the overall, always another brushstroke. The plaster is still moist enough to absorb the paint, and that would give it greater richness and durability. But the plaster dried much faster than we thought.

The frescoes do look good; Father Ormanno had been right about that. But he'd also made an excellent point. Generations, even centuries of worshippers might see the frescoes, even long after my brother and I have gone to God. They will look to it for inspiration, for education, over and over again. That idea both inspires and frightens me; but in the end, it's kept me going, day by day.

People may be looking at it every week, each time their eye finding some new flaw, something both my brother and I will overlook. It's too important to walk away without knowing for sure that every detail is as good as it can possibly be. I know that my work, our work, will be judged long after we're gone, and that we will be judged accordingly. It's one of the tremendous and terrible responsibilities of an artist's life. At least those who make something meant to last.

"Lucia tells me that you have invented a way to resist mold," he says, squinting at the plaster as if it might him help understand what I've done.

"We're… experimenting."

He nods at me and places a hand on my shoulder. "You have come a long way, L'Indaco."

"Thank you. But tell me… What is the latest? What have we missed in the city? What of your *gigante*?"

"The colossus," he says, then grimaces. A great sigh. But he doesn't say any more.

IN A FIELD within view of the country church, the Spanish merchants have packed up their mule cart to return home. They have spent weeks exploring the wonders of Florence, and I am still amazed that they find it worth their time to come back to us, in our modest chapel out in the green hills. I watch them load the carts in their convoy with stacks of wool samples, baskets full of unsalted bread and crusted cakes. A locked metal box full of elaborate gold baubles too fancy to pass our own sumptuary laws; instead, they've been stamped and approved by the goldsmiths' guild for export to Murcia.

To my surprise, Isabel, the Tuscan-speaking Spanish lady, has remained so enamored with my work that she has convinced her husband to let her give me a commission for a few small religious panels. I have completed a small Annunciation of the Virgin for their daughter, who is to marry, and a Virgin with flowers for the lady's mother. I have also made small pictures of saints, which Signora Isabel tells me will serve as *ex-votos*, placed at the tomb of her husband's brother, who died fighting the infidels in the south.

"You are quick and talented," she tells me. "The other ladies of Murcia will be jealous."

"Then you must tell them where to find me." I feel heat rise to my cheeks.

Though she did not ask for them, I have given her a few of my best drawings from my sketchbook. I have also quickly turned out my most popular street picture, a small, funny face made out of fruit. I am rewarded not only with her appreciation but also with her laughter, and I think that Filippo Dolciati, wherever he is, would be proud.

At sunrise, I run out to the field, my eyes watering in the warm swirl of wind that has rushed up from the south, causing yellow leaves to rain around me like gold. I take cover under the shade of a desiccated olive tree. From there, I raise my arm and wave a frantic goodbye.

≈

TO MY ASTONISHMENT, within weeks of the Spanish merchants' departure, I have two new commissions. It seems that Isabel's husband has complimented me among his wool-trading colleagues in my native city, and word has spread. When our frescoes in the country are complete, I return home to Florence with a contract for an oil on panel depicting a great battle be-tween Hercules and the Nemean Lion, along with a portrait of a wool trader's wife.

Soon after, a Flemish trader visiting a colleague's home sees the lady's portrait. He would like an image of Saint Barbara to take back to Flanders, as a gift to his ailing wife. Of this pic-ture I am especially proud, since the painters in the man's native land are especially accomplished, painting flowers and trees from nature with exceptional beauty and glistening surfaces like we have never seen in Florence.

And then, the wealthy wool trader who lodged the Spaniards gives my brother and me a major commission that involves painting mythological scenes and imitations of Florentine archi-tecture in the grand entrance hall of his city residence. The walls and even the ceiling will need fresco. We will need materials. We will need assistants. We will need space.

It is beyond my imagination that we might find ourselves in our own workshop, but the commission is large enough, Francesco says, for us to rent a small space in a disused storeroom in Santa Croce. Our patron gives us a budget for two assistants and materials. We are in business. We have a workshop, and we will no longer have time to work with Master di Cosimo. For now, at least, our fortunes have turned.

I stand in the middle of the newly rented storeroom, turning around in the speckled light. It is nothing fancy, but it is well lit, and cleaner and more beautiful than that of di Cosimo, which is more like a barnyard. We will work well here, my brother and me. Before long, our new apprentice—the polite younger son of the fishmonger who seemed eager to escape his father's trade—is smashing pigments with a mortar and pestle, and sweeping colored dust out the back door. Francesco and I sketch on large pieces of paper with silverpoint pens and charcoal. My brother says he has another contact with someone from our guild, who is inexperienced but works quickly and is good with a brush.

With the small pictures from the foreign customers and the new fresco commission, I allow myself the idea that I might soon have made enough money to be free of debt. Michelangelo has been out of my life long enough for me to feel free and accomplished on my own. Some days I have to pinch myself, for I cannot imagine how I have become the head of a painting studio, the head of a group, in charge of a fresco all my own, not working only to repay my debts or line the coffers of another master.

There only remain two problems to solve. Pay back the debt on the long-abandoned frescoes at San Pier Martire. And amass a dowry large enough for my sister to marry the man she loves.

⁓

AT THIS POINT, I can only see one way to raise a dowry large enough to marry off my sister: borrow it. And I can only think of one person who might lend money to someone like me who is not tied to the silk and wool trades. As I make my way toward the last Jewish moneylender left in Florence, my gut twists. Will Bonaventura Salomone lend me enough to make a dowry?

They say that Jews carry pestilence, but I don't believe it. Does pestilence not steal lives whether Jews live in our city or not? After they were expelled the last time, only two years ago now, bodies continued to pile up in deep, communal graves outside our walls. What difference did it make, in the end?

The Jews have been driven out of our city several times over the course of my own lifetime, not counting the many times before that. They were sent away from Florence along with their greatest supporters, the Medici, but our republican leaders soon realized how indispensable they were to commerce in our city and brought them back. Now, our wool guild hardly operates without them, but when they were recalled, only a few came straggling back. You could hardly blame those who stayed away, I think. Without the protection of our more powerful families, why would they return to Florence?

The Ponte Vecchio looms before me, its shades of yellow, orange, and brown glowing in the sunlight. I cross the old familiar bridge, but this time, I don't allow myself to linger at the top. I don't allow myself to contemplate the rushing waters beneath my feet. I keep my head down and follow the stone pavement until it disintegrates into the muddy, narrow alleys of the Oltrarno.

In the narrow pathways south of the river, goods spill out of the doorways as if the buildings have vomited their contents onto the street. Birdcages. A tangle of wrought iron. Cartons of wilted vegetables. A man repairs the cane seat of an old wooden chair. An old beggar woman sits in the filth of the street, her lined hand out, her gaze blank. A rancid, sour stench—rotted eggs or cooking cabbage?—fills the air. Above my head, gowns and overcoats with yellow stars hang to dry in the dampness of the alley. Boys kick rocks down the muddy alley, and a skinny dog skulks across my path, then weaves through my legs. I rustle its bony head under my palm. Finally, I find the doorway of the moneylender and take a deep breath before pushing it open. What is he to make of a man like me?

I find the moneylender asleep, sitting straight up on a stool, perhaps having dozed off after filling his stomach at the midday meal. He is a husky old man with a long, bushy black beard and a black cap. As I cross the threshold of his studio, he startles and presses his palms on the counter to keep from falling off the stool. In contrast to the bright squalor outside, his studio is dark but tidy, with large, leather-bound ledgers on the shelves and ornate brass lamps dancing with flame.

"Good day," he says, resting his eyes on me.

I tip my hat briefly in his direction. "Signore, I am looking for a loan."

"I see," he says. He opens up a large ledger, then picks up a small pair of spectacles and balances them on the end of his nose. "What is your name and profession?" he asks, peering down his nose.

"Torni. Painter."

"Registered guildsman?"

"Yes. My father was an illuminator. I trained under Master Ghirlandaio the Elder." I watch the moneylender make careful notations, filling the next blank line in his ledger with neat, minuscule script.

"How much do you wish to borrow?" I see his dark eyes watch me over the top of his spectacles.

I shrug. I have never negotiated a dowry, and I realize only now that I have no idea how much it will take to secure my sister's marriage. Wealthy men might have stashed away hundreds of florins in an account at the Monte dei Doti to secure their daughters' futures. What will Battistini the bookbinder accept from us?

A stab in the dark. "About fifty florins, I think."

Bonaventura Salomone strokes his long beard, and for a few moments, the only sound is the loud ticking of the clock.

Finally, he says, "A loan of that size could be proffered for a period of five years, at which time it would need to be paid back in full." I know that only the Jews are able to extract interest from Christians, as it would not be allowable for us to loan and charge amongst ourselves under pain of usury. "And what do you plan to use the money for?" he asks.

Of course I should have anticipated this question. I feel my feet shuffle against the stone floor, and I hope he cannot see my hands tremble. "You see…" I hesitate, for how can I tell him what has brought me to his doorstep? How can I explain that I must finally make something of myself? That it might take years of painting banners for Master di Cosimo for me to amass a dowry for Lucia, but that a dowry is the least I owe her?

"My brother and I…" I begin. "We are enlarging our work-shop, bringing on new assistants. And our sister… We want to complete her dowry."

The moneylender sets his piercing eyes on me, and for a sti-fling moment, I expect to be turned away. "A dowry." He raises his eyebrows and drums his fingertips on the ledger book. "A sum like that might mortgage a house. You have people—guild mem-bers—who can vouch for your good name, your commissions?"

"I… I worked with Michelangelo Buonarroti to design the giant in the cathedral workyard."

I have all but blurted this half-lie and immediately, I regret it. I would die of embarrassment if the Jewish moneylender went to Michelangelo to share the fact that I was groveling for a loan.

Plus, I do not know that Michelangelo would vouch for my character anyway.

"That sculpture!" he exclaims. "Well, we shall see if it survives. I'm sure you have heard that the *palleschi* plan to destroy it before it is even finished?"

"The *palleschi*..." At the mention of the Medici supporters and a plan to destroy it, my head spins. "I don't know what you mean."

He dismisses me with a wave of a hand. "Rumors," he says. "I hear a lot of them. Only rarely, they turn out to be true. You have worked with others?" he eyes me suspiciously.

"There is Master di Cosimo."

"Di Cosimo," he says, and I watch his bushy eyebrows rise. "A good man. Peculiar, but established in the guild. Do you owe money to anyone else?"

I shake my head, careful not to mention the gambling debt I owe to the city, my empty sections of wall at San Pier Martire.

"You are not bonded to any other moneylender?"

Again, I shake my head.

"Hmm," he says finally, and makes a few marks with a feather pen in his ledger. "I do not know you and have never done business with you. In order for our family to make the loan, you must put up some collateral of equal or greater worth."

"Collateral? Like what?"

He taps his finger on his pursed lips. "I do not imagine you would have a painting worth this amount."

Of course I don't. I don't have any paintings. I think of the silly work I've been selling on the street, of all my drawings and playing cards, charred by fire.

"No," I say. "All my paintings have been... commissioned."

"Understood. Often my customers put up property, either inside the city or in the countryside," he says, gesturing in the direction of the Porta Romana and the Tuscan countryside beyond.

"I only have my home," I say. "No properties in the country."

"Where do you live?"

"Santo Spirito."

I see the bushy eyebrows raise again. "Santo Spirito. Quarter of the wool traders' guild. You own the home?"

I nod. "My father left it to my sister, my brother, and me. In better times," I say.

He looks at me with his dark, intelligent eyes. I see the bushy, black beard move.

"I see. Well, there is a good probability I can arrange for your loan in exchange for mortgaging your house," he says. I feel myself exhale. "If we are able to arrange it, I will be able to disburse the loan in small sums. We shall go together to the notary to seal our bond."

I feel my shoulders tighten rather than relax.

The moneylender nods. "I shall hold a draft of the contract here. You will go home and locate the deed to your house. Bring it to me."

❧

ON THE WAY home, I stop at the gates of the cathedral workyard. The sun has already sunk below the horizon. Long shadows reach across the cobbles surrounding the cathedral and the merchants along the square have already battened their doors for the evening. I press my face in between the iron bars of the workyard gate.

Now, I regret not asking the Jewish moneylender more about the rumor he claimed. A conspiracy? Would someone really try to destroy the sculpture? If what Bonaventura Salomone has said is true, then it means people have already seen this sculpture as a symbol of our Republic—even before it has emerged from its wooden box.

༄

"I HAVE BEEN a burden to you. I am sorry."

I hardly know how to broach the subject, so I simply unload the heaviest weight of my heart.

"I don't know what you mean." My sister keeps her back to me. She reaches her hands into the basket carrying the wrung-out clothes, then pins them neatly on the line. Still, I see her pause. Where else would I find my sister besides the laundry line behind our house? The sharp aroma of ashes and quince apples, used to sanitize our clothes, fills the air. I heave myself onto a sagging bench in our bare garden.

"I mean that… It took me a long time to realize the reason you haven't taken a husband is that… that you felt responsible for taking care of me instead," I say.

She stops and turns toward me, her eyes narrowed to slits. "Who told you that?"

She waits for me to reveal it, but I only shrug. "As I said, I realize now I have been a burden."

She pauses, then says quietly, "You need help, Jacopo. Sometimes."

"Yes," I say. "I admit it. I have not been easy to live with. But look at us now. Francesco and me... We have our studio. We have patrons. We have paying work."

"Thanks be to God," she says, and she stops to wag her prayerful hands in my direction.

"I don't even need Master di Cosimo anymore." I huff in amazement. "I can start to save some money now. I can save up for your dowry. I want you to be able to get married, if that is what will make you happy."

Her eyes go wide but she continues to work. She turns her back to me again. "That would never work, Jacopo."

"Why not?"

"Do you have any idea how much a dowry costs? Besides, I am old."

"Well..."

She stops me from making a gross misstep in my response. "Any woman in this city with a dowry has had money sitting in an account at the Monte dei Doti for *years*. And a rich father who put it there, maybe even before she was born."

Clearly, she has already calculated such a sum.

"But Lucia..."

"I know you mean well," she says. "And I am grateful. Really I am. But I do not have false hopes. I would be long dead in the grave before you and Francesco were able to earn enough to put aside that many florins on my behalf."

"But that's just it," I say. "I have a solution! Hear me out... I have a source to borrow the money."

"What kind of source?" She narrows her eyes at me, and I know that images of the card and dice table are swimming in her head.

"It's not what you think! You see, I have found a way to borrow money against the value of our house."

"What? You would hand over the deed to our house? Are you insane?"

"Hear me! We don't have to sell it. We can still live here. It's just… We would be renting. Also, I can go on the road with Francesco. I am happy outside of Florence; I never knew that before. We can earn money in churches far beyond our city. Our skills are valued out there." I gesture toward the street.

She doesn't seem to hear me. "You would sacrifice our house, your work in the city. For me? Just so that I could marry?"

"I want to do what's right," I say. "What our parents would have wanted for you."

Lucia drops the shirt in her hand and turns toward me. "I am happy for you, Jacopo. I am proud that you have secured good commissions for yourself." She wipes her hands on a rag. "But what happens when you have another… spell of yours? When you need help? When you need… me?"

She has asked the real question, the one that matters. The only one for which I lack an answer. Now, I know my brother was right; she feels responsible for keeping me together; she has even put it above her own happiness.

I take the rag from her hands and drop it in the basket. Then I take her hands in mine. "So," I say, "this Battistini the book-binder… Tell me."

"Well." Lucia lets go and begins to pace, kicking up dirt under her worn leather shoes. For a few minutes she says nothing, but I can see her thoughts are moving like the whorl of a spindle. "Only if it worked, mind you… I would be able to contribute there. My skill with the brush and the pages, along with Stefano's bookbinding, not to mention his customers… It is a perfect collaboration. We already work well together, but with me inside his workshop, we could do much more. Think of it,

Jacopo! Yes, the sisters can still purchase my illuminations, but also so many more patrons!"

I feel as stupid as a donkey, not realizing that for all these years, my sister has carried the same dream as I: to make a living, a life with her hands.

"And Battistini... Stefano..." I hesitate. "He feels the same?"

"He doesn't care about a dowry. He doesn't need the money. He is not a Medici, but he has a very busy workshop. I can help him, and..." Her face flushes with the boldness of the thought. "And he wants me whether or not there is property and money attached."

"You're certain he doesn't care about a dowry?"

She shakes her head. "No, silly. I'm sure it's the farthest thing from his mind."

"Then you mean I'm the only thing standing between you and marriage?" I huff aloud and sink back onto the bench with the full weight of this realization.

"He knows that you... that I support you in some ways."

I meet my sister's eyes. "You love this man."

"Yes," she says, almost breathlessly. Almost laughing. "*Dio*, yes, I love him!"

"He respects you?"

She nods. "He is a kind and good man."

"Then you must not let me hold you here. Yes, I have had my moments when I needed your help, but you cannot sacrifice your own life for mine. Francesco and I, we will be fine here."

"I do feel better knowing that Francesco is at home with us again." Lucia steps over her laundry basket, presses both hands on my shoulders, and kisses my cheek.

"Still," I say, "I don't see why you think taking care of a man with four sons is going to be any easier than caring for a lunatic," and she laughs. "But if that's what you want, then I will help you."

"You are letting me go," she says, and along with her smile, I watch her eyes glisten in the dimming evening light.

◆

THE BOOKBINDER'S HAND is wide and calloused at the fingertips. Warm, nonetheless. I feel his grasp, sure and calm, in my own. The notary has instructed us to clasp our right hands, and with the joining of our palms, Battistini sets his large brown eyes on mine. Sincere. Determined. And surely relieved to hear that Lucia has been set free, at last, of her duty to care for her wayward brother. Around us, the bookbinder's studio is filled with the metallic fragrance of open inkwells, the scent of lamp oil and charred wicks, the overwhelming aroma of old books and leather bindings.

He is some twenty years Lucia's senior, I think, with a creased forehead and fine lines around his mouth, but in his eyes I see only kindness, warmth, compassion, sincerity—surely the things that attracted my sister to him, along with his mastery of his craft, his dedication to books. With the joining of our hands, we have promised that our families will soon enough be united.

I know my sister will be taken care of. She will inherit a small studio, four sons, and a chance at a respectable, stable life. It is more than she will ever get from me, more than she might get from another husband. To my mind, he will get more than she: an honest woman who can manage his household and work with him, making a life from beautiful books.

The two of us stand in attentive silence before the notary, who uses the bookbinder's worktable to lay out the pages of the marriage contract, which has now been negotiated. The men from both families gather around the bookbinder and me. There is our brother, who, like me, is watching the bookbinder's face; the bookbinder's father, a man with wispy gray hair who looks over our proceedings with interest; the bookbinder's second son, who holds his youngest brother in his lap; and the two other boys, who line up obediently against their father's bookshelves while they wait to sign over the details of a new mother. This is men's work, one of the only times in our lives when all of us will occupy the same room for the same task: the uniting of our families, our possessions, our offspring, our destinies.

In addition, there are two men whom we do not know, men from the leather guild who have been brought in as witnesses outside the families. They sit idly, examining their fingernails. Part of what the bookbinder is paying the notary will cover their time. Over small, round spectacles, the old notary turns the parchment pages one by one. He hardly needs to read all the legal language—after all, he himself composed it—but he reviews carefully before signing his initials at the bottom corner of each page.

There, in brown ink, all the gritty details of our lives are exposed. Compared to many families in Florence, we have little to show for our names, but what we do have is all there for public record: our house, thankfully, remains in our names instead of in the hands of the moneylender. There are the contents of our house. All of this, of course, shall stay with Francesco and me. I am relieved the debt does not appear anywhere on the document.

"Since there is no marriage broker involved in this case—and no dowry to speak of, apart from a chest full of linens and illumination supplies—and it is relatively straightforward, this will not take long," the notary says. "To be frank, I enjoy working on these alliances where there is no *sensale*, for it makes things simpler. Normally things are a bit more complicated," the notary tells us, and I know he is being kind, putting a positive stamp on our dour financial situation. "Even when there is a small dowry, it must be decided how many installments and what should happen if the bride dies within the first years…" He looks up from his papers to meet the bookbinder's eyes and stops speaking.

I already know the bookbinder cares little of the dowry; if he did he would not have wanted to marry my sister. Instead he wants someone to manage his household, his boys, especially the little one who squirms on his brother's lap and pulls mischievously at his brother's hair.

Next the notary turns to the bookbinder's possessions, and here, written in ink, it is more impressive than I had previously thought. There is the house in the Oltrarno, which, despite its location, is ample and well built. There is the workshop, which has been passed through several generations, with all of its tools and equipment. There is an inventory attached with an impressive lists of missals, breviaries, ancient texts, and other manuscripts housed in the workshop. Then there are lands outside of Florence, which have been passed through the mother's side. It provides a small extra income through the cultivation of grapes and mulberry trees where the silkworms breed. These shall stay with the family but shall be in part my sister's, and will go in parcel to any children they bear in the future, he says.

After that, the dates and details of the ring ceremony and the ceremonial trip from our house to the bookbinder's home, across the Ponte Vecchio, are established. With our signatures, the agreement is done.

We men shake hands again, thank the notary, and file out into the alley. The streets are muddy, the result of unusual

winter rains that have flushed detritus into the streets. We con-
gratulate one another, then disperse. I fall into step with my
brother as we head home, where I know my sister is anxiously
awaiting our return and the news of a successful *sponsalia*. She
will be relieved to know her brothers were capable of pulling off
such an exercise.

Throughout the city squares, Florence is preparing for
Christmas pageants. I imagine that Master di Cosimo is preparing scenery for nativity plays around the city. Elsewhere, there
are signs of Christmas. People have festooned their doorways
with lemons and oranges and lain boughs of greenery in their
deep window sills.

In the market, we stop at the fishmonger's table, where freshly caught river trout have been laid out artfully on the boards. I
stopped to admire the pink and light green scales of the fish on
the table. I think about bringing it home to my sister, but then
she would just have to do all the work to cook it.

We are barely back in our own neighborhood when I'm aware
of two tall men standing very close to me. I turn to look. I see the
dark brown eyes of the man before I register his uniform. "*Salve*,"
I say before realizing that he is wearing the uniform of the *otto di
guardia*.

"Jacopo Torni?"

Suddenly my heart speeds up.

"Yes, that's me," I say with hesitation.

The man grasps me under the pit of my arm, and then, there
is a second man I had not seen before. My other arm is lifted. I
feel my toes scrape the cobblestones.

"You are hereby arrested in the name of the Signoria."

I gasp. "Arrested! What on earth for?" Beside me, I see my
brother's eyes turn wide and as round as wagon wheels.

"For nonpayment of your debt to the Republic of Florence."

~

"LOOK AT THE baby walk away—awww!" Around me, a group of men, stinking like the street, howl with laughter as a tall, skinny man with long hair throws down his cards and walks off to slap his hands against a wall in a silent display of shame. I know the feeling.

I collect the mess of cards from the dirty floor, then bang them to reform the deck. The deck is worn and ragged, the edges of the cards turned soft, perhaps smuggled in under someone's tunic. The card game has ended as they always do—one victorious, many lost. None of us has lost any real money, of course. We use whatever we can on the floor or in our pockets—pebbles, scraps of wood, a moldy bread crust. In Stinche, you play cards to make a friend, to pass the time, to share a laugh.

It is something, I think, to make people laugh. Especially in prison.

Our city's most notorious debtors' prison, Le Stinche, is little more than a large stone box erected in a dreary, low-lying square northwest of Santa Croce. It is prone to flooding and infestations of mosquitos. It has no address, but simply squats in the piazza like a hulking container, nearly windowless, accessible by a single door you must duck under to gain entrance. A container for men, women, and children who cannot manage themselves in the streets of Florence.

Most of us debtors, it seems, have been confined to a large, barrel-vaulted hall on the ground floor, more of a monastery dormitory than a prison. But debtors are not the only ones within these walls, I am told. More illustrious prisoners occupy the upper floors: thieves, sodomites, dishonest slaves, unruly children being coerced to more appropriate behavior in their parents' homes.

I do not know whether it is night or day, not only because of the dimness but also because I have stayed wide-eyed, awake, when others have taken themselves off to their flimsy straw mattresses on the floor. Instead, I sit on the floor and deal cards from the various, ragged decks smuggled into prisoners' pockets. In spite of the many months in which I have not frequented the taverns, I must admit to myself that the thrill of the potential to win—long pushed down deep inside—is still there.

I am in good company. I recognize two other painters from our guild and another man who says he stokes the stoves that create the steam in the bathhouse in the Mercato Vecchio. He is an old man with a bald head and a sorrowful face. I recognize two other men from Il Fico. Filippo Dolciati has paid his due here. Card and dice players, those who have nothing to pay back gambling fines to the city. Like me.

While I am here, at least it is more of a party than a prison, for I am in good company. There are card and dice games—the prison guards seem not to care to stop us—among others. A young man, little more than a boy, proposes a game to see who will draw the shortest straw from the bundle in his hand. I recognize the straws pulled from the mattress stuffing. We give it a go. We guess incorrectly.

I stay away from the mattresses. Not only are they infested with biting insects, but as soon as I lie down, I only stare at the ceiling and everything comes rushing back into my mind. My failed frescoes. My inability to care for my brother and sister. My tangles with Michelangelo. My own failures. And now this! They still dragged me down, just when I was getting my life in order. I cannot bear to lie there and lick my wounds, so I get up and look for a playing partner among the pitiful sprawled on mattresses in the prison hall.

I try not to think too much about Francesco and Lucia, who I imagine must be so angry with me that they will never come to bail me out. Why would they? I deserve to do my time.

"Do you think I will make it out of here?" A small, round man asks me, a sincere look in his eyes.

"I know you will," I say.

"How do you know that?"

"Because I saw them fit a giant hay wagon through the prison gates. If a wagon of hay can fit through the gates, then you can, too!"

The men around us howl with laughter.

I can hold my bladder no more, so I stand and walk to the stinking latrines behind the hall. On the way down the narrow hallway, so low I need to stoop, there is a single, barred window. I stop and inhale a breath of fresh, cool air. On the horizon, I see orange light blazing.

Dawn.

The emerging light throws the red-tiled dome of Santa Maria del Fiore in silhouette. Our Lady of the Flower, the great symbol of Florence. I watch the swallows making frenzied loops around the dome, spiraling again and again. I think about the giant.

Before long, on one of those tremendous tribunes of the cathedral, Michelangelo's giant will stand, looming over the vast maze of streets like a guard. It will quietly observe the citizens of our city bathing, baking, embroidering, fighting, making love, gambling, sleeping. It will look down and judge me in my narrow bed, behind these prison walls.

IN THE END, my sentence in the Stinche prison only lasts a few days.

My fine has been paid up, the burly prison guard tells me, but I don't understand how that could be.

Outside, I recognize my brother's slight frame, his hands laced in the swirls of the prison's iron gate, as if he himself were clambering to get inside. Dear Francesco, so loyal to his older brother even when there is no justification at all.

"Jacopo!" he calls to me as I leave the dark coolness of the prison and squint into the stark brightness of the square. Francesco waves his hand frantically.

It is only when my eyes adjust to the sunlight that I see my brother is not alone. Behind him, pacing on the cobblestones, I recognize the familiar skulking, stooped figure. The greasy hair, the dirty shift, the gnarled forearms. I push through the unlocked gate.

"L'Indaco," Michelangelo says, pulling me into an embrace so tight I feel my ribs might crack, then slapping my shoulder so hard that it burns. "*Imbecile.*"

"What? It was a holiday in there. I played cards."

Michelangelo laughs, a loud bark, and my brother only shakes his head.

We begin walking home, the three of us, all the while my brother regaling me with the long story of how they tried so hard to get me out of prison, full of apology that it took so long.

"And just when we had your bail money, thanks to your friend," he says, slapping Michelangelo on the back, "well, then we learned you had another debt in process with the

Jewish moneylender." He stops walking and grasps my forearms. "Brother, why didn't you tell us? I could have helped you."

"The contract was never signed since Battistini agreed to marry Lucia even without a dowry." I hesitate sharing this information in front of Michelangelo, but by now, I suppose he's well apprised of my debilitated finances. "Besides, there is no help for me, Francesco. You should have let me do my time."

"But no! Brother. I saved every florin I made in Arezzo and Montepulciano. Didn't you know? Our master gave us lodging and good food—he was an honorable man and a fair boss—and so I had nothing to spend money on during my time there. I kept everything."

I stop walking. Of course. My younger brother. The responsible one. He has not made more money than I, but it turns out he has saved it all. He is not angry, for he has not endured my gambling as long as my sister has. And, for some reason he still looks up to me.

"I was saving to buy back Father's vineyard in the country," he says, "but clearly, your need was more pressing."

"I will repay you, I swear it," I say, wondering at the same time when I will go back and finish painting those accursed frescoes.

"But even after all that, they still weren't going to let you out of there," Francesco persists in telling the story of my daring rescue. "Not until the fine to the *comune* was paid. That's how I got your friend to help. He knew who to contact."

Michelangelo looks at the dirt alley as we walk, his hands clasped behind his back. If I had tried to put on any guise of success before, now it is too late. He knows everything now, all my dirty secrets.

"And the fine to the *comune*?" I prod my brother.

"You no longer owe it. Instead, you owe your friend a debt of gratitude," he says. I look at Michelangelo's face. He says nothing, only gives me a sheepish grin.

I stop and huff in disbelief. "But… you left your work, your giant, to come help me, to pay off my debt. I don't know what to say."

"Say you'll stop your nonsense, L'Indaco," he says, his black eyes finally meeting mine. His palms squeeze my shoulders tightly. "Your family needs you."

"Yes," says Francesco, grasping me. "Come back to the workshop, brother. We have work to do."

∼

AT HOME, THERE is a letter sitting in the middle of the table, a fine, folded piece of parchment with the Signoria's red berry of a wax seal.

I brace myself to face the wrath of the Florentine Republic again—or worse, that of my sister—but instead, it is Battistini the bookbinder who welcomes me. Standing behind him, Lucia only looks a little bit angry. Actually, she is glowing. My heart is lifted to see her there.

"Jacopo," Battistini says. He has a thick head of chestnut hair greying at the temples, and a ruddy complexion that seems out of place for a man who works inside. "Welcome home."

My sister has prepared a simple, delicious stew, and I am grateful to her and to the bookbinder for steering the conversation away from the troubles I have made for myself. While we eat, the bookbinder tells us how he lost his wife in the last plague, how he has managed to raise his sons all alone in his bookbinding shop.

They do well enough, he tells me, by crafting books for the monastic libraries around the city and for an old client of his father's from a big abbey in the countryside. It is through this contact with the nuns that he began working with my sister, he tells me, smiling at her from across the table as she looks down at her three-pronged fork. She will be an asset, he tells us, and I see clearly now that no dowry could have matched the value the bookbinder has placed on the skills our father taught her.

Over dinner, my brother tells us more about his work in Arezzo, regaling us with funny stories about his patron's eccentric demands. He tells us how he played a *beffa* on his coworkers by making them believe he was an Englishman. We all laugh, and for a golden few minutes it feels like the old times.

After dinner, I retire to my room, but I cannot sleep. I learn I have been in the Stinche for three days, but I have no knowledge of that for I was awake the whole time of my incarceration. I know now that I need to press into the comfort of my bed, into the abyss of sleep where I can feel nothing, know nothing of the pain I have felt and the pain I have caused others while the rest of my family gets on with their lives. I feel grateful to all of them for taking pity on me.

I listen to the familiar street noises of my childhood home, kids skipping rocks down the alley, people talking as they pass. The reality of my imprisonment, of my failed attempt to dower my sister, to gain a worthy profession, all hit me like a wall of bricks.

Finally, I dare to break the seal on the parchment. I lie back in my bed, running my thumbnail under the seal to crack the wax.

I open the invitation and scan the words.

I stand straight up and walk back downstairs, where my brother is helping Lucia clean the table. I stand before them with the open letter in my hand.

"What is it?" asks my brother.

"An invitation for both of us," I say, feeling the heat rise to my face. "An invitation from Gonfaloniere Soderini." I hear my sister gasp. She presses her palms over her mouth to stifle it.

"Soderini!" I see the bookbinder's eyes grow wide and glow in the candlelight.

I study the official-looking script again. "It seems they are asking for us to join a group of artists who will decide on the placement of the *David*."

⁂

IN A MEETING room of the Opera del Duomo, the air is filled with collective murmuring. My brother and I work our way into the small crowd of men. My eyes go instinctively to the ceiling, where an elaborate fresco imitates architecture; scattered throughout a pale blue sky with amorphous, pink clouds, *putti* stare at us from the spandrels. Quiet conversations, coughs, and laughter are amplified across the stone floor. Thanks to the large ceramic heaters in the corners of the room, my fingers begin to thaw.

I recognize many of my fellow guildsmen, their drab canvas shifts, paint-stained clogs, and scuffed leather vests an eyesore amidst the finely adorned cathedral consuls and brightly clothed representatives of the wool guild. Moths among butterflies. Master di Cosimo has cleaned himself up a bit, I see, with a deep rust-colored cape drawn over his round form. He is deeply engaged in a conversation with Master Davide Ghirlandaio, the brother of my boyhood teacher. So many familiar faces. Simone del Pollaiuolo the architect. Sandro Botticelli. Antonio and Giuliano da Sangallo. Andrea della Robbia. Pietro Perugino. Filippino Lippi. I see Salvestro the jeweler. Lodovico, maker of belts and saddles. My old associate Francesco Monciatto, leaning in close to talk with another woodworker, Bernardo dell Ciecha.

"Look!" my brother whispers in my ear. "Can you believe *he's* been invited?"

My eyes scan the room for the object of Francesco's surprise. Finally, they land on Master Leonardo. He presses through the crowd in a green velvet doublet and hat festooned with peacock feathers, hardly distinguishable from the dignitaries of the Arte della Lana, greeting fellow artists left and right.

And then, Andrea Sansovino, the man who nearly clinched the commission for the giant before I managed to convince Michelangelo to return home. He stands next to a window, his arms crossed. Perhaps a begrudging participant at this event? It seems that every artist of our city has been convened, whether they welcomed the opportunity or not. It is hard for me to imagine why Gonfaloniere Soderini thought my opinions worth seeking, but now I realize he has invited the majority of us in the city who are active in making things, even competitors for this very commission. I am one of many.

Michelangelo himself is notably missing. Where is he?

At a long table at one end of the room, several officials from the Opera del Duomo take their seats. Several of the men rap on the table with their fists or an open palm. Soon enough, the clamor quiets the echoing voices around the room.

"Signori!" the man at the center of the table cries. "*Attenzione!* Our proceedings shall begin." Across the room, men in small clusters now turn their attention to the front of the room. The men seat themselves along long, wooden benches that scrape across the tiles as we take our places. I watch a young notary seat himself at the end of the table with a pot of ink and a stack of parchment, pen suspended in the air.

"We have already seen the marvel that our native son, Michelangelo Buonarroti, has created for us," the man at the center of the table begins. "A work that has surpassed all of our highest expectations and dreams for how such a sculpture might be achieved. I need not convince all of you in this room, for you have seen it with your own eyes." The murmuring begins again, and two other men bang their fists on the wood to restore order. "From the outset," the man continues, "the *David* was destined to be a public sculpture. It was commissioned by the city, for the city, and would always stand somewhere in full view."

I think of the giant, the great boy-hero, still holed up in its three-sided box, still imprisoned behind the iron gates of the cathedral workyard for some four years. For the last two days, the *operai* have unlocked the gates so that those of us invited to be part of the committee to site the *David* might have one last look. But I have no need to look again. The sculpture is seared into my mind.

"Across our noble city," the man continues, "church façades, civic buildings, and public squares crawl with the bodies of thousands of stone figures. The question is, signori, where the *David* will fit in this cacophony of public works. It already stands out. The question, our mandate, is to decide where it will best fit in."

Already, I see that this meeting is to be nothing more than a farce, little more than a show of democracy when nothing in Florence is decided by consensus. All Michelangelo has to do is say where he wants the sculpture to stand, and they will agree.

But the man continues, scanning the crowd with piercing eyes. "As we begin our deliberations, I will ask those of you with a proposal for a location to please raise your hand. I will call on you to stand and make your case. Then we will discuss the advantages and disadvantages of such a location, and finally, we will call a vote. The cathedral fathers will make the ultimate decision. Who would make the first proposal?"

For a few moments that seem to last an eternity, silence ensues, punctuated only by the clearing of a throat. Who will cast themselves in the fire?

Then, the first herald of the Signoria stands, his small frame barely visible over the heads of the men.

"A decoy," I whisper, for I can only imagine this chief representative has been planted on purpose to steer the opening of the conversation. My brother nods.

"In my judgment," the small herald says, "there are two places that would be appropriate for such a statue. The first where the Judith is, that is, at the public entrance to the Palazzo Vecchio, where it could be easily viewed from the square. The second is in the middle of the courtyard of the Palazzo where Donatello's *David* stands." He pauses, then turns to make sure everyone can hear him. "The first because the Judith is a deadly sign and inappropriate in this place because our symbol is the cross and the lily, and anyway, it is not fitting that a woman should slay a man. But worst of all, it was placed in its position under an evil constellation because, since then, things have gone from bad to worse in our city, and Pisa has been lost."

His words bring on another uproar of murmuring, and another round of banging on the table to restore order. The herald continues. "Donatello's version of the *David*, in the courtyard, is an imperfect figure because the leg which is behind him is awkward; therefore I recommend that this new statue by the hand of Michelangelo be placed in one of these two places. But I prefer that of the Judith."

Finally, the herald sits, and there is a rumbling of words spoken among neighbors. The consul bangs on the table with his fist, then speaks again. "The notary has made note of the two suggestions—before the Signoria in place of the *Judith* of Master Donatello, and secondly, in the courtyard of the Signoria, in place of the *David* of Master Donatello."

I raise my hand but the official ignores me.

Next, I see Master Botticelli raise his hand tentatively. The official nods at him. "Master Botticelli."

"While those are good ideas," he says, "I would like to suggest that the sculpture by our friend Master Buonarroti might be best suited beneath the covered arcade of the Piazza della Signoria, which already houses many other large public sculptures. No matter what, it should remain in full sight," he argues, then quickly seats himself.

Leonardo da Vinci stands and the room falls silent. He hardly needs to raise his hand to command attention. "Signori," he says, casting a charming smile to his guildsmen. "To my mind, Master Botticelli has done well to suggest the loggia of the Signoria. There we might place it inside of a niche painted black."

"So that it will disappear," I whisper to my brother. Francesco nods in silent agreement with my assessment.

I see Giuliano da Sangallo stand next. "Master da Vinci is right, I think. Initially, I had in mind the corner of the Duomo, since there it would be seen by passersby. But since sculpture is a public thing, and marble is imperfect, being fragile and soft as a result of having been exposed to the weather, it does not seem to me that it would survive permanently in that location. For this reason, instead, I think the best place would be in the middle bay of the loggia, either centrally under its vault so it is possible to go around it; or closer inside near the wall, in the middle, with a niche behind it in the manner of a little chapel. If it is exposed to the weather it will quickly deteriorate, and it is better for it to be covered."

From the front table, I hear the frantic scratching of the notary's pen. Again, I raise my hand, but the official scans the room again with his eyes. Am I invisible?

Giovanni the fife player is next to raise his hand and stand, but he rejects Sangallo's proposal. "I would agree with what Giuliano has said, but only if the sculpture could be seen in its entirety in the central bay of the loggia. But there, the *David* cannot be seen in its entirety, signori. It is necessary to think of its purpose, its appearance, of the opening, of the wall, of the roof! All this is of consequence because it is necessary to walk around the sculpture in order to appreciate it. On the other side," he looks at Sangallo, "some wretch may attack it with a bar!"

Murmuring fills the air again.

"What is your proposal, sir?" the official at the front asks.

The fife player clears his throat. "Well, to my way of thinking, it seems better in the courtyard of the palace, as suggested by Francesco the Herald, in the place of Donatello's *David*. At least there it would be of great comfort to the roosters in the palace, being in a place worthy of such a statue."

The reference to Soderini and his entourage as roosters prompts laughter across the hall, and there is more rapping on the table to restore order.

Andrea Il Riccio is the next to stand. "I agree with the place of the loggia of the Signoria. At least there the sculpture would be well covered. It would be most highly regarded and most carefully watched against acts to damage it; and it is better to enclose it. But signori, I fear that such a thing in the piazza seems too threatening to we Florentines ourselves..." He hesitates. "I mean, that malevolent gaze of the *David*, I think it should not be directed to loyal citizens of our republic." Quickly, he sits down.

Signor Gallieno the embroiderer, stands next. "According to me, as I visualize it, and seeing the quality of the form of the statue, it would be better where the lion of the square is, having a base with ornamentation. This place is convenient for such a statue, and the lion might be placed at the side of the portal of the palace, where it might stand as a symbol of Florentine liberty and defense."

"Noted," says the official. "Anyone else?" I stand now, waving my hand above my head.

Then I see Master Ghirlandaio, whose uncle was my teacher, as well as Michelangelo's, stand. "In my opinion," he says, "Gallieno has indicated a place more worthy than any other. High on the balustrade of the palace is a congruous and suitable place for such a sculpture. Therefore, move the lion and make the *David* our communal symbol of Florentine defense instead."

"Why not in the square in front of the cathedral itself?" Cosimo Rosselli says, then quickly retakes his seat.

Francesco Monciatto stands next. "I believe everything is made for a specific purpose. To my understanding, the *David* was made to be placed on one of the outside pilasters or tribunes around the church. The reason one should not want to put it there I do not know, for there it appears to me it would serve well as an ornament. But since it is apparent that you have given up the first plan, then consider either the palace or the vicinity of the church. I defer to what the others say, since because of the shortness of time, I have been unable to properly consider the place that is most fitting."

I cannot hold my tongue any longer. I move into the aisle and blurt out, "These opinions... What is the point of this debate? It's... it's... ridiculous! Why not ask Master Michelangelo himself where to put the sculpture?"

My voice rings across the crowd. The room falls into complete silence. Surely they have thought of asking him before now? Of course I know the location Michelangelo desires, for he communicated it to me months ago when I first called him back home. He intended the statue as a symbol of our city and told me himself he wanted the sculpture sited before the Palazzo Vecchio. But now I hold my tongue.

It is Master di Cosimo who comes to my rescue. I watch him scratch the fine baby hair on top of his head. He stands. "Master Torni is right, perhaps. Might it not be appropriate for us to ask the creator for his input on where the sculpture belongs?"

My heart stops, whether from the sudden scrutiny of my peers or from the fact that di Cosimo has called me master, I do not know. My eyes dart around the room, trying to read the looks on people's faces.

Di Cosimo continues. "I think it is clear from the comments that this new sculpture of the *David* is to be understood as a symbol, perhaps even a symbol of Florence and we Florentines ourselves. In that case, it seems only reasonable to me that we might consult its maker on the matter of placement."

I see Filippino Lippi's head nod in agreement. "Yes," he says. "Why not ask the master of the *David?*"

Salvestro stands now. "I believe that he who has made it can give the best location, and I think it would be best in the vicinity of the palazzo. He who has made it, without a doubt, knows better than anyone else the place most suitable for the appearance and manner of the figure."

The man in charge of the meeting rubs his palm over his mouth. The two men flanking him lean in, conferring in whispers that echo through the room. Finally, he says, "Very well. It should be noted in the record that our committee shall consult with Michelangelo Buonarroti about the placement of the sculpture and will take that into consideration along with the desires of the cathedral fathers and the Signoria."

The suggestion has gone into writing. I press my back to wooden rungs of my seat, awash with relief that the proceedings are over. I know Michelangelo's will is stronger than anyone's here in the room. I know they will ask him, and of course I know the answer. If he makes his case, then the sculpture will be placed in front of the Palazzo Vecchio, the centerpiece of our city.

Above our heads, high up in the skinny tower of the Signoria, the old bells begin to clang the noon hour. On each loud peal of the bell, the image of the new sculpture in the Piazza della Signoria becomes clearer, more focused in my mind. With the sculpture placed in that location, Michelangelo will become revered. Forever, people will speak his name. The sculpture will live on. And as for Michelangelo himself, he will be remembered for generations to come. Loved. Adored. Admired. Remembered. Lauded. Celebrated.

Immortal.

⟆

AFTER THE PROCEEDINGS conclude, I go directly to Michelangelo's house with the news. I find him there in an agitated state.

Michelangelo's bedchamber looks more like mine than ever before. There are papers strewn around the room and a plate with an apple core and breadcrumbs littering the bed. A fat fly, drunk on the fermented juice of the apple, is buzzing around its core, landing, and then climbing slowly. I seat myself at a chair at a rickety table on the side of the room. Michelangelo is pacing back and forth, nearly making a line in the middle of the floor with the shuffle of his bare feet.

"And then Master da Vinci said he thought the sculpture should be put into a niche in the Loggia della Signoria, against a painted black background. Ha! That old crone." I thought Michelangelo would be relieved to hear about the committee meeting, but the more I tell him, the more agitated he becomes.

He shuffles back and forth and rubs his hand through his hair, gripping it with both fists. "He is only trying to mock me. Or make the sculpture invisible."

"Exactly my thoughts. But Little Michael Angel, I have told you they are going to ask for your opinion," I say. "You have nothing to worry about."

"I have no assurance they will ask me or that they will even listen to what I have to say." He continues to pace. "They did not even invite me. They could have asked me to start with and not come up with this silly game of soliciting everyone's opinion, bringing everyone in town to cast their judgement on my work!"

"I am not even sure how I got there myself," I say, shrugging my shoulders in his direction.

He whirls around. "How do you think you got there? I told them to include you on the list. I could not argue with Soderini. He was going to have this big show of artists no matter what I said. The only thing I could do was to recommend those who might speak in my favor."

I sit for a minute with the shock that he has chosen me.

On the table before us is a drawing of what seems to be another *David*, another man with broad chest and a slingshot in his hand.

"You are making another one?"

An exasperated gasp. "No," he says. "Again, Soderini. This French man—de Rohan is his name—is some sort of field marshal. He's got it in his head that he wants a *David* for himself. A bronze one. Against my better judgment I have agreed to do it, but it has caused me no end of aggravation."

I pick up the parchment and look at the muscles that he is drawn on the arms. "Then why do it?"

"How can I say no to Soderini and his crowd?" he demands. "The whole thing is ridiculous. They want a copy of Donatello's *David* in the courtyard. This French man… He has no idea what I have created inside that box in the cathedral workyard, and yet he says he wants his own."

I hold the drawing in my hand and immediately see the problem. In one instant, Michelangelo will make Donatello's *David* seem an antiquated joke of a sculpture. This French patron cannot even begin to understand what he has asked for and how ridiculous his own sculpture will look when the new *David* is unveiled.

"In the proceedings, they spoke of how the sculpture…"

"Again with the proceedings!" He dismisses me with the wave of his hand.

I continue, but he becomes more and more agitated. "I have an idea," he interrupts me. "They are selling delicious figs in the market at Santa Croce. Why don't you go down there and get some? Fill the whole bushel." From his pocket he produces a coin and tosses it on to the table where I am sitting. It skitters across the drawings of the French man's *David* and lands on top of them.

"Sure." I see he is tired of talking with me, or rather he is tired of hearing me talk. I pocket the coin and quietly exit the room. I have never been good at judging when people have had enough.

At the market, old women with their carts are bustling back and forth. The air is filled with the calls of the people selling fish and fruit. At one table, a man is extolling the virtues of cauliflower pulled from the country. Another is claiming that his family raises the best ducks on its farm in Tuscany.

It doesn't take long for me to find the fig seller. She is a sour-faced woman whose face looks like a ripe, old fig itself. I exchange Michelangelo's coin for a webbed sack of the plump purple fruits.

The market is closing, and darkness begins to fall. When I return to Michelangelo's street, the darkness has already covered the alley. His house lies in shadows, the candles already snuffed. Confused, I look up to make sure I have the right house, but I see the familiar stone decoration above the door and the bronze doorknocker in the shape of a lady's hand.

Normally I would walk right in, but when I try, the latch is locked. I use the brass door knocker and knock a few times. Silence. I bang on the door with my fist. I feel anger well up in my breast, and I glare at the sack of figs. Why didn't he just say he was sick of hearing me talk? Why didn't he just ask me to go home? Why did he send me on a fool's errand when he just wanted to wallow in his angst?

I dump the figs on the ground before his doorway so anyone walking in or out will squish them under their feet. I yell up to the window, "Thank you, my loyal friend!"

There is still no response. I find myself in a silent alley all alone.

"And keep your damned figs!"

❧

I DO NOT know what becomes of the figs scattered outside of Michelangelo's locked door, but the weeks stretch out before us: he holed up in his house, the whole of Florence waiting to see where the giant will take its place.

"You realize Michelangelo is never going to thank you for what you have done." Lucia watches me as she sews the edge of a cloth, part of the meager trousseau she is preparing for the day when she will leave for the bookbinder's home. Around the house, her things are being organized and packed. Her pens, brushes, and small tools have been stacked inside a discarded wooden crate, a poor excuse for a dowry chest. Still, she only thinks of me, of my own welfare. When I don't respond, she tries again.

"If you are waiting for his approval or his gratitude, you will wait forever." Her eyes follow me as I pace the kitchen. "Believe me, I know," she says, and her words stop me in my tracks. I see now that my sister has also given up on the idea that he might occupy our world. She accepted it even before I could. "Michelangelo will never bring you satisfaction," she insists before casting her eyes to the floor. "Only longing."

"That is easy for you to say," I respond, "when you have the luxury of staying inside the house. If you walk out of here," I say, gesturing to the door, "then you have only to walk five paces before you hear his name uttered. There is no more interesting subject on the streets, I assure you."

And there it is. The truth. For weeks, I have tried to rid my mind of him, to wash my hands of Michelangelo. Meanwhile, no one in town can talk of anything else. It is as if all of Florence has taken one big breath, holding it until the colossus breaks free of its box. Meanwhile, my brother and I spend hours scraping palettes, sketching ladies' faces, dabbing pigment onto a piece of canvas, panel, or wall. Quietly, we toil. No one, it seems, takes notice.

Perhaps my sister is right. I must learn to pursue my work out from under his shadow. It is just as well. I do not wish to see him or speak with him. "Understood. But I do not think it is right that he should achieve such wide recognition at the same time that he is an irascible, ungrateful recipient of such attention. Doesn't he realize the fortunate situation he has found himself in?"

But Lucia only smirks at me, teasing me with her expression. I realize that I have not seen things clearly. As much as I have focused on my own shortcomings, have I not fully understood that Michelangelo questioned his own worthiness, his own worth?

"He is not your enemy, you know," she says, and looks at me sideways.

I scuff the toe of my shoe along a crack in the floor. "No?"

She shakes her head. "You do not need another enemy, Jacopo. You, my brother, you are enemy enough for yourself."

The room is engulfed in heavy silence. Then, the door swings open, and our brother dashes in, his face flushed.

"The giant is coming out!" he blurts. "I saw it. They have taken down the Judith already, and there is a new platform at the entrance to the Palazzo Vecchio."

So the colossus will stand before the Signoria. "Then he has gotten his wish," I say.

"Yes," says Francesco. "They have announced that the giant will leave the cathedral workyard on the feast of Saint Florian. It's coming out at midnight. I think they were trying to temper the excitement, but it is too late. Word is already spreading around the city like a disease."

PART IV

THE PAINTER AND
THE SCULPTOR

Florence

1504

*I have gone drudging about through all Italy, borne every shame,
suffered every hardship, worn my body in every toil, put my life into
a thousand dangers, solely to help the fortunes of my house.*

Michelangelo Buonarroti, in a letter to his brother Giovan Simone

AT MIDNIGHT ON a full moon in May, the marble statue is finally revealed.

The moon hangs high in the sky, a great, white ball making wavering reflections along the Arno, lighting the streets as if it were day. A loud ruckus rises through the streets, the voices of rowdy men and boys, even women, shouting in the alleys as they make their way toward the gates of the cathedral workyard to see the spectacle. I watch children playing in the streets long past bedtime, and stray dogs skittering across the cobblestones as if they sense the nervous energy in the city. I watch wisps of clouds rush by as stars appear in the eerie aura of moonlight.

"Midnight seems a strange time to unveil a sculpture," Lucia says. She loops one hand under my elbow and another under Francesco's, so that the three of us might stay attached as the crowd grows in number. Together, we wend our way toward the cathedral to witness the spectacle as the chants grow louder.

"Long past the curfew," Francesco says. "The authorities probably wanted to avoid a public riot."

"They have failed," I say. The three of us pass a pair of drunks staggering through the crowd, hurling insults at a rouged woman soliciting from the door of a thinly disguised brothel. When we turn the corner near the Baptistery, we find that already, a crowd has pushed its way before the gates of the workyard. Men and women are pushing and shoving, joking and chatting. We find a spot near a wall across from the entrance.

I huff in amazement, for even after everything I have done over the past four years related to this statue, my heart fills with anticipation as I watch the hulking stonemasons guarding the iron doors of the cathedral workyard. Will this giant be all that it is rumored to be? We spy a group of workmen appearing alongside Michelangelo's wooden enclosure. The street clamor settles to a low murmur as the crowd presses forward. A lady alongside us lifts her young daughter high on her chest to try to catch a view through the bars of the workyard gate.

Then, Michelangelo himself appears. Even in the darkness, he is recognizable for his dingy smock, his greasy hair, and his stature, small yet somehow intimidating.

"Look!" Lucia presses against my back, standing on her toes to get a better look. Around us, the murmur in the crowd lowers to a hush.

The men gather around with their sledgehammers. It only takes a few moments. The wooden barriers of the box fall to the dust, and the sculpture is set free. They have destroyed the box that has hidden Michelangelo and his giant away from us for so long.

Now I see that an enormous contraption of beams, ropes, and pulleys has been erected around the sculpture. It looks complicated, as though someone has combined a gallows with the loading arms of the merchant docks on the river. Just inside the cathedral gates, a small group of laborers is slathering grease on some two dozen smoothly hewn logs.

The moving will go slowly.

For hours, my brother, sister, and I watch the crowd grow louder, rowdier. One of the men from the taverns elbows me in the side. Another produces a deck of cards. Proudly, I manage to refrain from joining them. Nearby, a ragtag game of *calcio* breaks out. Hours pass. Men lace their arms around one others' necks, singing the old chants of neighborhood bravado in unison. Someone illegally sets off a firework in a nearby square, a brief explosion of light and noise. No one in our city is at home in their beds.

After several hours, the glowing moon begins to sink in the sky. At last, it seems that the statue might be ready to roll out of the workyard, but there is a problem. The block and its contraption are too tall to fit through the opening of the gate.

"This is going to take some time," Francesco says with a yawn. "I'm going home to get some sleep, brother."

"I'm going, too," Lucia says. "We can come back again tomorrow to see if they've managed to get it out of the workyard. Come home with us, Jacopo."

But I'm not going anywhere. I do not feel the need for sleep, for eating, for drink. I feel the blood pumping faster through my veins, and I am filled with anxiety as if it were my own work trying to make its way through the gates. My siblings coax me one more time, then I watch them slip into the crowd and disappear. Alone, I push my way closer to the cathedral gates, where the disappearance of a few other onlookers has made the space for a better view.

☙

IT IS HOURS later, but still before the light of dawn, when a group of stonemasons is secured to break through the lintel of the gate. The stones fall to the ground, and the crowd cheers. At last, the statue appears in its full form. The *David* begins to roll out of the cathedral workyard.

At least two dozen uniformed officers do their best to push back the burgeoning crowd, as all of us watch the giant sculpture inch slowly forward, step by step, suspended in the air by ropes and pulleys.

Michelangelo has not seen me, but now, I have an unobstructed view of him. In the moonlight, I watch his eyes scan the crowd. Anyone unfamiliar might think he is scowling, but I see the nervousness, the anxiety written across his face. With every inch the sculpture takes forward, Michelangelo takes a step, a step toward the pushing crowds, toward the cheering, the excitement, the singing, the mayhem. His piercing eyes scan the high windows of the buildings bordering the square, as if he is watching for an enemy who might launch an attack from above.

No sooner has the idea of an attacker crossed my mind than I feel a great rain of dirt and dust across the back of my neck. Rocks. Someone is throwing rocks. I hear several small stones pelt the dust, scattering dirt and pebbles in the piazza like spilled grain. The crowd surges sideways, nearly knocking me to the ground. Why on earth would someone take that kind of risk? It has not been so long since we saw a man hanged on the walls of the Bargello for throwing dung at Our Lady of the Street Corner Shrine.

I turn around just in time to see a cluster of youths, boys no older than fourteen, slinking along the wall of a building bordering the square. One of the young men is clapping dust from his hands. I see another reach down into the cracks of the cobbles, dislodging a decent-sized stone. He's going to do it again, I think.

In a burst of energy, I rush my way into the crowd toward the boys. "Stop!" I yell. "What the hell are you doing?" I put my hands on the boy with the rock. He is bigger than I thought, already taller than I am. For a moment, we circle one another like a pair of street fighters. Just as I think we might come to blows, I feel a surge of power on my right side, and I am knocked to the ground. A sharp pain in my hip, my elbow. But I am not the only one. I turn to see two officers of the *guardia* tackle the boy to the ground. The other youths scatter, disappearing into the anonymity of the crowd.

For a few moments I sit stunned on the cobblestones, until a man standing nearby helps me clamber to my feet. I am only left to wonder whether Michelangelo has witnessed any of it.

❧

IT TAKES FOUR days for the *David* to move from the cathedral to its new place before the façade of the Palazzo Vecchio. Some forty brawny men work in rotation around the clock, employed to roll the logs joined beneath the wooden contraption, to grease them and move them back to front as the sculpture inches its way toward the piazza.

By that time, I have heard that four boys have been prosecuted for throwing stones. The *guardia* reveals their families' names: Martelli; Spini; Gherardini; Panciatichi. All four Medici partisans. Whispers on the street suggest their motives were political. I think they were simply impulsive children.

Most of the time, Michelangelo walks slowly alongside the great rocking, hulking colossus, both of them surrounded by a new round of officers who seem to me ultimately powerless to protect the sculpture. Occasionally, Michelangelo disappears for a time, perhaps to eat or sleep. As for myself, I have not slept or eaten. Apart from taking a piss in an alley, I have followed the giant every step of the way. I follow the sculpture's slow progress through the alleys to the Piazza della Signoria, some five city blocks to the south of the cathedral. I am swept up in the frenzy, unable to pull myself away.

Above the heads of the crowds in the street, the sculpture rocks slightly, side to side, forward and back. Antonio da Sangallo and his brother Giuliano have designed the contraption with slipknots that squeak and tighten under the weight of the marble, allowing it to swing gently as it moves slowly, ever forward.

Around the base, the *guardia* make room for the sculpture to inch forward, pressing people back from the rolling logs. All around us there is litter in the streets. Above, there is chaos, as people have gathered to watch the giant make its slow progress. Men, women, and children gawk from their upper-story windows and rooftops, cheering, waving dishrags, clapping, singing as the colossus inches slowly past their homes. Several industrious residents are collecting coins to allow people into the upper floors and roofs of their homes for a better view.

At first, I felt compelled to press my fingers in my ears so I would not hear all the accolades they heaped on the giant, on its maker. But by midday on the second day, hundreds, maybe thousands, of people have gathered around the statue, filled with wonder and awe. Eventually I become immune, and instead find myself wrapped up in the melee. I have sang and yelled so much that my voice is gone.

I push my way to the market hall of the Orsanmichele. I jog up the stairway, into the upper levels of the old building, so I can get a better view of the statue from a small terrace. I find a few of Master di Cosimo's assistants already clustered there, pressing on one another's shoulders. From this vantage point,

I can see the colossus moving through the street from above. I can pick out Michelangelo, too. The crowd swirls around him, around the contraption moving the sculpture. Residents stand in their doorways, clapping and cheering, placing two fingers in their mouths to whistle as it passes. A man has brought out a horn and is blaring in a deafening blast. People join the ruckus, then drop off, then return. The entire affair turns into a multi-day parade, a makeshift festival of barely controlled mayhem. Toward midnight on the second night, the crowd thins enough that I find myself walking only a few feet behind Michelangelo. If he knows I am there, he shows no sign.

"The head is too big," a voice behind me. "And also the hands."

"And the *pisello* too small," another one says. A flurry of laughter.

"Consider that it was originally going to be up high in the tribune. A different view."

The criticisms swirl around me, a chaotic tangle of commentary. Opinions. Criticisms. But mostly, people cheer or stand in awe as the sculpture passes.

At some point, for I have lost track of time, Lucia appears. "Jacopo, come home. Look at you! You're a mess." She brushes her hand across the front of my shift.

"I'm fine," I say, but it emerges as a whisper. I have lost my voice to two days of singing, whooping, chanting along with the crowds.

"Please," she says, "you will make yourself sick," but I don't let the sculpture out of my sight.

"You need to sleep, *fratello*," another voice says. "Come home with me." My brother. I know he has my best interest at heart, but this is important.

Then, Filippo Dolciati. "Buffo is taking on another contender from Arezzo in the piazza near the Porco tavern," he tells me, but not even a chance to double my coins lures me away. How can I leave at this point?

At noon on the fourth day, the *David* arrives in the Piazza della Signoria.

༄

WHEN I FINALLY sleep, I sleep for days.

༄

FRACTURED SOUNDS AND smells creep through my wooden shutters. Boys call to one another from windows across the alley. The wool looms and warping machines down the street clack their incessant rhythm. Mule hooves clop along the muddy cobblestones. Bread is baking in a neighbor's fire. The fishmonger curses her husband's name. A baby cries.

From the lower level of the house, I can hear the bookbinder latch and unlatch the door. My sister's whispers. Her muffled laugh. The clang of copper pots being put away in the cupboard.

When I open my eyes, I see my brother, sitting in a rickety chair alongside a beam of light that has found its way through a crack in the shutter. He pulls a nub of charcoal over a piece of parchment spread across his knee; he is lost in concentration.

Another time, it is my sister in the chair, pulling an embroidery needle through a swath of fabric. "I have brought you some water, Jacopo."

I close my eyes and surrender again to the black abyss.

⁂

HUNGER FINALLY DRAWS me from my bed.

After a meal of stewed mushrooms with bits of pork, Francesco squeezes my shoulders and leads me out of the house, into the searing daylight. We walk in companionable silence through the alleys toward our workshop. All is quiet. After the tumult of the giant's unveiling, our city has gone back to its normal rhythms. A shop owner sweeps litter from her stoop with a broom of twigs.

At the doorway to our workshop, I pause. Francesco waves his hand. There is a new easel constructed of fresh lumber. A stack of panels, one newly prepared with gesso. A long roll of paper.

In one part of my mind, I think it is amazing that anyone might call me a master, that I have my own place to work, for I do not feel that I have earned it, after all. On the other, I look at the space, dust-flecked light filtering through a window. The workshop is devoid of assistants, devoid of activity. Devoid of art.

On the table, there is only one work, a large series of parchment squares that have been glued together, a cartoon for a wall of frescoes. I watch my brother roll it from one side and put it away. But before the images disappear into the roll, I recognize a few familiar compositions: the folds of the robe of Saint Peter; the hand of an angel; a dove. It is the cartoon for my part of the fresco cycle at San Pier Martire, the project that burdened me beyond all reason, the one work I could not find it within me to complete.

"While you were sleeping," Francesco says, "I finished your fresco squares at San Pier Martire."

IT IS THE announcement of a new public competition that launches me back into the streets again.

"There is already a crowd outside Santa Maria Novella," Francesco tells me, steering me toward the church on the western edge of town.

"They are waiting... to see a drawing?"

"A *cartone*. Worth seeing," Francesco shrugs. "At least that's what I've heard."

Over dinner the night before, Francesco filled in the details. The Signoria sought to bring Michelangelo and Master da Vinci into the very same room, my brother told Lucia and me, his eyes wide and his hands gesturing wildly at our dinner table. The Sala del Gran Consiglio, one of the largest, most important rooms of the old town hall. Each man will paint his own battle scene on opposite walls of this great audience hall, Francesco explained. In preparation, each artist has been given ample space to prepare the giant paper *cartone* that will form the template for his design.

As for Master da Vinci, they've given the old man a disused refectory alongside the church of Santa Maria Novella. Michelangelo, on the other hand, has been provided with a large, former hospital hall at Sant'Onofrio, in a rundown section of town across the Arno. Each has been allotted a large budget for assistants, for paper, for glue. They have each been given months to prepare their drawings, Francesco has said, and Soderini has even claimed publicly that this commission will determine who is the greatest artist in the world.

Soon enough, we see that the rumors of the crowd before Santa Maria Novella are true. In the disorganized, murmuring queue, we recognize the familiar faces of some of our guildsmen, fellow painters and sculptors crowded among tradesmen, families, impatient children. Michelangelo Buonarroti is nowhere in sight, of course. It's Master da Vinci's name on everyone's lips now, and I am left to wonder whether everyone in the city has forgotten about our giant so soon. We file into the line behind several men I recognize from the taverns.

"L'Indaco," Paolo the blacksmith turns to us. My brother and I nod and tap fists with him. Many guildsmen call my brother and me by the same name, so we respond in unison. "Coming to get an eyeful, I see." The other men in the line chuckle.

"I suppose we're already on to a new spectacle," I say.

"I heard Master da Vinci has set aside all his other commissions," he says. "The monks at Santissima Annunziata aren't happy he hasn't finished the altarpiece they commissioned years ago."

The man next to him in line pipes up. "I heard that Francesco del Giocondo is planning to bring legal action against Master da Vinci because he hasn't finished a portrait of his wife."

The unruly line of people surges forward and we press into the cool shadows of the refectory. People fill the voids left by those exiting the great Sala del Papa. Finally, we catch a glimpse of what we have come to see.

A great drawing, covering many hundreds of sheets of paper glued together and pinned to the wall, is displayed for everyone to admire. The drawing progresses across several giant sheets of paper that had been fastened together to create a wall-sized preparatory cartoon. Guards from the Signoria have been stationed at each end of the cartoon to keep the crowd back, unsuccessfully.

"How could he be expected to work in these conditions?" Francesco mutters into my ear above the din. But there is no sign of the artist at all; only a jostling, admiring crowd—a crowd that suddenly seems to fade away as I lay eyes on the giant cartoon.

A swirling, chaotic mass of horses and men, some injured, others holding lances. The very heart of battle, an agonizing, horrific entanglement of human and animal bodies.

"A battle scene," I murmur back to my brother.

"Yes," Francesco says. "Look, the fight for the standard. The Florentine soldiers are taking the Milanese flag just before our victory at Anghiari."

"You suppose Buonarrotti's version looks anything like it?" Paolo the blacksmith presses in, breathing down my neck.

"We'll never know," Francesco says, "right, brother? You won't find any crowd like this over there. I would be surprised if he allowed any assistants at all."

"Don't think we can go and see it?" Paolo pushes.

"No chance," another man says. "Brother Bartolomeo told me that the Signoria has made its first payment and that paper has been delivered to the site to make the cartoon. No one else is in there. You saw how he worked on that giant."

"Well, Master da Vinci's seen it, at least that's what I heard. He's saying the Buonarroti created a scene with men so muscular they look like nothing more than a sack of walnuts." The other men howl with laughter.

"We must try to go see Buonarroti's work," Francesco says as we exit the monastery refectory.

"What for?" I say. "The old man has already said it probably looks like a sack of walnuts."

"You know he's only jealous," Francesco laughs.

Of course, I know it's not a sack of walnuts. It will be a work of genius and I am not sure I am ready to see it. More than that, I'm not ready to see *him*.

❧

THE RENTED, MULE-DRAWN carriage has been loaded with Lucia's meager trousseau: a discarded crate filled with our mother's lace, a set of copper wine cups from our grandmother's kitchen, a dozen books bound with parchment pages decorated by our father's hand. On top of this small hoard, Lucia has carefully folded the table and bed linens she has sewn or embroidered over her months of waiting. In another crate, she has carefully arranged her brushes, pens, and paper.

In less than an hour, we will arrive at the bookbinder's door. Francesco and I will reach for our sister and lift her from the carriage. By then, it will all be in the past—the blessing of our parish priest, the small gifts exchanged, the sharing of wine and bread at our meager feast, the gold rings hammered by Il Riccio the goldsmith. The entourage of neighbors will envelop the door to the bookbinding shop, and a round of cheers will rise into the air. Lucia will step over the wooden threshold. She will no longer be ours.

For now, she sits alongside Battistini, her arm looped through his, as the carriage bumps and rattles through the narrow streets toward his house by the river. From my position walking behind the carriage, I can't see her face, but in my heart, I know she is beaming.

They are my finest clothes: an old gown not worn since we buried our father, which is therefore clean. A pair of leather clogs I have polished with oil, but which are still stained with paint drips and the filth of the street. My sister wears a velvet-trimmed gown our neighbor has altered for her, surrounded by garlands of flowers our neighbors' daughters have strung together for the occasion. My brother and I trail behind the carriage, carrying the ends of the long strands of flowers.

It is a meager beginning, but no matter. My sister is happy. She will be welcomed by a loving husband, children to raise, the honest work of her hands. A life full of work and family. It is all she wants, and I am happy for her. Best of all, she will finally be free of caring for the likes of me.

Behind the carriage, Francesco and I look silly, I think, holding onto strings of flower garlands, which do little to mask the odor of the horses. Behind us, the bookbinder's sons follow. The oldest holds the hand of the youngest, and the third son skips and straggles behind, darting in zigzagged patterns, picking up small pebbles between the cobbles. Taking advantage of the fact that his father is preoccupied, he bats at a birdcage with a stick. The second son, Bartolomeo, trails close behind us. As part of our contract, my brother and I have promised to teach him the art of painting fresco, panels, and canvas.

We pass the Bargello, that hulking palace where I have seen countless bodies hanging from the battlements. But today, there is only celebration around us. Children skip alongside the carriage. From high windows along the street, people whistle and call out their well-wishes to the newlyweds. A shopkeeper rushes out and presses a container of honeyed almonds into Lucia's hand.

Today of all days, I should feel joy. I should feel pride for my family, satisfaction that Lucia has gotten her wish, at last. Peace that she has found love and will continue the work of her heart. But as we proceed toward the bookbinder's house, fear and anxiety begin to well up from somewhere deep inside. I am ashamed to admit how fully I have depended on my sister for all these years. I feel selfish. Ugly. Ashamed.

"Don't forget to pick the white blooms off the basil in the garden," she told me, just before we left the house for the marriage celebrations. "Otherwise it will taste bitter. And remember to use up the cured pork before it goes bad."

"But Francesco is a lousy cook," I teased her. "Surely we will only live on stale bread and swill."

"I rather think you know how to boil an egg," she said, reminding me of di Cosimo's daily regimen. "And anyway, it's about time that you two start doing your own laundry!"

"I can't promise that we will stay very clean," I said, "but we will manage."

Suddenly, my sister's brow knits into deep lines and she reached for my hand. "Jacopo. I do worry about you."

I only shrugged and sighed loudly, making a valiant effort not to cry. "I'll be fine. Plus, I'll make sure Francesco is here to do all the work."

She made a clucking sound, as if she knows my brother and I can never recognize what she has done for us. "You will have your hands full."

"No, *you* will have your hands full, Lucia."

"I rather think that caring for four boys plus a husband will be easy compared to caring for you." She pushed my shoulder, and I feigned injury, stumbling sideways. She pulled me back, and then stopped and grabbed the front of my gown.

"I am only a neighborhood away," she whispered, then pecked a kiss on my cheek. "Don't forget." Then she walked away. I hoped that she couldn't see that my eyes stung.

Now, around the carriage, neighbors and passersby have joined our procession, running alongside the creaking wheels, whooping, clapping, and offering their congratulations. As we turn into the area around the Mercato Vecchio, a group of patrons at the Porco tavern break out into a song. My sister and her new husband laugh and wave.

At last, the carriage turns into the Piazza della Signoria. Dozens of people are now following us, and the crowd rises into a roar of a communal song.

Before us, the giant. Around the clock, there are armed guards to make sure no one else tries to vandalize it.

My eyes follow the veins of marble, up to the intense face of the boy-hero, the one whose barely carved eye I peered into all those months ago. He is frozen in the moment when he spots his terrible enemy. It seems as if he is holding his breath. In the flash of a second, he will lower the sling from his shoulder and load the rock. A young warrior, apprehensive yet ready. Not some god of centuries past, but a modern hero for all of Florence. A small man doing something larger than life.

And whereas seeing the sculpture in progress might have made me feel like I myself was a small man who might do something big, today, as I walk my sister to her new home, I feel small again in the face of this massive achievement.

The *David* stands strong and defiant, facing Siena, where Michelangelo's frustrated patrons, the Piccolomini, still wait for his drawings—for my drawings. But *David* glares past Siena toward Rome, where the pope stands looking at his beautiful marble sculpture carved by a boy from Florence, and the Medici family resides in exile, perhaps planning their return. *David* stands in a posture of rest, but his brow is knitted in an expression of ferocious uncertainty. His fate is as unsure as our own, as mine, as all of ours in Florence.

But I am compelled to admit that this sculpture seems to have surpassed any others, even those of antiquity and perhaps of the whole of history. Michelangelo has taken the old theme of the biblical David and made him young and vulnerable, passionate and strong, ready to move. He is captured in the instant before the battle. David, at the same time an Adam and a Hercules. A man made in God's image. God made flesh. A stone that seems to breathe life. He is a victorious man, but only with the help and grace of his creator. He is unspeakably beautiful.

And there is a new word whispered in the streets. Few are talking about the sculpture when they say it. They only speak of its maker, the stooped little man—my tormented friend—whom they are starting to call *Il Divino*.

⁂

BETWEEN MY FEET, I watch the Arno rush by in a torrent.

From the railing of the Ponte Vecchio, I see that even though I slicked them with oil before the wedding procession, my clogs are still stained with paint and grime. I have loosened my collar and sit on the railing in my finest clothes.

My brother has returned home from the festivities, but by some twist, I find myself sitting once again on the railing of the Old Bridge, just like we did when we were kids, when I was trying to trick all those foreign visitors that Michelangelo might jump.

But this time it is no joke.

It would be easy to jump, I think, to sink slowly to the bottom as my lungs fill with green, silted water.

Just as when we were kids, I stare down into the water and imagine the fish swimming there. On the edge near the tanneries,

I see carts stacked high with tanned hides. I see the long, green grass clinging to the bottom of the brown riverbed and flowing swiftly southward toward Pisa, toward the coast. The day has turned hot, and I hear the cicadas making their infernal noises from the branches of the trees.

I think about my father then, when he was alive and what he expected us to do, and how I have failed to do it. My sister has been successfully married off to a husband better than I could have imagined. My brother will go on to be prosperous with or without me. And me? I am still here sitting on the bridge. In my mind's eye, I imagine letting the heft of my body sink, the euphoria of a moment's free fall, then the cool water, refreshing at first, then closing over my head.

It would be a relief, surely, for my sister and my brother, who would no longer have to live with my burdens. My sister would no longer have to worry about how I will take care of things all by myself. My brother will be free to go off into the countryside and pursue his livelihood without wondering how he will take care of his new burden, his older brother.

I push my hands into the stone railing and feel its cool hardness under my palms. I close my eyes and begin to heave my body forward. I feel the time suspended on the air.

"L'Indaco."

It takes me a moment to decide whether the sound is coming from my own head or from somewhere else outside of it.

"L'Indaco."

I hear it again. This time the gravelly voice is unmistakable. Just as I open my eyes and turn my head I feel his hands on me, pushing me forward and pulling me back, just as when we were boys sitting on this very bridge, teetering in that suspended moment when we didn't know if we would fall or be saved.

Does he want me to live, or will he help me die? Why will I bargain for life? What is there yet to live for? I wonder if he has the answer.

I feel him pull me back into his chest, his arms hard and tight around me. I open my eyes.

"Idiot," he chuckles, but I see his expression waver. Has he sensed my uncertainty? I swing my legs around, placing the bottoms of my feet solidly on the bridge.

"I have been looking for you," Michelangelo says.

"You have?"

"I caught sight of you at the front of the marriage procession, but then you disappeared. Come, you silly ox." He pulls me up to standing.

"What are you doing here?" I stumble, still reeling from the vertiginous feeling of sitting on the railing of the bridge. "I thought you were busy with that *cartone* for the town hall, anyway."

"A stupid project." For a fleeting moment, he casts his eyes southward, in the direction of Sant'Onofrio, the workshop the Signoria has given him to work on his plan for the town hall frescoes. Then he turns his eyes back to me. "I thought it was about time you showed me that workshop of yours. And anyway," he says, "I have news."

IN THE DIM workshop, I rummage through the shelves for an old bottle of my father's homemade wine, nearly turned to vinegar. I pour two glasses. We toast, then grimace as the sour liquid sears our throats.

"You are leaving for Rome." I study his face to make sure he's telling the truth. "Now?"

He runs a charcoal-stained hand through his hair. "I am done with this... this nonsense," he says, gesturing toward the door as if dismissing the entire world beyond my workshop.

I struggle to understand. "But why would you leave this all behind? You have the attention—the favor—of the entire Signoria. Of Soderini himself! Perhaps you already know that they are calling you the Divine One."

Now he dismisses me, too, with the wave of a hand.

"And the battle scene in the Palazzo Vecchio? The competition with Old Man da Vinci. You're just... walking away?"

He huffs, and I don't know whether it's meant to be a laugh or a scoff instead. "I'm *especially* walking away from that mess," he says.

For a moment I am speechless. I rake a wooden stool across the floor and sink onto it. "Well," I say, "at least you have made enough to live comfortably in Rome."

He shakes his head. "His Holiness will provide me with food and accommodations, of course. But otherwise, I am leaving for Rome empty-handed."

I sputter on the second sip of wine. "What? How is that possible?"

"Everything I have made I owe to my father and my family. We have also invested in two farms in the countryside. While I am gone, that and the fruits of those lands will sustain them. All those brothers of mine."

He begins to pace the studio, taking in the dusty shelves, the sparse walls. He runs his hands over our cartoons for the new fresco, then thumbs through a new set of drawings my brother and I have made for another fresco Francesco has secured for us.

"You had the magic in your hands all along," he says, turning away from the drawings to look around the workshop. "Look at this studio. You are deserving."

"You exaggerate—"

"No," he says. "I am serious. Do you want to know the truth? I have always been envious of you, envious of any guildsman who could just set up a workshop and hire people to work for them. I have never been able to do that. I make a big show of working alone, but things would be simple if I could just... do it in a normal way."

"Normal," I say. "Never heard anyone use that word in relation to your work."

He huffs himself down on the stool at my worktable, and I pour another glass of the soured wine. "Perhaps you are right." Somehow, a veil of angst has been lifted; we reminisce of old friends, the way our city used to be. We toast to my sister and her new family. The sun sets, and the workshop is cast into darkness. I empty the bottle and light a wick in an oil lamp.

"I am leaving you these." He places a sketchbook full of drawings he prepared, perhaps years ago, for that nagging commission in Siena. "They might help you."

I sit in silent shock, having never known him to share a drawing with another artist. "I don't know what to say." I run my finger over a delicate drawing of an architectural frame for a large-scale sculpture.

"Say you won't make it look like it was drawn by that stupid Sansovino," he says.

"My father always said I should draw at least three pages each day," I say, thumbing through Michelangelo's evolving designs on the Sienese altarpiece.

"Your father was a wise man."

"He also said the purpose of art is to make us immortal. Through it, we live forever."

"Does it make us immortal? Hm." Michelangelo's dark eyes look into the shadows of the workshop. "I do not know if my work will bring me immortality, L'Indaco." He meets my eyes. "Yes, art continues after we die. That much is true. But while we are here, it makes us a living. More than that. It brings us life."

He walks over to the narrow, wooden cot that stands under a darkened window. He sits on the edge of it, then stretches out and groans, pressing his arm over his eyes. "I haven't slept in days," he says.

I bring the last swill of wine in my glass, and heave myself onto the floor next to the cot. I sit on the stones, my back to him, listening to him breathe low and heavy. For a moment, I think he has already fallen asleep, but then I feel his hand light on my shoulder, and he speaks. "Do you want to know the truth, L'Indaco? I have always been envious of those who could paint. I could never be a painter like you are, as much as I might want to."

I huff. "You're lying."

"Maybe a little bit," he says. I see the corner of his mouth rise in a half-smile.

"What about the *tondo* you made for the Doni family? Or that little commission you got for the Battle of Cascina in the Palazzo Vecchio? That doesn't count as painting?"

He swats his hand again. "The whole thing is a joke. A public farce. Soderini just wants us to do his tricks like little monkeys on strings. No, I am done. Now, finally, I have a commission from His Holiness in Rome waiting for me. A giant sculptural tomb with some thirty or forty figures."

"But what about your other commissions? If not the Battle of Cascina, what about the twelve other marble sculptures for the tribunes, the contract in Siena?"

"When the Holy Father calls you to his side, what can you say, L'Indaco? I am going."

Once again I hear his breath heave, as he dances to the edge of deep slumber. Then he catches his breath. "L'Indaco," he says and reaches for my hand. I feel his bony, muscular fingers squeeze my shoulder. I place my hand over his, feeling his rough, callous knuckles. I stare into the dark shadows of the workshop.

"All the same," he says, "I have not been fair to you. You have been there to support me all along, but I have become... occupied. I neglected you."

His breath deepens into a ragged, regular rhythm. Soon enough, he is snoring loudly. Outside the window, the crickets have begun their nighttime symphony. Michelangelo's breathing and the chirping of the insects lulls me into a deep calm. For a long time I sit on the cold stone floor beside him, feeling his hand and watching the muscles in his face twitch and relax. I am running these things over in my head. After a while, I stretch my body out on the stone floor. Both of us succumb to the sleep of utter exhaustion.

When I awaken, the sun is high in the sky and Michelangelo is gone. Sunday. The streets are quiet except for the tolling noon bell at Santa Croce. I sit up and press my hand into the crumpled blanket of the cot where he lay. It is cold. I can still smell his unique scent, a combination of sweat and marble dust that hangs around him like a cloud.

Both of us have been running, I realize, chasing dreams that may have been only fantasies. We have not stopped to question what they mean, only longed to leave behind an imprint of our work, our existence in the world.

PART V

THE LETTER

Florence
May 1508

The stone unhewn and cold
Becomes a living mold,
The more the marble wastes,
The more the statue grows.

From a sonnet by Michelangelo Buonarroti

I UNLOCK MY workshop in the pale light of a spring morning to find a letter addressed to me, stuffed by a careless messenger under the crack in the door.

Even as I stare at the sealed parchment between my paint-
stained shoes, I recognize his handwriting. It has always been elegant and sure, containing all the confidence of someone trained
in copying ancient texts in the lushness of Medici gardens, script
so far removed from my own crude, incompetent scrawl. The
color of the ink has already turned brown after days in the courier's bag.

I set my bag of brushes down and pick up the folded parchment. I run my hand over the wax seal, a red cross I have seen
on other pieces of mail that issue from Rome. I feel my heart beat
faster. As I run my stained fingers over Michelangelo's looping
script, I feel his crackling energy, his presence, his fire.

But I no longer feel his burden.

As much as I toiled to bring him to Florence all those years
ago, it was only after he left for Rome that I was able to break
myself free of him, that everything turned out for the better for
me. My brother and I have continued to gain steady commissions

in Florence and in towns across the countryside. It was only with-out the shadow of Michelangelo's towering, tormenting presence that I fully realized that I had imposed my own burden on myself and that I was the only one who could tear it down.

I turn the envelope over in my hands.

Four years.

It has been four years since I have seen him, since he has crossed our threshold and laced his fingers through mine. Four years since I have felt him pull me close, then push me away. He feels far distant now. Without him, I have been able to find myself.

My brother is gone again, too, off again to the countryside to chase his fortune in Pistoia, this time with an old master and a new cycle of frescoes. I might have gone with him, but we have our workshop and new assistants. The house and the workshop are now mine and mine alone.

It is hard to believe that only four years ago, I pinned my very survival on the stability of my brother, on the potential of Michelangelo and his tormented brilliance, on my own flawed efforts to overcome my self-inflicted sufferings. Now, I no longer need them. Our workshop is thriving. We have successfully com-pleted the frescoes for the wool trader, which took longer than we thought. The Spanish wool merchants have returned for an-other season of trade. Their lady has asked for more pictures, and so my assistants are working on them. My workshop is a disaster, but at least now I have people to help me in designing decora-tion, paintings, even architecture.

I do not need to make myself immortal. I just need to work.

Our house is quiet now, except when my sister brings one or more of the bookbinder's sons to visit, or else her new baby girl, babbling happily on her hip. She is flush with joy and still young enough to continue to fill her house with children, not to mention shelves full of beautiful books.

I place Michelangelo's sealed letter on my worktable, atop a sandy surface covered with pages of sketches and rolls of fresco cartoons.

How silly of me to think that I might have played a part in the colossus that has now become an integral part of our cityscape, part of our collective identity. Over the past four years my envy and jealousy have moved away to make only more room for wonder. When I pass through the Piazza della Signoria, sometimes it is not even the first thing that catches my eye; it has faded into the background. All the same, when I do catch sight of it, I stand in awe.

In the meantime, the *guardia* sends two uniformed officers to patrol the square after dark; they do their best to thwart vandals who might try to defile the sculpture. Members of the goldsmith's guild have been engaged to gild the David's sling along with the tree stump at his feet. Master Botticelli has made a garland of twenty-eight gilded leaves to adorn the boy-king's loins. As a result, the *pisello* jokes no longer hold the same charm.

The bronze *Judith*, which once occupied the space where *David* now stands, was removed from the inner courtyard of the Signoria and nestled among the many mighty sculptures of the loggia. Paolo's foundry was tasked with building a foundation big enough to support the weight of the hooded woman wielding the sword over the head of Holofernes.

Many things have changed. Filippino Lippi and old Father Ormanno, whom I enjoyed visiting up until earlier this year, have passed on to the World to Come. Paolo the blacksmith fell victim to a plague outbreak that scourged the Oltrarno. And now, new artists have appeared in our city. The competitors are still at it, but I no longer pay attention. A new boy named Raphael Sanzio has come to town from Urbino, armed with a pile of letters of introduction. He is working with Ridolfo Ghirlandaio. He shows as much talent as Michelangelo, if I dare as to make an estimation, but he has a much nicer disposition.

And, I have learned that even giants fall. No sooner did Master da Vinci build a strange, accordion-like scaffold in the Palazzo Vecchio to begin transferring his impressive *cartone* to fresco that he made a decision to experiment with applying oil-based pigments in a bed of wax, then setting them with fire. He claimed in public that it was a time-proven technique used by the ancients, yet even I could have told him it was a terrible idea. All that public attention. All the scandal. All those beautiful images, running down the wall in a great mess.

No. Those men, those giants. They do not haunt me anymore. Not Master da Vinci. Not even Michelangelo. Still, I cannot avoid hearing about them from my fellow guildsmen, and if I am honest with myself, I cannot help but turn my ear when I hear my old friend's name spoken on the streets.

From this idle gossip, I have learned that Michelangelo has earned prestigious commissions in the Holy City, at the same time that he has clashed with Julius II, who decided in the end that it was bad luck to have his tomb created while he was still living. Michelangelo was insulted, but finally gave in and went to Bologna, where Julius II was camped as the commander of papal troops that had conquered the city. As far as I know, the Sala Grande in the Signoria—the room destined to have frescoes by Michelangelo and Master da Vinci—still lies abandoned, while artists across the city claim to have ferreted away small, torn pieces of Michelangelo's giant cartoon from the empty great hall of Sant'Onofrio.

Behind me, the door to the workshop creaks open.

"You're late, Bartolomeo," I say without turning to look at my new—and only—apprentice, the second son of Battistini the bookbinder.

"I stayed out late in the taverns."

I turn to look at him with as much of a piercing gaze as I can muster. "No good can come of showing your face there, son."

He shrugs, frame swaggering yet unsure. He deflects my critical gaze by redirecting my attention to my hand. "What is that, Master L'Indaco?"

My *blue boy*. The name has stuck.

I turn the parchment over. "Just a letter," I say. "From Rome."

I heave myself onto a wooden stool, and run my finger beneath the wax to break the seal.

My L'Indaco,

Perhaps by now you have heard what has become of my commission for that papal tomb in Rome. I know how word travels in Florence. It is a long story for another time.

I am writing to you because His Holiness has given me a new commission. I've agreed to paint the ceiling of an old chapel, one named for Pope Sixtus, near Saint Peter's Basilica. It is a building with spandrels so wide and so high that it will mean a tremendous contraption for scaffolds. I think it rather risky to bet on the eternal plans of these men, but that is not for me to decide. As I have said, it is inadvisable to turn down paying work.

You know that I prefer to work alone, but for a project of this scale I will need a team of assistants.

I tried to convince them that I am not a painter, but they did not seem to hear me.

Now back here in Rome, I am faced with this large project, and I will not be able to do it alone. There are so many I cannot afford to invite, but you are one of the only ones I can trust. You have proven yourself loyal. Besides, you know how to finish a fresco.

I know we have not always had the same way of seeing or creating. As you know, I am not a painter any more than you are a sculptor, and you are not a sculptor any more than I am a painter. But our patrons do not see that. They only want to be glorified. We must do our jobs to put food on the table, no?

I need you now. Think about it, my L'Indaco. My blue boy. Perhaps if your brother is still with you, he will come, too.

If you accept, I can promise that everything will be taken care of. You will have a place to stay and a salary that will make you comfortable in Rome. You will have access to the most important people here.

But more than that, it will be a chance for the two of us to work together as we used to, all those years ago in Master Ghirlandaio's workshop. You and me. Consider it. A chapel for His Holiness.

It will be just like old times. A chance for our work to live for future generations.

It is a chance to be immortal.

Consider my request and answer me as soon as possible.

Until then, I commend myself to you and may God protect you from evil.

Yours,
Michelangelo Buonarroti, sculptor in Rome

The letter slips out of my hand. I let it flutter to the floor.
I no longer need him.

I no longer need to work in the shadow of a giant. I know that now. I can stay here and be fruitful, in spite of, and maybe because of, his absence.

But as I summoned him all those years ago, he has now summoned me. It is my turn to answer a letter that appeared out of thin air.

By staying here in Florence, who am I deceiving? Only myself.

Before I have even reached down to grasp the parchment, refold it, and place it in the pocket of my apron to read again later, my mind is already reeling.

How would I get the news to Francesco? How would I convince Lucia that I will be fine on my own in the Holy City? How much will it cost to pay the mule driver? And how quickly can I arrange for a carriage to transport me to Rome?

AUTHOR'S NOTE

FEW BIOGRAPHICAL DETAILS are known about Michelangelo's friend Jacopo Torni, known by his nickname, L'Indaco—the "blue one." The sixteenth-century art historian Giorgio Vasari tells us that L'Indaco lived "in close intimacy" with Michelangelo, and that Michelangelo found L'Indaco the funniest and most entertaining of his friends. We also know that Michelangelo invited L'Indaco to work with him on the Sistine Chapel in 1508. According to some sources, it was a friend who convinced Michelangelo to return to Florence to take on the *David* commission in 1501, and I like to think it was L'Indaco.

Michelangelo is one of the most notoriously temperamental artists in history, and I wondered about this relationship of seeming opposites. It is this push and pull of two creative friends, in combination with the creation of two of the most seminal works of art history—the *David* and the Sistine Chapel ceiling—that drew me to this story and made me want to explore this complicated friendship further.

Vasari also provides a humorous anecdote that illustrates the nature of the relationship of the two men:

Now seeing that, as has been said, Michelagnolo used to take pleasure in this man's chattering and in the jokes that he was ever making, he kept him almost always at his table; but one day Jacopo wearied him—as such fellows more often than not do come to weary their friends and patrons with their incessant babbling, so often ill—timed and senseless; babbling, I call it, for reasonable talk it cannot be called, since for the most part there is neither reason nor judgment in such people—and Michelagnolo, who, perchance, had other thoughts in his mind at the time and wished to get rid of him, sent him to buy some figs; and no sooner had Jacopo left the house than Michelagnolo bolted the door behind him, determined not to open to him when he came back. L'Indaco, then, on returning from the market—square, perceived, after having knocked at the door for a time in vain, that Michelagnolo did not intend to open to him; whereupon, flying into a rage, he took the figs and the leaves and spread them all over the threshold of the door. This done, he went his way and for many months refused to speak to Michelagnolo; but at last, becoming reconciled with him, he was more his friend than ever.

In addition to working with Michelangelo on the Sistine Ceiling in Rome between 1508 and 1512, L'Indaco may have painted frescoes—now lost—in the church of Sant'Agostino in Rome, if we are to believe Giorgio Vasari.

From other sources, we know a few more small details about L'Indaco, enough to learn that his life was short but had a happy ending. After his stint in Rome, L'Indaco disappears from the records until he reappears about 1520 in Murcia, Spain, where he is documented as a master working on—of all things—sculpture.

He is also noted as the architect of Murcia's cathedral, which I like to imagine might have been one of his dreams.

We know that in Spain, L'Indaco was called Jacopo Fiorentino (Jacob the Florentine), and that he married a Spanish woman named Juana de Velasco, the daughter and apprentice of a noted woodcarver. He died around 1526, though the cause of his early death is lost to history. The couple's young son, Lázaro de Velasco, might have had little memory of his father, but took on the trade of L'Indaco's father as a manuscript illuminator. Lázaro would go on to find success both as an artist and a translator.

Although L'Indaco's surviving paintings are few and not well known, he is noted as part of Michelangelo's team of fresco painters at the Sistine Chapel, where he is credited for his contributions to protect the frescoes from mold. Michelangelo surely relied heavily on his assistants for the project, as he himself had little experience with fresco and never considered himself a painter.

FOR MUCH MORE ON MICHELANGELO'S *David*, Renaissance Florence, and the research behind this book (everything from Renaissance card games to the Stinche prison, as well as parades and pageants of the sixteenth century), visit my Research Vault at **lauramorelli.com/david.**

Register for my free online masterclass on Michelangelo's *David* at lauramorelli.com/giant

Excerpt from

THE NIGHT PORTRAIT

A Novel of World War II and Da Vinci's Italy

By Laura Morelli

PART I

WAR MACHINES

1

LEONARDO

Florence, Italy
February 1476

A DARK SHAFT in the hillside. In my mind, I see it.

Down the long passage, a forgotten recess beneath the city's fortifications, I watch men loading charges of black powder.

The best laborers for this task, I think, mine coal by day. These men are used to toiling in the thin air, in the darkness, with the careful use of the torch and the pick. Their fingers and cheeks are permanently black, their breeches stiff with soil and char. For them, what better occupation than in the service of siege?

They are brave, I think, to advance in the darkness, their lights held high. Quietly, unsuspected, they unload black grit into the farthest recesses of the shaft. When they emerge, the cannoneer turns the wheel noiselessly on its cogs, moving the machine forward into the mine. Citizens scatter amid the chaos and explosions of spewing rocks. The enemy is soon in the attacker's clutches.

The design lives only in my imagination, of course. I must admit that. Still, I am compelled to put it to paper. These thoughts, these machines. They keep me awake long past the hour when the sun turns the Arno to gold and then sinks behind the hills. These contraptions fill my dreams. I awake in a sweat, desperate to trap the images on paper before they dissipate like first morning fog on the river's surface.

The fact is that I am surrounded by my old room, with its smoldering fire in the hearth, with precarious stacks of parchment sheaves on the table, with inkwells and their metallic fragrance, with oil lamps and their charred wicks, with an ever-shifting arrangement of lounging cats. I have secured the iron latch on my door to deter those so-called friends who might lure me to the taverns. They can have it all.

I have more important tasks at hand. If I don't capture them between the pages of my notebooks, they flit away like colorful moths just beyond the reach of my net.

Never mind that troublesome distraction of the panel on my easel. There lies my improficient attempt to capture the likeness of a merchant's homely daughter. But she glares at me from across the room. Dissatisfied, as she has every right to be. Her father has asked me to make her beautiful before he sends the portrait to a suitor in Umbria. My heart is not in it, if I am honest with myself, but I cannot argue with the remuneration. It keeps bread and wine on my table. Still, the tempera pigments on my poplar plank have long dried hard. I pull the drape over the portrait so that the girl's reproving gaze will no longer distract me. I am anxious to turn back to my drawing. If only I could convince a patron to pay me for my war machines instead of replicating his daughter's profile.

Then there are my own parts of my master's unfinished works. An angel and a landscape for a baptism of Christ. The monks have been pestering Master Verrocchio for months. A Madonna and child—uninspired, if I am honest with myself—for a noble lady near Santa Maria Novella. She has written me another letter asking when it will be delivered.

How can I afford these distractions when there is so much for me to capture from my own imagination? I turn back to my notebooks.

Why the tunnels? They will ask me, these men who think as much of war as I. But I have already thought of that. How the enemy might be surprised when their attackers emerge from the earth to overcome them! They will see that the shaft driving the machine allows it to turn seamlessly, effortlessly, into the tortuous shafts below ground, without making a sound. And when these mines are not being exploded, what treasures might be hidden there from those who might steal them, deep in the underground reserves where there is copper, coal, and salt?

We must keep our enemies close. Or so they say.

But what do I know? I am only one who imagines such fantasies and puts them to paper. One who believes that sometimes, art must be put in the service of war.

I pick up my silverpoint pen and begin to draw again.

2

EDITH

Munich
September 1939

EDITH BECKER HOPED that the men around the table could not see her hands tremble.

On any other Thursday, Edith would be sitting before an easel in her ground-level conservation studio, wearing the magnifying goggles that made her look like a giant insect. There, in the quiet, she would lose all track of time, absorbed in the task of repairing a tear in a centuries-old painting, removing grime built up over decades, or regilding an old, crumbling frame. Her job was saving works of art, one by one, from decay and destruction. It was her training, her calling. Her life's work.

But for the last half hour, the eyes of the most important men of the Alte Pinakothek, one of Munich's greatest museums, had been on Edith. They watched her unwind the straps from each binder and remove folios one by one, each one representing paintings in the private collections of families across Poland.

"The identity of the man in the portrait is unknown," Edith said, passing around a facsimile of a portrait by the Italian Renaissance painter, Raffaello Sanzio. Edith watched their eyes scan the likeness of a fluffy-haired man looking askance at the viewer, drawing a fur cloak over one shoulder.

Edith was glad she had traded her usual faded gray dress and conservator's smock for the smartest outfit she owned, a brown tweed skirt and jacket. She had taken the time to make sure her hair curled evenly on either side of her jawline, and the seams up the back of her stockings ran straight. The men gave her their undivided attention: the curator of antiquities, the museum board chairman, even the museum director himself, Ernst Buchner, a renowned scholar to whom Edith had never spoken directly before today.

"There have been several ideas about the identity of the sitter," she said. "Some even believe it may be the artist's self-portrait."

Edith was the only woman in a room full of the museum's executive staff. She wished they hadn't asked her to abandon the peace of her conservation studio, where, for the last few weeks, she had been working to restore a large battle scene by the sixteenth-century Munich artist Hans Werl. At some point in the 1800s, another conservator had overpainted the human figures and horses in the picture. Now, working at a painstakingly slow pace, Edith was removing the overpaint with a small piece of linen soaked in solvent. She was excited to see the brilliant pigments that the artist had originally intended emerge from the canvas, one centimeter at a time. She wished they would let her get back to work instead of placing her at the center of attention.

Her eyes moved nervously around the table and finally landed on Manfred, a longtime colleague and museum registrar. Manfred peered at Edith over his small, round glasses and smiled, giving her the courage to continue. He may have been the only one in the room who understood how challenging it was for Edith to speak in front of the group.

Manfred, Edith realized, was also the only one of her coworkers who knew something of her life outside the museum. He understood the difficulty she faced in caring for her father, whose mind and memory had deteriorated, day by day. Manfred and her father had been classmates at the Academy of Fine Arts, and it was Manfred who had facilitated a position for Herr Becker's diligent, studious daughter in the conservation department. Edith knew that if she was to keep her job, let alone find any success as a professional woman at all, she had to protect her personal life from the others. She clung to Manfred's reassuring smile to help still her shaking hands.

"A masterpiece," said the board chairman, handling the facsimile of the painting by Raffaello Sanzio with care. "I see that the Czartoryski family had an impressive ambition to collect Italian paintings."

"Indeed." Edith, too, had been surprised to learn of the treasures locked away in castles, monasteries, museums, and private homes in the lands to the east. There were vast family collections, amassed over centuries, across the Polish border. Prince Czartoryski's family art collection alone served as a quiet repository of incalculable value.

And now, Edith was beginning to understand the point of all the hours, days, and weeks she had spent in the museum archives and library stacks. She had been instructed to pull together this research on paintings in Polish collections for the museum board. She didn't know why it hadn't become obvious before now. Someone wanted to procure these pictures. Who and why?

"And this is the last one," she said, pulling the final folio from the stack of images from the Czartoryski collection.

"The one we've been waiting for," said Herr Direktor Buchner, whose brows reached for the dark, wispy hair swept back from his high forehead.

"Yes," Edith said. "Around 1800, at the same time that Adam Jerzy Czartoryski purchased Raphael's Portrait of a Young Man from an Italian family, he also bought Leonardo da Vinci's Lady with an Ermine. He brought these paintings from Italy back home to his family collection in eastern Poland."

"And it remains there?" the antiquities curator asked, suspending his pen in midair as if it were a cigarette. The curator's old habit hearkened back to the time before the recent ban on smoking in government buildings; just months ago, Edith realized, the room would have been filled with smoke.

"No," Edith said, relieved that she had reviewed her notes before the meeting. "The Lady with an Ermine portrait has traveled often over the last hundred years. In the 1830s, during the Russian invasion, the family took it to Dresden for safekeeping. Afterward, they returned it to Poland but things were still unstable, so they moved the painting to a hiding place in the family palace in Pełkinie. When things calmed down, the family moved it to their private apartments in Paris; that would have been in the 1840s."

"And then it returned to Poland?"

"Eventually, yes," said Edith. "The family brought it back to Poland in the 1880s. It was put on public display then, to great fanfare. That's where many people first learned of the painting, and when historians began researching it. Several experts identified it right away as by the hand of da Vinci, and people speculated about the identity of the sitter. That's how it ended up"—she gestured to her stack of folios—"widely published and reproduced."

"Who is she?" asked Buchner, tapping his fat fingers on the tabletop.

"It is well accepted that she was one of the mistresses of the Duke of Milan, a girl named Cecilia Gallerani, who came from a Sienese family. She was probably about sixteen years old at the time that Ludovico Sforza asked da Vinci to paint her." Edith watched the facsimile of the painting circulate from hand to hand around the table again. The men pored over the girl's face, her bright expression, the white, furry creature in her arms.

"During the Great War, the painting came to Germany again," Edith continued. "It was held for safekeeping in the Gemäldegalerie in Dresden, but it was ultimately returned to Kraków."

"It is remarkable that the painting survived at all, given how often it circulated," Manfred noted.

"Indeed," said Herr Direktor Buchner, handing the facsimile back to Edith. She returned it to her thick binder and began to retie the straps. "Fräulein Becker, you are to be commended for your thorough background research in the service of this project."

"A senior curator could not have done a better job," the decorative arts curator added.

"*Danke schön.*" Edith finally exhaled. She hoped they would let her return to the conservation studio now. She looked forward to putting on her smock and starting on the stabilization of a French painting whose frame had been water damaged when it was placed in an unfortunate position under a plumbing pipe in a storage closet.

Generaldirektor Buchner stood. "Now," he said, taking a deep breath. "I have an announcement. In recent days, I have had a personal visit from Reichsmarschall Göring, who, as you may know, has been engaged by our Führer in the search for masterpieces like the ones we have seen here this afternoon. There is to be a new museum constructed in Linz. It has been fully funded by our Supreme Commander, who, as you know, has a personal interest in great art and its preservation. The museum in Linz, once it is complete, will be a repository for the safekeeping of all important works of art"—he paused to look around the table—"in the world."

There was a collective gasp. Edith let the idea sink in. Adolf Hitler had already opened the House of German Art, just a short walk away from her office. She and Manfred had gone to see the work of the officially approved contemporary sculptors and painters. But now . . . Every important work of art history in the entire world under one roof, all of it under the stewardship of the Reich. It was difficult—almost inconceivable—to envision.

"As you might imagine," Buchner said, giving life to Edith's thoughts, "this new vision of our Führer will be a massive undertaking. All of us in the art-related trades are being engaged as custodians in the service of safeguarding these works. As things become more . . . precarious . . . we must all do our parts toward this effort."

"But that's insanity!" the antiquities curator huffed out. "All the important works of art in the world? Germany will control the world's cultural patrimony? Who are we to be custodians of such a legacy? And who are we to take them from their current places?"

The room fell into nearly unbearable silence, and Edith wondered if the poor curator was already regretting his outburst. Edith watched Manfred press his pen firmly onto his page, drawing circular doodles, his other hand over his mouth as if to stop himself from speaking.

The museum board chairman broke the silence. "No, Hans, it is a worthy cause. I have good evidence that the Americans want to take valuable European paintings and put them in Jewish museums in America. On the contrary," he said. "The idea of a Führermuseum . . . it's ingenious. And anyway, you must realize that this is just a start. We are also making lists of important German artworks taken by the French and English in past centuries. Those works will be repatriated to Germany in due time."

Edith studied the director's face. Herr Buchner ignored the commentary, stood up, and calmly continued, though Edith thought she detected a twitch of the muscles at the base of his neck. "All of us will be receiving orders from officials at the Braunes Haus. We will be working with Germany's best artists, historians, curators, and culture critics. You will each be given jobs that match your specialty. Many of us, myself included, will be traveling afield to gather works to bring back to our storage rooms here, or to other German museums."

"But what about our work here?" Edith could not help but ask. "The conservation lab . . ."

"I'm afraid that our current projects will be mostly suspended. As for the museum itself, we have already begun rearranging our collections in storage to accommodate the works that will be coming to us, and we've secured additional space off-site."

"Where are we going?" asked the antiquities curator.

"We will be receiving our specific assignments later this week," the director said. "Fräulein Becker, I suspect that there is a very good chance you will be going to Poland." He gestured to the binders full of facsimiles that Edith had compiled.

Poland.

Edith felt her stomach seize.

"S-s-surely . . ." she stammered. "Surely we could not be expected to . . ."

"How long?" a curatorial assistant cut Edith's question short.

Buchner shrugged, and Edith saw the twitch in his neck again. "Until our work is done. As long as it takes. We are at war."

The director then picked up his stack of folders, nodded, and exited the room. The stream of museum staff followed.

Edith filed out behind the line of men. Reaching the familiar door to the ladies' washroom, she pressed it open and sealed it behind her. She dropped her box of folios onto the floor, sat on the toilet seat, and pressed her face into her palms. She gasped for air, feeling as if she might faint.

Poland? Indefinitely? How would she manage? Who would care for her father? What about her plans to marry, finally, after so many years of hoping? Was she really being called to the front lines? In danger of her life?

After a few long minutes, Edith stood and splashed cool water from the tap onto her face and wrists. When she emerged from the washroom, she found Manfred pacing the hallway.

"Are you all right?" he whispered, taking her arm.

"I . . . I'm not sure, if you want to know the truth. Oh, Manfred . . ." She exhaled, stopping to press her back against the cool tiles along the corridor wall. "What news. I can hardly believe it." Her hands were still shaking.

"I think we are all in a state of shock," he said, "even those of us who . . . who have foreseen this outcome."

Edith squeezed Manfred's forearm. She had seen little of Manfred's life outside the museum, but she knew that he had been an organizer in a Munich group that was known for opposing nearly all of the Reich's policies, their ideas disseminated in weightless leaflets left on park benches and empty tram seats.

"You knew what they were planning?"

Manfred nodded, tight-lipped. "The Generaldirektor has already purchased several truckloads of pictures confiscated from Jewish collectors across Bavaria. If you don't believe me, come up to the third floor. There are so many pictures in my office that I can barely walk to my desk."

Edith felt her jaw drop. "I can hardly imagine it. But you . . . Where will you go?"

"I'll bet they keep me here to catalog whatever comes in. They need me. Plus, I am an old dog." He shrugged and mustered a smile. "It could be worse. Out of the line of fire. But you, my dear . . . How will you manage? Your father . . ."

Edith pressed her hands to her face again. "I have no idea," she said. "Heinrich. My fiancé. He is also being shipped out to Poland."

"Ah!" Manfred said, his eyes growing wide. "Then you are headed to the same place at least."

"Yes, but . . . *Heiliger Strohsack!*" she whispered loudly. "This was not what I was expecting."

"I wish I could say the same, my dear *fräulein konservator*," Manfred said. "You are too young to remember the beginnings of the last war. And here we are again. All the same, what can we do? When the Führer calls, we hardly have a choice. They will issue us conscription papers. Saying no is not an option unless. . . ."

Manfred gestured toward a window at the end of the hallway, one that overlooked the square where Jewish-owned shops had been forcibly closed or even burned in recent months. At this moment, Edith knew, Jewish families were boarding trams—either by choice or by coercion—that would resettle them in another place, that would consign them to a fate beyond her understanding. The Nusbaums, a couple who lived with their two young children in Edith's apartment building, had left weeks ago. In the ground-floor corridor, under the sharp eye of their doorman, Edith had watched Frau Nusbaum piling worn leather bags and grain sacks full of their most precious belongings into a rickety barrow.

Edith knew that Manfred was correct in saying that refusing the Führer's call was not an option, but her mind raced, looking for a way out of the predicament. Was it too much to ask, to return to her conservation studio, to her humble apartment, to her father, to a new life with her husband?

"Well," said Manfred, mustering a tight grin. "Poland! Perhaps there is a silver lining. You will get to see all those masterpieces you've studied all this time."

3

EDITH

Munich, Germany
September 1939

EDITH WAS STRUGGLING with the lock on her apartment door when she heard her father shriek.

The fine hairs on the back of her neck tingled, and a jolt like a live tram wire ran down her spine. She had never heard that wrenching sound come from his mouth before. She rattled the door with all her force.

"Papa!"

Finally, the key clicked and the door opened. Edith nearly fell into the apartment. She dropped her shoulder bag, spilling the art books and folders she had brought home from work. Bookmarks and handwritten notes fluttered and spun across the worn, wooden floor. Edith rushed down the hallway, toward the loud voice of a radio broadcaster announcing that German troops had crossed the Vistula River in southern Poland. In the front room, she found her father seated in his chair, lashing out with his lanky arms and legs toward the slight woman looming over him.

"Herr Becker!" Elke, the woman who cared for her father while Edith was at work, struggled to grasp the old man's forearms. Her hair had come loose from its pins at the crown of her head. Her face was a contorted grimace. Edith's father's long legs lashed out again, stiff and uncoordinated, toward Elke's shins.

Then the smell of urine and excrement came over Edith, and she felt her heart sink.

"He refuses to walk to the toilet!" Elke finally let go of Herr Becker's forearms and turned toward Edith. "I cannot get him to leave that chair!"

"It's all right," Edith said, trying to steady her voice. "Let me talk to him."

Elke threw up her hands in exasperation and retreated to the kitchen. Edith strode across the room and switched off the radio, silencing the ranting announcer.

"Papa." Edith knelt on the rug before her father's chair, just as she had when she was a little girl, hungry for another one of her father's stories about counts and duchesses from long ago. The floral patterns on the arms of the chair had worn pale and threadbare, the cushion sagging and now surely beyond salvage. Edith did her best to ignore the stench.

"That woman . . ." her father said, his eyes wide with uncharacteristic rage, cloudy orbs rimmed in yellow. From the kitchen, Edith heard water running, followed by the loud clang of pots.

Coarse white hairs protruded from his chin. Edith imagined that Elke had been struggling with her father for hours. It was becoming a daily occurrence, Herr Becker's refusal to partake in the simplest tasks, from putting on a clean shirt to shaving. Getting him in the bath was close to impossible; in recent weeks he had developed an inexplicable fear of water. Edith felt pity for Elke, at the same time that she was frustrated that no one in the ever-changing group of caregivers that Edith had hired understood how to coax her father to cooperate. It required a high level of patience with a dose of trickery, Edith had to admit.

From the crease between the cushion and the frame of the chair, Edith excavated Max, the ragged, stuffed dog that had belonged to Edith as a child. Now, Max was her father's constant companion, its white fur matted and stained irreparably.

"It's all right, Papa," Edith said, putting her palm securely on his forearm, with its thin, lined skin marked with darkened spots. With his other hand, her father grasped the ragged animal tightly to his side. Behind them, the Swiss clock ticked loudly. Messy stacks of art books lined the walls, slips of paper haphazardly sticking out of each volume. Dusty, yellowed pages of scholarly catalogs and journals her father had once devoured now stood abandoned.

"Shall we get you cleaned up? I have a feeling that you might have a visitor."

Her father's eyes lit up as he digested her white lie, and Edith felt a pang of guilt slide across her gut. None of her father's friends was coming to visit. When her father no longer recognized their faces and could not recall their names, one by one, they dwindled away. Edith had watched wordlessly, powerless to stop it.

Her father no longer tracked time, but Edith knew that months had passed since their last visitor, with the exception of Edith's fiancé, Heinrich. And even that was about to stop. Heinrich would soon be boarding a train for Poland, assigned to a newly formed infantry division of the Wehrmacht. As soon as the invasion of Poland had been broadcast across the radio and newspapers less than two weeks ago, Edith had held her breath and begun to pray, but Heinrich's official orders had come anyway.

But Edith didn't want to think about that now.

In the bathroom, Edith ran her hand under the tap until the water warmed. She would never have dreamed that the barrier of modesty between father and daughter would have fallen away so completely. What else was she to do? When the caregivers she hired inevitably gave up trying to wrangle her stubborn father, who else but his only daughter would care enough to loosen his trousers, to blot a damp cloth across his shoulders, to carefully run a razor across his jaw? Edith's mother had been gone nearly five years now, and in moments like these, she missed her more than ever.

"*Guten abend!*"

Edith poked her head out of the bathroom doorway long enough to see Heinrich enter the apartment, greeting Elke as the stout nurse departed in a blur of blue raincoat and hat.

As much as her heart surged to see her fiancé, it also sank at Elke's abrupt departure. Tomorrow there would be a visit to the agency and another search for a nurse so that Edith could continue her work at the museum and put food on their table.

Heinrich pecked a brief kiss on Edith's lips. "What happened in here? It smells like a farm."

Edith pressed her face into Heinrich's neck and drank in his scent for a long moment. "I'm going to get him cleaned up now. I'm sorry. I don't know whether Elke ever got to preparing dinner. Have a look in the kitchen."

The voice of his daughter's fiancé in the hallway had lured Herr Becker from the front room. Now, the old man braced himself against the doorjamb, his trousers sagging, a sideways grin on his face.

"Greetings, soldier!" Heinrich smiled at his future father-in-law and rushed to steady him. Edith watched her father endeavor to give Heinrich a firm handshake. "Looks like you're in for a good shave from this lovely lady. Lucky man!" With gratitude and relief, Edith watched Heinrich steer her father successfully to the bathroom door.

Edith did her best to clean up Herr Becker, showing him as much patience and compassion as she could muster. When they emerged from the bathroom, her father dressed in clean pajamas, Edith saw that Heinrich had moved the soiled chair to air out by an open window and had brought a bowl of fruit and bread from the kitchen to the dining table. He was picking up the papers and books that she had spilled by the apartment door.

For a moment, she watched Heinrich kneeling over her satchel in the dim light of the entryway, a calm beacon in the storm. He was wearing the gray cotton collared shirt that brought out the sky gray of his eyes. She could hardly bear the thought of standing on a station platform, watching him wave to her from a small train window in a newly pressed field tunic.

"I'm sorry there is no dinner," she said, kneeling beside him to pick up the last sheets of paper from the floor.

"We have bread. We have fruit. We have muesli, reheated from this morning, but healthy all the same. More than many people have, surely."

Edith helped her father sit in his usual chair at the dining table and put a piece of bread in front of him. Finally, she took a deep breath and relaxed. She sat at the table and began peeling an apple with a worn knife.

"What's all this paper?" Heinrich asked.

"Research," she said. "They've asked me to compile a dossier of old master paintings in Polish collections. You remember I was telling you about all the library visits I've made in the past weeks? I had to give a presentation today to the director."

"Herr Professor Dokter Buchner?" Heinrich raised his eyebrows.

"Yes." Edith felt her stomach constrict as she thought about the room full of men, the Führer's museum, the news that she had no idea how to break to Heinrich and her father.

"I thought they kept you locked up in the back storerooms with a paintbrush and chemicals," Heinrich said.

She nodded. "Yes. It's not my usual place, but Herr Kurator Schmidt asked me to do it. He said I have special knowledge of Italian Renaissance paintings. You know I am happy to stay hidden away in my little scientific department, not standing before an audience."

Heinrich leaned back in his chair and thumbed through one of the large illustrated volumes that Edith had brought home from the museum library. Edith watched him nervously, wondering how to find the words to tell Heinrich and her father. How on earth would she break the news? When Heinrich reached a bookmarked, full-page color facsimile of a woman holding a small white creature, he stopped.

"Leonardo da Vinci," Heinrich read the caption. "*Portrait of a Lady with an Ermine*." He looked up at Edith. "What's an ermine?"

Edith shrugged. "Ladies in the Italian Renaissance kept a variety of exotic pets. An ermine is something like a ferret."

"No," her father interjected, raising a crooked finger. "There is a difference. Ferrets are domesticated. Ermines are wild. Their fur turns white in the winter."

Heinrich and Edith looked at each other, then laughed aloud at Herr Becker's assessment. Edith's heart surged whenever a spark of clarity flickered in the fog, when her real father came back to her, if only for a fleeting moment.

"Bravo, Papa. I had no idea," Edith said, but the flicker was gone, and her father had returned to spooning watery muesli into his mouth. "That's one of my favorite pictures," Edith said.

"Da Vinci painted it when he was still a young man, before he became well known."

"A strange creature," Heinrich said, tapping the picture with his finger, "but a beautiful girl."

This was what she would miss most, Edith thought, sitting with her father and Heinrich, talking of art. She wanted to hear her father's lessons again, random shards of information he pulled from the dusty corners of his brain, left over from years of teaching art history at the university, volumes of historical facts that he had transmitted to his daughter along with a passion for art. Was it too much to ask? She just wanted a laugh with her father and to eat a meal with the man she loved. She did not want to have to cobble together yet another caregiver to help her nearly helpless papa. And above all, she did not want to count the days left until Heinrich boarded a train. She pushed it to the back of her mind, stood, and began to clear the table.

Heinrich moved another armchair near the window and settled Herr Becker so that he could watch the lights begin to flicker from the apartment windows lining the edge of the park. He retrieved Max from the floor and pressed the old, ragged stuffed dog into Herr Becker's lap. Then Edith heard Heinrich talking softly to her father, telling him about something funny that had happened at his father's grocery market, just off the Kaufingerstrasse. She knew her father wouldn't remember any of it after a few minutes, but no matter. The next time Heinrich visited, his kind, familiar face would be enough to lure her father from his chair.

Not long ago, Edith would have sat with her father after dinner, listening to his impassioned opinions of current events, his critique of the greed and corruption of government officials. Edith wondered if her father had any inkling of what was happening beyond the walls of their apartment now. Continued reports of corruption. The dismantling of synagogues. The confiscation of businesses and apartments belonging to Jewish neighbors. The heightened surveillance by their apartment block leaders, who seemed to record her every move. The swift, unexplained departure of two staff members from the museum. Non-German books pulled from libraries and burned in the streets. New laws that would punish anyone who listened to a foreign radio broadcast.

Most of all, she worried about the disappearance of the little boy at the bottom of the stairway. Edith used to look for the Nusbaums' son every morning as she left for work. She'd find him sitting in the hallway with his pens and paper. She would stop to greet him and he would show Edith what he'd drawn that day. She would compliment him and tell him to keep drawing. But one day, he was gone, along with his innocent face and his fastidious drawings. The rest of his family were gone, too, simply walking away with the coats on their backs and a wobbly, wheeled cart.

While she did her best to stay focused on the details of her work and home life, Edith felt deeply troubled about how Munich had changed in recent months. More than that, she missed her father's commentary on current events, which might have provided her with a compass to help navigate her way through the disturbing events that swirled around them.

"Edith?"

She turned to see her father's wide, shiny eyes set on her, as if he had just recognized her face after not having seen her for a long time.

"Yes, Papa!" she said, laughing.

He held out Max the dog. "I believe this is yours."

Edith stared down at the button eyes that her mother had sewn and resewn many times over the years. Max had occupied her bed as a child, then was cast aside as Edith grew into a young woman. When her father had rediscovered Max one day, shortly after her mother died and he began to decline, he had latched on to it like a beloved pet.

"Max," she said, stroking the stuffed animal's matted fur. "But I wouldn't want to lose him." She pressed him back into her father's hands. "Will you take care of him for me?"

Her father settled the ragged stuffed dog back in his lap. "All right," he said, deflated.

"I love you so much, Papa," Edith said, squeezing her father's hands. She tried hard not to let her voice crack.

When her father began to doze off in his chair, Edith joined Heinrich in the kitchen. He dried the dishes with a frayed rag and stacked them on the wooden shelves above the sink. "She's not coming back, is she? The woman in the raincoat?"

Edith sighed. "I'm afraid not. I have to call the agency first thing in the morning. The problem is that he has become so stubborn! They are supposed to be professional nurses, but they don't know how to coerce him into doing the most basic things! I don't know what to do."

Edith felt Heinrich's hand on her back. She stopped and bowed her head, pressing her forehead to Heinrich's chest. She felt his hands go to her hips and rest there. For a few long moments, they stood there, holding each other.

"I have no right to burden you with this when you have bigger things to worry about," she said. "I'm sorry." Edith pressed her face into his cotton shirt and felt his lean, hard chest under her forehead. She inhaled his clean, male scent as she listened to the clock tick loudly in the hallway. How would she break the news that he was not the only one with official orders?

"Edith . . ." he began softly. "They have given me a date. I have to report to Hauptbahnhof Station in two weeks." He must have felt her body freeze under his grasp, he paused. "I just want you to know that, whatever happens . . ."

"Shh," she said, pressing a finger to his lips and shaking her head, her light brown curls hitting her cheeks. "Not yet. Can we just make this last for a bit longer?"

4

CECILIA

Milan
December 1489

"THERE IS A live one. I can feel it crawling."

"Where?"

"Just there. Behind my ear."

Cecilia Gallerani felt her mother's thick, calloused fingertips slide through her dark strands, unraveling the twists. Her mother pinched her frayed fingernails along the length of one hair, yanking so hard that Cecilia bit her lip. She heard her mother swish her hand through the small bowl at her side, a mixture of water and vinegar with small, white nits floating dead on the surface.

"Did you get it?"

An exasperated cluck. "It was too fast. Will you sit still?"

A slow ache was working its way across Cecilia's forehead. How many hours had they been sitting by the light of the window? Through its frame, Cecilia's almond-shaped eyes scanned the layer of cold fog that had settled in the inner courtyard. She watched a dove flutter from the bare branches to a high windowsill overlooking the empty, symmetrical footpaths below. Such a strange place, this hard, wintry stone palace, with its fortified towers and armsmen pacing the upper galleries. So far away from the blindingly sun-filled squares and raucous, bustling streets of home.

As their carriage had rolled through the streets of Milan the afternoon before, Cecilia had watched the flat, vapid landscape suddenly turn to a jumble of fine buildings and crowded streets. The slow crawl through the crowds afforded momentary views of the spiky white spires of Milan's cathedral under construction. She had caught fleeting glimpses of the city's women, their long braids wrapped in silk and transparent layers of veil, men with fur-lined leather boots reaching to the knees and their breath sending vapors into the cold air. Cecilia had marveled at their odd Milanese tongue, a dialect that sounded clipped and harsh, at the same time that it flowed from their lips like a song. She grasped a few familiar words, but they spoke too quickly for her to understand the meaning.

At long last, they had reached the Castello Sforzesco on the outskirts of the city. Guards armed with spears and crossbows had lowered the bridge over the moat, and their horses' hooves had echoed through the tunneled gatehouse into the fortified inner courtyard.

"Aya! I feel it moving again."

Another tsk of exasperation. Her mother ran the comb roughly through a tangle. "Honestly, Cecilia, I hardly see the point. All this hair will be shorn within a few days."

"That is not decided." Cecilia felt the familiar squeeze of dis-content across her stomach.

It made perfect sense. Of course it did. Her eldest broth-er, Fazio, their mother's greatest pride, as well as their father's namesake and successor, had laid it out in clear, logical terms. He had already made arrangements with the Benedictine sisters at San Maurizio al Monastero Maggiore. Cecilia should consider herself fortunate to have such an opportunity, they told her. It was only through her brother's position as a Tuscan diplomat to the court of Milan, a position that their father was never able to reach even after years of service as a petitioner at the ducal court, that the possibility was open to Cecilia at all. It's what had brought them to this wintry palace in the first place.

"Soon enough," said her mother, half under her breath. Cecilia caught sight of her mother's brown hand and forearm, as thick as one of the piglets in their courtyard back home in Siena. Cecilia felt a veil of shame and embarrassment cover the two of them sitting at the window. It was laughable, her stout, sun-speckled mother sitting here among the pale, elegant ladies of the ducal palace. What place did the two of them have here? In Siena, they held their heads high, the wife and daughter of a pe-titioner at the court of Milan. But here, in this northern palace, the seat of His Lordship's domain, Cecilia and her mother passed for little more than peasants. She felt certain that she could see the women in their silk gowns snickering at them behind their gloves and fans.

How quickly her fate had turned.

Only a season ago, her future had looked entirely different. She and Giovanni Stefano Visconti were set to wed, an arrange-ment that had been in place since she was barely old enough to take her first steps. It was a perfect solution, her father had said, to marry their youngest, the only girl, to the Visconti, a Milanese family with a noble legacy and ties to the Sforza ducal family. Giovanni himself was nothing so remarkable, little more than a lopsided grin of a boy not yet turned to man. A dusting of freckles spread across his nose, and the wide shoulders of his fa-ther's overcoat hung from his lanky frame, but Cecilia had been at peace with the safety and security of marrying into a respected

family. The two had already had a ring ceremony to commemo-
rate the commitment, as perfunctory and devoid of emotion as
it was legally binding. But Cecilia felt secure, content even, with
the arrangement. She was accustomed to being in the company
of boys and men, anyway. She had grown up in the chaotic tussle
of a house with six brothers. Spending the rest of her days inside
a cathouse of a convent sounded like the dullest possible fate.

But only months after her father was in the ground, the
magnitude of her brothers' foolishness had come to light. There
was no more hiding it. Together, her brothers had frittered away
Cecilia's dowry, squandering it on ill-advised investments, dice
games, and drink. Once things were out in the open, Giovanni
Visconti's father had burned the marriage contract in front of
her brothers' own eyes at the gates to their farm.

After that, there was a letter dispatched to her eldest brother, Fazio. Within a few days, Cecilia and her mother were loaded
into a small carriage rattling north toward Milan, where Fazio
had promised to make things right.

"But I don't see why I must go to the Monastero Maggiore,"
Cecilia said. It came out like a childish whine and Cecilia immediately cringed. Her mother yanked a little harder than was
necessary.

"Aya!" Cecilia clasped her palm to her scalp.

"You should count yourself fortunate to have such a chance,
Cecilia. We have already been over this. The cloister is the perfect place for a girl like you," her mother said firmly, ignoring her
daughter's yelp and letting another twist fall from the pile of hair
on top of Cecilia's head. Cecilia had heard the arguments; she
was intelligent, fluent in Latin, knew how to write poetry and
play the lute. She came from a respected family. As if she read
her daughter's mind, Signora Gallerani added, "You will be able

to do all those things you love—reading and writing and playing music. And you will be a woman of purity and high regard."

"Then I might find myself a highborn husband right here in this castle instead," Cecilia said. She had made sure that her brothers had signed not only her marriage annulment but also attested to her maidenhood before she had departed for Milan. She knew that she was considered a great prize as a wife; the beauty of Fazio Gallerani's only daughter, and her purity, was whispered about in Siena. "Surely I could use my talents to hold court in a great house instead of behind the convent walls, where I will have no audience."

Her mother crossed her arms across her broad chest and shook her head. Then she let out a sharp laugh that made her midsection jiggle. "What pride! Where did my daughter get such high ideas? If your father were alive, he would take a switch to your legs."

A soft knock fell on the door, then her brother's face appeared.

"My ladies," Fazio greeted them with a brief bow, and their mother's face lit up. She dropped the comb onto the inlaid table alongside the bowl of vinegar and dead lice, then clapped her hands together and pressed her palms to her eldest son's cheeks.

"My beauty," she said, stroking her son's face as if he were a favorite horse. Cecilia had to admit that her eldest brother, at twenty-six years old and ten years her senior, had indeed grown into a handsome, capable man worthy of more than their father's legacy at the court of Milan.

"They are ready for us at the midday meal," Fazio said.

"Santa Maria!" Signora Gallerani exclaimed, swiftly return-ing to Cecilia's back and weaving her hair into a tight braid. "Those pests have caused us to work too long." She quickly tied the end with a leather strap. Cecilia felt the braid thump down the length of her back.

"Fazio," Cecilia said. "If I must live here in Milan, then I want to stay here in this palace instead of a convent."

She heard her mother let out a guffaw. "She continues to talk nonsense," she said, picking up the comb and waving it at Cecilia as if threatening to beat her with it. "We must get her out of this overblown pile of stone as soon as possible." She cast her eyes to the gilded and brightly painted decoration in the coffered ceiling above their heads.

Fazio laughed. "Whatever do you mean, girl?"

Cecilia looped her hand through the crook of her brother's arm. "Surely you, with your high rank here, are in a position to find me a husband."

"A husband!"

"Yes," she said, patting his hand. "One with a large house and a court full of people, full of poetry and music." She did not dare to say it out loud, but the truth was that she also saw herself richer, cleaner, more elegant, just like the women she glimpsed outside the window, those whose lives she only imagined.

Cecilia saw her brother's face waver, and then he exchanged a wary glance with their mother.

"But it is already arranged with the sisters," he said, his brow furrowing.

"Fazio, you know well that I could be one of the most sought-after brides in our region. Plus, you owe me a new husband after what happened with the last one!"

For a few long moments, silence hung thickly in the air.

"*Vergogna!*" her mother broke in. "Prideful girl!" Her mouth had formed a deep scowl. "Your brother owes you nothing! He has already done more for you than you deserve. Besides, you will see. After only a few days with the sisters, you will understand that the convent is the right place for you, Cecilia. I have already told you—I have already told the prideful girl,

Fazio—you will get to do all those things you love. And most of all, you will be a woman of purity and high regard. You will bring our family honor and you will pray for your father's eternal soul on behalf of all of us."

Her brother, a skilled diplomat, stepped sideways. He offered his remaining arm to his mother and steered the two women toward the door. "Shall we go eat? Rice again, I'm afraid, but I saw the cook adding pomegranate arils and citrus. I'm famished."

Beaming at her son, their mother finally took his arm.

But no sooner had Fazio opened the door to the corridor than he stopped short, pressing the women behind him. A small crowd was making its way toward them from the end of a long corridor. As the cluster of courtiers approached, Cecilia watched her brother bow in deference. She and her mother attempted to follow his example, casting their eyes to the intricate patterns on the floor. Cecilia heard the hiss of silk across the marble and could only catch fleeting glimpses of velvet gloves and slippers, silk hose, polished buckles, transparent sheaves of black lace, ribbons of green and gold.

The man at the front of the crowd stopped, and the crowd circled behind him.

"Fazio Gallerani," the man said. From behind her brother's back, Cecilia could only see that the man was stout and black-haired, with a voice so deep that it sounded as if his mouth was full of pebbles.

"My lord," her brother said, his head and shoulders dropping still lower in deference to the man.

"You have brought guests," he said, the deep voice and his Tuscan words with their Milanese accent both strange and beautiful to her ear.

"Guests? Oh no, my lord. Just my mother and my little sister. They arrived last night from Siena."

"Let us greet them, then."

A few long, silent moments passed. Cecilia watched her mother stare down at her dress, where red earth was still caked to the hem and under her fingernails. She did not move from her place behind her son's back.

Cecilia pushed her way in front of her brother, where she found herself standing face-to-face with a man who could be no other than the lord of Milan. Though at least twice her age, Ludovico il Moro stood eye to eye with Cecilia. His face was angular but mostly invisible behind a richly oiled, black beard. His breast was covered in velvet and metal, each finger adorned with a colored gem. The front of his doublet hung heavy with jangling emblems, the sounds heralding his arrival as if he were a prized beast. He raked his dark eyes over Cecilia, then held her under a penetrating gaze for a few more long moments. Was he waiting for her to bow?

But Cecilia did not bow. She only met his dark gaze and smiled.

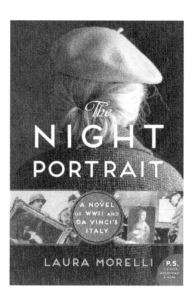

The Night Portrait by Laura Morelli

AN EXCITING, DUAL-TIMELINE historical novel about the creation of one of Leonardo da Vinci's most famous paintings, *Portrait of a Lady with an Ermine*, and the woman who fought to save it from Nazi destruction during World War II.

Milan, 1492: When a 16-year-old beauty becomes the mistress of the Duke of Milan, she must fight for her place in the palace—and against those who want her out. Soon, she finds herself sitting before Leonardo da Vinci, who wants to ensure his own place in the ducal palace by painting his most ambitious portrait to date.

Munich, World War II: After a modest conservator unwittingly places a priceless Italian Renaissance portrait into the hands of a high-ranking Nazi leader, she risks her life to recover it, working with an American soldier, part of the famed Monuments Men team, to get it back.

Two women, separated by 500 years, are swept up in the tide of history as one painting stands at the center of their quests for their own destinies.

Order your copy of Laura Morelli's *The Night Portrait* at lauramorelli.com/NightPortrait

ABOUT THE AUTHOR

LAURA MORELLI HOLDS a Ph.D. in art history from Yale University and is the author of fiction and nonfiction inspired by the history of art. She has taught college students in the U.S. and Italy, and is a TED-Ed educator. Her flagship shopping guidebook, *Made in Italy*, has led travelers off the beaten track for more than two decades. Her award-winning art historical novels include *The Painter's Apprentice*, *The Gondola Maker*, and *The Night Portrait*.

More at lauramorelli.com

Printed in Great Britain
by Amazon

61599254R00210